TARGET

CONTENT/TRIGGER WARNINGS:
Physical and emotional abuse from a parent to their teen child
Burn victim PTSD/memories
Gaslighting
Grooming
Trauma

TARGET

DARCI COLE
Ember Rose Entertainment

TARGET

Book one of the unbroken tales

Cover design by Kirk DouPonce at DogEared Design
Bow & arrow icon by Freepik, modified by Tiana Smith
Maps by Dewi Hargreaves
Formatting by S.D. Simper
Lex's notebook pages by Brandon Cole
Robyn's journal page by Darci Cole

An Ember Rose Entertainment Book
Published by Ember Rose Entertainment LLC
Mesa, Arizona

www.darcicole.com

ISBN 978-1-955145-01-5 (paperback)
ISBN 978-1-955145-02-2 (hardcover)
First Edition: October 2021
Printed in the United States
0 9 8 7 6 5 4 3 2 1

To Brandon.
For always believing in me.
Especially when I couldn't believe in myself.

TABLE OF CONTENTS

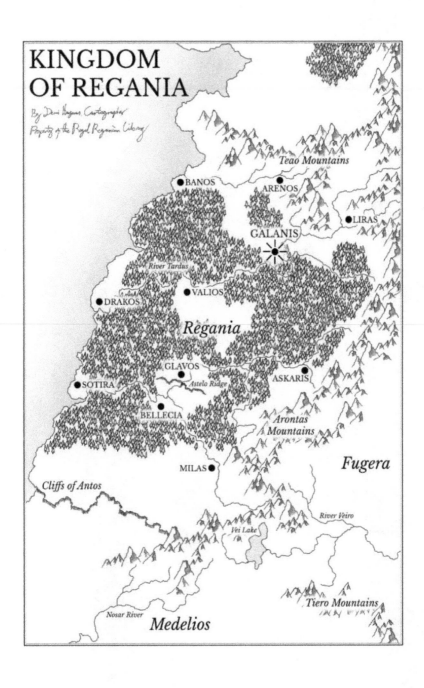

KINGDOM OF REGANIA

By Demi Hagues, Cartographer
Property of the Royal Regania Library

Teao Mountains

BANOS

ARENOS

LIRAS

GALANIS

River Tardus

VALIOS

DRAKOS

Regania

GLAVOS

Astelo Ridge

ASKARIS

SOTIRA

BELLECIA

Arontas Mountains

Fugera

MILAS

Cliffs of Antos

River Veiro

Vei Lake

Tiero Mountains

Nosar River

Medelios

PART ONE

THE MEETING

I forgot to write again. We heard of a conflict in which a shipment of wool blankets was being fought over and I was distracted.

I
LEX

His Royal Highness, Prince Alexander Galani of Regania, twisted the ring on the first finger of his left hand, trying to ignore the itching of his scars over his eye and shoulder. His anxiety was piqued, and he knew what was coming.

"Are you all right?" Enzi, his servant, asked beside him.

Lex sighed, keeping his gaze forward, ignoring the tapestries and guards and the view of the city through open windows. "No," he said. "I mean yes, I'll be fine."

He could almost hear the raise of Enzi's brow. As Lex's personal servant, Enzi would never directly defy him, but that didn't stop him from reacting.

"You know as well as I do what they're going to say," Lex said, keeping his voice low. "They've probably already chosen a wife for me."

"Probably," Enzi said.

"This is mucking stupid." He reached up to rub at the skin beneath the eyepatch over his left eye.

"Want some balm?" Enzi said, pulling a tin from his pocket.

Lex sighed, pausing in the corridor, and took some, rubbing it onto the agitated skin. Flanked by two guards, the doors to his parents' study stood twenty feet away now, and it was likely his entire future was already decided behind them.

He hated it.

"Prince Lex," Enzi said. "Can I ask you something?"

Lex straightened his robes, taking a moment. "Sure, what is it?"

Enzi looked to the floor. "Do you even want to be married?"

"Of course," Lex said, handing back the balm. "I've always wanted to, I knew I'd need to when the time came, but…it has to be the right person, doesn't it?"

"Then…why don't you like any of them?"

Lex blinked. "Them?"

"The ladies of court," Enzi said.

Lex paused.

"I mean," Enzi grinned. "I know you're not attracted to men, otherwise you'd obviously be with me."

"Obviously," Lex said, returning the smile. "So…what is it?"

Lex pulled Enzi away from the doors, out of earshot of the guards, then paused. "They look at me different, En. This," he said, pointing to his face. "You, my parents, my close friends, none of you flinch when I take off the eyepatch. You know me, you don't stare, you don't think differently…"

"But," Enzi said. "Isn't that something that'll come with time?"

"I've known most of these girls since I was ten," Lex said. "I've been to balls, festivals, feasts with them. I've spoken to them, played games with them, written letters to them, and yet not a single one can look me in the face without a slight cringe in their expression."

Enzi frowned.

"Maybe..." Lex sighed again. "Maybe I'm imagining it. Maybe it's all in my head. But I can't bring myself to marry a girl who I'm not absolutely sure has accepted me, scars and all."

"But," Enzi started. "But where will you—"

Lex gave a quick shake of his head, eyeing the guards nearby.

Enzi swallowed. "Do you have a plan?"

"The coast," Lex said softly. "The midsummer festival is happening in a week, maybe I can meet people, make friends, and if I'm lucky..." he trailed off. "En, I have to do this. Especially if my parents are about to tell me what I think they are. And I can't do it without your help. Can I count on you?"

Enzi sighed, and gave a short bow. "Yes, my lord prince."

"Thank you." Lex squared his shoulders, turning toward the study. As he approached, the guards reached out and opened the doors, revealing a simple room with a long rug down the middle, shelves lining the walls, and a fire in the far hearth. Lex stopped halfway across the room to avoid the heat, facing two soft chairs where his parents sat waiting, a third empty chair across from them.

The doors behind him closed, but he knew Enzi would be inside, watching. Three more servants stood at the far wall, awaiting their monarchs' needs.

"Alexander," Lex's mother said, standing to take his hands in hers. "Thank you for coming. I know you've been busy lately overseeing the canal expansion."

"It's nothing that can't wait," Lex said, placing a kiss on her cheek.

Larissa Galani was tall, golden-haired, and lovely even in her fiftieth year. The model of a Reganian woman. The scent of flowery perfume wafted off of her, taking him back to when she'd placed her hands so carefully around him after his accident—when the Cures hadn't worked fast enough and he was left with scars despite magic—avoiding the injuries, helping him fall asleep when the pain became too much.

She reached up and brushed his hair back. "I don't know why all you boys insist on keeping your hair so long in the front. I want to see your handsome face."

Lex laughed, then turned to his father, Stephan Galani. A tall, fit man who studied, who worshiped the God Sileo over the rest, favoring stability, keeping things running, steady and sure. The edges of the king's hair were greying, but his smile was as young and bright as it had ever been.

The king placed a hand on Lex's shoulder. "I heard you're doing well in your riding lessons."

"So they tell me," Lex said. "I've got a good mare, feels like we'll get along."

"I'm glad you're taking up riding again. Maybe we can go together soon, down to Bellecia, or maybe the mountains."

"I'd like that."

"How's sparring?" Father asked.

"Going well. Master Lyn says I'm improving each day."

"Excellent, excellent," Father said. "We're very proud of you."

"Lex," Mother said. She took her seat once more and gestured for Lex to take the chair across from them. "What about that meeting with Lady Arena? Oliver's cousin?" she asked. "Such a sweet girl, isn't she?"

Now they were getting to it. "Of course. She's very kind," Lex said.

"But…"

Lex sighed. "It's like I've told you before. I've spent time with every eligible young woman in the court, and it's always the same."

"Son," Father started.

"You don't know what it's like," Lex said, standing again and stepping away. "People look at you and they see perfection. A model marriage, the ideal king and queen. They look at me and—"

He ran a hand through his hair, tugging a bit, letting the pain there distract from the stretching of his scars.

"Surely if they were to spend more time with you," Mother began.

"Maybe," Lex said. "But, how long? I've spent at least a few hours with each one in the past six months, since you both have been pushing this so strongly. And more with many of them, especially those I've known since childhood. None of them can even look me in the eye."

5

He turned to see the two of them exchanging a sad look. Not pity, his parents would never pity him. But something close to heartbreak. Should he tell them? Ask?

"Lex," Mother said, standing. "What we want most is for you to be happy. But you are a prince, and with that comes responsibility."

"I know. I know that, but…" He paused, took a breath. "Let me look outside the nobility."

"What?" Father said.

"Just as an experiment," Lex said. "I hardly spend time around the common folk, maybe I could find someone—"

"Son," the king said, cutting him off. "You've been eligible to marry for nearly two years. There are many lovely young ladies—"

"No, you're not listening to me. None of them—"

"We hoped things would happen naturally, of course," Father said, turning toward the fireplace. "It was so simple for us, we didn't worry for you. However. You turn eighteen in one month's time, and you have not yet chosen a wife."

Lex pressed his teeth together. *Here it comes*, he thought.

"We've been discussing the possible options," Mother said. "And we truly believe Carina Valio is a wonderful choice."

Father paused near the fire. "Unless you choose a different young lady yourself, you will meet with Lady Carina and accept the proposal she's offered in two days."

Lex's jaw dropped. "Two days?"

"Yes," Mother said. "Two days. You've known these ladies for a long time, and that is plenty of time to choose who will be best to have at your side."

"Mother," Lex said. "I don't love any of them. There are only a handful who can barely tolerate *me*. Why would you force me in this choice?"

"You will choose a bride," Father said firmly, "in two days, or you will agree to marry Carina Valio."

"Why the deadline?" Lex asked. He'd argued this line before but they'd never answered the question to his satisfaction. "My birthday isn't for another month, and for that matter why does it have to be by my birthday? And why can't it be someone outside the nobility?"

Father turned, his eyes narrowed. "We have talked about this—"

"Not enough," Lex snapped. "You've said it's *tradition* to do things that way but the tradition obviously hasn't worked for me."

"Alexander," Mother said. "Do not shout."

"Why not?" Lex said. "You haven't listened to anything I say on this matter. You trust me with renovations and overseeing the guards but on this one thing that will affect the rest of my life—"

"Enough."

Lex clamped his mouth shut.

King Stephan stepped softly, but his shoulders were stiff. "You will do as we say."

"Or what?" Lex said.

His mother gasped.

Lex found it difficult to care. He was beyond arguing with them. What they asked him to do was not worth the sacrifice of being with someone he didn't love.

7

"To your rooms," Mother finally said, breaking the silence. "Until you agree, or in two days' time."

"What?"

"We won't accept the proposal for you, Alexander," Mother said. "But you must understand this is important. We're getting old. We want to see you situated for success with a good woman as your future queen and an heir of your own."

Lex opened his mouth to argue, but his father cut him off.

"This is not up for debate, son. This is how things are done."

Lex said nothing. Frustration building in his chest, he turned on his heel and left the room. It was time for drastic measures.

I'm certain I sent a note to give half to each, but the towns claimed
they both needed the entire lot despite my instructions.

2
LEX

Lex woke himself moments before midnight as he'd planned. Having an internal clock was a gift he'd never take for granted. Sitting up in bed, he reached for his eye patch, craning his ear toward the door.

"Boy's mad, I tell you," one of the guards said.

A swear, shuffling. "You can't say that about the prince! You're gonna get us executed."

"He's got his pick from the finest ladies in the kingdom, and he doesn't want any of them? I don't care if he is the prince. You can't convince me he's not a mucking fool."

Maybe I am a fool, Lex thought, adjusting the strap around his head while the other guard swore under his breath. *But I won't be a fool who sits around and does nothing.*

House arrest. Because of course there was no way he could escape from the palace he'd been living in for nearly eighteen years. Bad Prince, go to your room until you get engaged.

9

Ridiculous.

He'd have thought his parents would know better. He was a prince; he knew his obligation was to marry and produce an heir. Take care of the kingdom, ensure its continued prosperity. Seeing his parents' love for each other had always made him look forward to marriage. He would do it, and do it gladly.

But when all of his prospective brides flinched at the sight of him?

Carefully, slowly, Lex slipped out of his bed, feet meeting the cool marble floor. Through the open columns that made up one side of his room, bugs chirped their nightly calls to one another, and the wind sent a chill over Lex's skin.

The room itself was large and airy. Paintings and sculptures lined the walls between his personal belongings—mostly books—which were haphazardly organized. The door being guarded was heavy dark wood, and locked from the outside. But he wouldn't be going that way anyway.

Lex knelt beside his bed and retrieved a length of rope Enzi had hidden there. Still straining to listen to the guards, Lex quietly tied the rope to one of the thick columns. That done, he went to his wardrobe and began to dress. Sturdy wool wrap, a soft leather tunic to protect him from the humidity, belt, and oilskin trousers. He shifted awkwardly in the trousers; he'd worn them before, but they always itched at his legs. Formal attire in the palace was a simple sleeveless robe—a chiton—gathered at the shoulders and belted at the waist. But he couldn't ride his horse wearing a chiton. That would not turn out well.

Sandaled footsteps approached outside the door. Lex paused.

"About time, boys," one of the guards said.

Nicholas Belleci, one of Lex's two friends, laughed. "Apologies, sir. This one had a stomachache and needed some attention."

"He all right now?"

"I'm fine, sir," said Oliver Arena, sounding a bit annoyed.

The guard grunted. "Just don't let him through these doors, understand?"

"Yes, sir," they said together.

The two older guards' footsteps retreated, echoing in the polished stone corridor. A moment later, three tiny knocks sounded. The lock scraped, the door opening silently in the moonlight.

"Lex?" Oliver called.

"Here," Lex said, padding over to them, his feet still bare. "Thank you."

"Your parents will know we helped," Nick said.

"Maybe," Lex nodded. "But I doubt they'll punish you for it. Just follow the plan. You don't know where I'm going."

"You're crazy," Oliver said. "You do know that, right?"

Lex smiled. The fact that they weren't trying to stop him meant more than they'd ever know. "I'll be fine."

Nick looked down the hallway before turning back. "You are sure about this, then?"

"Yes," Lex said. "You know this isn't a whim."

"Right," Nick said. "I just..."

Lex watched them, noticing a tension to their expressions he hadn't before. "What is it?"

Oliver sighed. "We're worried."

"What? Why?"

"Lex," Nick said. "You've hardly been outside the palace grounds your entire life."

"That's not true," Lex snapped. "I spent weeks running around the orchards with you as a kid."

"What he means," Oliver said, "is you've never traveled on your own. Never had to sleep on the ground at night."

"Look." Lex held up his hands. "I'll only be gone a few weeks, then I'll come back. It'll be like it never happened."

Nick and Oliver exchanged a look. Lex gritted his teeth. He had to do this now, or he'd never get another chance. "Anyway, thank you. Close the door, and—"

"Wait," Oliver said. "Here."

He reached into a pocket and pulled out a handkerchief, opening it to reveal a single gold coin with a hole punched through it, glowing with a soft blue light. He offered it to Lex.

"Is that—"

"My father's," Oliver said. "He had it filled this morning, no one's touched it since. Take it."

An ache growing in his chest, Lex pulled a gold chain out from the pocket of his tunic. Two rings swung there—his grandmother's wedding ring, and the Prince's Seal.

Carefully, Oliver helped him wind the chain through the coin. If he touched it, Life magic would flow into him and grant him strength.

It wouldn't fix his old injuries, those had closed off, healed years ago within weeks of the accident. He remembered the pain, the endless heat that raged through him. And the Life Vessels—Cures—sitting by his bedside day after day, one hand in a barrel of water, the other on his body, trying to heal his injuries before they had a chance to close naturally. But Lex had been near death, and even the Master Cure, his parents' personal priest, could barely channel enough Life to keep him breathing through the burns.

Ever since, the things he thought he'd excel at had changed. The heavy scars that lined his left shoulder, neck, and side of his face were permanent in more ways than magic could help. The least of which was his habit of bumping into things on his left side because he couldn't see that way, or being unable to raise his left arm higher than his chin.

He'd gone from a bright nine-year-old who spent his time sparring to a bright nine-year-old who spent more time in the library than he needed to. He'd come to accept it, or at least he told himself he did. He stared at this coin now, wondering.

He shook his head, pushing aside the memories. The magic wouldn't heal him, but it *would* make the scarred muscles less sore, grant him more endurance. This small vessel wasn't much, but it should at least help him get out of the capital.

He slipped the chain around his neck and met Oliver's eyes. "Thank you."

"It's the least I can do."

"Lex?" Nick said. "Be careful."

Lex looked over Nick's blue eyes, olive skin, and golden hair, so like his own that people had often asked if they were brothers. Oliver's paleness and dark hair—inherited from his Ignatian mother—made him stand out.

He would miss them.

Lex forced a laugh. "Why does this feel like a goodbye? I'll be back, I promise."

The other two put their fists forward and Lex did the same, meeting in the middle.

"Use it well," he said.

"Use it well," they repeated.

He nodded his thanks and closed the door. The lock clicked back into place. His determination renewed, Lex hurried to wrap his feet in oilskin and put on his sandals—a thick-soled variety that would hold up in the rivers and mossy forests of the Reganian wild. He latched a dark cloak around his shoulders and pulled the hood up, then took up a small pack filled with extra clothing, his writing notebook and pencil, a small kit of healing supplies, and a couple of daggers. Then he went to the half wall.

Wind pulled at his hair, and the distance from where he stood to the ground looked farther than he remembered. He shook his head, then pulled the gold chain from his collar and stared at the coin.

"No turning back after this," he whispered.

He put the coin between his teeth, letting his lips close around it.

Energy flowed through him, and the soreness in his shoulder and neck was gone. The itching behind his lost eye that he barely noticed anymore was relieved. He breathed in, revitalized. The air was like a river flowing through his blood, granting him power. He had to move quickly. Letting himself over the edge, he gripped the rope and descended hand over hand the forty feet to the ground. He passed one other window like his own where servants lay sleeping. The Life helped him keep silent, and not a soul woke.

So far it's working, he thought. The servants would be the ones to raise the alarm in the morning, and by then, Nick and Oliver would be off duty and hopefully not suspected.

He spat the coin from his teeth, and felt the weight of his injuries hit him like a battering ram. Stumbling, he caught himself on the palace wall, swearing. He should've thought of this. He was used to having Life magic heal minor injuries, but he'd never used it for added strength before.

Muck, that hurt! When he finally caught his breath, he stared down at the coin. If this happened whenever he used it, he needed to be more careful.

The palace sat on a raised hill, above the banks of the River Tardus, which served as a moat. The river was thirty feet across and ten deep, and ran through the capital, Galanis, named for Lex's family. Lex made his way down to the river to a granite walkway that followed the shore. Trees and shrubbery lined the walk, easily used as cover to avoid being seen by patrolling guards.

A few hundred feet along the river, and he came to the first canal that brought water through the rest of the city. Deep grooves in the ground, human-made rivers, flowing between homes and businesses, then out into the surrounding fields to water crops and groves. Not that nature needed much help; Regania was riddled with rivers.

He turned at the fourth canal from where he began. This would lead him straight to the southern wall. He made his way slowly, carefully, his scars and pains feeling brand new. He was tempted to use the coin again, but pushed the thought away, forcing himself to focus on his surroundings.

The canals, like the one he ran beside, were more for convenience than anything else. Running water and indoor plumbing helped the people stay healthy and happy. It was a luxury Regania invented that other countries had yet to copy. As he continued, Lex couldn't help smiling, knowing his kingdom was so well off. Part of him had worried there might be negative consequences from his leaving tonight, but seeing the comfort and prosperity of Galanis from close up like this, he was reassured. The kingdom would be fine without him for a while.

Sticking to the shadows helped him stay unseen, and within minutes he'd made his way through the entire city. Another rope waited for him at the outer wall, hanging from thirty feet up. Lex took a breath. He'd never make it with his bad shoulder. Not without the coin. His jaw clenched, then he bit down on the gold once more.

Climbing was as easy as lowering had been. At the top, Enzi waited.

"You're late," Enzi said, hurrying to move the rope to the outer side of the wall.

"Blame Nick and Oliver," Lex said, still holding the coin in his mouth.

"We have seven minutes," Enzi said. "Your horse, sword, and extra supplies are there in the trees, near those boulders. You have to get down the other side and into the shadows before the guards come by."

Lex began to climb over the edge. "Will you get away safe?" he asked, his words muffled through the coin between his teeth.

"I'll be fine," Enzi said. "You, get out of here."

Lex sighed, grateful for his friendship. "They'll throw you in the dungeon."

"Maybe," Enzi shrugged. "So long as Andre sneaks down to visit, I'll be happy."

Lex laughed.

"You be safe," Enzi said, turning serious.

"I will," Lex said. "Thank you." Hand under hand, Lex lowered himself to the ground once more. He ran for the trees the moment his feet hit soil, and was in their shadows in a matter of moments. He looked back then to see Enzi pulling the rope back up and carrying it away. In the distance, guards made their way toward the now empty spot.

He'd done it. He was out. And it would be hours before anyone realized he was gone.

A thrill filled his chest. The thought of the midsummer festival on the coast, filled with food and colors and normal people, surely he would meet someone...surely.

A few yards into the trees, Lex's horse was picketed. Pepper, a dappled grey mare, shook her black-maned head at him as he approached. Lex braced himself, then spat out the coin and collapsed against her neck. He wasn't a weak person, he could lift a sword and hold his own in a fight, but he'd become so used to dealing with his limitations that he'd never considered how strong he *could* be. How much he was missing. That line of thought could be dangerous for him, though. He knew the coin gave him more than what was humanly possible though; anyone would probably feel weak after that amount of strength. Still, it shook him. He had to be mindful, only use the magic when he absolutely needed it.

Lex lifted the chain over his head and tucked it into the saddlebag. He didn't need it now. What he needed was to get far away from Galanis before anyone woke to find him missing. If he rode through the night and into the day, he should be able to lose anyone looking for him. What would his parents think of him running away?

I'm not running away, he thought. *I'm running* to *something. Someone.*

With a great deal of effort, Lex mounted his horse and patted her neck. "All right, Pep. If there's a girl out there for me, let's pray the Gods lead us to find her."

He kicked her flanks, and disappeared into the forest.

TRAINING

- smile
- be mindful of the Priests
- never yell (except when I'm old?)
- ~~don't go to~~
- problems - good for Father
- Ignore the [illegible]
- I should get a cat. A big fluffy one
- or maybe a bird
- [illegible] hardly one nice
- Father is doing my training for me
- ~~I thought I was supposed to be~~
- Sword practice that's afternoon
- Library after that
- dinner after that with Mother and Father
- Midsummer Festival in three weeks
- what does Growth Magic feel like?

- clothes
- healing
- daggers
- food and water (Enzi)
- extra sandals
- sword (Enzi)
- need a rope

A stupid someone who will remain unnamed tried to get me alone today. She asked for a private word, for me to meet her in an alcove off the main hall. I told her no. She's one I've talked with many times and I honestly don't even care anymore what she thinks of me. I mean I care about her as I would any citizen, but no, I'm not going to follow her anywhere just because she pouts her lips at me. Does that actually work on some men? Seems like a horrible inconvenience to me...

I hate the way their eyes trail me
As though I'm something ~~bad~~ wrong to see
Then why they ~~try to~~ go and play pretend
As though we've always been close friends
No, those I ~~always~~ only have a few
And trust when I say – they're not you.

This has been my most difficult struggle: helping people who begin to feel I owe them something.

3
CARINA

Carina paused, her hands suddenly cold, and she balled them into fists to get her blood moving again. With a deep breath, she nodded to the servants, and the heavy doors opened before her.

She strode through the arched doorway onto the portico. Cool night air wrapped around her face and bare arms, causing bumps of chill to rise all over her. She took a small moment to revel in the view. Her family's palace sat on a small hill, overlooking the central fields of Regania, the wild forests, and looming mountains beyond. Below the palace were homes of lower lords, knights, and peasants who lived under the protection—or lack thereof—of Carina's father, High Lord Maximus Valio.

The thought of him brought her back to herself, and she blinked before looking to him. He stood in the center of the space, staring down at the fire pit with his back to her. His shoulders were tense, and his jaw stiff. He wore the same style chiton as she, belted at the waist and hanging to the floor, but his was deep blue and hers scarlet. The colors fit them, he being slightly lighter in complexion though still the olive-skinned tone of most Reganians. But Carina displayed the deep brown skin of her Medelian mother.

Carina shifted slightly, her sandals scratching at the stone floor. The silence made her heart race.

"Carina?" he said.

She gasped, but thankfully kept it inaudible. "Yes, Father?"

The tension in his body eased away as he sighed. "I am only relieved to hear your voice, child. I am glad you chose to dine with me tonight instead of in your room."

She swallowed. "Why is that?"

"We should hear word on the proposal this evening. I have high hopes, and have ordered a fine feast in your honor."

Carina paled, grateful he couldn't see. She'd nearly forgotten about the proposal. The palace was only a twelve hour ride away on a fast horse in good weather, so they ought to hear the same day a decision was made. She thought of Prince Alexander. She didn't know him well; they'd spoken once or twice, had an official outing together that was supposedly her audition—at least that's how she thought of it—to be his wife. He'd always seemed nice enough, but she felt no desire to be attached to him. It was all her father's idea.

"I am certain you shall live a happy life at the side of our dear prince," he said, a slight hint of bitterness in his tone. No one else would have caught it, but Carina knew it well.

From a door to her right servants began carrying in platters of fruits, breads, and cheeses. Carina joined her father at a long table set up on the far side of the fire pit, overlooking the small city of Valios, and beyond, the fields and moors that made up central Regania.

Carina ate quickly. Something about her father's presence told her she didn't have time for a leisurely meal. Aside from the rare clink of silverware against plate, there was only silence. They never prayed over their food, especially not since Mother died. Carina had never been especially faithful on her own but she'd always worshiped with Mother. When she died, Father continued to take Carina to services but his heart was never in it. She'd tried to speak to him about it, but those times had not ended well.

Halfway through their soup, a rich blend of tomatoes, marjoram, and fish, a servant entered. She curtsied low. "My Lord, Sir Zivon is here for you. Shall I have him wait?"

Carina froze, her spoon halfway to her mouth.

Father didn't notice, only wiped his mouth gingerly. "No, no. Send him in."

The door opened wider and a tall, thick man strode through. Zivon was her father's personal servant, a Callidian man who had sworn himself to Lord Valio.

Carina looked up once to take in his appearance. Black trousers under a short black riding robe with silver buckles. One piercing brown eye, the other covered with a patch. His skin was slightly darker than her own, his hair a stunning blue. He had worked for her father for nearly five years—since right after Mother died. She didn't know much about him. And she didn't want to.

"Master," Zivon said, his deep voice resonating even in the open space. "I wish I had better news. It has been confirmed today, the prince went missing yesterday."

Carina's eyes widened, staring at her soup.

Her father stood, slowly, calmly. "What do you mean?"

"Rumors say he ran away, Master," Zivon said. "His quarters were found empty, a rope hanging from the pillars of his room. The king's best hunters were sent to find him."

Father began to pace, one hand running through his golden hair. "The boy is smart. Capable. He'll have gone as far as possible to avoid being caught." He paused, looking at Zivon. "Can you find him?"

"Of course, Master."

"Do it, then. Before the king's guard do. And bring him here."

"Yes, Master." Zivon bowed, then turned to go.

Carina stole a glance as he left, part of her wishing to be dismissed as quickly.

"Leave us," her father said.

Carina froze. A moment later all servants and staff had fled the room.

She took two deep breaths.

Her father's hand gripped her arm and hauled her from her chair.

"After everything I've planned," he growled, low enough that his voice would not be heard through the doors, "everything I worked for, the prince runs away at the very *thought* of marrying you!"

She tried to plead, but only whimpers escaped her.

He threw her to the ground, her shoulder scraping against the stone floor, pain shooting through her arm. Her head was so close to the fire pit she could feel the heat on her cheek.

A moment later his sandaled foot slammed into her ribs. The breath was knocked from her, and she gulped at the air to refill her lungs, but another kick followed, making her slide away from the heat. She retreated, curling in on herself, trying to let the pain be a thing she observed rather than felt.

"You have the *best* education money can buy," he said. "You've been trained in arts young women only dream of, had the best stylists in the kingdom design your very appearance, yet you are *still not good enough.*"

Carina choked as air returned to her, letting her head rest on the cool floor. All she saw was her father's feet and lower legs, the rest of her vision was a blur.

She screamed as he landed one last kick, this time to her lower abdomen. Perhaps in an effort to assure he received no grandchildren. The thought didn't upset her nearly as much as it probably should have. He stepped lightly around the fire pit. Carina closed her eyes, sucking in air, listening.

"I am so tired of living under those soft-hearted, slow-thinking monarchs," he muttered, more to himself than her, she knew. "Stephan and Larissa don't deserve the crowns they wear, and that brat Alexander only shows his ineptitude by running when he ought to be forming alliances. Stupid imbeciles."

She'd heard all this before. She'd known his intentions were to wed her to the prince, then run the kingdom from behind the throne. She'd gone along with it—hadn't had a choice to do otherwise. Still, as she lay on the cold marble,

24

forcing air into her lungs, she wondered whether she *had* been the reason for the prince's escape. He didn't seem like the kind to leave her without an answer, but perhaps she'd misread him.

"I have spent nearly all our resources getting the loyalty of the church, the king's guard, even the mucking lower lords here are with me. If I can only get control…."

She opened her eyes, staring at the flames licking up into cool summer air. Her father still muttered, circling the fire pit, his sharp features made sharper by the shadows and flickering before him. He looked like…like Carina used to imagine a Virus—those Vessels who channeled the power of Death and Shadows. She'd never met one, and didn't want to, but that couldn't stop a child's imagination from inventing things.

Another knock sounded, and the same servant entered. She did not spare a glance for the crumpled daughter on the floor, and Carina was glad of it. It would only make things worse.

"My lord, the local High Cure is here to see you."

"One moment," Father said. Without explanation, he lifted Carina from the floor like a doll and placed her in her seat. She forced herself to sit straight as he arranged the folds of her dress and laid her hair over one shoulder to hide the scrape she'd just received.

"Lovely as always, my dear."

Carina shivered.

The High Cure was the head of the church's local branch, over the Life Vessels. Carina had met the man a few times, but doubted he'd noticed her. Midnight blue robes trailed after him. A silver line ran down each sleeve to mark his position in the church's hierarchy.

"Good evening, Lord Valio."

"Good evening indeed, Father." Carina's father was now the epitome of piousness. "To what do I owe the pleasure of your company?"

The Vessel smiled. "I wished to thank you in person for the generous donation you sent last week. Because of the faith and charity of people like you, this kingdom might continue to prosper."

"Might, you say?" Father asked. "Regania is a strong and self-sufficient kingdom. Is there any doubt?"

The Vessel sighed—rather dramatically, Carina thought. "It is only this ordeal with the prince, my lord." The man looked from side to side, as though checking for eavesdroppers. "The royal family has chosen no heir in the event that the prince does not return."

Valio frowned, leaning forward. "Do you mean to imply that he may not return?"

"There was rumor of a note saying he would, but no proof. The church in particular is in an awkward position. We speak for the Gods, and we support the crown, but we cannot support an heir who is not acting as one."

Valio rubbed a hand over his trimmed beard. "Will the monarchs choose a second heir?"

"Doubtful, my lord. Though they are being encouraged to do so."

Valio nodded. "Then let us pray they will choose the person best suited for it."

"Or that the prince will return safely," the Vessel added.

"Of course, yes. Thank you, Father."

The Vessel bowed and left the room. Carina did not move. She did not eat, nor barely breathe. Her father continued to circle the fire pit, eyes narrowed, muttering under his breath. She caught words such as *prince* and *heir* and…she couldn't have heard…*kill?* No, her father would never…would he? She shoved her fear aside and tried to listen more carefully.

"Carina," her father said in his full voice.

She jumped in her chair, but stood shakily. "Y-yes, father?"

"Go see if Zivon has left yet. If he has not, send him to me. I have more instructions for him."

"Yes, Father," she said, curtsying.

"And a scribe. I need to act quickly."

"Of course, Father."

For some nobility, being sent on an errand like this would be embarrassing. But Carina was through the doors in the space of a heartbeat.

Carina always did as she was told. But she could imagine otherwise when no one was watching.

Her bedroom was fully enclosed, on the north eastern corner of Valio Palace. It had windows, but at the moment they were covered by heavy curtains. Her doors to the main colonnade and to her baths were closed and locked. She sat on the carpeted floor before a modest fireplace, wearing nothing but her underclothes—linen shorts and a wrap around her torso. She breathed deeply of Fugeran incense she'd lit before her. It wasn't as energizing as her scented oils, but it would do until she could distill more. Her shoulders fought to droop, but she forced them straight.

After leaving her father, she had indeed found Zivon preparing to leave, and sent him back as he was about to mount his horse. She'd then come straight to her room to apply doctorbush oil to her scrape and bruises. She was nearly out, and would need to send for more of the flowers from the southern Reganian territories. There was no Cure serving at Valio Palace, only Carina and her oils. And she was not about to go out into the city to find treatment. That would mean admitting what was happening. She was certain all the servants knew.

She closed her eyes, focusing on her breath. After Mother's death, Father had changed. He'd never been particularly compassionate before, but it seemed sometimes as though she were living with an entirely different person. He shut her out and found release with his mistresses.

The poor girls, not much older than Carina, who he closeted away for a few months at a time and then threw into the streets when they were too weak to function. Carina felt for them. They were harmed far more than she, and in far worse ways. She was sometimes able to slip poison to them, in case they wanted an easier way out. She knew that feeling too. The place where dignity no longer mattered, and worth was a thing of the past.

She shook these thoughts from her head. For the moment, she needed to close her eyes and clear her mind. She thought of the color of her hair—deep Medelian black, with thick streaks of Reganian gold. Something in the Medelian blood caused it to mix with others in this certain way, and Carina could never decide if she was proud of it, or embarrassed. It certainly made her stand out in the Reganian court, which was not always what she wanted. But imagining the smooth texture and dramatic coloring helped her calm herself, and slow her heart.

She stood, pushing the incense toward the fireplace, and went to her wardrobe. Everything was in its place. She could have easily done this blindfolded. She removed her sword from its spot behind her training armor, and drew it from the sheath. The handle was deep grey steel wrapped in black leather, embedded with a small ruby at the pommel. A gift from her mother on her tenth birthday. She'd out-grown it after Mother died, and thankfully Father had it re-forged using the same materials and design. It was made for her. Fit her better than any other sword ever had. But there had always been something off about handling it. Like it could be slightly better, and was missing something.

She went back to the open space before her fire, and took up a practice stance. Her feet stable on a thick soft carpet, she raised the blade before her and began to move. Slowly at first, then with more speed as she finished the dance and began again without pause. Her muscles began to burn, sweat trickled from her hairline. Her thin clothing stuck to her the more she worked.

When she danced, her mind was clearer than any other time. She went over everything she'd heard at dinner. The Prince, her father, Zivon...how was it all connected? Dare she even continue this line of thought?

Three times through the dance, and she stopped abruptly, holding the sword before her as she had when beginning. She held that stance, her muscles burning, until her heart had again slowed, then finally released her sore and tired muscles. Sword back in sheath, sheath back in wardrobe, Carina closed the doors and rested her forehead against the wood. Nearly half an hour had passed, and she still felt unsettled.

A knock sounded at the door to her baths. "My lady?" Adia, her handmaid.

"Yes, I'm here," Carina called.

"Shall I draw up your bath now?"

"Yes, please. And thank you, Adia."

"My pleasure, lady."

Carina went toward the doors, and paused before opening them. Something warm tickled her cheek, and she wiped it away. A tear. How odd. She never cried anymore when her father hit her, and rarely at any other time. She couldn't remember the last tear to fall from her eyes. She stared at her fingertips, the tear smeared across them.

She couldn't stop her father. She knew that. Not that she would be brave enough to try.

I want to help them, I truly do. I've been where they are.
I still am, in a way.

4
LEX

Lex dropped the reins and let Pepper walk while he turned awkwardly to his saddlebags. Digging through, he took out a piece of dried meat, and grimaced. It had only been what, a day and a half? And he was already tired of the only food he had?

Pampered Prince, he was.

He sighed out loud.

Pepper nickered, ripping grass from the ground below.

"I can't eat grass," Lex said, disgusted. He dismounted, looking around and rubbing his chin, hoping for scruff to come in soon. At least enough to disguise him should he need to go into a town.

Kneeling down, he examined some plants. He knew which were safe to eat—he'd specifically studied them before embarking on this journey. After a few minutes of searching he spotted a small bush of sunsetberries—his favorite—and hurried to pick as many as he could find. Granted he ate half of them as he did, but at least he'd have something in his stomach.

31

He took a moment to unfurl the map Enzi had packed for him—taken from the royal cartographer himself. Lex liked to imagine Master Hargreaves frantically counting the copies of his maps only to find one missing, a thank you note and a few coins from Lex in its place. The man had always been kind to him, more than most. Lex hoped he'd understand.

Now, Lex tried to discern where he was. He'd ridden mostly west and somewhat south since leaving Galanis. Avoiding towns and farmsteads, he'd favored small trails that wound through Regania's dense forests, the foliage of which was far thicker than he'd imagined from reading of it.

Heavy moss hung from branches everywhere, and one morning he woke to a cloud of fog and couldn't continue on until the sun revealed its presence and burned the haze. The trees were another thing entirely: huge trunks, ten feet or more across, and a hundred feet high. The tallest trees he'd ever seen were those surrounding Galanis, and they barely passed the thirty-foot city wall. These giants fascinated him. He'd written a few pages in his notebook just describing them.

He'd been surrounded by these for the past two days, but the landscape was beginning to shift around him now. The trees slowly thinning, opening to grassy flatland with a wide river running west through it. The map showed this, the River Tardus, with a main highway running alongside it, until it reached another section of forest perhaps five miles away.

Lex looked up to find the sun, low in the sky. He should look for a shelter soon. He would probably have to risk entering a town or village as well if he wanted to keep going. Remounting Pepper, they began to walk through the tangled forest, when a snap sounded behind him. Hoof beats? Footsteps? Or had he imagined it?

A huge horse burst through a thick web of moss and stopped, pawing the ground. Lex stared at the rider. The thick man was obviously Callidian, with dark skin and rich blue hair that hung in a long braid down his back. But what was a Callidian doing in the middle of—

"You are here, then," the man said. He too wore an eye patch over his left eye, and for a moment Lex wondered at the rarity of two of them in one place. "My master orders me to bring you in."

Lex blanched. In an instant he knew that this man was not one of his father's guards sent to "rescue" him. This man's dark clothing bore no seal, no colors. Only a heartbeat had passed before Lex kicked hard at Pepper's flanks and tore down the road.

Wind whipped past as Lex bent low over Pepper's neck. He pushed her harder than he ever had. If he could get a lead on him....

A fist slammed into Lex's scarred shoulder—coming at him from his blind side—knocking him from his saddle. He flipped, hit the ground hard, and cried out in pain. Pepper stopped only a few strides beyond, and kicked at the loamy ground. Lex gritted his teeth. He had the token, the vessel. Maybe he could get away if he just—

Lex struggled to get his feet under him as the Callidian man dismounted nearby. But dizziness from the fall made Lex's vision a blur, he couldn't see where Pepper was....

A thick hand gripped Lex's tunic, pulling him over and dragging him. He blinked, not fighting anymore as he was pulled across the forest floor.

He shook his head, willing his mind and vision to clear as his body was tossed about. For a moment he feared he might become totally blind and he'd be lost in the Reganian forests until he died. Or was killed.

With great effort, he raised his head. A man was moving around nearby. Blue hair. Eye patch.

Oooohhhh, Lex thought, his mind beginning to clear. He'd been captured. Had gone unconscious for a bit, but not long. Less than a minute if his internal clock was correct.

He shifted, or tried to, but couldn't because his arms were tied down. His back against a tree. His lower back ached from where he'd landed after falling off Pepper. Pepper! His head snapped up fully and gaze darted around the space, landing on the dappled grey mare to his right. He sighed in relief.

The man across from him was striking flint to start a fire, blowing on the early embers. Lex swallowed at the sight, forcing his gaze away.

"You had enough rope to tie me to one of these?" Lex said, nodding to the huge tree behind him, in an effort to distract himself.

The man didn't reply.

"Who are you working for? I know you're not one of my father's men. What does your employer want with me?"

Still, nothing.

Lex sighed, slumping against the tree. The ropes rubbed against his shoulder, irritating the scarring there. Suddenly, he felt more stupid than he ever had in his life. Why had he thought he could survive on his own? He was still at least a week away from the coast and had no food, no experience hunting…he'd assumed his parents would send people to track him, but it hadn't occurred to him that others might want to capture him as well.

It seemed so obvious now that it had happened.

The fire before him caught, the large man adding small sticks one at a time to fuel it. Bumps rose on Lex's arms. He was six feet from the flames, he would be fine. Despite knowing that, however, he found himself curling against the tree as much as the ropes would allow. Then his stomach gave a hearty growl. The man across from him looked up with a raised eyebrow.

Lex cleared his throat. "Do you have any food to share?"

The Callidian rolled his eye and stood. He went to his horse and pulled something out. A strip of dried meat. Lex's captor approached and knelt down to loosen the ropes slightly to free one arm, then handed him the food before re-tightening the ropes.

"Thank you," Lex said.

The man only grunted, and returned to his seat slowly adding more wood to the fire. Lex watched, fascinated and terrified. Not by his circumstances, but by the heat he was beginning to feel emanate before him. In another attempt at distraction, he took a bite of the meat.

When he did, he let out an involuntary hum of satisfaction. It tasted *amazing*. Spiced and tender, it melted in his mouth and seemed to restore his energy and clear his mind. "This is incredible!" he said. "What is in this?"

The man's mouth quirked with an amused smile. "Spices from my home country," he finally said through a thick accent. "With the deer of your kingdom it goes well. We have few of them in the East."

Lex took another bite savoring the unfamiliar and delicious flavors. "I've read about Callidian food," he said through a mouthful, "but I never imagined it so rich."

The man raised a thick brow. "Take care, highness. You'll drip on your fine clothing."

"I'm not a prince here," Lex said, swallowing. "That much is evident from my being bound with ropes." He paused, eying the man, and the fire. "Will you tell me your name?"

"So that after you escape you can hunt me down?"

"So that I can feel as though we've been introduced," Lex said.

"I have you captured."

"You seem a decent fellow."

"You can persuade me not to turn you in, you think?"

"If it's a matter of payment, I'm sure an agreement could be reached."

The man's expression darkened. "No. Payment in coin is of no use to me."

Lex watched him carefully, trying to discern the reason for his shift in mood. He'd seemed to be bantering before, and had now looked away as though…ashamed, perhaps?

Lex ate a bit more as the silence grew heavy, and the fire larger. He couldn't get away from it, the heat beginning to warm his feet.

Was this the Gods' idea of forcing him to face his fears? He hadn't been this close to flame in years. Even in his own rooms, the fireplace was fifteen feet from his bed and desk, and fully guarded by glass, monitored hourly by servants to make sure it didn't get out of control. His heart was beating a frantic pace inside his chest, willing him to get away from the flames.

"Are you sure you need the fire that large?" he finally said, his voice higher than usual.

The Callidian looked up. "This is not large."

Lex swallowed. "Would you mind moving me, then? Particularly if you're planning to make it bigger."

The man frowned. "How did you lose your eye, prince?"

"Huh?" Lex blinked, refocusing.

"I said: how did you lose your eye?" The man pointed to his own eye patch. "Mine was a job gone wrong. A girl put an arrowhead into my eye."

Lex gaped. "You…what?"

He shrugged, but it seemed forced. "Job was mostly done. Kill her family and collect her. The girl fought and got away."

Lex shuddered, his throat tightening. This man wasn't only a kidnapper. He was an assassin. Lex thanked the Gods that the girl had escaped, but…how long would *he* last?

"And you, young prince?" the man asked. "Your lost eye?"

Lex forced a smile onto his face, though he didn't feel at all amused. "I was six. There was a…cooking competition of sorts in the palace courtyard. Many people, fires and huge…huge pots of water and oil. There was one stall, making fried bread desserts with sugar and honey. They were my favorite. But I…" He paused, the memory catching in his throat.

37

"Was it fire?"

"No," Lex said. "Not exactly, anyway. It was oil. A pot of hot oil spilled over me. My whole body, I remember...for days all I could see was the red of light shining through my eyelids."

"Should have killed you, that."

"It nearly did," Lex said softly. "I was immediately doused in cold water, my face and neck wrapped in salve and bandages. The Cures focused on the worst of the burns, over my legs and torso, but that meant the ones up here," he pointed to his eye and shoulder, "healed over before they got to them."

The Callidian nodded in understanding. "Once a wound heals itself, there's no healing it with magic."

"Exactly."

The man paused, and Lex felt a weight to the stare. "You have had a difficult life for a prince."

Lex scoffed. "No...no I was lucky. If it had been any other child, they would've died."

"Still."

"I thank the Goddess Amplia every day for sustaining her Cures in healing me as much as they did," Lex said. "They were at my bedside for weeks, taking shifts as they got tired. Workers worked night and day to carry fresh water to them to pour Life into me. And I thank Sileo too for keeping my thoughts clear through the healing, or I'd have lost my mind along with my eye."

The man nodded solemnly. "To channel that power, it is a great gift."

"Indeed." Lex frowned. He simply could not read this man no matter how hard he tried. One minute he was hard and angry, the next tender and sad. "Are there Vessels in Callidia?" Lex asked.

"Of course," the man said, seeming to shake off his mood. "It is like here, only—"

An arrow shot through the clearing. It grazed the Callidian man's cheek, drawing blood. Lex had barely registered the shot when the man had stood.

"What was—"

Another arrow flew through the space.

The Callidian man's gaze darted from Lex, to where the shots were coming from. Then with a grunt, he mounted his horse and kicked hard, flying into the trees in the opposite direction from the arrows.

Lex sat, stunned, and suddenly remembered how close to the heat he was.

A swear sounded from the darkness, and a man twice Lex's size entered the firelight.

"Did I hit him?"

Lex stared.

"*Did I hit him?!*"

"No!" Lex said. "Ah, grazed his cheek is all?"

"*Damn* him to Muxai!" The man kicked at the ground, showering dirt and dead leaves over the fire.

Lex flinched away as bits of burnt ember flew into the air. He would be fine. He would be fine. There were other people here, no one was going to let it get out of control.

The newcomer went on swearing colorfully, and shortly an entire group had crowded into the light, leading many horses and even drawing a cart full of food sacks. Lex wished he had some way to hide or seem not so conspicuous, but every person there stopped to consider him when they arrived. Following which they ignored him completely. He was grateful for that, as it gave him a chance to force his heart to slow. The gathering group babbled to each other excitedly, and Lex tried to focus on a central conversation.

"Did you tell her?" the first man asked of a small, dark-skinned woman with long copper hair. Her curves were accented by tight-fitting trousers and a flowing brown tunic belted at her waist.

"Only that you'd gone," the woman replied. "She's on her way, but she won't be happy when she learns you missed. You should've waited."

The man sighed, running a hand over his face. He and the woman had the same round face and dark eyes, and Lex guessed them to be siblings.

"Who's this?" the woman asked, raising a brow at Lex.

The man turned and looked Lex over. "No idea."

"Hm." She tilted her head, considering him. "Fine clothing, no marks though…are you from the capital?"

"Um, I—"

"Jee," the man said. "Wait to question him until Robyn gets here."

Lex blinked, trying to process everything that had happened to him in the past hour. The others went back to their discussion as they cooked and prepared their camp, a few people coming to monitor the fire and cook on it. The small woman was one of these.

"So, come here often?" she asked with a smirk.

Lex frowned.

"Wow," she said. "Can't take a joke, all right."

"I—no, I just...sorry. You caught me off guard."

"I get the feeling that happens to you often," she said, eyeing the ropes around him.

At this, he did crack a smile.

"Don't worry," she said, spearing a piece of meat on her knife and holding it over the fire. "We'll probably be able to untie you soon, but...no promises."

Lex nodded. It made sense. They didn't know him, had to make sure he wasn't a threat. Part of him couldn't help but feel grateful to these people, whoever they were, for driving away his captor. He settled back—still tied up—and watched them work. The group was made up of men and women from all over the Unbroken Lands. About a third of them looked pure Reganian, but most had features of other races mixed in as well.

He finally learned the first man's name was Mitalo, and the woman was indeed his sister, Jianna. Perdonian names. They seemed perhaps in their thirties, and looked to be in charge of the rest of the group, yet still made exceptions to certain things someone else would have to address. After eating most of them went to sleep. It was nearly an hour before two more figures entered the light.

Both had the slim fitness of youth and looked to be about Lex's age. One was a wiry boy who, like Lex's captor, had blue Callidian hair. It was long, and tied in a tail at the base of his neck. The other's face was shadowed by a hooded cloak which, along with their clothing, was entirely coated in mud and grass. Quietly, they approached Mitalo and Jianna.

"Get it?" Mitalo asked.

"Yes," the hooded one said. "And we need to plan. Now."

Lex frowned. The one with a hood sounded female, but he couldn't be sure.

"What is it?" Jianna said, standing from her spot by the fire. Her playful face turned serious.

"It's Valio," the Callidian boy said, handing them a piece of crumpled paper.

"He never does this," the hooded one added. "He's usually predictable, but this is not. I have a bad feeling about it."

"We trust your instincts," Mitalo nodded. "Suggestions?"

"We need to listen in," the hooded one said. "Maybe get someone to pose as a servant and find a way for us to eavesdrop."

"I can go," the Callidian boy said. "I'm a faster rider than all of you, and I need less sleep. I can be there tomorrow if I take two horses."

The hooded one paused. "If I let you go," she said, "you have to follow orders exactly, do you understand? I'm tired of having to babysit you."

"Come on, Robyn," the boy said. "Give me a chance, I can do this."

The hooded one, Robyn, seemed to consider, then finally nodded.

"I'll send Chess on ahead with the shipment," Mitalo said. "The people of Liras know her, and she's ready for more responsibility anyway. The three of us should see this through."

"Good, I agree," Robyn said. She turned to the Callidian. "The three of us should arrive in a couple of days, and that will give us enough time to form a plan."

The boy nodded. "I'll get my things together, then." He hurried away, and Mitalo and Jianna came to the fire, Robyn following them, finally lowering her hood.

She was tall and thin, almost unhealthily so. Her hair, face, and forearms were stained with dirt, but she walked with her shoulders squared, eyes bright and focused.

"Oh, you should know," Jianna said, now to Robyn, "we uh…have a prisoner of sorts."

Robyn looked to where Jianna pointed—at Lex. She frowned, looking over his form from scarred face to feet tucked under him to avoid the fire's heat. He felt exposed under her gaze, as though she could see right through any deception he might try to offer. She seemed to be looking him over, searching for something. Perhaps weaknesses or potential dangers.

"The assassin had him?" Robyn asked.

"Yes," Mitalo said. "He was tied up when I…missed."

Robyn's frown deepened. "I did tell you to wait if we caught sight of him."

Mitalo glowered.

"Regardless," she said, turning her full attention to Lex. "Who are you?"

Lex swallowed, his mind racing frantically. He couldn't tell them who he really was. They'd either turn him in or use him as blackmail—he'd learned that much from his first captor, hadn't he? Still, he'd better stick to a familiar name. "I am Sir Lex, my lady. A knight of the Belleci house."

Her eyes narrowed.

"Should we untie him?" Jianna asked.

"Not just yet," Robyn said, her eyes still on Lex.

He said nothing, worried that if he did the lie would unravel. She watched him for a few moments before finally turning away.

"Is Damari gone yet?" Robyn asked, looking around.

Mitalo shrugged. "Don't think so."

"Tell him to come back here a moment." She turned back to Lex and crouched between him and the fire, level with his gaze. "What do you know of the Valio house?"

"Ah," he shrugged. "Not much. Only things I've learned through word of mouth."

Damari approached, leading two horses. "Who's this?"

"We have a knight," Robyn said proudly. "And he's going to tell us everything he knows about Valio and his palace, or we'll leave him tied up here for the bears."

Lex's brows shot up.

"Or maybe we can use him as bait for the assassin. He wants him for some reason." She paused. "Why does he want you?"

"No idea," Lex stammered. His mouth had gone dry, his skin itched. "I've never met the man before."

"Hmm. He doesn't do anything without a purpose. Well, never mind that. Tell us everything you know about Valio."

She waited, expectant.

"Lord Valio is ah…excessive," he said, tempted to make things up just so he'd have more to say. "Rumors say he spends everything on fine clothing and food, or décor for his palace. He has one daughter, Lady Carina. Age sixteen. She's kind, but very quiet. Doesn't come to many social functions. Lord Valio proposed a marriage between her and the prince but that's

44

probably not going to go through. Though Lord Valio did seem very adamant about it in the proposal letter. More so than most…from what I heard."

Robyn's eyes narrowed. "How do you know all this?"

"The king reads things like that publicly for two hours each day," he said, continuing with the truth. "I was in court when it was read." He left out that he was on the throne while it was read, sitting in his father's place for an hour. Training.

She relaxed. "What was that about his daughter? You say she's quiet?"

Lex nodded. "I've spoken with her a few times. She's a lovely girl, but doesn't speak much even in conversation. Very twitchy, too. I remember I offered her my hand to escort her to a dance and she flinched away for a moment." He had thought she'd been offended by his offer, but instead she'd turned out to be a little high-strung.

At this information Robyn's expression hardened. She stood. "Damari, learn what you can about this girl. She might be interested in helping us."

Damari's chest swelled with pride. "Yes, my lady."

"Be quick about it."

Damari mounted one of the horses and was gone in moments.

Robyn turned back to Lex. "Listen well, friend. We can work with you if you're willing to help us, or we can simply let you go. On principle, I don't trust nobility, but you could be of great help to us should you earn that trust."

Lex frowned, trying to decide what she meant. "You're asking me to…come with you? I don't even know what you're doing."

Her serious expression cracked slightly, a smirk lifting one corner of her mouth. "Come with us, show me you can be trusted, and I'll tell you what we're up to. You must've run away for a reason, so maybe you aren't as pompous as most nobility I've met."

Lex raised a brow. "Have you…met many nobles?"

She did not answer.

Lex cleared his throat. "If staying with you will keep that assassin from coming after me again, then I'd appreciate the chance to travel in a group."

"Good," she said, standing. "We head west at sunrise. We will untie you and feed you, but we will also keep a close eye on you. We don't want our runaway knight running away from us."

We only take the barest of essentials for ourselves.
I suppose it doesn't help that I've acquired weapons
in the time I've lived out here.

5
LEX

A kick to Lex's boot shook him awake. He blinked, his vision blurry.

"Morning your lordyship."

He looked up to see Jianna kneeling beside him, and the events of the previous day came to mind. He scrambled away and she let out a sweet-sounding laugh.

"Time to get up," she said, standing.

Her eyes did the thing that everyone's did when looking at him without his eye patch on, trailing the marks coloring his face, covering where his left eye had once been.

Lex turned away and hurried to slip on his eye patch. He hadn't let anyone see him without it for years, and the embarrassment burned inside him.

He never went anywhere without his patch on. It was humiliating at the best of times, and the embarrassment felt heavier now since he didn't have a place to escape to. Perhaps only worse was the time he'd been teased at age fourteen for his scars. The memory was clear; a friendly tournament of swordplay, not for glory, only for fun. He was the worst of them, and his peers had laughed at him for it, then a few proceeded to make jokes about his appearance. The king of course made laughing at the prince an offense punishable by imprisonment, and Lex never lost a sword fight again.

What would he do now if he were forced to use his sword? Surely he was more talented than these three. He had been trained by the best, after all. And by the time he grew and gained more strength he'd become rather proficient, even if the others did let him win anyway.

Stuffing his things into bags, he took a moment to be grateful that the bounty hunter had at least left Pepper. Lex saddled her and tied his bags down before realizing that the clearing was nearly empty. Jianna was kicking dirt over the fire, and Robyn and Mitalo stood a short way off, speaking softly. But the twenty-odd others he'd seen the night before, the horses, the cart, all were gone.

"Where is everyone else?" he asked, rubbing his eye.

"Gone," Jianna said. "They had a schedule to keep. Not everyone can sleep until midday like you Life-Drinkers."

Lex frowned, watching her cover the fire. "Life-Drinkers?"

"That's right," she said. "You've got your own personal Life Vessels, don't you? A single strong Cure working for each noble family? I'll bet you take in a bit every morning with breakfast."

Lex smiled and tried not to laugh at the assumption. "No, actually. The only time I've ever used it was when I was sick."

He left out the vessel he'd used to escape the palace. That was certainly an exceptional circumstance.

Jianna however only raised a brow.

"You don't believe me?" Lex asked.

"I don't trust you," she said. "Robyn decided to keep you around, and I trust her judgement, but that doesn't mean you're free and clear."

Lex swallowed, then nodded.

"Alright, noble," Robyn said, approaching and drawing him from his thoughts. "Who are you, really?"

Lex looked from one to the other of his three new companions, confused. "I told you last night, I—"

"And I know you lied," Robyn said. "Now tell me who you are. What noble house?"

Lex sighed, and tried the other name whose family he knew well. "Arena. In the north."

Robyn stared for a moment, and Lex stared back. She had a thin scar on her left cheek he hadn't noticed the night before.

She shook her head. "Still lying. Fine. You'll be told nothing until you decide to be honest. You should know that escape isn't an option for you. We know these lands far better than any noble, so don't try to ride away from us. We'll only catch you and then we'll be angrier and you don't want that. Understood?" She said all this very matter-of-fact, her expressions not revealing a single emotion aside from annoyance.

Lex only nodded. He'd never been so thoroughly silenced in his life.

"Good. Then let's get moving. We need to be at Valios in less than a week."

Lex couldn't believe how beautiful his country was. He'd seen drawings and paintings but visual art couldn't capture this. The sound of clear water bubbling over rocks, the fresh smell of growing things, the touch of mossy tentacles when they passed through thicker parts of the forests where the trees grew tall over the road, forming a silent tunnel—he wanted to look everywhere at once. He would write as much as he could later, maybe a poem about the way that moss looked almost alive.

For hours, Robyn set them to a pace that was quick, but seemed to not tire the horses. By the time they stopped at midday Lex noted happily that Pepper was winded, but not exhausted. He took the opportunity to reach for a strip of dried meat from his pack and shove it in his mouth before Robyn began to order them around.

"We're coming up on a settlement," she said, her voice hard. "We will walk the horses through, we will not stop for supplies."

Lex looked up at her in surprise. "What? Why not?"

For a moment Robyn said nothing, her lips forming a hard line. Then she took a slow breath and said, "There is a larger town farther on where we will resupply. This one needs everything they have."

50

"But…" He paused, taking a moment to process her words. *Needs everything they have?*

Robyn seemed to sense his confusion. "Just…please. Let me do the talking."

Curious, Lex nodded, and they moved on.

For a moment, he considered breaking away. Pepper was stronger than they thought, he was sure. If he could just outrun them enough to hide, then maybe he could continue on his way to the coast and keep his original plan. For the moment, they were taking him in the right direction, but what if they changed course? He'd have to leave. But would they let him?

His curiosity about this group grew with every interaction, though. Why was Robyn—a girl his age, he was fairly certain—the leader of this band? And who were they? And what about all of the carts and people they'd had the night before?

As they entered the small town, he shook himself out of his thoughts and looked around, keeping his head low and hood pulled down so as to not be recognized. He was surrounded by small shacks built of branches and mud, covered in sheets of ragged canvas. The stench of mold and refuse made bile rise in his throat. He cringed at the sight of small children running completely naked over the damp earth.

Shock made his breath catch in his chest. This could not be normal…he had never heard of living conditions being so terrible anywhere in Regania. Where were the sewers and canals? And why didn't these people move to where they could have better lives? What kept them in such a terrible state?

A clatter came from a hut ahead of them, and a woman stumbled out to the path where they rode. She wore a dingy chiton that looked as if it might have been white once, but was now deep grey. Only a length of rope was her belt. Her hair was matted, her face streaked with mud. Yet she had shining blue eyes full of hope, staring up at Robyn as though she were an angel.

Robyn's face had been stern and focused all morning, an expression bordering anger—but now, the lines around her eyes softened. Her shoulders slumped a little.

Robyn met the woman's gaze, shook her head, and said simply, "Soon."

The woman's face fell a little, and she gave an understanding smile before ducking back into her hut.

Lex said nothing. They moved through the homes—hovels was a more accurate description—at a slow and steady pace. Small patches of earth had been cultivated, gardens growing tomatoes, grapes, corn, even asparagus and potatoes. But the plants seemed frail and small compared to those Lex had seen in the fields surrounding Galanis.

Twice more, people came from their dwellings to look at Robyn with hope, and twice more she only said, "Soon." Lex would have to get some answers from her about this. It was obvious she knew more than he did, and it broke his heart. Maybe if he knew why this was happening, he could find a way to help when he returned home. Surely his parents knew nothing about this, or they'd never have allowed it to happen.

They were nearly to the edge of the settlement when a tall girl came bursting from a hut to their left. With skin dark as night and hair of deep blue, she looked Callidian, like Damari and that assassin. Her eyes were bright, and sweat beaded her brow.

"My Lady! Thank the Gods you're here," she said between gasping breaths.

"Miss, I have already told others," Robyn said. "We don't have anything today, but it will be here soon."

She shook her head. "Please, Lady Robyn. We have three very sick children, and the Cures of the cities refuse to come unless we pay in advance, but we have nothing to give." Her face was pleading, desperate. "Have you anything, *anything* we can use to secure their services?"

Robyn's posture wilted. Her mouth opened to speak but no words came. She looked herself over, then Mitalo and Jianna. She glanced at Lex, but her eyes did not linger.

With a sigh, she began to unbuckle one of the daggers at her waist.

"Rob," Mitalo said. "You need—"

"Not as much as they do," she snapped.

Three sick children. How long had they waited already? With no help to come? Lex frowned, but he understood. And he knew how he could help.

"Stop," he said.

Robyn turned to him, a line of confusion between her brows.

"Take mine," Lex said.

He quickly removed one of the two daggers from his side, uncomfortably aware of the people watching him. These had been gifts from his parents, and it pained him to give one away, but he was certain the king and queen would understand why he did it. He passed the sheathed weapon to Robyn, whose eyes had taken on a confused cast. Her thumb ran across the sapphire chips embedded in the handle.

She met Lex's gaze with a look that was surprisingly tender, and nodded her thanks. Then she handed the dagger to the young woman, whose eyes widened at the sight.

"Remove the stones and melt it down," Robyn said. "Trade the raw materials in exchange for coin. It should be enough to bring the Cures."

"Th-thank you, my lady," the girl said, then looked to Lex. "My lord, your generosity—thank you!" She ran back into the hut.

Robyn pushed their horses into a loping canter while cheers filled the air behind them. And as they rode away, Lex felt a knot forming in the pit of his stomach. What else didn't he know about his kingdom?

Lex was consumed by his thoughts for the rest of the day. He hardly looked up as they resupplied, only bought a few things for himself and followed the others without comment. Pepper nudged him a few times while he walked, apparently aware something was bothering him. And it was. This larger town was quite different from the poorer one he'd seen earlier that same day, and they were barely two leagues on.

Why?

Robyn didn't want to stay in the town, and Lex was only too glad to be away from prying eyes. He thought he recognized a member of the royal court, but was mistaken. Still, he didn't want to chance it. He assumed most of the kingdom knew of his disfigurement, and while his image had never been widely publicized, he still didn't want to draw attention to himself.

They rode a few more hours, until after the sun had set. Finally, Robyn led them off the road and through the trees to a clearing where they began to set up camp. Without a word, she went to a nearby tree and climbed up like a wildcat.

"How—" Lex began, staring after her.

"She's had a lot of practice," Mitalo said, laughing softly. "Come on, boy. Let's gather wood for a fire."

They left Jianna to start a cook fire, and Lex was only too glad to fall into step with the hulking Mitalo. Silence fell between them, the only sounds a snap of twigs or rustle of ground as they gathered wood.

Lex breathed in the cool night air, the smell of pine, and let it calm his nerves. He'd hoped he would be a match for the wild, yet he knew he'd be dead if it wasn't for these people. He still didn't know who they were. Merchants, perhaps?

As he walked he picked up stray sticks to use for kindling. Staring at the forest floor, his mind turned back to the girl in the town. How her cloudy eyes lit up like she'd seen the sun for the first time. Lex's dagger had been that sun. The chance for three children to survive despite terrifying odds. A lump formed in his throat. Regania had once been prosperous, hadn't it? Lex had thought it still was.

Nearby, Mitalo swung a large axe at the branches of a fallen tree. Lex continued gathering twigs and some small branches until he had an armful of wood, and Mitalo had a larger armful. As they walked back toward their camp, Lex's curiosity got the better of him.

"Are you merchants of some kind?"

Mitalo chuckled. "No, sir knight. We're outlaws."

"Outlaws?"

"Every one of us has some price on our heads somewhere in the Unbroken Lands," Mitalo said, stepping over a large log. "It's just easier to stick together. People expect outlaws to be solitary. When they see us in a group, they think we've got a purpose."

Lex nodded. That made a certain amount of sense. Then the question he really wanted to ask tugged at him. "Why do the people look to Robyn that way?"

Mitalo raised an eyebrow, but said nothing.

"Those people should be depending on their lord for protection, shelter, and goods. Why are they living like that? I'm certain the king knows nothing of it, or it wouldn't be that way."

Mitalo scoffed, but again did not speak.

Lex watched him, frowning. "You've been ordered not to answer me, but I can make deductions as well as anyone. Those people love Robyn. They trust her, I saw it in their eyes. Why? Why should an outlaw command so much respect from them? What does she do for them? She can't give them silver daggers every time she comes through."

"That dagger was silver?" Mitalo said, smirking. "You're even more well-off than I thought."

56

"You're avoiding the question."

"Yes, I am."

Then something in Lex's mind connected. The cart of sacks, a schedule to keep, the people's looks of wild anticipation followed by humble acceptance....

"She provides for them," Lex said. It was a statement of fact. They worked, grew and cultivated what they could, and then went not to their lord for help, but her. Why? The lords certainly came to the king for everything, and Lex knew they had enough food in the royal storages to feed the entire kingdom for at least a month. Why, then, were his people living in such bare circumstances?

"She didn't intend for it to happen."

Lex looked up. "What?"

"It was a muckin' accident," Mitalo said, his voice rough. "We were traveling, she saw one village had a surplus where another village lacked. The lords don't do a mucking thing to help unless it suits them, so their people go wanting. We even those odds."

Lex looked at the man more closely. He had strong features, a kind smile, and laughter lines around his eyes that made Lex want to trust him. He shook his head and stopped walking. "So, you move things around right under the noses of the nobility?"

"Mostly," Mitalo said, stopping as well. "Regania is a big kingdom, vast resources. Everyone can live comfortably, but only if things are done right. We take excess from the people before the lords take their taxes. Started off small and gradually took more so they never noticed it missing. Then we give it to other towns and villages who need it in exchange for excess of theirs. You'd be surprised how willing people are to give when they know they'll receive something in return."

Lex didn't doubt it. "And…Robyn came up with all this?"

"That's right," Mitalo said with a shrug. "She never planned for it to become so large a project, but it's grown and we've learned to manage it."

The note of pride in his voice made Lex smile.

A creak sounded above them, and they both jumped slightly. Mitalo looked one direction, Lex the other. And he saw Robyn, perched above them and to his left. He met her gaze and held it for the second time that day.

Something about her steady stare made his heart pound so hard he could feel it in his ears.

"See anything?" Mitalo asked.

"Um…" Lex said. "No?"

Robyn watched him.

And he watched her. The memory of her dealings with those townspeople made him want to trust her despite—and perhaps because of—her suspicion of him. Which, he reminded himself, was perfectly valid. He was not being honest with her, and she had no reason to trust him. Not yet.

His usual perfect posture deflated, and he looked away from her, scratching at the band of his eye patch. "I never knew a dagger was worth so much."

Mitalo's eyes softened. Lex remembered his father's doing so at times when he was younger. "I won't lie, things are bad for people. You wouldn't see it, living in Galanis, serving under the king. He and the queen take far better care of their people than the lords do. Some treat their commonfolk well, others…the peasants might as well be dead."

Lex felt as though someone had gripped his heart and squeezed, tighter with every word Mitalo spoke. He had been raised to care for his kingdom, to love this uncountable, incomprehensible group of people he'd never met. And he did. They were his responsibility. He knew that.

And with that knowledge, he knew what he had to do. He still wanted to marry, and he would, but the midsummer festival could wait. Finding a wife could wait, returning to the palace could wait. He would send a note to his parents as soon as possible, explaining what he'd seen, and that he wanted to help. They would understand.

He met Mitalo's eyes. "You have my word, I will do everything I can to help."

Mitalo smiled—the first Lex had seen, and it suited him. "We'll gladly accept any help you can give."

As they began to walk again, Lex turned back to look at Robyn. She stared after him, her brows pulled together with a crease between them. He nodded to her, trying to convey an understanding. Something they had in common.

Whether she understood all that, he didn't know. But he felt her stare long after he'd turned away.

Surely they understand though?
I must protect myself.

6
CARINA

Carina held her skirts up as she bent down to examine the tiny rose bud fighting for life on a wild bush. It was at the base of a mostly-ignored wall on the western side of Valios Palace, sheltered from the cool mountain winds, and last to bid farewell to the setting sun each day. She leaned close and breathed in the sweet scent. She was distilling oils today, and had gathered many roses for that purpose. But this one, she left to grow. It would give more oil when older.

"My lady?" Adia said, approaching.

Carina turned and smiled at her Ignatian servant, her friend. They were as different in appearance as could be, yet she felt a kinship to the girl who helped her every day.

Carina stood and added her armful of stalks to Adia's basket, now overflowing with roses they'd gathered.

"This should be plenty," she said. "I can take these to my room, if you'll bring the ice?"

"Yes, my lady," Adia said with a curtsey.

Carina took her time through the halls, open to the elements. The palace itself was shaped like a box, missing one side. The open side faced east, to the city. The western side was reserved for Carina and her father—their private rooms, a small meeting hall where her father entertained large groups of guests, their private dining portico.

The northern arm housed workers and servants, with a few workshops for tradesmen and the stables below, and the southern arm was a granary, food cellar, and kitchens. These she passed now, on her way to her rooms. Every so often she could peek through a door, and see out another on the other side of the room, to rows of twisted olive trees in the south, and open fields where huge herds of cattle and sheep grazed.

To her right was the palace courtyard; a beautiful square of green grass, bright flowers, and grape vines climbing up the marble pillars. She loved to sit there in the evenings, watching the sky shift from blue to purple over the mountains. She was lucky to have so much beauty close at hand, when the rest of her life sometimes felt like a nightmare.

In her room she went straight to her desk, where her oil distiller was set up. It was her most prized possession, the one thing she knew she was good at. She never moved it for fear of it being damaged.

With a length of burning wood from her fireplace, Carina lit an oil-soaked wick above which was mounted an empty hourglass with tube-like openings closed by corks. All this was supported by a delicate steel frame. Into the lower chamber, she poured a measure of water, and into the upper, she inserted as many rose petals as she could fit.

She was nearly done when Adia returned and wordlessly dumped the ice into a second container.

When the water below began to boil, Carina smiled and watched as steam rose through the petals, making them wilt. At the top of the second glass sphere, the steam gathered and flowed through a small tube to the next chamber. The steam, now carrying with it oil from the rose petals, floated through a second tube surrounded by the ice, condensing into water and rose oil, before the substances exited through a third tube into the final container. The water and oil would part here, and Carina could collect both separately through spouts at the top and bottom of the collection chamber.

"Am I needed, my lady?" Adia asked.

Carina was so focused she jumped at the speech. "No, Adia. Thank you again for your help."

The younger girl bowed and left the room. Carina would need more ice, but not for an hour or so. She sat on her bed to read as the scent of rose oil filled her room, helping her to relax. It had been twenty minutes when a knock sounded at her door.

She stood, smoothing her skirt. "Come in."

Her father entered, dressed in a chiton of fine Somnurian silk, belted at his waist with a golden chain. For anyone else it might be their finest wear, but for him it bordered casual. He took a deep breath through his nose and released it with a sigh. "Ah, such a divine hobby you have, my dear. Roses today, is it?"

She nodded, a tentative smile appearing on her face.

"Wonderful," he said. "Your oils fetch fantastic prices across the border. The Fugerans are obsessive over their scents, you know."

She did know. It was the one thing she did he seemed to value.

"Darling, Hector Drako will be arriving tomorrow," he said, striding to the door. "I expect you to be presentable when he arrives, and you are to entertain him between then and dinner, unless he sends you away. Is that understood?"

Entertain? She hesitated. "I had hoped to distill more—"

"You will do as I say, and not argue, Carina."

Her shoulders drooped. "Yes, Father."

He nodded, took one last deep breath of the sweet air, and left the room.

Carina laid back on her bed and tried to return to her book, but could not focus. She stared up at the crimson canopy of her luxurious bed, wondering what she would do to entertain Lord Drako. The gardens, surely, would be of interest. Perhaps he would like to see their fields and livestock, as she'd checked on earlier. There was art and tapestries in the meeting hall, and servants to bring him whatever he wished. Certainly that would be enough to impress. She sighed, feeling better about it, and rolled rather ungracefully off her bed. She checked on the ice, and decided she'd better replace it soon.

Leaving her room, she made her way down the open portico toward the kitchens. The basement there held an ice box they'd worked to build all winter. No need to call the help when she could do it herself. Her robes swished over her legs, along the smooth floor, and she took her time, enjoying the walk and a slight breeze over her skin.

A yell shattered her silence. It was her father. She threw herself against a pillar and crouched low. He burst from his rooms farther down the hall, and shouted, "CARINA!"

What have I done?

He saw her and advanced. "Get up you little devil," he said, grabbing her hard by the arm.

"Father, please, you're hurting me." He smelled of peppermint.

"Look at my neck, child!" he gripped her jaw and forced her to look at him. "It burns! What has your devil oil done to me?"

His skin was red and splotchy. She tried to feel relieved that it wasn't anything more serious, but the pain in her arm was unbearable. "Y-you should have diluted it first, my lord."

He threw her against a pillar.

She crumpled.

"I SHOULD HAVE?" He cursed her under his breath, pacing the hall. "This is your fault, you little monster. Tell me how to fix it, now!"

She tried to find her voice, but before she spoke he kicked her in the chest, knocking the wind out of her and sending a jolt of agony through her body.

"TELL ME!" he screamed.

She heaved on the air, fighting to not exhale until her lungs were full. Her voice was small and weak when she found it. "C-carrier oil..." she whispered. "There should be olive oil in a bigger bottle near the peppermint. Apply it liberally, it will dilute the peppermint and ease the burn."

He grunted, landed one more kick, to her leg this time, and returned to his rooms, slamming the door.

She cowered on the floor, specks of dust floating before her eyes, lit by bright sunlight. When her heartbeat returned to normal, she stood and limped down the corridor.

She still needed ice.

If I don't, they wouldn't receive their goods at all.

7
LEX

Robyn pulled her horse to a stop, holding a hand up behind her.

"What's—"

Lex was cut off by glares from the other three. In the time he'd been with them, he had learned one thing for certain: don't argue. Her hand called for silence, and that's what they gave. If a little grudgingly, in Lex's case.

Their travel had been all work, eat, and sleep, with some sparring thrown in at night. There was little time for trivial chatting or questions. Lex found himself almost missing the palace life if only for the freedom it gave him to talk to people.

Now, he watched silently as Robyn slipped from her horse to the ground in one fluid movement and began to creep forward. She drew three arrows from a quiver on her mount and put one to her bow string, holding the other two between the remaining three fingers of her right hand. Her feet moved over the sodden earth, soft-soled sandals barely whispering her presence. And then she disappeared around a bend in the road.

Lex looked to Jianna and Mitalo, trying to ask without words whether they ought to follow. Jianna shook her head, her dark eyes narrowed in focus.

Lex began to sweat.

Then a shout, and a soft whistling sound reached his ears, and he looked up. One of Robyn's arrows flew toward them, planting itself in the ground at their feet. Not a second later Mitalo and Jianna had kicked their horses forward, and Lex followed behind them.

They rounded the road to find Robyn surrounded by a group of at least ten armed men. They leered at her, trying to get close. But she held her bow raised, one arrow left in her hand, poking at them whenever they came near.

In a flash, Mitalo had drawn his sword and flung himself from his mount, barreling toward the group. "Stay away from her!"

The men turned and some of them flinched away from Mitalo and his drawn sword. But one man took advantage of the distraction and rushed toward Robyn, knocking her bow and arrow aside before he clamped his hand down on her upper arm and put a knife to her throat.

Robyn froze.

"Let her go!" Jianna cried.

"No," the man said, his voice a growl that sent chills down Lex's back. He quickly drew his own sword, then joined the others. He'd just met these people, but he wasn't about to watch them get hurt.

"You let her go or you'll be sorry she didn't stick you on first sight," Mitalo said, teeth clenched.

"As though she could have," the man said. "Anyone who comes through here pays us, or dies, got it? Now I see a number of shiny things around here, just hand them over and we'll let her go."

Mitalo grunted. "You expect us to believe you?"

The man holding Robyn sneered. "Guess you'll have to do as I say and find out."

"Listen," Robyn said, her voice a whisper. "You don't have to do this."

"Shut up," the man said, grabbing her hair and yanking her head back.

Lex's anger rose in him like a thunderstorm. Before another thought could pass through his mind—of caution or sense—he ran forward, sword raised. The man must have loosened his arms, because Robyn quickly slid out of his grip and to the ground. Lex flew at the man, his sword running through the man's chest in a sickening way before he could think to draw a weapon.

Lex pulled his blade from the body—no time to think about what he'd just done—in time to block another attack from one of the bandits. Part of him noticed Mitalo, Jianna, and Robyn engaged in fights across the road as well. Lex gritted his teeth as he parried blow after blow, his muscles sore from riding and lack of practice.

He managed to slash at one attacker, forcing them back, then backed away a step or two himself, trying to get his bearings. But the man he fought was ruthless. In the midst of the fight, Lex noticed the man's gold hair and olive skin so like his own, just before another swipe nearly met Lex's chest.

His arms were tiring, especially the left, and in a moment he would be completely useless. His blocks were coming slow. He would miss the next strike.

An arrow appeared in the man's chest, the momentum pushing him back a step. Lex sucked in deep breaths, watching in confusion as the man fell to his knees, then to the ground.

Lex closed his eye, letting out a sigh in relief.

A moment later, silence overtook the scene save for the surviving bandits mounting their horses and hurrying away.

Lex's arms drooped at his sides, weak and limp. Now that the adrenaline was gone, he remembered vividly the tension and heaviness of plunging his sword into the other man's chest, the slick weight of pulling it free. Even now, his blade was wet with freshly shed blood, his own blood coating his fingers, neck, chest, the tang of it creeping in through his nose and mouth.

He turned, and vomited.

Wiping his face, pressing a hand to his neck, he stood and turned to see Robyn lowering her bow, a glare on her face as she approached him.

"Are you hurt?" she asked.

"What? I—"

"Are you mucking hurt?"

"N—no, I don't think—"

"Then you'd better have a mucking good explanation for what you just did here."

Lex frowned. "What I…did?"

"Do you see what you caused?" she said.

Lex frowned. He looked over the scene. Four bodies lay dead. He turned away, but it was burned into his mind. His hands were shaking. She was right. This was his fault. He'd jumped forward without waiting for orders. All these deaths....

"They were only doing what they thought they had to do to survive," she said. "If I'd had more time I might've been able to convince them to join our cause."

Lex's jaw dropped. "Robyn, he was about to slit your throat, how can you say—"

He was cut off by the look on her face, the sudden brightness in her eyes. She stared at him, and her voice was low when she spoke. "Everyone deserves a chance to choose a better path."

"I'll be honest," Mitalo said, "I agree with him. I've never seen anyone get that close to hurting you, Rob. If Lex hadn't jumped forward when he did, I was about to anyway, so the result would've been the same."

Robyn glared at him. "Sure. You're willing to kill *now*."

"I told you, I missed. I was—"

"*I* wouldn't have missed," Robyn said. "Regardless, now there's four lives lost, unnecessarily." She went to her horse. "Mount up. We need to be far away from this blood bath before any patrols come around."

She led them fast and far from the scene. They rode until long after dark, and Lex was exhausted—physically from such a long day, and mentally from the memory of his sword forcing its way into a man's chest. Grinding against bone, sliding through muscle. He shook his head; he needed to distract himself. Pepper's mane was getting knotted. He would brush it tonight.

They finally settled into a camp in the middle of a stand of willow trees. Their leaves hung long and thin to the ground, the trunks covered in moss. Jianna started a small fire, and soon the clearing was warm, the heat being held in somewhat by the thick trees. Robyn and Mitalo stepped away into the darkness.

Lex gathered wood and water as was his usual task now, and set them near Jianna at the fire before taking a seat farther away against the trunk of one tree. He'd grown used to sitting and sleeping on the ground in the past few days—something he hadn't expected to be so frustrating. He honestly did miss his comfortable bed, but he wasn't about to say that out loud.

At the fire, Jianna was cutting up a dried vegetable Lex didn't recognize, and dropping it into the pot for their nightly stew. The thought of fish and carrots *again* made him a little sick, but he would eat it without complaint. While Jianna worked, Lex took out his notebook, hoping to take his mind off his first kill.

"So are you writing or drawing?" Jianna asked.

Lex looked up and smiled. "Writing."

"What are you writing?"

Lex shrugged. "Descriptions, mostly. The trees, the sunset, the sky...." *Blood, swords, Robyn's eyes as she stared down at me....* He cleared his throat. "Mostly I try to turn them into poems."

"That's a gift," Jianna said. "Do you write stories, too?"

"No, no," Lex said. "I'm not that talented."

"Says you," she said. "Can I read some?"

Lex nodded, and she came over to sit beside him. He handed her the book, a small twist of nerves in his stomach. She flipped through a few pages. Lex took the moment to watch her. She was short, which was a contrast to her brother's huge size. But her hair was a coppery red, and fell in thick waves over her shoulders. Her features were soft while she perused his words, but he'd seen her turn hard as stone in a tense situation. Like today.

"You're better than you think," she said, handing the book back. "For bad poetry that's pretty good."

Lex smiled. "Um...thank you, I think." He watched her return to the fire, and sat in silence a few seconds more as she stirred the soup. "Jianna, can I ask you something?"

"Sure."

"Did I do the right thing today?"

She sighed. "I'm the wrong person to ask. You'd be better off asking Mitalo about morality and right and wrong. He's the religious one." She looked at him and smiled. "Don't worry too much. She doesn't like killing. That fight threw her off more than you think."

"I...should've waited."

"Probably," Jianna agreed. She smiled, blinking through thick lashes.

It took Lex a moment to realize he was staring right at her. He blinked and looked away, clearing his throat.

Jianna laughed. "Men. You're all suckers for a pretty face."

"Jee!" Mitalo called. He and Robyn stepped into the firelight.

"What took you so long?" she asked.

"I need to burn off some steam," Mitalo said. "Care for a spar?"

Jianna jumped up, fetching her sword. A minute later, Lex found himself alone, ten feet away from the fire, with Robyn close by sharpening one of her short swords.

He watched Jianna spar, her long hair swaying as she moved, and couldn't help admiring the sight.

Then there was Robyn, whose short hair was caked with dried mud, face smeared with dust and sweat. Whatever she'd done to get so covered in grime, he didn't know. Neither Mitalo nor Jianna were as dirty, and he'd been over a week without a bath and still hadn't reached her level of filth. But as he watched her sharpen her swords, there was something about the focus she held. Some depth to her eyes that made him unable to look away.

Until he realized he was staring again. He went back to his notebook.

Mitalo said Robyn was the mind behind a kingdom-wide operation. But how could Lex get her to talk about it? If he said anything, wouldn't she get annoyed? He *had* made her angry. Before he asked her anything, he would need to apologize. At the thought, his heart sped a little.

"Robyn?"

"Yes?" she said, not looking up.

"I'm sorry."

She paused, her whetstone held in midair. "Go on."

He swallowed, trying to squash his nerves. "I acted rashly today, and without thought. I put us all in danger, and you had every right to simply let that man kill me. But you didn't."

She finally looked up to meet his gaze. He'd never been close enough to tell, but her eyes were bright blue. In the firelight they looked like the midday sky reflected in the ocean waves, rippling, but steady and constant. For a moment Lex forgot what he'd been saying. His breath quickened under her stare.

"Ah…" His voice had come out higher than normal, and he cut himself off, clearing his throat. "I mean, I'm sorry I did what I did. And I'm in your debt for saving my life. Please, if there is anything you wish of me, you need only ask. If it's within my power, I will see it done."

The corner of her mouth lifted in the first smile he'd ever seen on her. "Bold words from a runaway knight."

Lex breathed a nervous laugh, nodding his agreement.

"Still," she said, "they're quite pretty words. Thank you for the apology, and the pledge. Those men didn't deserve death though, and I can't say I'm not still angry about it. Along with that, I still don't believe you've told us the entire truth about yourself, but everyone has their secrets, I suppose." She looked him over, and gave a single nod. "You'll do."

This simple statement rang in Lex's ears as Mitalo and Jianna rejoined them. After they ate and the fire had grown low, Lex found himself repeating the memory over again. Robyn's simple nod, her smile that was so small yet changed her expression entirely.

He was coming to know them, and they him, but they still didn't know who he truly was. The thought of telling them the truth...Lex wasn't sure he could do it just yet, but the time was getting near when he'd have to, or risk breaking their trust by revealing it.

Sunshine gleams green through ~~leaves~~ boughs above
the ~~trees~~ shimmer like gold
leaves
Forests of peace ~~make~~ me feel small
I am no more than a speck but more

How is the sky so blue   the land is far
So bright   wider, wilder,
It goes on forever   than ever knew
daggers
eyes ~~that~~ pierce my ~~heart~~ here   How the sun sets
~~orange~~   turning blue to pink
I am only   to orange to black
                                           I see the sunlight
                                           Shimmer like gold
                                           The boughs above
                                           Gleam bright and bold
                                           A land far wilder
                                           Than I knew
Why is black so dark   Glows bright with stars
When ~~everything~~ is so good?   In a dark so blue
That's stupid. Let   Then with one stroke
Why is black so dark?   I seal my fate
                                           A life is gone
                                           Remorse too late

I'm sure M could keep it up for a while, but he gets distracted too easily. And he has a family to think of.

8
LEX

They rode hard the next day, again trying to put as much distance between themselves and the previous day's fight as they could. They stayed on the road, fording streams and crossing bridges, heading west. Lex tried to slip bits of dried apple and grain to Pepper whenever they slowed. He was tired enough, he couldn't imagine how the horses were taking it. So it was little surprise to him when Robyn's horse collapsed in the muddy bank of a river.

"They're all exhausted," Mitalo said, rubbing the mare's leg. Then he paused, touching and pressing the horse's stomach here and there. "Well no wonder she's the first to go. She's got a foal on the way."

Robyn stared at him. "But...when would she have—"

They both turned to Jianna, who folded her arms and stared at her horse. A stallion, he was pawing at the ground, his hooves making deep furrows. Lex smiled. The horse looked slightly ashamed.

"You just had to have her, didn't you?" Jianna said. "Mucking beast." But contrary to her harsh words, she hugged the stallion's head and scratched at his ears.

"She won't be able to go much farther today," Mitalo said. "I don't think she's too far along, but making a baby is hard work in any case. We should find a place to rest."

"Jianna," Robyn said. "See if you can spot any landmarks nearby."

Jianna jumped into the trees, climbing with slightly more effort than Lex had seen Robyn spend. Robyn sighed. "How long do you think we have until sunset?"

"Bit less than two hours," Lex replied, rubbing the nose of Mitalo's horse. He paused, feeling an awkward silence rise between the others. He turned to see both Robyn's and Mitalo's eyes narrowed at him.

"How," Robyn started, "could you know that without looking at the horizon?"

Heat rose in Lex's face, and he looked away. It wasn't normal, what he could do. He knew that. "I've always known the time. I can wake myself up at a specific time, or tell myself to do something at a specific time, and I remember when that time comes. I've done it since I was little."

"But how?" Mitalo asked, crossing his huge arms.

"I don't know," Lex said, shrugging.

Robyn nodded. "Well, that may come in handy."

Jianna landed from the trees then, and dusted off her hands. "There's some smoke only about a hundred yards southwest of us. Looks thick enough it could be a settlement or a wilderness temple."

Robyn nodded. "Will you all help me get this girl standing? She can rest when we get a fire going for her."

Together the four of them got the mare to her feet, and led their horses toward the smoke Jianna had seen. It wasn't long before Lex could easily identify it as a wilderness temple. The building was rectangular, raised three steps off the forest floor, with one side enclosed for a living space. The rest was left open, the roof held up by columns and forming a square. The floor was marked by a four-pointed star with circles marking each point, in which stood an altar and statue representing each God or Goddess.

Lex tied his horse and Mitalo's at a hitching post, then stepped onto the platform to pay his respects. He knelt before Amplia, the Goddess of Life, whose Master Cure and High Cures had healed him so much as a child. He felt the closest kinship to her, and a warmth rose in his chest as he ran his fingers over the Life symbol at the base of her statue: a circle made of an ocean wave.

He also knelt before Crescere, God of Growth; Sileo, God of Stability; and Fina, Goddess of Death. He always told himself he wanted to be on the Gods' good side, in case he ever really needed something. And right now, he prayed for some way to help Robyn's efforts.

He hadn't considered it much, but the thought had occurred to him. If Robyn was given more resources—for example, *royal* resources—what kind of good could she do? How many more people could she help?

Behind him he heard footsteps. He stood, turning to see Robyn approach.

"You worship?" she asked.

"I do."

"Hm," was all she said.

"I take it you don't?" Lex asked.

"Why should I pay respects to someone I've never met?" She shrugged. "Come on, we need your help getting my mare to lie down." She turned and stepped down from the platform, Lex following behind.

"Did I hear visitors?" a voice called from behind them.

Lex turned back. Behind them, a door opened to reveal the living quarters and a young man—not much older than Lex—stepping from them. His eyes shone a silvery grey, at odds with his dark black hair and a shadow of scruff on his jaw. But his smile was bright and kind, and he wore the blue robes of a Cure, with a white stripe down his sleeves.

"Good day, Brother," Lex said, bowing in respect.

The Cure waved a hand. "Good day, yes, good day. Now what are you doing here?"

"Ah," Lex stuttered at the direct question and lack of formalities. "We were traveling by when one of our horses collapsed, and then we discovered she's...ah, with child."

"With child my foot," the Cure chided, hurrying forward to the horse. "It's called a foal you idiot. And what are you doing riding a pregnant mare into the middle of nowhere? No wonder you had to stop, she's probably about to bite the heads off the lot of you!"

Robyn snorted a laugh. In anyone else it would've been a small thing, but her face shifted with a suppressed smile. Even though he knew it was at his expense, Lex smiled back. He

80

noticed then that she was near the same height as he at about six feet. And her laughter emphasized sections of her face that were darker than the rest. He'd assumed it was dirt before, but it looked different up close.

"Sorry," she said, straightening her face. "I know it was me who rode the mare out, but that was a grand bit of insult he put to you."

Lex shook his head, grinning. "I can't argue with that." They made their way to the horse. Together the five of them got her to lie down, and they watched as the Cure worked.

"Well," he said after ten minutes of prodding, checking her nose, mouth, ears, and hooves, "she's completely healthy, if very tired, but she's near six months along if my guess is right. By the look on her face I'd guess she'd rather not be ridden for a while."

Lex looked and saw that the mare had fallen asleep on her side, completely exhausted. Robyn petted her gently, apologizing under her breath for pushing them all so hard.

"I can give her some Life to perk her up," the Cure said. "But if you'd like to leave her here, I have a good horse you can take in trade. This temple is occupied most of the time, you can come back for her whenever you like."

Robyn sighed, then nodded. "I hate to leave her, but she'll be happier resting."

"Onward, then," the Cure said. He drew from his robes a small flask and a clay bowl. He poured water into the bowl and set it on the ground near the mare. "Everyone please, step back."

They all watched as he closed his eyes, placed one hand in the water, and the other on the horse's chest. A moment of nothing passed, then his hands began to glow with a pale blue light. Robyn and Jianna gasped. The water's power activated; it flowed into the Cure's body, then out through his hand and into the mare. A moment later, the mare blinked awake, but didn't rise.

The light faded, and the Cure stood without a word, going back to the temple. Mitalo, Jianna, and Robyn stared after, as though he'd performed a miracle for them. To them, Lex supposed, he had.

"Should we camp here tonight, then?" Lex suggested, shaking them all from their amazement. It had never occurred to him that anyone could go throughout life without seeing the Gods' magic used. They immediately set to starting a fire and making dinner, to which the Cure contributed a loaf of freshly baked bread from his oven. Lex ate his share slowly to savor the soft cloud-like feel of it in his mouth. He hadn't known he'd miss it so much.

The Cure had also offered to resupply them, saying he had so much food here it would likely go bad, and he didn't need any payment in exchange. At that, Robyn asked if he would visit the town they'd passed through two days prior, and help them there. He'd nodded, smiling, and agreed to leave first thing in the morning.

Since there was still light, Robyn climbed a tree to check their position, and Mitalo and Jianna set off to search for berries or other food they could take with them. Lex was left once again ten feet from the fire, scribbling in his book.

Sitting on the steps of the temple he realized he was running out of descriptors for the beauty he saw in nature. Lovely, perfect, beautiful, gorgeous, exquisite, brilliant...pretty didn't begin to describe anything he saw, and he knew his words would never do it justice.

He tried to recall how Robyn had looked when she had laughed, just for a moment. How her entire image seemed to shift from its usual gloom and focus to simple enjoyment. The words weren't cooperating, though. He kept scratching them out and trying again.

He didn't notice her until she was already sharpening her short swords. She'd taken a seat on the ground across and to the right of him, enough that he could see her clearly in the firelight. Without thought, Lex turned to a new page and began to write.

"Lex," Robyn said. "Why are you sitting so far away from the fire? Aren't you cold?"

He paused a moment, his mind still reeling from writing. He'd never had to explain this before. "Well, I don't like…heat."

"Heat?"

He nodded toward the fire. "A little is fine, but too much and…well, I'd rather not be near it is all."

She frowned, her head tilting to one side. "Is that how you got your scars? Fire?"

"Hot oil," he said, turning back to the page. "It's less about the flames and more about the heat. The fear it might get out of control."

She hummed an understanding, and turned back to her swords.

Lex scribbled with a kind of frantic desperation. Robyn herself wasn't in the details, but in feel, in mood. He tried not to stare, but took quick looks that he hoped went unnoticed. Blink up, blink down, think, write.

Cross that word out, there had to be a better one. The strap of his eye patch began to itch at his skin, but he forced himself to keep going. He might not get another chance. They sat in silence for five minutes, her whetstone sharpening the sword, his pencil scratching on paper.

When he finally stopped, he breathed a sigh of relief. What he had before him resembled a poem, though had a prose feel to it as well. The descriptions had a mood to them, more than anything he could remember ever writing. It was as though the words themselves were shadows from the fire, the trees behind her, and her, intent on her sword, doing the best job she could. Calm, focused, intense.

Robyn wasn't sharpening anymore. Lex looked up to see her watching him.

"Are you all right?" she asked.

He nodded, smiling. "Fine, um…why?"

"You stopped your scratching. Made me feel like I was intruding on the silence."

He laughed a little. "Actually. I ah…I'm sorry, I should've asked first, but I sort of…I wrote a poem. About you."

She arched a brow.

Lex cringed slightly in embarrassment. "Would you…like to read it? If you don't like it, I can toss it into the fire."

She hesitated, then said, "Sure."

He stood and circled the fire, and was pleasantly surprised when she stood as well, meeting him halfway.

He handed over the book. She took it with a reverence he hadn't anticipated, and stared for a moment, as intent on the page as she'd been on her sword. Then she frowned, that line between her brows appearing again. "Is that really how you see me?"

He hesitated, looking between her and the words. "I...I think so. I thought you looked rather peaceful, personally."

"I'm a complete mess." She ran a hand through her short-cropped hair, knocking out bits of dirt. Her fingers got stuck. She sighed. "A sad state indeed."

Lex couldn't help smiling. "Honestly I've grown used to you like this. But out of curiosity, why are you so much dirtier than the others?"

She rolled her eyes, handing the notebook back. "We were trying to get away from patrols. I ordered the others to run, but I wanted to stay back and listen, see if I could learn anything. So I buried myself in a muddy riverbank."

Lex pressed his lips together to keep from laughing.

"Well. They didn't find me." She shrugged. "And I just haven't had the opportunity to bathe properly since."

"Well, that explains..." He let his gaze drift over her frame, suddenly noticing how close she was to him.

"I suppose," she said, "we could stop in the next town for the night and actually sleep in real beds. We're getting close to our destination anyway, and I'd like us all to be properly rested."

"And clean?" Lex asked.

"Yes, and clean," she said, nodding. "You know, Lex, for a noble you're not as bad as I expected."

"Well, for an outlaw you're much more brilliant than I would've expected."

She cocked her head like a curious bird. "Brilliant?"

He nodded. "I guessed you were distributing food and supplies, and Mitalo confirmed it for me. He said it was your idea."

She blinked up at him, and something about the way she looked at him put his entire body on edge. He swallowed, his mouth suddenly dry.

Then Robyn cleared her throat. "More of a group effort, really," she said, moving to her pack. "I came up with the theory but I had no idea how to carry it out. I was lucky Mitalo and Jianna knew people all over already who were willing to help."

Her sudden move away sent a shock through Lex that he hadn't anticipated. He ran a hand through his hair, shaking his head. "How far does it extend?"

She'd been untying a rope that held her bedroll and now paused, watching him. "You're not going to turn us in, are you?"

"I may be a runaway knight, but if you need a secret kept, I can keep it."

She thought for a moment, then nodded. "It extends through all of the lordships, though we're able to do more in the inner circle than the more distant ones." She frowned at her rope, picking at a knot.

"What do you transport?" Lex asked, moving toward her

"Crops, mostly. Sometimes supplies like wool or tools. Anything the people produce that the lords take taxes in. Are you not familiar with taxes?"

He shook his head. He'd always been on the receiving end.

She sighed, sounding exasperated. Lex couldn't tell whether it was from the troublesome knot or his ignorance. He nodded to the knot, and she gestured for him to try.

"Well," she said, "the Lower Lords require a certain percentage of the total produce as a tax from the knights who govern the people. They're required to pay or be thrown in prison. Two-thirds of that goes to the High Lords, and two-thirds again is sent on to the capital. Some territories are virtually starving because they can't produce enough to support themselves and the tax, while others had excessive amounts of food that went rotten before it could be eaten. Someone just needed to see what was excess and redistribute it. In the last two years it's grown to cover almost all of Regania."

Lex couldn't help smiling. This was the most she'd spoken to him since they'd met, and she sounded quite proud of her accomplishments. As she should be.

"You have an illegal smuggling organization going on right under the noses of the nobility." He'd undone the knot.

She nodded, smirking.

"Absolutely brilliant."

She smiled, her cheeks darkening a bit.

They were once again very close. Lex pulled back, putting some distance between them. "I'm sorry, I didn't mean to—"

"It's all right," she said. "Thank you for your help."

Now it was his turn to blush. He had a sudden awareness of his eye patch, his scars, the mutilated muscles.

Standing, he went to unroll his own bed. "Robyn, what if you took your ideas to the king? Got his support? I mean how many more people could you help?"

She shook her head. "Not an option."

"Why not?"

87

"If I did, every lord in Regania, high and low, would accuse me of robbery. And they would win. Who is the king going to trust? His closest advisers, or a dirty outlaw?"

"Well…" Lex muttered softly, "what if you had support? Someone closer to the king to vouch for you?"

The corners of her mouth twitched. "You mean like a runaway knight?"

He smiled at the irony. The reminder that she didn't know who he really was hit him like a punch to the chest, and made him just as uncomfortable. "Point taken."

"Look Lex," she said. "I appreciate you wanting to help us. But things are working fine the way they are. We take a great risk trusting you as it is. Now if you know anything about how to get into Valio's palace, that would come in handy."

She turned and unrolled her bedroll beside the fire. Soon, Mitalo and Jianna returned and followed suit, and as Lex curled up under his blanket, he thought of the lies he'd spun already. These people were telling him information, opening up to him. Perhaps they weren't truly friends, not yet, but the trust was beginning to form. He could feel it.

And he was already betraying it.

TARGET

Focused. Calm. Always ~~watching~~ observing.
Listening. Watching. Cool under ~~fire~~ stress.
She is the pale white of a Hovering petal,
the edge of a blade when danger is near.
She is the darkness of secrets & hope
the confidence ~~radiating~~ of a lioness feeding her brood.
She is in the trees, the wind,
the sound of a warzone on steel.
~~Sharp~~ The brightness of a flame
with none of the fear
A spark in ~~a~~ the night
A brushed-away tear
~~She is not simply~~
She is bravery, grace, a note, on a scale
~~She is more than~~
A bolt of lightning, a feather on the ~~breeze~~
She cannot be contained in a single word
She is more, all in all.

   She is real.

How I envy him that. I've come to trust him in the time I've been here. He's been like a father in many ways.

9
CARINA

Carina stood in front of a tall gold framed mirror as Adia gathered the silky chiton and buckled it at Carina's shoulders. Rain fell lightly outside, and thunder shook the air, making her heart race. The gardens wouldn't be an option today, then. The galleries though, and the dining portico. Those would be fine. Her hair was pulled into a tight twist at the back of her head, making her temples ache, and her makeup done so she appeared to blush. She tried out a few smiles in the mirror.

Nothing looked real.

"All finished, my lady." Adia stepped away.

"Thank you, Adia. Will you send word to my father?"

"Yes, my lady." She curtsied and left the room.

Carina twisted her hands before her. Entertaining Lord Drako? She'd never been given such a task before. Nerves made her heart race, and she tried to calm herself. Her job tonight was to smile and look pretty. Nothing more.

A few minutes later her father stood outside her door, dressed in his finest chiton of black velvet. Gold clasps at his shoulders, a necklace of thin gold squares draped around his neck. She took his arm and he led her through the hallways to the palace's entry hall—a small room that took up the south east corner of the palace. He did not look at her. He had her sit on a cushioned bench to wait, then stood beside, silent.

The space was large, but not open to the air. Two servants stood at large wooden doors, waiting for the order to open them. Soft brown carpets lined the stone floors. The walls were decorated by tapestries and gold sconces, with a grand chandelier of crystal and candles in the center. Carina had always wanted to swing from the thing as a child. Even now, she watched as it moved slightly in the breeze from open windows, wondering how she would get up and down.

A lookout appeared in the window above them, from a balcony outside. "My lord? They're approaching."

Valio nodded. He motioned for the servants to open the doors. Outside was a courtyard, a small area of which was covered by a roof. A group of riders galloped in, slowing once they were out of the rain. Carina watched her father greet the foremost among them.

"Hector! I'm glad you could come."

Lord Hector Drako dismounted and pushed his hood back from light hair and a square jaw. Carina had seen him before, but it had been years. He looked as though he had once been handsome, and the slicked hair and tight clothing made him appear as though he were trying desperately to hold on to his youth. Servants took their horses and cloaks, and even removed muddy sandals and wiped their feet before the men stepped inside.

"My, being indoors feels good after that ride, Maximus," Drako said, shrugging his shoulders. Then he saw Carina and looked her over appraisingly. "And who might this beautiful young woman be?"

Carina stood as her father offered his arm again. "May I present my daughter, Lady Carina Valio."

Drako bowed low, taking her hand to kiss it. She had to force herself to not pull away.

"It is an honor to see you again, lady. You have grown up since last we met." His shallow eyes took her in; he began at her feet and stopped at her eyes, lingering in places between.

Her bare arms felt cold, and she wished she'd worn a cloak to cover herself. She swallowed and curtsied. "The pleasure is mine, my lord."

Valio snapped at a servant. "Put these men in the empty servants' quarters. Carina will show Drako to his room near the dining portico," he said.

Carina balled her hands into fists, trying to calm herself.

"Dinner will be served in an hour. Time enough to clean up and get comfortable, yes?" He gave a stiff nod and turned through an archway.

One of the servants, a tall young man with Callidian-blue hair and olive skin, approached Drako and said, "Shall I accompany you with your trunks, my lord?"

"No," Drako said, his eyes never leaving Carina. "You are to stay here, and I'll send for you. I'd like some personal time to become acquainted with Lady Carina."

The tall servant looked from Drako to Carina, and met her eye for a moment. He looked tense. She tried to beg him with her eyes to insist on joining them. Instead he nodded. "Yes, my lord." He and the other servants and men-at-arms took the hallway going west, leaving Carina and Drako alone. She watched the servants go, wishing they hadn't.

Looking back, Lord Drako's eyes were more penetrating than before. Warmth crept up her cheeks at the hungry look in his eyes. She cleared her throat and straightened her dress. "Shall we?" she asked, motioning to the hallway heading north.

The corner of his mouth lifted in a crooked smile that said far more than she wanted it to. He offered his arm.

She took it reluctantly and they walked. Carina struggled not to limp—her leg was still bothering her—as she pointed out various treasures of the palace. Here was a painting of her great grandfather. This tapestry was of the finest Somnurian make, shipped from over a thousand leagues away. That rug was painted by Carina's mother a few months before her passing. At each one, Drako nodded and returned his eyes to her without apology. She wanted more than ever to run.

When they reached his rooms she sighed with relief and released his arm. "Here you are, my lord. Inside there should already be a bath drawn for you and I will make sure your things are brought in." She curtsied.

As she turned to leave, he snatched her arm. His hands were warm and damp with sweat. "Oh, don't go, my lady. Please, won't you show me around my rooms?"

Fear flooded her senses. She couldn't breathe, couldn't move. He opened the door, pulled her in with him and flipped the lock. Was this what her father wanted her to do?

Entertain?

The apartment was decorated in greys and purples, but Carina saw red. She paused in the doorway, not letting him bring her any farther.

"Forgive me," she said, trying to pull away. "I really should go." Her voice was so tiny, she could barely hear herself.

He chuckled and spun her around, pressing her against him. He reeked of dampness and mold, his clothing wet. Bile rose in her throat.

"My lord? Lord Drako?" a voice rang out.

Drako cursed and shoved her away. She caught herself on the door frame, her heart pounding against her ribs.

Lord Drako stepped out of the room. "What is it?"

Two young men ran forward. "My lord." The taller of the two, the same servant from before, bowed. "Valio's servants have lost the horses. We caught most, but yours and three others aren't coming to the stable hands. They asked if you would come gather your mount? The animal trusts no one but you, after all, sir. Theo here can show you the way."

Drako's face went from impatient, to angry, to smug within the course of the explanation. He nodded. "Yes, all right." He turned back to Carina. "My lady, if you'll excuse me?" He bowed to her, and left the room, led by the second servant.

When they'd gone, the tall young man looked to Carina. His voice quiet, he asked, "Are you hurt?"

Without her consent, tears pricked her eyes. She blinked them back and took a shaky breath. "No. I'm all right."

He closed his eyes and sighed. "Good."

She watched him, still trying to calm herself. After a few moments she stood straight and rearranged her chiton. She met the servant's gaze. "I won't ask if you released his horse on purpose, but whatever the case I'm glad you interrupted when you did. Thank you."

He smiled, and she felt her heartbeat skip. His long blue hair was held back at his neck by a strap of leather, but a few strands hung loose to frame green eyes. He was thin, but his short-sleeved riding robes revealed muscular arms. The black and yellow of Drako's family crest were emblazoned on his tunic.

He bowed to her and offered his hand. "May I escort you somewhere?"

She put her hand in his, assuming he would place her palm to the back of his hand, or wrap it around his elbow. But he laced their fingers together and let their arms relax at their sides as he began to walk. Still shaken from her encounter, this felt too intimate to be appropriate, and she pulled away.

"Oh," he said, eyes wide. "I'm so sorry, I forgot my manners." He held an arm out, as propriety dictated. After a moment's hesitation, Carina placed her hand on top of his. It was probably different in Callidia. Perhaps holding hands was considered formal there.

They walked through the halls without speaking. She wasn't sure what to think of this young man. At her door, he lowered his hand, leaving hers warm where they'd touched. He bowed and began to leave when she stopped him.

"Wait?"

He turned to face her. "Yes, my lady?"

"What is your name?"

"Damari, my lady."

"And, you are a servant of Drako's?"

He opened his mouth to speak, and hesitated. "Not exactly."

She waited for him to continue. He didn't. She could have probably ordered him to speak, but it felt like some betrayal of trust to do so, since he had just rescued her.

"Well," she finally said, "thank you for your help, Damari."

He smiled, and her heart stuttered again. "My pleasure, my lady. Is there anything else I can help you with?"

"No, I'll be all right. Thank you."

He bowed once more, smiling that smile, then he was gone.

Carina stepped into her room and bolted the door, a knot twisting her stomach. She didn't want Drako thinking he was allowed in here.

She summoned Adia to help her into a chiton with a higher neckline and less-flattering shape. She even found a short cape that would cover her shoulders and arms to a degree. She did not want to be so exposed during dinner. Not that her being covered would make much difference to Drako. Really, she didn't want to go to the dinner at all, but she knew her father would have none of that.

What would she have done if Damari hadn't come when he did? How would she make it through Drako's stay? And what about the rest of the lords who would come? She couldn't depend on Damari to rescue her every time…though, she hoped there wouldn't be another time.

The more she thought, the more her anger and hurt boiled in her chest. Had her father meant for Drako to bed her? He'd never allowed anything like that before. Then she remembered the manic look in his eyes when he'd beaten her after the prince's escape. How he had snapped about the oils. He seemed to be losing his mind faster than ever, but what could she do?

Run away.

"No," she said out loud.

"No, my lady?" Adia asked.

Carina took a slow breath. "Nothing, I…it's nothing."

Running. The thought had crossed her mind before, and never had she entertained it. She would never make it beyond his reach. Would she?

And besides, what would he do without her? He'd already lost his wife, could he stand losing his daughter? How much more anger could he hold? But it wasn't as though she'd be dead, just…gone. She took a deep breath and faced herself in the mirror.

What do I want?

And then a voice sounded in her mind, shockingly similar to her father's: *What you want doesn't matter.*

Adia finished her clasps, then softly spoke. "Shall I send for an escort, my lady?"

97

Carina looked at her. The young girl's eyes said everything. Drako's actions were known by the entire household at this point. Carina felt a flash of shame that the news had spread, and yet, a comfort in the knowledge that perhaps this was where the staff would draw the line. She wondered if Damari had anything to do with it.

"Yes, please."

Adia bowed, stepping out for a moment. When she returned, she fixed Carina's hair a bit and said, "It may not be my place, my lady, but if you ever need someone to talk to…"

Carina turned to meet the girl's eyes. They stood in silence for a moment, before Carina looked away.

"It's not your fault," Adia whispered.

One of the house guards knocked on the door. Carina hurried to leave with him as tears pricked her eyes, Adia's words echoing in her mind.

The hallways felt cramped, stuffy, as she made her way to dinner. Lord Drako would be there, and her father, and in a few days, the rest of his allies. How she wished she could have nothing to do with any of them.

A few months ago, his sister joined us. Seeing them together makes me wish I had a family of my own.

10
LEX

Riding in the rain made for misery and not much more, but Robyn kept them going until they arrived in the next town. It was only afternoon, but they stopped at an inn of Jianna's choosing and paid a stable boy to take their horses to be fed and their belongings to their rooms.

"Why this place?" Robyn asked, shaking out her cloak in the entryway.

"I've got a friend here," Jianna said, doing the same. "I might be able to get us a good deal on the rooms."

"Is it Astra?" Mitalo asked.

"Maybe," Jianna said, smirking.

Mitalo looked to Lex. "Astra's her girlfriend."

Jianna smacked his shoulder. "She's not my girlfriend."

"Not yet," Mitalo muttered.

Her cheeks darkening slightly but still wearing a smile, Jianna made her way into the inn's tavern without them.

"I'll see about our rooms," Robyn said. "Go get us some food, will you?"

"Of course," Mitalo said.

"And don't tease her too much."

"Wouldn't dream of it."

Lex couldn't help a grin as he followed Mitalo into the bar. It was a huge room with a low ceiling, a scent of must and stagnant moisture lingering in the air. Round tables filled most of the space, which was lit by flickering candles on fixtures hooked to the ceiling beams, and a few musicians played stringed instruments in one corner.

"Drinks?" the barman asked when they finally reached him.

"Ale for me," Mitalo said. "And—Lex? What for you?"

"Do you have mulled wine?"

"Aye," the barman said.

"That, thank you." Lex pulled his hood down and scratched at his beard. It was finally starting to fill out, though he could feel places where the old scars at the back of his jaw prevented growth. Mitalo ordered them some food as well. Lex ate it, but it turned out to not taste nearly as good as what Jianna made on the road. He turned to look for her, wanting to ask what the difference was.

He found her seated at a table in the far corner of the room, leaning close to another woman, slightly taller than she with light gold hair and dark eyes. They looked deep in conversation, their hands intertwined on the table before them.

Lex turned back to his food. The question could wait. "Mitalo," he said, turning to his right. "How old are you?"

"I'm thirty-three. You?"

"Nearly eighteen," Lex said. "What about Robyn and Jianna?"

"Robyn's just nineteen, Jee will be twenty-eight in two months."

Lex nodded. "Do you have any other siblings?"

"No, just Jianna. Our mother died crossing the Arontas Mountains to get us here. Before that it was only the three of us for a long time. Our pop died when I was twelve, Jianna five. But that was back in Perdonia. She doesn't remember him much."

Lex turned back to look at Jianna. She looked at the other woman with such adoration, an expression Lex had only ever seen shared between his parents. Seeing it made him feel as though he were intruding by simply being in the same room.

"You all right, boy?"

Lex shook himself. "Yes, sorry."

"You have a problem with her?"

"Jianna? No, Gods no. It's just..." He paused. "Have you ever wondered whether there's a person out there for you? Destined love, like in the fairy tales?"

Mitalo gave a knowing smile. "I think everyone wonders that at some point in their lives. Took me a few tries to find mine though."

"Yours?"

"My wife."

"You're—" Lex dropped his fork. "You're married?"

"Aye."

"Then what are you—I mean—"

"Why am I helping run illegal smuggling operations?"

Lex laughed. "Yes, that."

"I'm an outlaw," Mitalo said. "We all are, as ordered by the high lords who declared us so. I can't ever go back to Sotira, for example. That's where I was arrested for stealing food to feed Jianna. My face is up on all the notice boards all over that lordship. Jianna stays with me, but she's not technically illegal. To be honest, Robyn shouldn't be here in Valios, but you can probably tell this mission is important to her."

"What's important to me?" Robyn asked, joining them on Lex's left.

"Is it safe for you to be seen in Valios?" Lex asked.

She waved a hand. "Everyone in the smaller towns who matters knows who I am and what I do. They won't turn me in. We just can't go into the bigger cities. Ale, please?" she said, flagging down the barman. When he brought her drink she tilted it back and chugged the entire contents in one breath. Lex stared.

"Big drinker, eh?" he asked when she'd set down her mug.

"When the occasion warrants it," she said, wiping the corners of her mouth.

Lex smiled back. "And, what occasion might that be?"

Robyn began to speak, but was shoved into Lex by a man on the other side of her, nearly falling to the floor. Lex managed to catch her, and part of his mind noted he'd never been this close to a woman before. The man who had pushed her was calling for a drink.

"Are you all right?" Lex asked.

"I'm fine," Robyn said, sounding out of breath.

Lex helped her stand, then glared at the intruder—a thin, wiry man wearing furs, a thick knife at his side—who chose that moment to look back at them.

"What's your problem, one-eye?"

Lex shrank back as though he'd actually been hit.

"Apologize," Robyn snapped.

"For what?" the man asked, his speech slurring.

"For that vile comment."

"And for shoving her," Lex added, stepping forward.

"Piss off," the man said.

Before Lex could do more than open his mouth to reply, Robyn grabbed the man by his arm, spun him around, and shoved him into a wall where he crumpled to the floor.

"Hey!" A second man was standing from a table nearby, another trapper by the looks of him, drawing a blade.

"Lex, get down."

Lex obeyed, ducking under the bartop as Robyn and Mitalo drew their daggers, facing five men dressed the same as the first. One flew forward and knocked Robyn's blade from her hands, pulling her away from the bar. A moment later the entire room was in chaos, feet and legs blurs as Lex tried to stay out of the way. And then something flew high enough to knock a few candles from their perches above.

Hot wax and flame caught on Lex's robes, sending heat washing over him in his spot beneath the bar. His entire body froze. The fire was free, out of control, and too close. Flashes of phantom pain raked his shoulder. He shoved himself along the wall behind him, trying to get away. He gripped at his cloak, struggling to find something—anything—to hold onto.

Something to ground him. The entire left side of his face seemed to scald as his heart pounded in his ears.

Blackness crowded his vision. He closed his eye, tight, tighter. Not enough. He could still feel it. The memories burned, flowed, wouldn't stop. He couldn't stop it. Tears pricked at the corner of his eye.

Not again. Please, not again…

"Lex?"

No. No, he couldn't look. It would only get worse.

"Lex, what's…oh Gods. Put that out! Now!"

The heat lessened. And then, soft hands framed his face. He couldn't open his eye. Couldn't. Not—

"Lex," a soft voice said. "It's all right. It's gone."

"No," he said. "Please."

"Lex, it's all right." The hands stayed steady, waiting, even as sounds of the surrounding tavern returned to him. And slowly, a visceral fear still raging inside him, Lex opened his eye.

Robyn knelt before him, her crystal eyes shining like rays of sunlight through the dark clouds of his terror.

Lex forced himself to breathe, following her breaths as her shoulders rose and fell.

"Can you stand?"

He nodded, and she offered a hand to help him. He was unsteady, and took hold of the bar to balance, giving her a nod that he would be all right. As he did, it seemed as though the entire world came crashing back down onto him, sound and smells and a funny sensation of knots in his stomach.

"Get out," the barman said. "All of you."

"Excuse me?" Robyn spun to face him. "We were defending ourselves from an attack."

"And they won't stay either, I promise," the barman said. "But I won't have anyone staying here who is so quick to draw a blade as you all. Get your coin at the desk, get your things and go."

Robyn's face went red with anger, and she stormed out of the bar. Lex followed, and could hear when Mitalo stopped at the desk for their coin and belongings. A rushed conversation had Jianna running to gather the supplies they'd meant to get the next morning.

Robyn however didn't stop outside. She kept walking down the road, mud and rain pelting her since her hood still rested on her shoulders, heading west as they had been from the beginning.

Lex caught up to her, but said nothing. Even if he'd wanted to, he couldn't think of what to say. He simply followed, trying not to get too covered in mud.

By the time they reached the other end of the town, Mitalo and Jianna were riding up, leading their horses. Lex mounted Pepper and tried very, very hard not to think about the memories he'd just had returned to his mind.

By the time the sun set the rain had passed them by, and Robyn managed to find them a clearing right on the banks of a deep stream where the ground was surprisingly dry.

"I still need a bath," Robyn said, "and I'm determined to get it. I'm going upstream." Without any objection, she set off, a towel, soap, and fresh riding robes in hand.

"A bath sounds amazing after that storm," Jianna said.

"We're bathing here," Mitalo said to Lex. "You're welcome to stay, or you could head downstream. You'll get all our filth though."

Lex shrugged, rummaging through his pack for his things. It didn't make much difference to him. "I'll head downstream. I need some time to think anyway."

His hand struck something hard in the middle of his clothes, and he paused. Pushing aside a tunic, he saw a wooden carving of Amplia, the Goddess of Life. Her hair and dress seemed to flow like waves, even though it was made of wood. Lex ran a finger along the smooth curves.

At the touch, Life flowed into him. He recognized it immediately, and drew his hand back. His bruises were already almost healed by that single touch. There had to be a huge amount of magic stored there, though the thing was hardly taller than the palm of his hand. Who would have put it there?

He wrapped the carving in one of his shirts so he wouldn't accidentally touch it again, then stuffed it to the bottom of his pack. He'd have to work out later who gave it to him.

As he walked down the banks, his mind felt scattered, somehow. As though too many things were happening at once and he couldn't make out how to handle them.

He'd now been captured twice, nearly killed in that fight with the bandits, and had his life saved twice as well—first from the assassin, then from the bandits—three times, if he counted Robyn pulling him out of his flashbacks.

That hadn't happened to him in so many years…he'd been so careful at the palace, staying away from the fireplaces, away from the heat, preferring the cold in many cases. He would gladly take a dozen blankets to keep him warm rather than a fire in the hearth.

It used to be his mother who would help him when he got too close to heat. Her gentle hand taking his, wrapping him in her embrace, telling him she was there to help him carry the fear.

Had he ever really thanked her for that?

Reaching a spot he hoped was private, Lex began to strip out of his travel clothes. The water felt freezing at first, but once he was in it didn't feel so bad. His thoughts shifted to his place in this journey. He'd intended to go to the coast, mingle during the midsummer festival, and meet his one true love. His plan had been to befriend many, and find one who would love him despite his scars, despite his crown, even.

That seemed like such a naive idea, now. How had he expected to form a lasting relationship with a complete stranger so quickly? He sighed, reminding himself he'd set that goal aside. He had agreed to help these new friends, and he wouldn't desert them to go chasing some unknown bride. They were his allies now, and he wanted to help make his kingdom better. Marriage could wait.

He rubbed soap over himself and through his hair, and washed his clothing as well as he could. When he finished scrubbing, he lay with his back against some rocks, the river's current flowing over his shoulders. What was he doing out here? He'd never imagined going so long without a bath, nor that he might bathe in a stream in the middle of nowhere with his only comrades being three outlaws he was only beginning to know. He really hadn't thought this through as much as he'd thought he had…that thought in itself was confusing.

He closed his eye and ducked under the surface, letting the water flow over him. The cold felt good against his scars, and comforting to his mind. Submerged by cold water, heat couldn't find him.

Reluctantly, he pushed himself up to break the surface and went to the bank, taking the towel and beginning to dry off. He slid on his trousers, then pulled his riding robe out and paused.

His gold chain fell out. He'd taken it off to not risk losing it, and had tucked it into this clean robe. He lifted the chain and glanced at the coin there that Oliver had given him, briefly wondering how much magic it had left. Without thinking why, he found a boulder and sat, staring at his two biggest challenges in life.

The Prince's Seal.

His grandmother's wedding ring.

He had a responsibility to Regania, to think of the greater good. To that end, he had to marry. He knew that. Still, he'd rather choose for himself than let his parents choose for him. For the first time, he wondered why they'd chosen Carina Valio for him. A nice girl, certainly, but he didn't know her very well. Much like the rest of the ladies at court. They were all either uninterested in being queen or *too* interested. And most of them wouldn't even look at him.

Being out here, with these outlaws, he felt…different. It wasn't as though they ignored his scars, but they didn't make him feel less because he had them. Even his parents had somehow not managed to do that, coddling him and over-protecting him until he was old enough to ask them to stop it.

It felt liberating to be among people who accepted him. Or at least seemed to…it had only been a few days, he supposed. But he couldn't forget the way Robyn had helped him just a few hours ago….

He stared at his grandmother's ring.

He was a prince. And he was in the company of outlaws who'd made him feel more like a person than he ever had at the palace.

He had to tell them the truth, and hope they would understand. Hope Robyn would forgive him for the lie she already saw.

He shrugged on his clean riding robe, leaving it open to the cool night air, still half thinking about the chain and the responsibilities looped through it. He tucked it into the pocket of his trousers, then he returned upstream to where a fire was already crackling in the darkness—smaller than usual, he noted. Was that intentional?

Before he entered the light, he paused and stared.

Robyn was part Somnurian. He hadn't realized before, thought the lines on her skin were part of the dirt that had covered her since he'd met them. But her heart-shaped face was pale-skinned with freckle lines that framed her features like a tiger's stripes. They lined her arms as well, and, he imagined, the rest of her body. The thought made heat rush to his face.

Along with the freckles though were scars. Cuts that looked like practice accidents on her arms, and one jagged one along her left cheek. Her hair was cut short, the longest strands only reaching to her jaw. He'd guessed that much before but it had been hard to tell for certain.

And the color—again, he'd guessed it would be light but had assumed it was gold, like his. With it cleaned, he saw it was pale white, like a Fugeran. So white, it looked like strands of silk that fell across her eyes. She must've had one parent from each country. Unusual, but not unheard of. Lex watched with amazement as she talked with Mitalo and Jianna, their Perdonian and Somnurian roots showing as strongly as ever. They were easterners, all of them—or their parents at least—from the other side of the Reganian mountains.

"Lex?"

Robyn. She was looking right at him. He froze. Had she seen him staring?

"What are you doing in the shadows?" she said. "Come on, the food's ready."

Lex swallowed and tried to rearrange his face to look casual. When he stepped into the light the other three stopped talking to look him over. Immediately he regretted not tying his robe. The tangle of scars on his chest were there for all to see, and he couldn't change it now. A part of his mind couldn't help comparing himself to them…he was marred in a way they were not, even Robyn with her own scars.

Jianna cracked a laugh, breaking the tension. "Well, we know our runaway knight takes care of himself. You've got some muscle under there, don't you, boy?"

"Jianna!" Robyn said, her face turning bright pink.

"What?" She laughed. "It's true, look at him. Well, you already are, aren't you?"

"Jee," Mitalo said, warningly.

"I mean," Jianna continued. "I'm not even into that but I can appreciate it, can't I?"

"Jianna," Mitalo said, obviously trying to hold back a grin. "Let the boy eat."

Lex swallowed, feeling heat in his face to mirror the blush on Robyn's. Had she been looking at him…like Jianna said?

He quickly closed his robes and put on his belt, trying to be discreet about it, then took a seat on a fallen tree, a few feet from Robyn and ten feet back from the fire. The warmth still sent a shudder through him. When he looked up at her once, she was fully focused on her food.

They ate in silence, all too tired to say much. After her second bowl of stew Jianna stood and asked Mitalo to spar with her. Lex was grateful. He wanted to tell them the truth about who he was, and he really should tell Robyn first. He didn't see this going well either way, but he'd rather not have an audience.

"Robyn," he said, turning toward her. "Can I talk to you?"

She didn't look up, but nodded. "Are you going to tell me the truth?"

His heart began to thud inside his chest, nerves rising. She was usually so firm, but had been incredibly tender with him too…he had no idea how she would react to this.

At his silence Robyn looked over, meeting his gaze. "The truth, then. It's about time."

Lex swallowed a lump rising in his throat. He respected her. He wanted her to trust him. For some reason he was finding it much more difficult to speak to her now that she was watching him so intently. Her short white-blonde hair fell over her face, shielding her eyes from him. She stirred her stew in the bowl, not eating. Waiting.

"I'm not an Arena."

Her lips pursed. She was thinking. "If you're not of House Arena," she said, her voice low, "which house are you from?"

He swallowed, staring at the ground. "Galani."

Her head snapped up, her face gone pale except for the freckle stripes. "What did you say?"

He met her eyes. "Galani."

Her entire body was tense, and he could tell part of her wanted to reach for her dagger, though there was a sadness to her eyes he couldn't parse.

"Robyn," he started.

"Who are you, truly?"

"I swear I mean you no harm."

"Tell me," she snapped. "A cousin to the king? Tenth in line to the throne and bored at court?"

Lex drew the chain from his pocket and passed it to her, holding out the Prince's ring. She examined it carefully, her breathing slow and intentionally measured, a tension to her jaw.

Lex closed his eye, waiting for the anger. Surely she'd be furious to know she had the heir to the throne in her company.

Maybe he should have gone on pretending.

Mitalo and Jianna had noticed their conversation and returned, watching in silence. Robyn sat, tension taut in every muscle, staring at the chain and ring in her hands, not speaking. Lex couldn't take it anymore.

"I didn't want to keep on with you thinking I was something I'm not," he said, standing to pace as he spoke. "You're my friends now, I can't –"

"You have the power to change this kingdom," her voice was low, angry, almost pleading. "Yet you sit in your palace and do nothing."

"I didn't know," he said. "I never knew. Not even my parents know how bad things are. They're being lied to by the high lords—men like Valio, like you said—they're the ones—"

"How did you end up captured by the assassin, then?" she asked, standing as well. The chain dangling from her hand. "Why were you even outside the capital walls?"

"I—" he paused. How could he explain his plan without sounding like more of an idiot than he already did?

"I don't believe this," she said. "You made a promise to help us, and now I don't even know if I can trust—"

She blinked, her words cutting off. Then turned to look into the trees behind them.

"Riders coming," she said.

"How many?" Mitalo asked.

"Six, maybe?"

"What do we do?" Lex asked.

"*You* stay calm and say nothing," Robyn said. "I'll talk to them."

Then a voice called out from the darkness, and Lex's mouth dropped open.

"Ah," Lex said. "I need to go." He turned away from the riders' approach and into the trees, taking Pepper with him into the night.

"Lex!" Robyn hissed. "Where are you going?"

"Trust me!" he said back.

"Unlikely," Jianna sang.

"I'll be right back, I promise," he said, "but I can't let them see me."

Unless he was mistaken, and he didn't think he was, those were the king's men, and Oliver Arena, Lex's best friend, was among them.

If my feelings for my parents and Ravin are anything to judge from, it is the strongest bond in existence.

II
LEX

Lex crept as close to the camp as he could on silent feet, staying in the shadows. As he'd thought, Oliver was there. Mounted and in full armor, he was chastening them for the bar fight in town earlier.

"I was told there were four of you," he said. "One with a cloak is missing."

"There was a cloaked man in the fight, but he wasn't with us," Robyn said, sounding as though she were working very hard to keep from losing her composure. "Some do-gooder who had to step in and help without being asked. He's the one you want to find. He started the whole thing."

"Do you have any idea where he might've gone?"

Please lie, please lie, please lie….

"Not really," Robyn said. "He left town same time as us, but he turned south at the first break in the road. Didn't say where he was headed."

"Very well," Oliver said. "What were your names?"

"I'm Robyn, this is Mitalo, and Jianna."

"Thank you," Oliver said. "We're taking your names down as disturbers of the peace. If it happens again you'll be fined, a third time and you'll be imprisoned. Am I understood?"

They nodded, and Oliver signaled his men to leave. Lex was about to breathe a sigh of relief when Oliver turned back to Robyn and asked, very quietly, "You haven't by chance seen a young man in an eye patch traveling around here, have you?"

Robyn's eyes narrowed. "Perhaps."

Lex's heart stopped. What would she tell them? Would she turn him in?

"Have you, truly?" Oliver said. "Is he well?"

"Why?" Robyn asked. "Who is he to you?"

"A good friend."

"He's well," she said. And after a moment's consideration added, "At least he was the last I saw him. He was riding off into the night without a word of explanation."

"When? Where?"

"Days ago, farther east," she waved a hand vaguely.

"Oh," Oliver said, obviously disappointed. "Well…if you see him again, tell him a friend said, 'use it well.'"

Robyn frowned at that, but nodded.

Oliver gave a nod. "Have a good night."

"Mmhm," Robyn said.

As soon as Oliver was out of sight, Lex crept to Pepper and led her back to their camp. There, he found Robyn pacing back and forth beside the fire, his chain dangling once more from her hand. Mitalo and Jianna were across the fire from her, obviously pretending they wouldn't listen.

"Care to explain yourself, your highness?" Robyn said, straightening. Her light eyes blazed, a line between her brows narrowed in anger. "Who was he, and how does he know you? What does 'use it well' mean? And why did you leave without giving us any warning?"

Lex took a breath, trying to slow his heart's racing pace. "First, that was Oliver Arena, he's one of my best friends at the palace and a member of the king's guard. Second, 'use it well' is a sort of…code phrase we use to tell each other to be careful or watch out. It's a reference to my eye."

Robyn blinked, but gave no other reaction.

"And third," Lex continued. "There wasn't time to give you warning. Oliver knows I'm gone, he helped me get away from the capital in the first place. But I can't be recognized. With his soldiers surrounding him like that, he would've been obligated to take me back, and possibly bring you all in as suspect of kidnapping me or something."

Silence fell between them. Lex glanced to Mitalo, who seemed pensive but only gave Lex a shrug.

Finally, Robyn shoved his chain back into his hands and turned away. "You need to leave."

Lex's head shot up, staring at her. "Wh-leave? Why?"

"You said yourself, you are putting us all in danger," she said, pacing closer again. "I can't trust you with our safety, or with any more knowledge of our infrastructure."

His hands began to shake. "But if we take the right precautions—"

"You also attacked those bandits, stabbing their leader and forcing the rest of us to fight them, leading to unnecessary deaths."

"I know that was stupid, and I apologized—"

"You're putting us all in danger and you have yet to prove you won't go running off at the first chance we give you."

Lex's heart beat a frantic pace. "Robyn, I gave my word—"

"You are a runaway prince, probably being tracked by every guard, knight, and bounty hunter in the kingdom and could easily betray us at a moment's notice."

"I've only tried to help, I don't intend to—"

She spun to face him. "It doesn't matter what you intend! You are nobility, and therefore a danger to us by your very nature."

"How does my birth make me dangerous? I haven't—"

"It's not what you've done, it's—"

"WILL YOU LET ME FINISH?"

She staggered backward.

Lex took a deep breath. His hands shook. He'd never lost control like this. It was something he'd seen his father do frequently before the accident, but Lex had tried for so long to not be that way. He forced his voice to stay even as he spoke.

"I promised I would stay and assist your work in any way I can. Knight or prince, I meant that promise and I intend to keep it. I'm under the impression that we're going to Valios for something, but I have not asked what or why, and I'm perfectly happy waiting for you to be ready to tell me. But I can't demonstrate my honesty unless you give me a chance."

He reached out to her, but she pulled away.

"I can't," she said, her eyes calmer now, but wary. "I need to think on this."

His shoulders slumped. "Why are you so afraid to trust me?"

That made her pause. She looked to Mitalo and Jianna, but neither of them were watching. Her eyes came back to Lex, and he wilted slightly under the stern gaze.

"Don't pretend you know me just because you've had an expensive education. I could slit your throat in your sleep."

He looked directly into her eyes. "I don't doubt it for a second."

Her anger melted into something less tangible. Her mouth tightened into a thin line. Then she turned and ran into the trees.

Lex sighed, his shoulders falling.

"Well. That was nicely handled." Jianna said.

Lex joined them, sitting back from the small fire. The sky was fully dark now, and mist was coming off the river.

"What have I done?" Lex muttered into his hands. "I know I've only been with you a few days, but I believe in what you're doing. I want to help. I want her to believe I'm sincere when I say that."

"You know she's right, though," Jianna said.

"I know," Lex said. "I'm sorry. I've been stupid. But why is that any reason to send me away? I avoided being caught, didn't I? I thought I was doing the right thing."

"I mean, learning the truth about your parentage," Jianna said, shrugging, "She was already on edge, and then those guards came and you took off…. She likes control, Robyn. Doesn't want variations on the plan."

Lex sighed again. "I certainly wasn't part of any plan."

"Don't be too hard on yourself, boy," Mitalo said. "She's got a vendetta for people like you."

"Like me?" Lex asked.

Jianna scooped a bowl of stew and handed it to Mitalo. "She doesn't like nobility. Everything about them makes her nervous." Lex waited for her to go on, but she shook her head. "That part of the story is hers to tell."

"Why now though?" Lex stood and began to pace. "She seemed comfortable enough around me before but now I'm suddenly too dangerous?"

Mitalo tilted his head. "That's a good point you make. Nothing's really changed except what she knows about it."

Lex sat against a tree, far from the fire. "Why did she bring up the bandits when she'd forgiven me for it already?"

"Ammo," Mitalo said. "Bitterness, pettiness, her temper. Sometimes she wants to stay mad for a while."

"She'll come around, though," Jianna said. "Give her time."

Mitalo eyed Lex carefully. "I think you did the right thing, boy."

Lex sighed, staring up into the branches above him. "Sometimes it seems like she's only ever happy when she's in the trees. She's like a bird."

Mitalo laughed. "She'd take that as a compliment."

Lex's mind suddenly came to the right question. He leaned forward. "Why is she unhappy?"

The siblings exchanged a look that didn't say much except that they were debating whether to answer him.

Finally, Mitalo looked up. "You want to know why she's unhappy? Look around. Do you think she wants this muckin' life? I mean, I'm sure she's content, proud of what she can do to help people."

"And she's tough," Jianna added. "She'll put up with a lot more than most, that's for sure."

Mitalo nodded. "Right. She's strong, and smart, and adaptable. But..." he sighed. "This isn't what she wants."

Lex frowned. "So, what does she want? If it's money or comfort I could make that happen for her, and she'd still be able to run her organization. She could have guards and wagons and anything she wants."

He sat against a tree and slumped. Why was he so determined to do this? He now knew his people needed help and he wanted to fix that, but there was something about Robyn that made him crave her approval. He ran a hand over his face.

"What does she want?" Jianna asked. "She hardly ever talks about it. If you asked her, she's selfish for wanting what she does."

Lex looked up, his brow creased.

"Safety." Jianna smiled sadly. "Security. A family. Her own children. She'd never admit it, but we know she thinks about it."

"Every day." Mitalo nodded. "It's in the way she watches the little ones in the towns we pass. I've seen her catch a married couple hug each other at the end of a long work day, and her eyes say everything. Sure, she's muckin' tough. She's had to be. It was take care of herself or be taken advantage of. But if I had to wager, I'd put all my money on her wishing she didn't have to."

Lex blinked. How hard a life had she led? Why was she in the forest in the first place?

"So…she wasn't always a forest-dweller?"

Jianna laughed. "Of course not. None of us were. We've been on the road since I was five though, so it's really all I've ever known, and I enjoy it. Robyn, she was born and raised in a town not far from here, actually. Then…"

"Something happened," Mitalo took over. "It wasn't her fault, but she was forced to leave. She found us, proved herself useful, and eventually she took charge. She's been out here for three years."

Three years? Lex had barely been out a few days. Silence fell over them, and he couldn't help wondering what the rest of Robyn's story was.

Lex couldn't sleep. He knew Robyn was out there in the trees, probably still angry. He sat up and saw the dark form of Mitalo leaning against a tree, something lighting his face.

"You awake?" Mitalo asked.

"I am. Are you smoking?"

Mitalo grunted. "Waterweed. Don't always have it, but it's all over this riverbank. Helps me stay awake. But if you're up for it I'll let you take a turn.

"Sure," Lex said. "Where's Robyn?"

122

Mitalo pointed upward.

Still in the trees, then.

Mitalo clapped a hand on Lex's unscarred shoulder. "Wake Jee when you start to feel tired."

Lex nodded, adjusting his eyepatch. Mitalo tapped his pipe against the tree behind him and stomped the glowing embers until they were smothered. As Mitalo lay down, Lex stood and began to pace quietly, watching where he placed his feet in the waning moonlight. He looked skyward and guessed it was probably sometime past midnight. Sighing, he walked into the trees.

After about ten paces, he didn't try to hide his presence. His footsteps were clear, if light, in the silent darkness. Then a soft *thump* sounded behind him, and he turned.

Robyn straightened, one hand on the dagger at her side.

"Good evening, Lady Robyn."

"Hello, Lex."

"How are you?"

She took in a deep breath. "I overreacted earlier. I'm sorry."

He looked at her. Her light hair was made whiter by the moonlight. Feathery and soft now that it was clean, it fell across her eyes. Though her thin scar called for his attention, it wasn't hard to focus on those eyes.

"Thank you," he said, then spoke with care. "I want to apologize as well. I should've told you the truth earlier, warned you that there would be people looking for me."

She crossed her arms. "I can't say I would've done differently, had I been in your position. But that doesn't mean I like it."

"I don't blame you for being angry with me," Lex said. "Or concerned for your safety. The fears are legitimate."

"Even so, I shouldn't have told you to go so flippantly," she said. "You were right, you've only been trying to help, and you made the right call when you avoided being seen." With a gesture for him to follow, she began to walk and he fell into step beside her.

"Has Mitalo or Jianna told you where we're going or what we're doing?" she asked.

He shook his head. "Like I said earlier, I'm fine if you don't want to tell me yet."

"I've decided I do," she said. "You finally told us your truth, I'd like to be honest in return. Besides, I think you might be able to help us."

"All right," he said, stopping. "So, we're going to Valios?"

"Yes."

"And what are we doing?"

"We intercepted a message about a meeting there. Though the message only mentioned three, we suspect he's inviting six of the other high lords—his closest supporters. And if he is, he's likely up to something we'll need to stop."

Lex frowned. "What do you mean 'something you'll need to stop'?"

"Remember the small village we went through? If you thought that was bad you haven't seen Valio's lands. He treats his nobility the best and his commoners the worst. And…I have reason to believe he may be harming his own daughter."

"Lady Carina?" Lex said. "What makes you think—"

"Something you said the night we met you," she paused. "I'm sorry, I interrupted you again."

Lex held in a smile. "It's all right, go on."

"You said Carina was quiet, and always kept her head down, trying not to be seen." Robyn swallowed. "She's in danger."

He still didn't understand. "Jianna said you dislike nobility…why are you so concerned about Lady Carina?"

"Lex," she said. "I've seen what Valio in particular is capable of. I need you to trust me when I say this: Maximus Valio is an evil man."

"And you think he's abusing his daughter."

"Yes," she said. "Though, I would love to be proven wrong."

Lex nodded. "But that's secondary, right? You said you got word of a meeting?"

"Yes," she said. "Some kind of conference. I don't know more than that, but I have suspicions. Lex, Valio has already hurt this kingdom far worse than you can imagine. If he has any plans for aspiring to greater status, gaining more support, stealing, lying, or cheating his way into something, then he must be stopped."

"You think…" Lex paused, repeating her words to himself. "You think he's trying to gain the throne."

"I think it's a possibility that should not be ignored."

"But…." A thought came to him, and he stared at Robyn. At her scar.

"Did he—Valio, did he—" His teeth ground together, staring at that scar.

"One of his servants," she said, putting a hand to her cheek. "That assassin who captured you, actually. When I refused to become Valio's mistress."

Lex's chest boiled with anger.

"So you see," she said softly, "I know better than most how bad nobility can be."

He looked up to see her eyes had hardened to him. No, this declaration was not made in trust, but in spite.

He bowed his head to her. "Whatever is going on, we'll find out. If it's dangerous, I'll help you stop him."

She relaxed slightly, but her eyes remained sharp.

"We will, I promise," he said. "You have my word."

She arched a brow. "The word of a runaway knight?"

"No," Lex said, his smile widening. "The word of a Reganian Prince."

I wish I could allow myself the freedom to love
fully and openly, or even passionately,
but I fear it too much.

12
CARINA

The portico rang with the clatter of silver forks and knives on silver plates. Carina sipped her wine sparingly. She didn't want it to cloud her mind, not with all of her father's allies staying at the palace, a few of them constantly trying to get her alone.

She hadn't found proof yet, but believed her father was promising them power and control in exchange for their help. She was just a pawn in this, something that could guarantee them closeness to her father if they courted and married her.

Maybe she was making it all up, blowing it out of proportion, but the thoughts kept her awake at night. Now, she kept her head down, avoiding the gazes of the men around her.

Her father, dressed in a chiton of black and red, took the head of the table. Carina sat at his left hand, dressed in the same colors. Lord Askar, Valio's most trusted friend—if indeed he had such feelings for anyone—to his right. Around the table sat the Lords Drako, Bane, Sotir, Milar, and, beside Carina, Glavan. Their hair varied from deep gold to white or blond, and their ages differed by decades in some cases.

"Maximus," Lord Askar said between bites of roast venison. "We are all eager to know. What is the purpose of this gathering?"

Valio answered, holding up a finger. "Ah, ah, ah, too many unwanted eyes and ears are present at the moment," he said, glancing around at the servants. "We shall speak of it in the morning...in private." He gave a nod to the rest of the lords to signal the topic closed.

As the conversation shifted to crops and the peasantry, Carina flinched at his use of the word *unwanted*. He was referring to the servants, but had told Carina she wouldn't be invited either. Still, just because she was banned from the meeting didn't mean she wouldn't hear what was said.

Her father knew about most of the good eavesdropping locations where spies might slip in, and therefore placed guards around them, but there was one she'd been able to keep from him. The meeting would be held in his private council room. He would have guards posted in the hallways twenty paces from each door, threatened with death should they be caught any closer. Even the chimney would be guarded on the roof, again, from a distance. But Carina didn't need either.

There was a small crawl space—a drainage tunnel for flood water from the roof—that wound through the walls between the council room and her father's chambers. It was too small for a man, but just right for a thin lady—as long as pretty clothes were left behind, of course.

She'd found it as a child while playing hide-and-find with one of the servants, and whenever she wanted to be alone, that was where she went. It was a bit of a climb, but she'd managed it many times.

There were tunnels like it all around the palace, but that one had been her favorite for a long time, when her parents were happy. She could crawl inside and listen to them speaking softly, hear her parents talk about her, their land, their people, or important political discussions. The only time she'd regretted her discovery was when her father brought home his first mistress. She'd never eavesdropped after that. But perhaps the fate of the kingdom was a good enough reason to try again.

She finished as much of her meal as she wanted, and placed her silverware on the plate parallel, pointing away from her, signaling her completion.

"Would you like dessert, my lady?"

She looked up to see Damari standing over her, now wearing her house colors, one corner of his mouth turned up.

She blushed. "Yes, um…that would be wonderful."

He nodded and took her plate, leaving toward the kitchen. She watched him go, a smile teasing her mouth. When he was out of sight, she felt someone watching her and turned to see Lord Drako level a glare at her. A chill ran through her entire body at the gleam in his eyes. She looked down, the smile gone.

Damari returned with a small slice of cake. When he placed it in front of her, she looked up to thank him, but he was staring at her neck. She reached a hand to the spot and winced. Her father had beaten her again when she'd asked to attend the meeting. He'd been so angry, his usual perfect form of marking where her chiton would cover had failed him.

She met Damari's eyes for a moment, then looked away, ashamed. She tried to eat her cake, but it was like sand in her mouth. No amount of wine helped. Moments later, she placed a hand on her father's arm. "My lord, might I be excused? I'm feeling quite ill."

"Of course, darling," he said, patting her hand. "Take care of yourself. Would you like me to send for a Cure?"

"No no, I think I just need a bit of rest." She stood and kissed his cheek and turned to curtsy before the visiting lords. She did not look at Drako, but could tell he was still watching her.

As soon as she was in the corridor, she haphazardly rearranged her hair in an attempt to cover the offensive bruise. She ran down the passage toward her room, tears threatening behind her eyes. What would Damari think of her? Why did she care what he thought of her? A poor little courtier who lets her father hit her. Hoping someday he might come to his senses and apologize, realizing he loves her…

Which might never happen.

She made it halfway to her room before collapsing against a column, sliding to the floor. She hated it. Hated when people knew, when they saw how weak she was….

Footsteps closed in on her before she could react. She stood to run, but was met by a strong set of arms wrapping around her. She didn't know who it was, but she fought them anyway.

"Let me go," she whimpered.

"Carina," he said. "It's me."

Damari. This made her try harder to tear away. He couldn't know. But he was too strong. His hands held her upper arms firm, just enough to keep her there. The flight drained from her. She slumped against his chest. She shivered when his arms wrapped around her back and pulled her close.

She hadn't been held like this in so long…

"Lady Carina," he whispered, stroking her hair. "Who did that to you?"

She stiffened. He didn't know. Hadn't guessed.

"Did what?" she asked, shoving him away. She moved her hair to cover the bruise. "I don't know what you mean."

He frowned. "Yes you do. If someone is hurting you, I want to help."

She hugged her chest and turned away slightly. "That's kind of you, but you can't stop it."

From the corner of her eye she saw his shoulders sag. "Why not? Why do you let it happen?"

She shivered. Those words sounded so like the ones in her mind. She closed her eyes, trying to hold in her emotions. She paused, then looked up at him. His expression was so eager. He reached out and ran a hand down her arm. She flinched away, and immediately felt silly. The contact was sweet, wasn't it?

And yet…it wasn't seemly for a servant to treat her so…tenderly. Still, it was unlike any she'd ever felt from anyone, man or woman. Even her mother had always been aloof, despite genuine expressions of love. Carina had never thought about it much, but she now realized part of her longed for someone to touch her gently. Swallowing, her voice came out breathy and hitched. "It's my father."

He stiffened, she looked away. She didn't want to see his reaction. It wouldn't change anything. Damari was only a servant. Not a lord, not a knight, no influence, not important at all. Except for the odd pull he had over her, something that made her both curious, and afraid. He put a hand on her shoulder, and a small sob escaped her. Before she could protest, his arms were around her once more.

She felt him shift. Lifting her head, she saw him gaze up and down the colonnade before looking back to her. Such sympathy in his bright emerald eyes. He bent down and picked her up, cradling her in his arms. She should tell him to put her down…but would that be rude? And she didn't want to cause more of a scene than she already had….

Moments later, he laid her in her own bed. Heavy blankets were drawn over her, and her tears wiped away. His hand ran along her cheek, making her shiver, then continued down her neck to the bruise.

"Carina," he whispered. "I knew your father was cruel, but I never knew he did this to his own flesh. I'm so sorry."

"It's not your fault," she said, the words soft.

"No, but I know how to stop him." His jaw set, a bit of anger flashed in his eyes. "Get some rest. In three hours, will you come with me to the stables? I'll introduce you to some people who can help."

She knew her face showed fear, because he said, "Don't worry. We know what we're doing, and we want to help. But if you agree to help us, we can be so much more effective. And I…I want you there."

His declaration made her melt, her whole body relaxing. A small section in the back of her mind flashed a warning, but she shoved it aside. It had been so long…so long since anyone had shown any compassion for her….

"I will come."

The statement felt wrong to her ears, as though someone else had spoken it.

But Damari smiled. "Thank you. Can I get you anything before I go?"

She shook her head. "Just lock the door, please?"

Nodding, he leaned over her. She nearly pulled away, before he pressed his lips to her forehead. Carina wished she could pull away, but she was blocked from moving by him. He lingered there, his face inches from hers. "If you need me, I'll be in the kitchens. Send for food and I'll come."

She forced a smile. "Thank you, Damari."

He sighed. "My name on your lips is the most beautiful thing I've ever heard."

She inhaled, anticipating what he might be about to do…what part of her feared, and another part hoped he would.

"Carina," he whispered. "May I kiss you?"

The focus in his eyes made her breathless. "Yes."

The distance between them, which was so small already, shrank. His lips were soft, and eager. She wasn't sure what to do, but let his mouth move hers, following his lead. Danger flashed in the back of her mind, and she was just beginning to hope he would stop…when he pulled away.

"Rest now," he said. And then he was gone.

She lay awake for a long time, wondering what that kiss meant.

Carina did rest, but not for long. She watched the water-powered clock on her wall. The time passed by at an infuriating pace. When she had five minutes, she put on her cloak and opened her bedroom door to see Damari approaching.

He immediately wrapped his arms around her, placing a kiss on her head, before taking her hand and leading her through her own home.

The halls were dim, most of the lamps extinguished for the night. They crept from shadow to shadow. When someone passed around the corner, Damari pressed her against the wall, holding her back with one arm.

It was a guard. This was ridiculous. She lived here, why should she be sneaking? Still, she didn't want to run into any of the lords or her father, and Damari seemed to know what he was doing.

Two minutes later, they reached the stables on the north side of the palace. The large space was covered by a high barn-like roof, but was open to the elements between walls and ceiling.

Damari paused before they got far, turning to face her. "Are you all right?"

Carina nodded.

He looked down the aisle of stalls, seeming wary. "I want you to know, I shouldn't hold your hand or anything while we're around my friends. They won't understand. But that doesn't mean I don't care."

Carina frowned. What was he saying? She didn't have time to think though, so she nodded, which seemed to make him happy.

They separated, making their way through the stalls, which were occupied by only horses, until about halfway down. A tall blond girl dressed in riding robes stood as they approached.

"This is Lady Robyn," Damari said. The tone of his voice when he said her name made Carina turn to him. He was looking at her with admiration plain on his face.

Robyn shook her head. "I'm not a lady like you, they just call me that. It's a pleasure to meet you, Lady Carina," she said, extending a hand.

Carina shook it, then pulled back, wrapping her arms around herself. What had she agreed to?

Robyn looked her over and said, "Now, you're in an uncomfortable situation regarding your father, is that right?"

Carina's eyes flew to Damari.

"No, no, he didn't tell me anything. I guessed." Robyn extended a hand. "It's all right. I understand. We want to help."

This tall, powerful-looking girl understood what it was like to be beaten? Carina looked her over more carefully and noticed the scars. Small, nearly invisible until she looked carefully, they were there. The one on Robyn's face made Carina stare. "You do?"

Robyn nodded. "We also know your father has hurt many more people beside yourself, and we hope to put a stop to that. Do you know of the meeting taking place tomorrow morning?"

Carina still felt hesitant. How was she lucky enough to meet more than one person who wanted to help her? And in a matter of days? It seemed impossible luck.... Nevertheless, she did know of the meeting, so she nodded.

Robyn smiled. "Is there any way you can help us listen in on it?"

The small passageway came to mind, and Carina knew Robyn at least was thin enough to fit inside. She nodded again.

"Perfect," Robyn said. "Follow me."

I fear the feelings I cannot control, the impulses,
the vulnerability, the complete trust one
must place in their partner.

13
LEX

Two days had passed since Lex told the truth. Now he stood by Pepper, hiding near the river with Mitalo and Jianna as they waited for Robyn to return from Valio's palace. He wasn't sure what to expect from Robyn moving forward, but he did know that he wanted to make good on his promises. He would find a way to help.

The forest ended at the northern bank of the River Tardus—the same river that ran through Lex's home city. And beyond stood the small hill on which the Valio city palace was situated. A single story in the shape of a square with one side missing. They'd circled around to the back—the western side—which looked to Lex like nothing but a wall with some drainage pipes. Beyond the palace lay the city Valios, which Lord Valio ruled over. Clean and extravagant. The fine homes of lower lords and Valio's knights were lined up in perfect rows leading to the forest line to the east. But outside the city walls, where the fields grew and the farmers who tended them lived, the buildings were little better than the huts he'd seen in the first village he'd entered. It seemed as though Valio cared what his central city looked like, but left the rest in his lands to rot.

It made Lex sick to his stomach.

When footsteps sounded nearby, he turned to see Robyn approaching with two people. The tall Callidian boy he'd seen that first night, and a petite girl—Lady Carina. Lex pulled off his hood. They had talked before Robyn went in and agreed that her man—Damari—would likely be bringing Carina out to help them, and if Lex wanted to stay informed, he'd have to let her see him. He let out a nervous breath.

"We have a visitor," Robyn called. "May I present Lady Carina Valio."

Lex met Carina's gaze. The color rushed from her face and she fell to her knees.

Then Damari looked at Lex, his brow furrowed.

Robyn waved a hand at Lex now. "This is Lex, he's a prince."

"Prince?" Damari said. "What's he doing here?"

Robyn raised a brow. "He's offered his help."

"But he's nobility," Damari sneered. "I mean, Carina at least has a good reason for helping us, but he's just as dishonest as Valio and the rest. A muck-drooling mudspot who doesn't have the decency to—"

"He has proved himself willing to help and able to keep a secret, Damari. If you have a problem with that, you can leave."

Damari's eyes widened. "Leave?"

"Or play nice with the prince," Jianna said, smirking.

Robyn nodded. "Your choice."

Damari looked taken aback. Lex was too, for that matter.

Damari nodded. "I'll stay."

"Good," Robyn said. "Now, Carina. You say you know of a way for us to eavesdrop on the meeting tomorrow?"

Carina nodded.

"And in exchange, we will do what we can to stop your father from hurting you."

Carina nodded again, a stiffness to her movements this time.

Robyn offered a kind smile. "Please, tell us about how we can listen in."

Carina took a deep breath. "There's a tunnel...a sort of...a drainage shaft, that runs over the entire palace and empties into the river here. It passes between my father's chambers and the council room where the meeting will be held. I've...I've tried it before. The sound is very clear."

"Perfect," Mitalo said. "You can show me how to get in."

"Actually," Carina said, "it's quite small. Forgive me, but you would not fit."

"I guess that means me," Robyn said.

Lex turned to her. "What?"

"Well, if none of you can fit, that means I'm going."

"I'm not much taller than you," Lex said.

"Um, hello everyone. I'm shorter than all of you," Jianna said. "I will be the one going."

"Forgive me again," Carina said. "But it is a very thin shaft. Height is of little matter if one cannot fit ones width inside. You may be short, my lady, but your shoulders and hips are wider than I think will fit."

Jianna raised a brow, but said nothing.

"Of the four of you," Carina continued, "Lady Robyn will have the easiest time moving through the space, provided she leaves behind any large weapons."

Lex looked Robyn over. The quiver at her waist, her short swords crossing her back.

"If she can't take weapons, she's not muckin' going in," Mitalo said.

"Yes, I am," Robyn argued. "I can take my daggers in hand, if nothing else. That won't take up much space. Will that do?"

Carina nodded.

Lex shook his head. "Robyn, what if he sees you?"

"So?" she asked. "What if he does?"

He turned from the others and lowered his voice so only she would hear. "What if he recognizes you?"

She glared at him before turning away. "Listen, all of you. If Carina thinks she can sneak me in without being seen, then I believe her. No one but her will even know I've been there."

She met their eyes one by one, making sure they understood.

"Good," she said. "Now, Carina. Shall I go in tonight, or early morning?"

"Very early morning is quieter. Perhaps four or five hours from now?"

Robyn nodded. "That's the plan, then. Damari, take Carina back inside. I'll go to the stables in four hours. For now, everyone ought to get some sleep."

They parted, and Lex watched Carina go. She looked back at him once, then whispered something to Damari before she drew away, and came to Lex.

She inclined her head. "Highness, I wondered if I could ask you something?"

Lex smiled. "Feel free, my lady."

"Well, my father sent you a proposal, and...I was curious to know if that was what made you run away from the palace?"

"Oh no, my lady. I mean...it wasn't you in particular...I'd sort of been planning it for a while. My parents have been pushing me to marry for over a year, and I didn't feel ready. I needed some time alone. It's only fate that's brought me here now."

She nodded. "I was actually grateful. I've only been sixteen for a few months, and I don't feel ready to marry either."

"I'm glad it's worked out for both of us, then."

She smiled. With a quick curtsy, she turned back to join Damari, who still glared at Lex, and disappeared into the dark trees.

Behind him he heard Robyn and the others shuffling around. He turned in time to be offered a piece of dried meat, and some stale bread. He took both gratefully. No fire tonight, they were too close to the city.

Lex lay down, but couldn't sleep. His leg started bouncing at one point, and he had to concentrate to keep it still. Mitalo paced, Jianna sharpened her sword, and Robyn stood to shoot her arrows for a time. Lex watched, and couldn't help but be impressed. She shot with such speed. An arrow per second, when she held many prepared in her draw hand. Lex had never seen anyone use that particular style. After she'd gathered them and sat down to sharpen the heads, he spoke.

"You're a very good shot."

"Thank you."

"How long have you practiced archery?"

She shrugged. "My father started teaching me when I was five, so…fourteen years?"

"That's a long time. And you enjoy it?"

"Very much."

"I couldn't see what you were aiming for. Did you hit it?"

"Every time."

Lex smiled. "You pride yourself on good aim."

"Of course. Practice when calm means perfection under pressure." She paused to check the sharpness of one arrow. "Besides, if I only land one shot in all the rest of my days, it will be Valio." She looked up at Lex. "And that is one shot I refuse to miss."

The determination was clear in her eyes. Lex nodded, and she went back to her arrows.

After a half hour of silence save for Robyn's sharpening, she stood. "I think I'd like another bath. You all stay here, I'm going over to the river."

They nodded, and she quickly left.

Lex lay down on top of his blankets, staring up at the stars. He made out some Life constellations as they moved across the sky: Wave, Geyser, and Waterfall, but he never seemed able to find the ones relating to Stability or Growth or Death.

He thought back to the priest they'd met…was it two days ago? Three? The carving of Amplia still sat in Lex's saddlebag, untouched except the occasional brush of a finger. He'd thought about it and was certain the only person who could have given it to him was that priest. Maybe he should start carrying it on his person. It was small enough, it'd fit in a pocket.

He shook his head. What good would it do if he used it all up? He stood and looked around. Mitalo and Jianna were lounging against a couple of trees, Jianna sharpening weapons and Mitalo carving something. Robyn still wasn't back yet. Lex looked up, checking the time. She'd been gone for nearly half an hour.

She was probably fine. She could take care of herself.

Still, he couldn't sleep. He stood, stretching. "I'm taking a walk," he said.

"Don't do anything stupid," Jianna said in a singing voice. Mitalo said nothing.

Lex wound through the trees, not really paying attention to the direction. He fiddled with the rings and the now-empty-of-magic coin around his neck as he went, thinking again of his grandmother, and now also of his father. Lex could still see the look of pride on his father's face as he smiled and spoke of how important the ring was, the Prince's seal and what it represented. That Lex be honorable, and kind, and honest. He'd always tried his best to do those things, to be who his father expected.

Then he took up the engagement ring. In this one thing he'd failed. He was sure he hadn't met every eligible lady of court, but he'd met a good portion. None of them were right. Then there was the last ball he'd attended. His parents made him promise to dance with a different lady for each song played, and he'd stupidly agreed. On his first dance, he tripped, sending himself and Lady Andris into a table. She'd stomped out of the hall trailing wine, with bits of carrot and olives skittering from her skirts.

No. Even if he'd wanted to, none of the courtiers would look at him now. If he was going to marry someone, he wanted to connect with them on a deeper level than "polite indifference."

Who would his parents want him to marry? What kind of woman? If they hadn't been limited to the court, would they have chosen Carina? He was glad now, that he'd left. Knowing what Robyn said, he didn't want Valio anywhere near the throne.

Moonlight glinted off the blue stone and gold band as he twisted it in his fingers. In his mind's eye, he pictured a faceless bride. He imagined taking her to the palace, bringing her into the throne room and announcing they were to wed. His mother would beam with joy, and his father would shake his hand. They would both embrace him and the girl, of course.

He slid the ring onto each finger, giving his mind free reign. He took a moment, trying to picture this woman in wedding garb, and his lips curved in a smile. Whoever she was, she was beautiful. Hair smoothed, with stray strands falling across her eyes. A flowery scent filled his lungs, and he saw a shy smile on her lips as he placed the ring on her slender finger.

A veiled face and cream-colored gown filled his mind, and he couldn't seem to make them disappear. This woman, standing with him, as he took her hands and drew her to him, before kissing her gently....

He stopped, staring at the ground. Kissing. What if he was bad at it? How would he know? How would she react if he couldn't kiss right? Not to mention...the rest. He knew the basics of course, but he'd never *done* it....

His shoulders slumped. He was hopeless, and he knew it. No woman with any sense would ever—

Water splashed nearby, and Lex looked up.

He hadn't meant to see her. He'd been so focused on his problems he hadn't realized where he was walking. So lost in thought that he took in her silhouette before realizing what he was seeing.

Submerged to her hips, Robyn stood facing away from him in the swift current, water flowing smoothly around her. Her pale hair glowed bright in the light from the full moon. Her back was marked not with scars, but the same freckle stripes that framed her face. She looked at peace.

Lex's face burned, trying to ignore the heat growing in the pit of his stomach. He stared at the ground and backed away, placing his feet carefully.

He hadn't seen anything, not really, an outline, and her bare back...smooth, unscarred skin....

His hands shook as he made his way back to the camp.

And yet, I want it.
An irony, I know.

14
LEX

Lex slapped his face, trying to regain his senses. Wasn't he just telling himself how honorable and honest he was? What was he supposed to do now? By the time he got back to the camp, his accidental indiscretion had put him in a sour mood.

Mitalo looked up and glared. "What did you do?"

Lex balked at him. "Nothing!"

Jianna raised a brow. "Doesn't sound like nothing."

Lex paced in front of them. "Nothing, it's nothing. I went...for a walk. It's fine."

Mitalo and Jianna shared a look.

"What?" Lex asked.

"Did you see Robyn bathing?" Jianna asked.

"I didn't...I mean—"

"Did you muckin' watch her?" Mitalo said, standing.

Lex's heart jumped to his throat. Mitalo was intimidating even when he wasn't trying to be. Lex backed away, stammering. "I may have...accidentally...seen her."

"Accidentally?" Mitalo said, his voice a low growl.

"Yes, accidentally," Lex said, running a hand on the back of his neck. "I was thinking as I walked and lost track of the...where I was, and I happened to see her in the river. I backed away and came straight here."

"So she doesn't know you saw her?" Jianna asked, a grin appearing on her face.

"I don't think so, no."

Mitalo stomped forward and took the front of Lex's tunic in his thick fists. Lex tried to back away, but Mitalo directed him toward a tree and pinned him there.

"What are you—"

"What are your intentions?"

Lex stopped struggling. "What?"

"I said, what are your muckin' intentions?" Mitalo's voice was low and serious.

"I...I don't," Lex started.

Jianna stood and came to stand behind Mitalo's shoulder. "He wants to know whether you intend to court Robyn or not."

They looked like guard dogs, these two siblings. Lex's heart beat in his chest. "C-court her?" he asked. "No, I...I mean I hadn't thought...even if I had feelings for her, which I don't, she'd never be interested in me, I mean look at me."

Mitalo's eyes narrowed.

Blood pounded in Lex's ears. He hated knowing that people looked at him and thought he was less-than. That he was slow, or weak, or incapable....

Mitalo kept him pinned for a few moments, staring. Slowly, he released his grip to let Lex slump against the tree.

Then Mitalo backed away, crossing his arms like Jianna. Waiting. The three of them stood in a deadlock, Lex unsure of what to say or do.

"I," he started, trying to think. "What do you want me to say?"

"You really think," Mitalo started, "she'd care about some mucking scars?"

Lex looked away, focusing on some moss near his feet. "Everyone else seems to."

"I've seen the way you look at her, boy," Mitalo said.

Lex balked. "What do you mean the way I look at her? I look at her the way I look at anyone."

Mitalo rolled his eyes.

"Look," Lex said. "I would never want to put her in a position she's not comfortable with."

"Good," Jianna said. "Go on."

"I do admire her," Lex said. "Of course I do. But I've never thought of her as...in that way, and I swear I didn't look on purpose!"

The two eyed him. "Fine," Mitalo said. "But you'd better decide before things get too messy, because prince or no prince, if you break her heart, I *will* come for you."

"I'm not a prince here."

"Why'd you leave your pretty palace, then?" Jianna asked.

Lex sighed. "Does it matter?"

"Does to us," Mitalo said.

"Because I wanted to," Lex said, getting defensive. "Can't a prince travel his own kingdom?"

"'Course he can," Mitalo nodded. "But I'd imagine they usually do it with a guard, and riding in a carriage. There's another reason you're not saying."

"So what if there is?" Lex said, barely managing to keep his voice level. "Would you believe me if I told you?"

Mitalo rocked on the balls of his feet. "That depends on the reason."

"Fine." Lex turned to face him. "I left because I was being forced into something I didn't feel ready for. More specifically, because I didn't want to marry. Not any of the ladies I had to choose from."

"Why?" Jianna asked. "Aren't they all more beautiful than all the stars in the sky or some muck like that?"

"Oh, they're beautiful," Lex said. "They're even good people, the ones I got to know well. Smart, strong, kind, at least they appeared to be in court anyway."

"So why—"

"It's the way they look at me," he snapped. "You wonder why I don't think anyone would want me because of this?" he asked, pointing to his face. "It's because I've never been given any reason to believe otherwise. Sure I have close friends who don't flinch at the sight of me, but I've known most of these girls since I was at least five. I've danced with them, tried to get to know them, had dinner in their homes...but there's always something off. A cringe, a flinch, when they see me." He shook his head. "I could be imagining it. Maybe they're not doing it and it's just that we don't share enough interests or none of them have ever really shown interest in me as a person instead of a prince. I just…can't bring myself to marry a girl who can't look at me."

He'd begun to pace while he spoke, and while his voice had grown softer, his chest heaved with deep breaths. The silence that met him was thick with shock. They stared at him. Mitalo's brow raised to such an extent, Lex wondered if his face would ever return to normal.

Jianna recovered first, shaking her head. "Seems pretty rude for a bunch of high society ladies if you ask me."

Mitalo only nodded.

Lex shook his head, running a hand over his face. "My parents told me before I left that I had to choose someone or they'd choose for me. They're getting old, and Mother couldn't have children after me, so of course they want an heir sooner rather than later. I mean I understand where their impatience is coming from, I do. And I want to marry. But I couldn't let them choose for me. I decided the best way to find someone who would love me for me, and not for Prince Alexander, was to get out and leave the title behind. So…here I am," he ended with a shrug.

"Hmm." Mitalo eyed him now. "And have you found someone?"

Lex's face burned as Robyn's silhouette reappeared in his mind, followed quickly by the way she'd looked at him when he'd shared his poem, and the softness of her hands on his face, helping him come back from his pain….

He shook his head, unsure.

"Well good luck," Mitalo said. "You'd be lucky to find a wife half as good as mine though."

Lex's curiosity piqued. "What's she like, your wife?"

"Oh, don't get him started, please," Jianna said, rolling her eyes with a smile.

Mitalo gave a half-smile, and his eyes became distant. "Beautiful. Dark hair, almost blue in the moonlight. She's mostly Perdonian, like me, but she's got a bit of Callidian that comes through. Eyes deep brown as a good strong tea. One look from her can make anyone smile. And her laugh makes you want to laugh along. Gave me a little girl too. Got me wrapped around her fingers. I sent her a bow and some arrows for her birthday last month, and she's learning them. She's only nine, but...by the Gods' graces, I hope she learns to protect herself."

Despite her teasing, Jianna was smiling. Content. "Best sister and niece anyone could ask for."

Lex offered to take first watch, promising through their teasing that he would make sure Robyn was safe. Once they fell asleep, he faced the problem of telling Robyn the truth. He didn't want to delay.

He circled the camp, shaking his hands and arms to try and relax. He watched the moon, marking the passage of time. After half an hour, he wondered if he ought to check on Robyn again, but decided not to. He didn't want to make things worse for himself. Another half hour later, she stumbled into camp, her eyes soft and tired-looking.

He sighed with relief. "Robyn, it's been more than an hour. Are you all right?"

"Mmmhmm," she nodded. "Sorry, the water and sounds were so soothing and I fell asleep." She yawned. "Oh, but I needed that."

He nodded, wondering for the millionth time how he would tell her.

"Are *you* all right, Lex? You look a little shaken." She came closer to him, focusing on his face, and the scent of soap and lavender drifted over him.

He swallowed. He just had to say it. That's all.

"I-I'm sorry."

She stared at him. "For what?"

He couldn't hold still. He wrung his hands, put them behind his back, through his hair, on his hips, before he crossed his arms over his chest.

"What's wrong?" She frowned. "Did something happen?"

He couldn't speak. "I—that is, it was an accident, a-and I-I didn't mean to. I walked right away. But I, I did want to tell you because...well, I didn't want to lie again and—"

"What are you talking about?" she asked, though her tone suggested she had guessed.

"I-I swear I didn't see much, I—"

"Lex."

His gaze snapped to hers.

And he was shocked to see a lift to the corner of her lips.

"You saw me?"

He swallowed. Nodded.

"Unintentionally?"

"Yes."

She looked him over, her eyes pausing as she seemed to evaluate him, the way she'd done when they'd first found him tied up.

"You're forgiven," she said. "Be more careful, though. I might not be so merciful a second time."

She put a hand on his shoulder as she passed, before jumping up into the trees to sleep.

Lex let out a slow breath, putting his own hand over where she'd touched his shoulder. That…had gone far better than he'd expected.

He leaned against a tree and watched the Valio palace until the lights had all gone out. Soon Robyn would go in there, risking her life to make sure Valio wouldn't succeed in whatever he was planning. Lex let his mind wander, and soon thoughts of his parents came to him.

Had he hurt them by running away? He'd intended to return soon, assuming he could fall in love quickly. He'd been so stupid to think that.

His mind returned to what Mitalo had said…Lex hadn't actually considered Robyn in that way until that moment, but would she ever fit into his world? He barely fit in here, in hers.

He tilted his head back and looked up through the trees. They had to be worried about him right now, his parents. He wished there was a way to tell them he was safe. Well, relatively.

Of course they'd sent out search parties for him, if the sighting of Oliver was any indication. He knew they wanted what was best for him. While he loved them for it, he also knew they wouldn't understand. He'd learned so much already from being out on his own. Most importantly, how much his kingdom, and his people, meant to him. How much they needed him.

He had to find a way to fix things.

I want so much to trust someone in that way,
but my heart has been betrayed.
I've never actually written that story down.

15
CARINA

Carina woke to a quiet knock on her door. Damari. It was still very dark outside, no hint of sunrise yet. She blinked and rubbed the sleep from her eyes. After slipping on a plain woolen chiton and a shawl, she peeked out the door to see Damari waiting. Her father had told her to stay in her room all day, but at least no guards were posted. He trusted her that much.

Seeing that she was awake, Damari took her hand in that intimate way she had withdrawn from the first time they'd met. Now, she held on. That first time, she'd been shaken by Lord Drako's advances. This felt protective.

They turned down the hallway toward the stables once more. The palace's living quarters were quiet in these early hours. As they crept by, the kitchen workers were already busy warming fires and preparing breakfast. They rounded the building in silence, then Damari kissed her forehead and whispered, "Good luck," before slipping into the kitchens.

In the stables, Robyn waited at the back of an empty stall. She stood when Carina approached, two daggers held in her right hand. "Ready?"

Carina nodded.

She led the way in silence, around the northern building toward the entrance to the tunnel on the west. Robyn followed close, mimicking Carina's every step with exactness. Whoever these people were, they were well-trained. Then it occurred to her that they'd likely never had training as she had, but learned from experience. Carina had never been hunting, nor had she ever fought anyone outside of practice. Glancing back, she caught a glimpse of Robyn. The taller girl had muscles just as toned, movements just as sure.

They passed several small openings, and Carina began to wonder if Robyn would fit. The girl was quite tall, and her height masked how wide she really was.

Halfway down the side of the building, Carina stopped at a tunnel marked by three large stones surrounding the opening. "Hurry," she whispered, letting Robyn duck in before her. It was cold inside, and damp from the recent rainstorm. Through the darkness they climbed. It was only about thirty feet before they reached a landing, of sorts, where the space opened slightly and they could curl up to sit. Here, surrounded by stone and darkness, small cracks in the building allowed sound to travel, and they would be able to easily hear what was going on in the council room.

"Unless they're making noise, we'll have to be silent," Carina whispered, "Or they'll hear us as clearly as we hear them."

"Understood," Robyn said.

And they waited. It was pitch black, and cold as a cave in winter. Or, what Carina imagined a cave in winter would feel like. She brought her knees to her chest and hugged them. It was big enough for her to lean against the wall with her head ducked a little. She couldn't tell how Robyn was positioned, but she imagined it wasn't comfortable, her being so much taller.

Before too long they heard the sounds of servants preparing the room: clangs of plates and silverware, carts of food and flower arrangements.

As the sounds below grew loud enough to hide their voices, Robyn spoke low. "Your father beats you."

Carina stayed silent.

"When we first met Lex," Robyn whispered, "we asked him what he knew of the Valio house, and he told us about you. Said you were jumpy, always trying to keep out of sight." She shifted in the darkness. "I know that feeling."

Carina looked toward Robyn and glared, knowing she couldn't see it. Was this girl really trying to get Carina to spill her heart? At a time like this? Even if they weren't stuck in an enclosed space, Carina would have been hurt by the forwardness of such comments. "How can you possibly know that feeling? I'll bet you haven't hidden a day in your life." She hugged her knees tighter and scowled at nothing.

Robyn gave a humorless laugh. "Just because I don't slouch doesn't mean I'm not hiding."

Carina's brows knit together. She'd always wished to be strong and powerful. It didn't make sense that someone with those things would be hiding behind them. "Why would you hide behind strength? What more could you want than to be strong?"

The silence felt thick. Carina waited.

Robyn sighed. "I want what I've always wanted." But that was all she said.

Carina's heart broke a little at the hopelessness in her voice. After a minute's silence, she asked, "Why haven't you found it yet?"

She heard more than saw Robyn shrug. "I have trouble getting close to people."

Carina nodded. This she could understand.

"What is it you want?" Robyn asked.

Carina opened her mouth to speak, but nothing came. The truth was, she'd never thought about her own wants. Except for her oils and her sword, she had little to call her own.

Then, the sound of huge doors thudding open came to them. It was so clear that Robyn jerked and landed a kick to Carina's leg. She groaned a little and rubbed at the spot while Robyn apologized in a hush.

"Yes, in here. Everyone please take a seat and I'll have breakfast brought in."

Carina tensed as her father's voice came to them, crisp and official. Plates and silverware clinked as the food was brought in and the men began to eat. Carina sat still as the stone around them and listened with all her might.

After some time and meaningless chatter, Valio commanded, "Leave us."

Doors opened and steps receded as the servants left the room. The sound of a chair being pushed back, then more steps—slow, measured—began to circle around the room.

"For the Gods' sake, Valio. Don't keep us in suspense." Carina recognized Lord Drako's voice. "Why have you called us all here?"

The pacing stopped; a throat cleared. "I can't speak for everyone, I'm sure, but I have been quite unhappy with the way this kingdom is run, particularly in the last twenty or so years. I pushed it aside, tried to ignore it, until my wife died of a plague the Royal Family didn't contain in time."

Carina groaned to herself. Her mother died of consumption, not a plague.

But he went on. "Since then, I have thought long and hard about ways in which I could exact changes. At first, I went through the proper channels, submitting my thoughts to the king and queen via proposals and such, but that was pointless. Trying to convince them to alter their traditions was an effort in futility. They are opposed to change, and pay little more than trivial devotion to Crescere, God of Growth. The kingdom is void of color, void of prosperity, despite their praise of Amplia. And those who worship Sileo and Fina are only weights against our progress."

A chorus of Mmm's and Aahh's sounded in agreement. Carina frowned. Was it really so hard to propose change to the king? Or had her father's proposals been refused for good reasons? And, she'd thought he was indifferent to the Gods. Yet here he was, using them to manipulate his followers into trusting him.

"My next endeavor was to see my daughter married to the young prince. I thought, how better to improve the kingdom than through the soft hand of love? Unfortunately, the boy ran at the thought."

Carina gritted her teeth. The lies stung as much as the beatings. Tears burned behind her eyes, and she gripped the fabric of her dress. In the darkness, Robyn's hand found hers and Carina held it, welcoming the offered strength.

Silence seemed to ring in the chamber below them. Carina felt bumps rise on her arms, fear pricking at the back of her mind.

"All this said," her father continued, his voice low now, and Carina strained to hear. "I hold no animosity toward our monarchs. They are doing their very best, I'm sure. I am, however, concerned for the...welfare of the throne itself. Our crown prince is gone, and our king and queen grow more frail with each passing day."

The concern is his voice sent a pang of agony through Carina's chest. He'd sounded just like that in the weeks before Mother died....

"I invited you all here to simply propose...shall we call it a contingency plan? Something to agree on, should anything happen to our dear leaders. We wouldn't want the kingdom to be without guidance, would we? It's our responsibility as the leadership of Regania to choose the *best* possible candidate."

Carina winced.

"As I'm sure you're all aware, in the event that there is no heir to the throne the high lordships are summoned to the palace to vote on a new king or queen from among them." He paused. "I am certain we can all agree who the best man would be, should this obligation arise."

Carina could see him in her mind's eye, gazing at each of his allies in turn, assuring himself of their loyalty as he implied the worst should they prove untrue.

"Maximus," a voice muttered, followed by the creak of a chair against the marble floor. "You do realize the kings' guard will put up a fight? They'll believe the prince is still alive until he is proven dead. They'll never allow you to—"

"The prince *will* be dead, if he isn't already," Valio said. "And I'm certain if you take a moment to do the math, you'll realize that between the seven of us we have nearly three times the number of soldiers as are stationed in the capital."

"Are you suggesting," Another voice snapped, low and eager, "that we storm the capital to get you onto the throne?"

"I am suggesting," Valio said calmly, "that we simply be prepared."

Low muttering rumbled through the stones; a chill ran down Carina's spine at the thought of her father as king.

"Specifics, Valio," Carina heard Lord Drako say. "When? Where?"

"One month," Valio said. "Sooner, if you can. Stay hidden, if possible, until you receive orders from me. Do not invade, but prepare. Have your forces at the capital in four weeks' time."

Another voice spoke, "And the king and queen, Valio?"

Her father did not reply right away, and she could almost feel his eyes scanning the room. "You know of the doctorbush?"

Silence, though Carina could imagine the nods being given.

Valio spoke stronger then. "You just bring your troops; I'll handle the rest."

Carina shuddered.

"Are there any questions?"

By the time the meeting adjourned around midday, Carina longed to stand straight and stretch her muscles. Chairs scraping and men talking, eating, or drinking drowned out the sounds their crawling made. They were halfway out when Robyn finally spoke.

"Do you have any ideas how your father might try to kill the monarchs?"

"Assassination, poison perhaps, I don't honestly—wait. He mentioned the doctorbush."

"What about it?"

Carina grunted as she crawled. "It's potent in its oil form. I've made it many times.

"You have an oil distiller?"

"Yes. And doctorbush oil, it's only to be used topically for bruises and sore muscles, but if taken by mouth, in food or drink..."

"It would kill them?"

"Yes."

A moment passed. "How much do you care for your distiller?"

A pang of regret hit Carina in her chest. "Very much."

"I was afraid of that."

"You want me to break it?"

"It would help."

Carina bit her lip as she crawled.

"I can't. Please don't ask me to."

Robyn paused ahead of her. "You're right. He would suspect, or take his anger out on you. That's the last thing I want."

Carina felt a lightness in her chest at Robyn's words. "I...the best I could do is dilute it with another oil, something safer. That way they wouldn't be getting the whole dose. At the very least it could buy us time."

"Let's plan on that then," Robyn said. "I'll speak to my crew and send you a message with more details when we know them."

They crawled in silence for a time, and didn't speak until Carina could finally see a shaft of daylight below.

"Carina," Robyn said, "You seem like an observant person. How much do you trust Lex?"

"Enough, I suppose. I don't know him well enough to put my life in his hands, but he's never been dishonest toward me."

"That makes one of us."

"From what I've heard of him he's always very genuine," Carina continued. "He doesn't pretend to be anything he's not, he's just...himself. Some people don't like that, though."

"Hm," Robyn said. "And Damari? Is he taking care of you?"

Carina frowned at that, though Robyn couldn't see her. "He...he is kind, and helpful."

"If he's been a comfort to you, I can have him stay."

Carina didn't answer that. Every touch of Damari's felt both exciting and forbidden, and dangerous. With a sigh, she slid out of the tunnel and into bright sunlight. Blinded for a moment, she rubbed at her eyes and blinked.

Steel-tipped arrows were pointed at her. She was surrounded by archers.

Fear gripped her. *He knew.*

Robyn was out of the tunnel before Carina could warn her to stay back. At the sight of her, the bows tightened, drawing back.

"Take Lady Carina to her rooms," Zivon said from behind the line of archers. "The tall one will visit Master Valio."

They grabbed Robyn by her arms even as she threw punches and struck out with her daggers. Carina saw her manage to slice the jaw of one man before kicking the knee of another. Carina wanted to scream. Reach out and hit, something—anything—to help Robyn. This girl, her friends, the prince, had trusted Carina. And she'd gotten them captured.

Robyn kept fighting. Cutting at the armor of her captors. An arm here, a leg there, before her wrist was twisted and the daggers fell to the ground. Then one of the men pinned her arms and put a cloth to her mouth and nose. A moment later, Robyn's form went limp.

Hands gripped Carina's arms. Her breath wouldn't come. Her whole body was shaking as she was led to her rooms. The doors closed; her shock gave way to panic. What would her father do to Robyn? Carina's door locked; she was trapped now. She couldn't sneak out to check, or eavesdrop or ask the servants to spy for her. She could do nothing. She paced on the carpet before her fireplace, too warm in the heat of summer, walking back and forth, her arms wrapped around her chest.

Then a sound that made her crumple to the floor.

Screams.

PART TWO

THE TRUTH

I was fifteen, eligible to marry in three months. I was being courted by a young man named Markus. He was handsome and kind, a friend of my brother's.

16
ROBYN

Robyn kept her mouth shut. Her teeth ground together in pain.

She would survive. Her friends would come. They would. She knew them, she trusted them. They would come.

No one came last time.

The whip cracked against her back. She arched at the sting of it.

She'd been drugged, and woken up to pain. After that first scream, the feebleness of it, the fragility, she was determined not to make a sound again. She'd never been whipped before, but she'd had plenty of injuries. This would just be a lot at once.

She would survive.

"It is wonderful to see you again, lovely," Valio said, pacing past her.

She ignored him.

She hung suspended between two wooden poles, her arms stretched tight to either side. There were no windows, so…underground. Her thoughts were thick as river mud. Wading through them was sticky and pointless. She focused on remaining relaxed. Limp in her bonds. Maybe she could make them think she was unconscious.

"I was quite disappointed when I heard you'd refused me a few years ago," Valio said. "Even when I'd taken care of everything else for you."

This bastard…Robyn spat at him.

He stepped aside, clicked his tongue. "Not the greeting I'd hoped for, I admit."

She ground her teeth together.

"Little Robyn," he said, coming closer. He put his hand under her chin and lifted her face to examine. "You were a sweet young thing. So innocent and brave. So…passionate."

He leaned closer to her. His breath hot on her face.

She flinched. "Get away from me."

"Oh, I don't think so," he said. "You see, you owe me." Then his lips were on hers, his hands at her hips, pulling her against his body.

Robyn bit down hard on his lip, drawing blood.

Valio screamed, backing away. But instead of anger, she saw a smirk appear on his bloody lip. "We're playing that way, then?"

Again, Robyn did not reply.

His hand flew, striking her across the face. She swayed, her vision blurry. She clung to her bonds for balance.

"When I ask a question," he crooned, "you will answer. I am your master now, do you understand? You will never see the light of another day."

Robyn glared at him, her vision clearing enough to see him straighten his clothing. He took a handkerchief from his pocket and soaked up the blood from his lip, staining the fabric like he'd stained her life. What he'd done could never be forgiven.

Mitalo will come. Jianna was watching the tunnel, they'll have seen. They can get me out.

"You know," Valio continued, pacing in front of her. "I heard you wanted to accept my proposal, but that your parents wouldn't allow it. I assumed you needed help getting out, so I sent my man to fetch you." He motioned to something behind her, where she assumed his servant stood, wielding the whip.

Finally, she looked up, met his eyes.

"Such a shame," he said, emotionless, stepping closer once more. "I had hoped you'd come to fulfill your desires."

Bile rose in Robyn's throat. That she had ever considered this man worth admiring made her nauseous. She didn't hold it back, and let herself be sick all over Valio's clothing.

He jumped back, swearing. Disgust plain on his face. Without a word, he came back and slapped her across her face a second time. She swung limply with the blow.

"Fifty lashes," he hissed. "And when you're done, bring her to my room. We'll see how proud she is after a night of being broken in." With that, he strode from the room, and pain erupted again on Robyn's back.

Stay alive, she told herself. *Stay alive. They'll come.*

I wouldn't say I had a grand connection to him,
but I was content to marry him if he asked.

17
LEX

Lex wiped sweat from his brow, following behind Jianna as quietly as he could. Robyn was inside. Robyn was with Valio. He took her. They had to get her out. What about Carina? Jianna said she'd heard a Callidian man tell the guards to keep quiet about Carina's involvement, that he could twist the truth to make it seem that Carina had been leading Robyn into the trap on purpose.

It would be all right, though. They could get Robyn out. They had to.

"Eight minutes," Lex whispered, counting the time since Robyn had been taken.

Mitalo paused at the end of a hallway. He peered around the corner, then held up three fingers to Jianna. She then pointed one at herself, and two back at him, and he nodded. In two seconds, they were around the corner and struggling with three guards. In twelve seconds, the guards were knocked unconscious, lying in a heap on the floor.

"Come on," Mitalo said.

Lex felt helpless. He couldn't fight, could barely sneak, and had no way to help at all. He might as well have been back in the trees, except they needed someone to lead Robyn out again, since she'd been knocked out when she was carried inside. So Lex paid attention to his surroundings, each turn and hallway, so he could get her out as quickly as possible.

Two more groups of guards and they reached the dungeons where Jianna had seen Robyn's captors descend. Mitalo opened the door and they went down a set of narrow stone stairs that spiraled in on itself, making Lex dizzy.

"Thirteen minutes. What do I do when we're out?" he asked, trying to focus on anything but the stairs.

"Meet back at the tree line to the west," Mitalo said. "We'll likely have to split up from there, leave multiple trails, but we need to hear as much as we can from Robyn to know what our next steps should be."

Lex nodded.

"Shhh," Jianna said, waving a hand to silence them. They'd reached the bottom of the staircase. Lex turned his right ear toward the door and could hear snapping behind it. His face went pale.

"Fourteen minutes."

"You cannot be seen," Jianna reminded him.

Lex nodded, pulling his hood to shadow his face.

"We'll keep everyone off you," Mitalo said. "You just get her out, understand? We'll lead them off and meet you later. Then we can deal with the rest when we know she's safe."

"It's not much of a plan," Lex repeated.

"We don't have time for anything else."

Lex nodded. Then Mitalo shoved the door open and hurled himself inside.

There were only two guards here. Lex stayed in the shadows, unseen in the chaos that ensued. Along with the guards was the one-eyed Callidian who had captured Lex so many days ago.

Mitalo engaged the Callidian man while Jianna fought off the two guards. Forty-two seconds in, Lex got his chance. He ran to Robyn, who hung suspended by ropes in the center of the room.

For a moment, he paused in horror. Her back was torn apart. Stripe after stripe cut her clothing and skin—skin he knew had been perfect and unblemished only hours before. Anger tore through his chest. Anger for Valio and this Callidian who worked for him, who would dare to hurt anyone like this, especially Robyn who didn't deserve a fraction of it.

One minute...

Shaking himself back to sense, Lex hurried to the ropes that held her. He undid one, and she slumped to the floor. He tried to slow her fall, but she landed on his left arm, so he didn't help much. Instead he lifted her onto his knee, braced against the second pole, so he could loosen the second rope. Her arms free, he began to drag her toward the door. She seemed to rouse slightly then. His arm around her waist, and hers around his shoulder, they made their way up the spiral stairs that seemed to last forever.

No guards came.

They made their way down the hall, toward the river where their horses waited.

Still, no one stopped them.

Lex began to sweat again, hurrying, expecting something to come. Valio himself, perhaps, to appear and stab him in the chest so he could take the throne.

But no one came.

Lex made it to the horses and helped Robyn onto hers, where she slumped forward and held tightly to the mane. In a moment of clarity, Lex pulled the Amplia carving from his pack and shoved it into Robyn's hand. Her eyes fluttered open a fraction. That was enough.

"Robyn, hold on to the horse. Can you do that?"

Sluggishly, she nodded. Lex pulled the trinket back from her. He couldn't let the wounds heal fully until he had a chance to clean and treat them.

Mounting his own horse, he took hold of Robyn's reins. He looked back once to see whether Mitalo and Jianna were on their way—they weren't. Fear dug a hole in his chest as he put the river to his right and turned them west.

He reached the tree line and rode for five minutes before the sound of two more horses approached. Lex turned to make sure it was Mitalo and Jianna, before pulling up on the reins.

"We don't have much time," Mitalo said. "Is she all right?"

"Doesn't look like it," Jianna muttered.

"She's weak," Lex said jumping down from his horse and going to his bag. He drew out the carving again and took it to Robyn, placing it in her hand.

She held it for a moment, before it slipped from her fingers.

173

Lex swore. He picked it back up and placed it on Robyn's shoulder. That gave her enough strength to blink her eyes open.

"Robyn?" Lex said. "Can you ride?"

"Valio," she muttered, her voice slurred. "He's going to...attack—"

Lex looked to Mitalo and Jianna. Worry was clear on their faces.

"—kill the...king and queen..."

"What?" Lex said. "Kill? When? How?"

"Let her talk," Mitalo snapped.

"He's bringing...armies." She groaned through her pain. "Four weeks...maybe less, if he knows we know."

Mitalo swore. "He's going to kill the king and queen then attack the city?"

"The armies," Robyn said, "just in case." She sighed, leaning forward on her horse, losing consciousness.

Lex withdrew the magic. He'd have to tie her onto her horse and heal her when they could stop. But for now—

"We have to stop this," he said, turning to the others. "He can't kill them, they haven't done anything wrong."

Jianna snorted. "That's debatable."

"Jee," Mitalo snapped. He turned to Lex. "What do you have in mind?"

Lex took the moment to return the carving to his pack, wondering. He knew which lords were in that meeting...could he get the rest to side with him instead?

"What if..." he began, his brain whirring. "How quickly can you make it to the northern lordships?"

174

Mitalo frowned a moment, but Jianna caught on immediately.

"That's not a bad idea," she said.

"What's not?" Mitalo asked.

"Listen," Lex said. "If we can gather support from the other lords, muster enough knights, I could meet Valio's troops and stop him from taking the throne."

"But why not just go back to the palace?" Jianna said. "Warn them before he gets to them."

"No," Mitalo said. "That puts Lex in the center of Valio's target. We may not like nobility, but you've proved yourself honest, boy. I'd much rather have you on the throne than Valio."

"Thank you," Lex said. "But Jianna is also right, we should warn my parents."

Jianna's eyes went wide. "You want *us* to tell them?"

"They'll never trust us," Mitalo said.

"No," Lex agreed. "But I could send them a letter. You deliver it to the capital, that's all."

"Then what?"

"I'll write two more notes. You ride northeast to the Liras lordship, and have them send the last note to Arena by carrier hawk. They'll know I sent you, have them gather troops. I can go south to Belleci. We'll meet up at the southern bend of the River Tardus in…it'll have to be three weeks."

"It's not much of a plan," Jianna said, "but it's all we've got."

Mitalo rolled his eyes, but tightened his grip on the reins. "Well get writing, that tracker is going to be on us any minute. One for your parents, one each for the two lordships, and one for Carina."

"Carina?"

"We need to tell her what's happening. Quickly!"

Lex jumped at the command and pulled out his notebook. Quickly scribbling—trying to keep his writing legible—one longer note to his parents, two shorter for Liras and Arena, and a fourth for Carina, he tore the pages out and dug out the prince's seal ring, and frowned.

"I don't suppose either of you has any seal wax?" he asked.

Jianna raised a haughty brow before pulling out a stick of brown wax.

Lex let out a sigh of relief as she even lit a bit of tinder for him to melt the wax. Once the four notes were sealed, he handed them to Mitalo.

"I hope you know what you're doing, boy," Mitalo growled. "And you take care of her," he said, nodding to Robyn.

"Wait," Lex said. "You're not taking her with you?"

"We have farther to go than you as it is," Mitalo said, turning his mount north. "Besides, you've apparently got that magic—use it."

One day, I came home to see a fine war horse outside my home.
I could hear shouting, and when my name was mentioned,
I hid by a window to listen.

18
ZIVON

The girl, Robyn, was gone. Zivon stood from his examination of the forest floor, where prints of hooves and sandals mixed with each other in a frenzy of lines and shapes. Follow her, find her, Master Valio had said. But there were two trails leading from this place, and Zivon had no way to know which path the striped-Fugeran girl had taken. He did not want to follow her, but the master might order it so.

Zivon made his way to the palace. Master Valio would want to know right away, in case he would like Zivon to follow one trail or the other. Perhaps he would know better where the girl was likely to go. Zivon never asked any questions. Not why he was sent after the prince, or this Robyn, or why he'd had to whip the poor thing to the brink of death. An exaggeration, of course, she was likely fine, especially if she had found a Cure nearby. Fine or not, Zivon had chosen to avoid her for a long time already. He did not want to cross her now.

He entered the palace's main hallway and went toward Valio's private rooms. The palace staff made way for him. They knew the things Valio made him do…he hated it. Would they think all Callidians were so ruthless as he seemed to be? His home country was across the world from here. He missed things, sometimes. That was why he purchased spices from the rare merchant who carried them. It reminded him of the rolling green hills and the warm southern sea. Nothing like the cold breeze that came off the mountains here. One had to always wear a cloak to avoid getting chilled.

The master's rooms were locked, but Zivon had a key. He entered without announcement, and heard sounds from the bed chamber, through an archway to his left. Sounds that made him sick to his stomach. Zivon stayed out of sight and closed his heart to it. It was not his business what Valio did, or how he lived his life. Zivon had a debt to pay, and he would pay it.

"Zivon?" Valio called. "Was that you?"

"Yes, master," Zivon answered. "I tried to track the girl, but there are two trails leading from her departure point and I couldn't distinguish her direction of travel. Would you wish me to follow one of them? To the north or south?"

The bed creaked, and a moment later Master Valio stepped through the archway, tying a robe around himself. All business. "North or south, you say?"

"Yes, Master."

"I've had reports that her base of operations is in the north, but she's done deals with people in the Belleci territory as well." He waved a hand. "It's no matter. She'll come around again. Soon, I'd wager."

Zivon nodded in obedience. "Then what do you wish of me, Master?"

Valio turned to a decorated side table where a decanter of wine stood with a few glasses. He poured himself a generous serving, then held it to his nose and breathed deeply. "I have work for you, but it will need to be timed carefully. For now, check to make sure my daughter is in her rooms, and then you are free to take some time for yourself. Dismissed."

Zivon bowed low in the Callidian style, one knee to the floor, and the opposite arm across his chest. Valio didn't know the significance of this, Zivon was sure, but he knew. It was about loyalty. It made a difference.

The Lady Carina was indeed in her rooms when Zivon checked, guarded by four men outside her door. Zivon stepped inside and saw the tiny girl curled up at the fireplace with—

A Callidian boy?

Zivon frowned. He had never seen this boy before. He wore Valio's colors, the clothing of a respected servant. His hair was blue, tied in a tail at the base of his neck, not quite long enough yet to braid.

The boy looked up, his eyes widening, and Zivon noticed his skin was lighter than a pure Callidian.

"You are mixed?" Zivon asked.

The boy nodded. "My mother was Reganian."

"Who was your father?"

The boy looked away.

"Traitor anyway," Zivon said. "Better not knowing. Only those chosen by the Council have permission to marry outside our land. Your father was an adventurer, I imagine."

"I don't know," the boy said. "I never knew."

Then Carina looked up, and her eyes widened at the sight of Zivon. "What do you want?"

"I was sent to make sure you were in your rooms," Zivon said.

"Did you...does he know?" she asked, her voice low.

Zivon shook his head. "He suspects only the girl Robyn, and she got away."

Carina sighed, leaning more heavily against the boy.

"But I would urge you, Mistress, to stay here, where the master wishes you to be."

She shook her head. "I don't have a choice."

Zivon said nothing. She was right. Master Valio was a strict man, and would not tolerate disobedience, even in his own daughter. Zivon nodded to them, and left.

Time for himself was something he rarely received. He walked the halls, staring out into the courtyard, wondering what he should do. He would likely need to return by dinner time, and that meant he had a few hours. He took a path leading out, and north. Away from the palace and into the trees. The wide River Tardus ran here, shallow, and perhaps twenty yards across, and covered with round rocks at the bottom. Everything on the shore was covered in moss, but the river stones were clear and smooth. Zivon sat in the center of a clear space, where soft grass grew. His eye closed, and he thought of Callidia. His friends. His home.

There was a blacksmith there, a woman of strength and skill to match any craftsman he'd ever seen. Would she still be there? Her eyes had been a deep green, like the forest at midnight…. And there was the council, on which he'd sat for five years, leading the people to the best of his ability. That was when his son was young.

Moriz.

His face was still clearly visible in Zivon's mind. Young, bright, brilliant. He'd broken the laws; strayed from the path he'd been taught. He had committed murder, and Zivon loved him still. Even in death. Wasn't that a parent's duty? To love unconditionally? To fix wrongs? He'd tried.

For five years Zivon served the man whose wife Moriz had killed. Lady Arianna Valio took a knife to her chest, though she was dying anyway. Zivon soon learned that no one expected Lady Valio to live more than a few months. Yet Moriz had been paid and ordered by the Assassins Guild. And when he tried to back out afterward, he'd been killed himself.

Zivon opened his eye, his brows now furrowed in anger at the unknown man who had brought his son to murder and death. The guild themselves didn't know, they only received the order and acted on it.

He removed a paper from a pocket in his cloak and unfolded the brittle sheet. It was small, and read only, *Arianna Valio is near death. End her life. Enclosed, 500 gold crowns.*

A signature followed, but it was completely illegible. It looked like nothing more than a line going up and down with abandon. There wasn't even a break for a first name and surname, just one long signature. This had another line, struck through it running up and down at a slight angle. Zivon guessed it to be the cross of a T or something similar, but no matter how many times he stared at it, he couldn't make out the name.

He returned it to his pocket, careful as always. Moriz had hurt this family, broken it. It was up to Zivon to help heal them. Was the death necessary? All the killing he was now required to do since offering his services to Master Valio? Zivon now killed to make up for the one death his son had committed.... He didn't think it was right, but the Powers knew better than he. He would serve, until Master Valio said his debt was paid or the Powers gave him another sign.

Silently, he prayed, *may it come soon.*

*My parents had received a proposal from the lord of our land
to take me as his mistress. His wife had recently passed away,
and I had heard of him taking mistresses before.*

19
LEX

Lex pushed the horses off and on through the day and into
the night. When his internal clock told him it had been over
eight hours, he called it well enough. He made their way into
the forest and stopped at the first stream he found. As he landed
on the soft earth his entire body screamed to be still. He would
care for Robyn first. Then rest.

Robyn's bedroll, plus every blanket they had, he laid out on
a patch of grass. He had to pry her fingers off the horse's mane
to get her down, and as he saw her injuries again, he understood
the cost. Her back and saddle were coated in dried blood, and
the cuts cracked as she moved. She stayed asleep while Lex laid
her on her stomach, unconscious whimpers of pain slipping
from her lips.

The sound broke his heart. He got her onto the blankets,
then unsaddled the horses before kneeling down beside her. The
sight of her mangled skin made him want to look away, but he
stared at it. Remembering how perfect it had been before.

He was exhausted, but this had to be done first or he'd never forgive himself. He went through his pack to find the Amplia carving.

Carefully, he lifted the trinket with a cloth, laid it on Robyn's blankets, and moved her hand on top of it. Slowly, imperceptibly, her skin began to heal. Branches creaked around them as he saw a tear slide from Robyn's eye. Lex gripped the grass beneath him. It was for the best that it be done. He watched as Robyn's skin started to knit itself together. Then, one of the cuts began to heal around a strip of her robe, the cloth still inside.

Lex jumped to move her hand off the vessel. He cursed himself. Should have cleaned her up first, he'd known that. Muck, he was tired.

From his pack he took a dagger and a waterskin, grimacing as he knelt beside her once more. Noises came to him from the surrounding forest, making the hair on his neck stand up. He stared down at Robyn.

"Please stay asleep for this," he muttered.

The fabric made no sound as Lex slowly pulled it away. Piece by agonizing piece, Robyn's robe came free. He had to cut one strip to get it off her back, because it was one of the only pieces that ran the whole way across. Another, he had to extract from a deep wound. Carefully as he could, he dripped water across the cuts, wiping them clean with one of his own spare tunics.

He wasn't a healer, nor a Cure, but he'd read enough about medicine to know the cuts needed that much. If they were closed without cleaning, there could be infection. And that was far worse than scars.

Thirty nine.

He hadn't meant to, but he counted the cuts.

Thirty-nine separate lashes, though some looked as though the spot was hit twice. Twenty-nine times they intersected. Lex's vision blurred with tears and exhaustion, but his fingers were steady. Slowly, the cracks and snaps of a forest at night had turned to the soft rustle of a breeze through leaves in the morning sun, and Robyn's back was free of blood. The cuts were still there, but the skin surrounding them was clean. Lex felt himself nodding off. Shaking his head to focus, he moved the carving to Robyn's hand once more, and began to watch.

It was slow, so slow Lex could barely see it happening. He fell asleep more than once, but always woke. At one hour past dawn, then two, then three. By midday, Robyn's skin was finally closed. It still bore a red gleam, and angry welts, but she would be fine.

Finally satisfied, Lex sighed with relief as he drew the carving from her, touching it once to try to get a sense of how much magic was still there. He felt no difference, and that made him pause. It had to have taken a great amount to heal her, yet it felt like there was still a huge source. Putting it away, he wondered yet again why the priest had slipped it to him. Regardless of the reason, he took a moment to be grateful, and send a prayer of thanks to the Gods.

He checked to make sure Robyn wasn't lying on anything uncomfortable, then laid another blanket over her, and curled up nearby under the last. With a fleeting thought of hope that they wouldn't be found, Lex let himself fall into a deeper, whole sleep.

When Lex woke, the sky was purple. Dusk. A fire crackled nearby, and he sat up, looking around.

"It's all right," Robyn said, holding out a hand. "It's small, and contained. I promise."

Lex slumped back to the ground with a sigh. He stared up through the trees for a moment, watching the stars make their appearance in the black depth above him. He'd slept all day.

"Are you hungry?" Robyn asked.

Lex turned to see her sitting close by, wearing a whole, clean riding robe and leggings. Her arms were bare, striped freckles lining them, angling toward her hands. There was no sign of blood anywhere on her, and for a moment he wondered if he could forget the whole thing had ever happened.

"Are you a Cure?" she asked.

Lex frowned, then realized she'd probably not realized he'd used the vessel. He sat up, reaching for his pack to take out the carving, wrapped in cloth.

"No, I'm not a Cure. I used this," he said, handing her the carving.

"What is it?"

"A vessel," Lex said. "It holds magic so you can use it later."

She frowned. "I didn't know that was possible."

"Cures, Claritys, Shifters, and Viruses are all human Vessels of the four various types: Life, Stability, Growth, and Death, respectively," Lex said, his studies taking over. "They have the ability to use their magic directly on someone or something, but they can also channel the magic into an object, if they wish, and that power can be used by anyone. It tends to run out very quickly, and isn't usually as strong or as fast as if a human Vessel had performed it, but it's effective enough."

"I feel as normal as it's possible to feel," she said. "I almost wonder if yesterday was a nightmare."

Something cracked in the darkness. Lex shook his head. "I wish I could tell you it was."

"Where are Mitalo and Jianna?"

"They rode north," Lex said. "You came around enough to tell us Valio plans to kill my parents, so Mitalo and Jianna are going to get help from the lords there who are loyal to me, and we're heading south to do the same. The plan is to meet up at the southern bend of the River Tardus in three weeks, with as many soldiers as we can muster."

"How are they supposed to gather soldiers?"

"I gave them letters for the high lords there. Liras and Arena will help."

"So we're stuck together."

"Yes."

She nodded, staring at the fire. "I suppose there's worse company." Then she looked up at him and smiled.

Something in Lex's stomach made a fluttering motion he couldn't remember ever feeling before.

Robyn stood and went to her horse's saddle where her bow and arrows lay. "How do Vessels happen? The human ones, I mean."

Lex cleared his throat, trying to shake off the fluttering whatever it was. "Ah…the great majority are born that way," he said. "No one is certain whether it's the manner of birth that causes the power, or the power that causes the manner of birth.

But Vessels always have extreme circumstances when born, and the way they're born is a sign to the church that they need to be trained."

"And those who aren't born to it?"

"It takes many years of study, from what I've heard. As well as an act that embodies the power's essence. It can take years, decades."

"Keep talking." Robyn nocked an arrow. "I need something to think about besides yesterday."

Lex went on, his textbooks coming back to him. "When a Cure is born, they remain en caul, meaning their birth sack stays intact even after exiting their mother's body; Claritys are born breech, always with their feet first; Shifters are born months prematurely, tending to grow faster in the womb than others; and Viruses are born with their umbilical cord wrapped three times around their neck. From what I've read, those are the most frightening. They're nearly always not breathing when born, and are sometimes assumed dead before they finally take a breath."

"How do you know all this?" Robyn asked, shooting another few arrows. "I had an education, but I've never learned this much about the Gods' magic."

"Books, mostly," Lex said. "But any priest can explain it too. There are stories in the histories about people who studied and researched Vessels for years, gathering information from parents and friends about every aspect of their lives to try and find out what causes them."

"Hm." She went to gather her arrows. When she returned, she said, "You really believe they exist, don't you? The Gods?"

"I do," Lex said. His chest warmed with comfort and something like pride.

"I mean," she said, "I know the powers exist, I was healed by it. But you believe they're connected to real people? People like us?"

"Well, I'm sure they're more…omnipotent, I suppose. But otherwise, why not?"

She shrugged, then stumbled a little, though she wasn't walking.

Lex stood, taking her arm to help her balance. "Are you all right?"

"Dizzy," she said.

"Blood loss," Lex said, helping her sit. "You shouldn't push yourself too much."

"I have to. You can't fight off attackers."

"Neither can you in this state."

She looked up at him with a glare, and he fully expected her to tell him off. Instead, she let out a long sigh. "Fine. You're right."

"Look," he said. "We rode hard all afternoon yesterday and last night. If we ride for another six or eight hours now, we should be able to lose anyone who might be following us. Then we won't have to worry about defending from attackers, right?"

"Right. Then let's get moving."

Tired though they felt, they were well enough to ride. Lex knew he couldn't do much, but he watched Robyn closely as they rode, intent on catching her should she fall.

While it wasn't the marriage I'd always dreamed of,
it was an opportunity few girls would get.

20

CARINA

Carina sighed, pushing her hair back from her face for the tenth time. The distiller sat on her desk, waiting to be lit. The small doctorbush petals formed a long thin tube before opening into a five point star, squared at the edges. Tiny pollinated stamen filled the center with a light blue color. They were on a lump of bushy branches. Her father had given them to her, saying he needed it for the people in Valios. He said the Cures there needed extra help, and had specifically requested her oils.

Gloves on, she tore the petals from the doctorbush. If she hadn't known he was lying, she might've been flattered. The way he spoke, so confident and sure, made her wonder what other falsehoods she'd believed.

Pouring clean water into the lower chamber of the distiller, she thought of Robyn. Of Alexander, and their companions who had made it their business to stop her father. She trusted Robyn because Damari did. And she trusted Damari because…well, because he cared for her, didn't he? That seemed obvious by the affection he showed. He seemed to care for her a great deal, though she wasn't sure why.

She lit the burner, remembering. Zivon had caught Carina eavesdropping, but only turned in Robyn. Luckily, she escaped. Though Carina didn't know how. And even luckier, Zivon hadn't told Carina's father about her betrayal. He'd laid the blame squarely on Robyn's shoulders, and Valio had no idea Carina even knew the plan. So, she would go through with what she and Robyn discussed. She would make the oil, and dilute it with olive oil before giving it to her father. Even in a large dose, the king and queen should heal on their own, especially if they had the help of Cures.

Shaking her head, she adjusted the flames to the right temperature. She had to focus. Five minutes passed, then she took up the doctorbush petals and grouped them in the upper chamber.

Then she waited.

Soon, the smell radiated throughout the room. It was a pleasant scent, though thick and heady, making her head spin. She opened her windows to release it into the night. She still wore the same clothing she'd been in all day, reluctant to change into her nightclothes when she knew she had to be awake all night. After an hour, she removed the wilted flowers and replaced them with a new batch.

As she finished the first exchange, a knock sounded. Damari stood outside her door, holding a tray of fruit, cheese, and wine. He stared at her for a moment before he blinked and looked over her head. He cleared his throat and said, "I wondered if you'd like some company?"

"What do you mean?"

He met her gaze, his mouth quirked up on one side. "I could help you stay awake. Or we could take turns sleeping and watching the distiller."

She tucked a piece of hair behind her ear. "Yes, that's a good idea. Come in."

Damari nodded, entering and placing the tray on a small section of her desk that wasn't taken up by equipment. She quickly explained the distiller and what they needed to keep track of, then resumed her post on the bed, watching the water bubble and the flowers gradually wilt above.

Damari paced in front of the fireplace. "I got a note from Lex."

She looked up to him.

"He left it before they ran."

"And?"

"They plan to travel to the outer lordships and gather an army," he said. "They believe your father is not to be underestimated."

"They're right to do so. I hope it works." After a few more moments of silence, she asked, "Are you going to walk all night, or come sit down?"

"There aren't any chairs." His words had a smirk to them. His confident air made her heart race, but she tried to keep her voice calm.

"No, I had them all taken away. I've no need of them."

He didn't move.

"There's a bed." She patted the blankets next to her.

He stepped forward, but went to the desk. He peered down at the flowers. "How long do they need to stay in there?"

"An hour," she said. "I just put in a new batch."

He looked at the clock. "Are you hungry? Or tired? You can sleep for a while and I'll wake you when it's time."

She shook her head. "Neither. I'm too nervous."

"Nervous? Why?"

She smiled. "I don't want to do anything wrong. I always seem to…well, I want to finally do something right."

His face fell a little, then he came and knelt in front of her. His hands took hers, and she watched the play of skin tones they exchanged. Hers a dark coppery brown, and his a lighter olive. She smiled; they looked nice against each other.

"Carina, that's your father talking. You are lovely and smart. He blames you when bad things happen, and he shouldn't. You deserve better, I—" He sighed and looked away.

"What's wrong?" she asked.

"I hate it," he said. "I hate that he hurts you, body and mind, and there's nothing I can do about it. I wish I could just…take you away."

The thought sparked in her mind like flint on steel. She quickly smothered it.

Damari looked up, then moved to sit beside her on the bed. "Why not? Why shouldn't we leave?"

"I couldn't," she said, a blush rising in her cheeks. "I mean not now, after agreeing to help. The king and queen are good people. I don't want to see them die at my father's hand, I…I want to *do* something."

Damari scoffed. "But it's you I care about. The thought of your father hurting you…I get so angry…."

His words trailed off, but she didn't know what to say to this. She didn't want to comfort him; his frustration was nothing to her own. So she said nothing. The only sounds were the bubbling of water, the cracking of fire. She could smell him. It was leather from the stables, and something spicy…probably from the kitchens. She breathed it in deeply, letting it tickle her nose.

A knock sounded at her door, and Adia stepped in carrying a bucket of ice.

Carina jumped up. "Thank you, Adia."

"Of course, my lady," Adia said, eyeing Damari. "Is there anything else I can do for you?"

"Just make sure the fire stays stoked tonight, if you could? I'm going to be awake for a while."

"Of course, my lady," Adia said, kneeling before the hearth to add fuel to the fireplace.

Damari stood then, and helped Carina pour the ice where she needed it, though she could tell he was thinking something.

Finally, he said, "Why do you let him?"

"What?"

"Why do you let him hurt you?"

She flinched at that. "I don't…*let* him. He's my father," she said. "I don't have any other choice."

"Carina," he started.

"No, Damari." Her voice was steady. She wasn't angry, but he needed to understand. "He's my father. The only family I have left, and I love him."

"There has to be a way—"

"What would you have me do? Do you think I haven't asked him to stop a million times already? When it started, I used every combination of words I could think of. Nothing worked. So I stopped. Once I even tried to…run away. But it was only worse after."

She'd been about to say something far more terrifying, but she'd never told anyone about that. As much as she liked Damari, she didn't feel quite comfortable revealing that particular weakness.

She fell silent and turned away from him. She noticed Adia was still in the room, kneeling by the hearth and trying to look invisible, as she was meant to.

Carina closed her eyes tightly.

Damari didn't speak, but wrapped an arm around her shoulders. She let him pull her into his chest, savoring the touch, even if he had just said such hurtful things. He was warm, and soft.

A few minutes passed before Adia stood. "My lady, would you like me to stay?"

Carina's heart pounded in her chest.

What did she want?

"No, thank you," she said. "You're dismissed."

Adia left, the door closing behind her with a sudden finality that sent a shiver over Carina's skin.

"Carina," Damari whispered into her hair.

A rush of heat flooded her at the sound of her name. His hand rose to her face and lifted it to meet his. He kissed her softly at first. He seemed hesitant, but soon his touch grew more firm. She wrapped her arms around his neck and pulled him closer, pressing her lips hard against his.

The back of her mind whispered danger, but she was so starved for touch...she'd never been kissed, and it felt good, even while it felt wrong.

Damari pulled away for a moment, his green eyes bright against his olive skin. His chest rose and fell with each deep breath.

He stared at her, then brushed his fingers along her face, pushing her hair back. "You are so beautiful."

His voice had deepened, gained a gravelly texture to it, and the warning in the back of her mind flared bright.

"Stop," she said.

He paused, his lips hovering over her neck. "What?"

"I said stop."

He straightened, confusion in the furrow of his brow. "Why? Did I do something wrong?"

Her hands shook as she pushed him away. "I'm sorry, I just—"

"Sure," he said, shoving away from her. His hands were in fists and there was a sharp angle to his brow she hadn't seen before.

"Damari, I—"

"It's fine," he said, putting up his hands, cutting her off.

"You can stay, I just—"

"I brought you food," he said with a forced smile. "Just wanted to keep you company."

"You can, I only meant—"

"Maybe later, then?" he asked, walking to the door.

Carina couldn't think of what else to say. She let him go, wondering how that exchange had gone so very wrong.

I expected my parents to accept, but they did not.
I didn't ask them about it, but sat confused
as I watched the messenger ride away.

21
LEX

Over the course of the following day, Lex's shoulder and scars began to ache far worse than he was used to. The muscles stiff, and an itching underneath the skin that drove him crazy. He'd been diligent about applying the salve Enzi usually carried for him—at least when no one was looking—but part of him suspected the weather was about to change. He tried to hope otherwise. That, combined with his worry for his parents, was making him more tired than he'd ever been in his life.

They rode all night and into the next day, then rested for a few hours, and went on again. Lex thought he knew the way to Bellecia, the home of Nick's family, but Robyn was taking him on a cross-country path he didn't recognize. It was sunset of their fifth day, when Lex thought he might fall off his horse from exhaustion, that Robyn stopped them early to camp. Lex forced himself to unsaddle and brush the horses, making sure they had water and grass, then joined Robyn for a cold supper of dried meat and nuts. Neither of them spoke, and all Lex could think about was his parents, the last time he saw them.

As he laid his bedroll out, Robyn took up her bow and arrows and walked into the trees.

"Where are you going?" he asked.

"To shoot."

"Well…stay where I can see you."

She waved a hand he hoped was in agreement.

He stood to watch, crossing his arms and leaning against a tree. The stream nearby bubbled wild over the rocks, splashing everywhere. Robyn's silhouette was barely visible in the darkness.

"Lex?"

"Yes?"

"See any sticks or pinecones on the ground?"

He blinked, looking around. There were some around their small campsite, and he gathered a handful.

"I've got some."

"Good," she said. "Toss one in the air."

Lex raised his brows. Was she going to try to hit them? "All right…"

He gently tossed the first stick high into the air, into the center of the small clearing. As it fell, an arrow whizzed past and snapped it in two.

Lex stared.

The two halves and stray splinters littered the ground like fallen snow.

"Again," Robyn said.

Again, Lex tossed a stick into the air, and again she snapped it into pieces.

Amazement bringing a grin to his face, Lex didn't wait for her command, but threw a pinecone next, and another stick right after.

She hit both.

He kept going until he ran out. Of fifteen marks, she'd only missed one.

Robyn approached him with a smile on her lips that looked like she was holding it back. Lex raised a brow. "Impressive," he said. "But you already knew that."

Her cheeks went pink. "Thank you."

On the other side of the clearing, all fifteen arrows had lodged into trees fairly close by.

Lex helped gather them, pulling them out carefully to not damage the heads. When the arrows were all removed, he handed them to her. She took them, but he held on, catching her eye. Her eyes went wide as she met his gaze.

"I mean it," he said. "I've never seen anyone shoot like that."

Her smile returned, and she blinked, breaking their eye contact.

He let her take the handful of arrows. Robyn sat to re-sharpen her arrowheads, and Lex's exhaustion flooded over him once more. The adrenaline of helping her practice gone, his soreness returned with a vengeance. He watched Robyn work, trying to ignore the pain. Minutes passed before he gave up and took out his notebook. It was the sights, and describing them, that helped him relax at night. Otherwise, he'd have worried about his parents instead of sleeping.

And he was worrying about his parents enough already.

"You said he's going to poison them?" he asked, breaking the silence.

"Yes," Robyn said.

Lex shuddered, but tried to cover it up by rolling his shoulders and stretching. If Valio stuck with that plan, then they had time. It would take weeks, maybe months to properly poison them slowly to make their deaths look natural.

But did Valio know how much Robyn heard? Would he change his plan?

How much time did they actually have?

Lex found himself writing these questions in his book as he thought them. It felt as though his fear was bleeding onto the page through his pencil.

With a sigh, he closed the book, looking around. Robyn was still sharpening her arrowheads.

"How ah…" He cleared his throat. "How long does one live after being hit with an arrow?"

Robyn paused and looked up from her work, meeting his eye. "It depends on where they're hit."

He nodded, motioning for her to continue.

"If it only pierces muscle, they're certain to survive," she said. "A shot to the head, from a distance of more than a hundred feet or so, will do damage, but probably won't be lethal unless it hits in the eye. A shot to the stomach or pierced lung…that is usually deadly, but if Cures get to it before death, it *is* fixable. The only shots I'd be worried about are a hit to the heart, or to the neck, here." She pointed to a spot beneath her jaw. "If done right, a person can be dead in less than a minute."

"Done right," Lex breathed.

"You know what I mean," she said.

He waved a hand. "I know, I know. But what if Valio changes his plan? What if he uses a dagger, or an arrow or something else? I just…I can't stop thinking about my parents."

"We could go back," Robyn suggested. "Go to the capital and warn them."

Lex shook his head. "I considered that." And he had, during the last day or so since leaving Valios. "If I went back now, it's entirely possible that I could get poisoned along with my parents. Possibly even multiple others in the palace to make it look like a contagious illness." He shook his head. "I can't risk that."

He stood, tossing his notebook to his bedroll behind him. He began to pace, rolling his left shoulder to get some of the stiffness out. He imagined his parents sitting by the fireplace in their rooms. Would they be drinking wine and relaxing? Or poring over reports of his disappearance? Or had they been given the poison already and were weakened? Lex rubbed at his face. His finger caught on the strap of his eye patch, and without thinking he yanked it off, throwing it aside with a growl.

He bent his knees and squatted, rubbing his fists in his eye and the skin-covered socket. It felt good. It felt normal, like he could open his eyes and see through both once more. He couldn't even remember what that was like.

"Lex? What's wrong?"

"What's wrong?" He laughed. "What's *not* wrong? My parents are in danger, and here I am traveling in the middle of nowhere with an outlaw I hardly know. I'm not helping anyone. I'm useless. As usual."

She stood and came to him. For a moment his heart sped up, wondering what she intended by getting so close.

"You *are* doing something," Robyn said, putting a hand on his arm. "You're going for help. That's the only option you have unless you want to risk going back to the capital. As of right now, Valio doesn't know where you are, and that means you're safe."

"Until his people find me, anyway—"

"Which we're doing our best to make sure doesn't happen," she said, her voice rising. "You know I have little love for nobility, but as much of a muck hole as this kingdom can be, I don't want to see your parents dead because that will put Valio in charge, and that will be a hundred times worse."

Lex nodded, trying to calm himself.

"If you do go back, you could try taking precautions," Robyn said. "Arrest Valio, don't accept drinks from anyone you don't explicitly trust…but I agree that you're safer out here. By revealing yourself it's possible you'll get shot with one of these." She held up an arrow, the point right between them.

Lex stared at the arrowhead. The stone was a little ragged in places—he could tell she'd made them herself—but it was sharp as any knife Lex had ever handled. She twisted it before them, and he shifted his gaze to meet hers. Her eyes were shining, as though tears were welling up, but not let out.

"You know how I feel about killing," she said. "The last thing I want is for arrows to be found in the bodies of people I care about. That includes you, and that includes your parents."

He lifted a hand. He wanted to reach out and embrace her. It meant so much to him to know that she was worried too, that it wasn't weighing on him alone. But instead, he rested his hand on hers, the one holding the arrow.

"Thank you," he said.

She smiled. Not a big smile, in fact it was rather sad, but a true one. And Lex felt his chest expand with hope.

As she stepped away and went to climb a tree for the night, he remembered he wasn't wearing his eye patch…but she hadn't flinched at him. The realization hit him hard. Staring at his scarred half-empty face did not make her draw away. For some reason, that made him feel…vulnerable. He had exposed a part of himself without realizing it, and she had actually seemed *more* comfortable.

He turned his eye skyward to try to find her in the mangled tree limbs above, but it was too dark to see anything. He wanted to thank her again. To tell her he knew he was difficult, but that she was helping him and he was grateful. Her strong pace, her determination, her kind words and compassionate heart, had lifted him up tonight. Lifted him so much that he didn't feel so worried.

He still felt sorry, that he'd unknowingly left his parents in so much danger, but he couldn't control that now. He could, however, try to help them. And Robyn was right, they were on their way to get help. She was pushing him, and encouraging him, and making him be better than he was before.

And somewhere in the back of his mind, Lex knew: he was falling for her.

"LEX!"

He shot up from sleep and looked around in the darkness, vision blurry. Robyn's voice was still above him, but he couldn't see her.

"Look out!"

He was surrounded by lantern-wielding soldiers; they wore the tunics of knights in training but no armor, and they wore no colors. One of them lifted him by his shirt and threw him to the ground. Damp earth covered his face, and entered his nose and mouth. A kick in the ribs knocked the wind out of his lungs. Then a fist came down on his head and he splayed out on the ground. They laughed.

"He's out. Take care of the girl."

No...

Lex rolled onto his side and kicked at one man's stomach, but the man grabbed his foot and spun him. He crashed into the ground, knocking his breath out again, and he gasped for air. Another man grabbed Lex's arms and held him up. He hung between two men like a curtain.

"You think you can take all six of us?" the leader of them sneered. Lex made out a tall, strong young man, but didn't recognize him. "We know who you are. Lord Valio's promised a high price for your head, *your highness*." He drew his sword and set it on Lex's shoulder. "And we're happy to take back nothing but your head."

Lex fought them. He twisted his arms, making the skin raw. He shouted for help, but they shoved a cloth in his mouth to muffle the sound and it made him gag. The men at his sides twisted him until he knelt in the dirt. They pressed his face into a fallen tree trunk. Finally, Lex spat out the cloth and shouted as he struggled. "This is treason! You swore loyalty to the crown, not to Valio! I command you to stop this!"

They weren't listening. A royal order wouldn't do any good with no one to enforce it. He saw the man with the sword raise it high. His heart pounded in his chest. He closed his eye, and for an instant remembered the day Robyn had saved his life, and how close to death he thought he'd come at the hands of a bandit.

Thwip.

The man grunted, his sword dropped, clattering against the rocks. He fell to the forest floor.

Thwip.

Lex's arms were released. The man at his back fell onto him.

Thwip. Thwip. Thwip.

Three more men stiffened and fell, crying out in pain.

The last man looked around at his comrades and backed away, turned, and broke into a run.

"I'm sorry," Robyn's voice whispered.

Thwip.

The last man collapsed mid stride. Chills broke out all over Lex's skin. He stood, shoving the motionless body off of him.

Dead.

They were all dead. The first two by arrows to their throats, just as Robyn had described earlier. Three lay on the ground, whimpering, not quite dead yet, and the last had taken an arrow to his neck. He, too, twisted in the distance, and Lex felt his stomach churn at the sight around him.

Blood.

Blood was leaking from every man. The scent of it burned in his nose, and bile rose in his throat. He backed away from the scene, still reeling, and not fully awake.

Robyn hopped down from a branch, bow over her shoulder. The quiver at her hip swung with each step. Tears flowed from her eyes as she pressed both her hands to his face.

"Focus," she said, her voice breaking.

His gaze darted between her and the dead bodies that had almost killed him.

She slapped his face.

"Aah!"

"Lex!"

He rubbed at his cheek, still staring at the death around him.

"Look at me! Are you all right?"

His mouth hung open. He could only nod.

"Good. Get your things. Let's get out of here."

He didn't argue.

They saddled the horses and rode for only a few hours, on the road to make better time, until the sky began to lighten with sunrise. Robyn pulled her horse off the dusty path and behind a large outcropping of rocks. Lex followed. The small spot would be shaded for a few hours yet.

"We ought to be able to sleep for a while here," Robyn said, her voice raspy. "Let's hope no one finds those men until later, and by then we'll be gone."

Lex nodded, not trusting himself to speak.

"I'll go cover our tracks a bit," she said.

In the sky, grey clouds hovered on the horizon and a chill breeze blew through his hair, the cold making his scars tighten.

Yes, the weather would turn soon. By the time Robyn returned, Lex had laid out their bedrolls side by side. A pile of grain was before each horse, which were unsaddled and brushed. Robyn ran a hand over her face as she laid down on her blankets.

Lex looked her over. "Are you all right?"

Her cheek lifted in a slight smile. "I'm fine. Just tired."

Lex went to their mounts and rubbed their noses. Pepper and this unnamed mare were going through a lot for them. He hoped they understood his gratitude. He stared at the mare they'd gotten from the priest back at the wilderness temple.

"Does this girl have a name?" he asked.

Robyn shrugged. "We weren't told one."

The mare was completely black, except for a small diamond patch on her forehead. Lex wasn't very imaginative when it came to naming animals, but he believed they should be named anyway, even if it was a silly one.

"I'll call her Midnight," he said.

Robyn gave an "as you wish" kind of shrug, and tucked herself into her bedroll.

Lex lay down in his blankets next to Robyn. They hadn't been this close to each other since they'd started traveling alone, and his thoughts from the previous night made the tightness in his chest return.

The shade made it feel like dusk. The air cooled his sweaty brow, making him shiver. The smell of lavender drifted to him on a breeze, and he let out an audible sigh.

"What is it?" Robyn asked. When she rolled to face him, the scent was stronger.

He shook his head. "Nothing, just…getting comfortable."

She nodded and lay back down.

"Robyn?"

She didn't move. "Yes?"

"Thank you."

Her head turned. "For what?"

He rolled his eye, even though she couldn't see. "For saving my life. Again."

"Hm." She shifted beneath her blankets. "You do seem to be making a habit of needing to be saved."

"I do, don't I? I should work on that."

"Or…" she said softly. "You could keep people around who can help when you need it."

Lex smiled. "I do like that idea."

She breathed a tiny laugh, and he fell asleep to her unexpected flowery scent.

The darkness is oppressive sometimes. And not just the trees at the night... The stars are like Tiny rays of hope in an otherwise desolate blackness. The branches above me shudder in the wind, but at least I have company to keep me safe.

Does Valeo know how much Robyn heard of his plans? He mentioned Person, but that could take months, and he plans on leaving an army at the capital in one month... that means we only have that long to get there. Seven days to Flick's house, and two weeks north with Angeli's forces, ... Gods...

Troops are so slow!

Maybe Robyn and I can move faster?

What I wouldn't give for a carrier hawk!

Will Valeo change his plan though? What if he guess his forces there earlier? We might not stand a chance... how much time do we really have?

A few days later, I was washing clothes in the stream nearby,
when the High Lord himself approached me. He was respectful,
very much a gentleman. He flattered me.

22

CARINA

Two days. For two full days the diluted oil had been consistently slipped to Lex's parents. Carina had waited as long as possible before actually giving it to her father, but it was still only three days she'd managed to stall and now it was five days after the meeting, and her mind ran on and on with her nerves, unable to separate one thought from another, knowing Robyn and the others should at least be near the other lordships, if they hadn't already arrived, and it would still be a week or more before they would gather again.

She had, of course, been confined to her room since the meeting. Now, she paced in front of her fireplace, occasionally staring at the water-powered clock that seemed stuck at five minutes past midnight. Damari would bring her news soon. Her father received updates on the king and queen's status every six hours, and Damari always listened in on the reports. Six hours ago, things were looking as they should; the monarchs were slightly dizzy, but nothing dangerous was imminent. Though this pleased her, the anxiety was renewed with each messenger.

When her door slid open, Damari entered and came straight to her, wrapping her in an embrace. As angry as he'd been the night she'd sent him away, she let him hold her as long as he needed to now.

Her cheek against his chest, she couldn't contain the words anymore. "Did the runner come? What's happening?"

He smiled, pulling away. "Yes, the runner came. And he said they're barely showing dizziness, not even confined to their beds yet. The Cures keep saying they're not sure why the spells continue to come back, but they're certain they'll recover soon. I think we're all right."

She slumped in relief, resting her face in her hands. "I hope we did it right."

"We did, don't worry." He put a finger to her chin and tilted her face towards his for a kiss.

A knock sounded at the doors, and they jumped apart as Adia entered.

"My lady?"

"Yes, Adia?" Carina said, ignoring the girl's confused looks at Damari, who stood against the wall with his head down.

"I'm sorry for the lateness of the hour, but your father has summoned you."

Carina felt her shoulders slump. Damari lifted his arms, she assumed to comfort her, but lowered them right away.

Adia spoke again. "Shall I escort you?"

Nodding, Carina squared her shoulders, faking confidence she didn't feel, and followed Adia out of the room, leaving Damari behind.

Through the colonnade, she watched lightning bugs hover in the garden. Lanterns hung among the plants, casting sharp shadows between the flowers and shrubbery. Her mind ran through possible reasons why her father would summon her…and so soon after receiving word about the poison's status. She fought to keep her back straight, but the prospect of being alone in her father's presence pulled her down like a sea monster in the deeps.

"My lady?" Adia said softly.

"Yes?"

"I realize it…it might not be my place, but…are you certain this new servant is…safe?"

Carina frowned. "Safe?"

Adia cleared her throat. "What I mean, is…he seems…dangerous."

Carina shouldn't have laughed, but the thought was so absurd. "I am perfectly safe with Damari," Carina said. "He has been nothing but kind."

"But—"

"I appreciate your concern, Adia, but you are correct: this is not your place."

Adia curtseyed. "Apologies, my lady."

Carina squared her shoulders once more, and continued on her way.

She entered her father's office and saw him standing behind his desk, his back to her. Adia announced Carina's presence when they entered. The room was more closed-in than most, with only a single small window behind the heavy hardwood desk. The walls were lined with shelves, on which lay books and papers, records of some kind, and a thick scarlet carpet covered the floor. As Adia left, Carina's entire body shook with the door's vibration, trying to hold her shoulders straight and stand tall.

He stood stiff, his hands clasped behind his back. When he turned, he plucked a slip of paper from his desk that looked like it had been rolled, then flattened out, its corners still pointing upward. His blue eyes met her brown, and she wilted. Something in her chest collapsed like glass underfoot, and she could barely breathe. She hadn't been alone in his presence since the day Lord Drako arrived.

"Carina," he crooned. "I hope I didn't wake you?"

"No, Father."

"Very good. I wanted to thank you for distilling the doctorbush oil. I've received word that it has been put to good use in Valios City. You've helped many, my dear."

"Thank you, father."

As he spoke, he moved around the desk, coming closer to her. She didn't move.

"However, there has been a slight problem."

"Yes?" Her voice sounded like a mouse's squeak.

"The Cures have reported that the oil is extremely weak. Not producing the desired effects."

Carina swallowed, keeping silent.

"Do you have any ideas why this might be?"

She shook her head, trying to look as cool in her lie as she knew he did. "No, Father. Perhaps the plants were simply weak? I did as you told—"

"Liar," he said.

Carina's eyes went wide, just before his hand met her cheek.

She fell to the ground, holding her face. But before she could react, his foot collided with her stomach. She curled around the pain, a wave of nausea rolling through her body, cold, then warm, and not at all pleasant.

"What did you do to that oil, Carina?" His voice was soft, slow, stroking her wounds already.

Her words came in gasps. "I distilled it as instructed, my lord."

He backhanded her face. She reeled at the impact, and her head hit the floor with a *thud*.

Tears formed behind her eyes, but as usual, they did not escape. "Perhaps...perhaps the Cures are simply using it incorrectly. I could instruc—"

He gripped her upper arms, lifted her, and slammed her against the wall. Her feet weren't even touching the floor. When he spoke his voice was calm, and that frightened her. He'd always lost his temper when beating her. Never had he sounded so lucid, and still hit her. "You did something to it or you did it wrong, intentionally. What do you know?"

She tried to shake her head, say no, but fear froze her. It was all she could do to breathe in and out.

He dropped her, letting her to fall to the ground.

Carina closed her eyes, trying to focus on her breathing.

Her father began to pace the small room, muttering. She should have listened, but her chest and arms were too hurt; she could barely move. "You," her father's voice finally broke through her haze, "to your room." He kicked her side.

She cried out in pain and wrapped her arms around herself. Surely that was a broken rib.

"No visitors except your servants," her father continued. "I don't know how you found out, but your actions will not change anything. Foolish child."

Her entire right side felt numb. Her ribs ached, her lower abdomen cramped in pain.

He called for Adia. The girl helped Carina stand, and practically carried her to her room. When she came through the door, Damari was still there and came forward immediately. He lifted her into his arms and laid her in the bed, asking Adia to get ice for Carina's injuries.

"Carina, what happened?" He pushed hair out of her face and kissed her softly. She winced when he leaned against her side. Anger flashed in his eyes and he moved to stand. "I'm going to—"

"No," she choked. "You're not—going to do anything." She had to force the words from her, it hurt to breathe, and speaking was excruciating.

"He can't keep doing this to you!"

"But he knows…" she said in a hiss. "He knows."

"He knows what?"

"He knows," she wheezed, "the oil didn't work how he'd planned. He's going to change the plan. I don't know how. How could I let this happen?"

"No, no, no," he chided gently. "You did all you could. This isn't your fault."

"But what if they die? What if we can't help?"

"Then…they die. And Lex will have to deal with it."

Tears that had formed in her father's office finally poured from her eyes. She buried her face in the pillow, muffling the sound. Damari climbed up onto the bed and curled himself around her. She didn't have the energy to send him away, so she fell asleep to the uncomfortable warmth of his chest against her bruised shoulder.

I remember blushing, smiling; feeling, for the first time, a heat rise in my body. He made me feel like a grown woman.

23
LEX

Lex leaned into the wind as rain pelted his hood, and pulled his cloak tighter around him. Forcing his scarred muscles was like driving on rusted wagon wheels. At least, he suspected as much. Mucking arm would barely move in the cold.

He rode next to Robyn, following a muddy track. They needed to find shelter. If his calculations were correct, they should be nearing Glavos, the city of High Lord Glavan.

"Robyn," he shouted over the rain.

She turned to him, pulling her hood further forward to block the rain. "What?"

"We need to figure out where we are. We can't just march up to Glavan's palace or he'll capture us both."

She nodded, looking around. They were in an orchard, olive trees lined up around them, but it might as well have been a jungle, for as much as they could see. The rain blinded them beyond thirty feet.

"There's nothing here," Robyn shouted. She dismounted and removed her cloak, holding it over her head and motioning for him to come down too. "Get out your map."

He did, keeping it beneath her awning as he unrolled it from its water-safe tube. Still, drops slipped through and hit the parchment as he found where he thought they were. The Astelo Ridge marked the boundary between the Glavan lordship and the Belleci, and Glavan's keep sat only a few hundred yards from its upper edge, nestled there beside the Eiri River, with his city sprawling to the west.

"We've been going through these fields for hours," Robyn said, pointing. "We ought to be close."

Lex looked around. The olive trees were mere shadows, the ground around them had been churned dirt for miles. "We are close," he said. "Any closer and we might have gone too far."

She looked up at him. "We need to avoid the city."

He blinked. She was standing very close, her face mere inches from his. "Y-yes, but the road down the ridge is beyond it. We need to circle around to the east."

"But that could take all day!"

"You want to risk the ridge off-road in this weather? Mudslides and floods? It's dangerous enough on the prepared path, but no one will be there with it raining like this."

Her expression froze for a moment, then she shook her head. "No, you're right. We'll have to cut through the fields, then follow the river."

"Exactly," he pointed to the map. "We'll go east until we find the river, then south until we reach the ridge. Then we can follow that back west to find the road."

"Agreed."

He replaced the map in his pack,

"We should walk," Robyn said. "The horses will slip in that mud anyway, let's not make it harder for them." She took

Midnight's reins and strode through the trees. Lex followed, mud flicking up at him from Pepper's hooves and adding to the weight of his soaked clothing.

They followed one row of trees, heading east. It was tedious work, and they never saw the city. After an hour, the wide Eiri River appeared before them, raindrops leaving ripples on its calm surface.

They turned south. They both wore oilskin wrapped around their legs, and sturdy sandals, but Lex doubted they'd been intended for an experience such as this. His legs were weighed down with thick layers of heavy mud. His muscles burned with the effort of lifting over and over.

He told himself they would find shelter on the ridge. There were caves there, he'd played in them as a child. He squinted into the falling water, not wanting to accidentally step too far and fall down the ridge. Luckily, the orchard ended first and they stepped onto hard packed dirt that was still muddy, but not as soft.

His legs were shaky after so much exertion. He bent over to wipe clumps of mud away. "Do you see anything?"

Robyn nodded. "The edge is about a hundred feet that way," she pointed south. "I can practically hear the waterfall. Let's head back."

How she could see or hear a hundred feet in this he couldn't fathom. He followed her, and not five minutes later they reached the road and the rain had started to let up. Glavan's palace was now to the north, its city beyond, and Lex frowned as he caught sight of it.

"Soldiers," Robyn said.

"A lot of soldiers," he agreed.

The earth around the palace was not churned for planting, but by boots, hooves, and wagon wheels. Piles of weaponry stood high enough to be made out from only a few hundred strides away. Lex shivered.

"Let's get down the ridge before we're spotted," he said.

Robyn turned, pulling Midnight by the reins, and Lex followed with Pepper. The road cut back and forth on the side of the cliff—barely thirty feet from the waterfall—though the road was wider now than he'd remembered.

He traveled here a number of times when he'd first befriended Nick. Lex's parents had hoped he would eventually take to the Belleci's daughter. Instead, she'd become like a sister to him. He smiled a little that he'd be seeing them soon, then refocused on the road.

They were halfway down when Robyn slipped. Her cry rang in his ears, louder than the rain. He shouted her name. She fell. The reins slipped from her hand, and she tumbled down the muddy road. Then over the edge.

"ROBYN!" He let go of Pepper and made his way down the road to where she'd fallen. She lay fifteen feet below, stopped by a huge rock, rain still falling over her. He let out a breath in relief. One step at a time, his whole body screaming for rest, he made his way to her. She'd been knocked out by the fall, but was already blinking back to consciousness.

"Robyn?" He brushed the hair from her face. For a moment, she looked like she was sleeping. Her face calm, at peace.... Even splattered with mud, she was beautiful.

Not the moment, Lex, he told himself.

"Concussion," Lex said. "Robyn, wake up. Do not fall asleep. Can you hear me?"

"Yes," she said with a groan. "Oh, it hurts."

"Stay here," he said. "Don't move, I'll find us a place to shelter."

She nodded. "Stay awake, don't move. Got it."

Lex looked around, then took off his cloak and laid it over Robyn. He had to find a cave for them. The first he found had a wide entrance, but was too small to fit the horses. The next was harder to get to, and he'd never make it carrying Robyn, nor would the horses be able to get to it. But the third…just below the road line and behind the waterfall, easily accessed from the road, a large but hidden opening that went upward first before turning downward into a wide cavern.

He made sure the horses were still on the road before going back to get Robyn. She mumbled something when he picked her up, but didn't complain. His left arm couldn't support her without pain, so he flung her rather unceremoniously over his right shoulder. He clenched his teeth, trying to focus on the sound of dripping rain all around him.

In the cave, he laid her down, clinically examining her for injuries. Aside from a bump on her head, her right ankle seemed swollen, but he couldn't tell with her boots on. He'd give her the Amplia vessel soon.

He covered her with his cloak again and hurried to get the horses. Before bringing them inside, he searched for flint and steel and a candle he knew Robyn had in her pack. He only prayed the wick wasn't soaked with water. After a few tries, he got it lit. The horses then stepped carefully around Robyn as he led them to the back of the cave where, blessedly, there was a small pool of water that drained back into the earth below.

He took off the packs, laying things out that needed to dry, then unsaddled and brushed the horses down quickly.

When he returned to Robyn, she'd closed her eyes.

"Robyn? Robyn!"

She snapped awake, rubbing at her head with the sudden movement.

"You cannot fall asleep right now," Lex said. "Please."

"Right," she said, closing her eyes again. "No sleeping."

Lex sighed. He'd have to talk to her to keep her awake.

"Well, now that we're out of the rain, I'm changing into dry clothes."

"I'll keep my eyes closed," she said.

Lex rolled his eye. "That's kind of the opposite of what you're supposed to do when you hit your head."

"Do you *want* me to watch you change?"

He leveled a glare at her only to see her pressing her lips together to hide a smile.

"I'll change in the entry, behind the waterfall," he said. "Keep your eyes open."

"Yes, your highness."

The tone of her teasing sent his stomach fluttering again. So that's what that was...

He took his clothes into the entry tunnel and changed, and by the time he returned, Robyn was standing and tying her own clean robes on as well.

"Robyn," he said. "You should be lying down."

"Well, I wasn't about to have you help me dress," she said. "And I needed to. Where are the bedrolls?"

Lex didn't argue the point, and she seemed to be recovering well enough.

The rain continued to fall outside, thunder booming every few minutes. The storm was growing worse, but they would stay dry in here. He gathered both bedrolls and laid them out as one, then took a seat across the cave.

Robyn frowned. "What about you?"

"I'll be fine." He picked up their wet clothes to wring the water from them and lay them over some outcropped rocks to dry.

She watched him work, a question in her eyes.

He frowned at her. "What is it?"

"Thank you," she whispered.

He bowed his head to her. "You're welcome."

She looked away sheepishly. "I'm...not used to people helping me much. Except—"

"Mitalo and Jianna?"

She smiled.

"It's as useful as I've been so far," he said. "Though you probably would've been fine without me."

"No, I wouldn't."

He met her gaze. There was something new behind her eyes as she looked at him, something that hadn't been there hours ago. Lex drew a deep breath and nodded. "Then I'm glad I was here. Now sleep. I'll wake you in an hour."

As she drifted off, he studied the knot forming in his stomach. The crack that had formed in his heart when she fell over the cliff edge and healed when he saw her eyes flutter open again.

For a moment, he let his tired mind loose. How she moved when firing her arrows. How light and soft her hair looked when it was clean, so soft he imagined it would feel like silk between his fingers. How she carried herself even in ragged clothing. She was smart, confident, resourceful, gracious….

He blinked.

In most things, he did not believe in fate. But in this, his search for the person he would spend his life with, he'd placed all his hope in chance. In the Gods being able to help him. He'd run away from home, got captured, joined a band of outlaws, and was now trying to stop a plot to assassinate his parents, and all of it began because he'd wanted to find the one he was meant to be with.

If he was trusting in luck, Gods, faith—whatever it was called—then Robyn was the only option. Not only that, she was the *best* option. More than any lord or lady of court, Robyn was what Lex was looking for. She was the one. And with that realization, Lex felt his whole future crash down upon him.

She would never come.

She was perfect. She was brave, and beautiful. He could love her, if she wanted him to—it would be so easy to fall—but she would never let him. She was too close to the forest, too set on revenge against Valio. She always put up walls, and Lex wasn't sure he could convince her to open any doors for him.

He took a few deep breaths, calming himself as he laid out the last of their wet clothes. Robyn lay curled up beneath all their blankets, shivering slightly.

Lex blew out the candle, then approached and slowly lay down on top of the blankets beside her. A moment later, she burrowed into him in her sleep, and he, heart pounding, rested an arm around her waist. Robyn flinched slightly, waking, and Lex pulled his arm away, looking to her eyes.

They were open, staring at his chest before her. She did not move.

Lex moved to rise. "I'll go—"

Robyn gripped his shirt. She pulled him back down.

Lex swallowed.

"It's cold," she said.

Her eyes closed, and Lex slowly laid his arm over her once more. It was only the cold. She had been injured, and needed the warmth. That's all.

*I see now how manipulative he was, tugging on the emotions
of an impressionable young girl. I was too inexperienced
to understand what was happening.*

24
LEX

Something shifted against him.

"Lex?"

"Hm?"

"What time is it?"

He opened his eye to darkness. Blinking a few times, he noticed dim moonlight filtering in through the cave opening. Robyn sat up next to him.

"Are you awake?" she said.

"Yes, I'm awake." He cleared his throat, sitting up and moving away from her. "It's um…a few hours until dawn."

He heard her shift in the darkness.

"Where's that candle?" she asked.

He felt around. It took a few minutes before he placed the bright light beside them on the dirt floor.

"Thank you," she said. "I could've done that."

"Yes, but I knew where it was already," he said, glancing at her. The soft light played over her face, giving her skin an orange cast that, with her freckle stripes, truly made her look like a tiger. Lex stared for a moment, then turned away reluctantly. "Are you cold?" he asked.

"I'm all right."

"Are you hungry?"

She pulled a leg in and sat on it. "A little."

"I think I saw some berries outside; I can go get some."

"Don't we have supplies?"

"Sure, but why use them if we don't have to?"

She shrugged.

"Are you sure you're all right?"

She nodded, then looked away, blinking.

"I'll be right back," Lex said. Putting on his cloak to stay dry, he left the cave and slid out from behind the waterfall, looking around through the now softly-falling rain. Then he spotted the bushes he thought he'd seen before. The berries were dark shades of red and blue, two tones on each small round fruit, giving them their name: sunsetberries. His mouth watered. Leaving his cloak on, he removed his short riding robe and piled the fruit into it. The chill rain raised bumps on the bare skin of his chest.

As he entered the cave, he slipped. His feet flew up. His cloak caught under him and the clasp snapped, the fabric making him slide down the short entrance before sprawling over the floor. Sunsetberries scattered everywhere.

"Are you hurt?" Robyn said, hurrying to help him.

"Fine," Lex grunted, half-laughing and rolling onto his side. He squashed some berries in the process, which made him sigh. "Help me gather these up?"

Robyn was silent for a moment before replying. "Yes. Yes, gather."

He looked up to see her turning away, bending down to gather tiny blue-red berries around the floor. Lex picked up handfuls and placed them back on his robe, soon piling them high again.

Robyn brought her handful over and poured it out with his. She paused for a moment. Lex glanced up at her. She was staring at his scars.

He froze. His robe. His cloak…he hadn't even put on his eye patch since the night he'd thrown it off in frustration. Now she was seeing him like this? He felt something like shame well up in his chest.

"Sorry," he said, standing quickly. He went to the clothes he'd laid out to dry, to put on his other robe. It was still wet, but it would have to do.

"Lex, stop," Robyn said.

He paused, but didn't look at her. He knew his face was red with embarrassment. Somewhere in the back of the cave, water dripped onto rock.

"Those clothes are still wet," she said. "You shouldn't put them on, it'll make you sick."

Shocked, he stammered a little. She was right, but surely he should wear something to cover himself….

"It's all right," Robyn said.

Finally, he turned to her.

"Everyone has scars, Lex," she said softly.

The way she looked at him…. She met his gaze. And when she did look at his scars it wasn't with distaste, but curiosity, even interest.

It was an expression he'd never seen when anyone looked at his scars.

"They're kind of beautiful," she said, her eyes running from his eye, down his neck and shoulder, to where the scars ended just above his bicep.

"Beautiful?" he asked.

Her eyes widened. "I'm sorry, I didn't mean...I know it must've been so painful, and no one should ever have to go through that. I just..."

Her voice trailed off as she looked up and met his gaze. Lex was prepared for flinching, for staring, for disgust...he hadn't been prepared to hear that his scars were beautiful.

"What do you mean?" he asked.

"I mean it's terrifying what happened to you, I—"

"No," he said, waving a hand. "What do you mean 'beautiful'?"

She opened her mouth, then closed it again. Her eyes were drawn back to his shoulder and neck.

"Well...I mean the colors, and the way they flow. It...it's distinctive." She twisted her hands before her. "I hope that's not hurtful."

"No," he said. "No, I've just never thought of them that way."

She smiled, then turned back to her blankets, taking a handful of berries with her. "I suppose it's too dangerous to try to go down this ridge in the rain?"

"Yes, I'd say it is," Lex said. To force his emotions aside, he took a berry for himself. It burst across his tongue with the sweet, tangy flavor he remembered from his childhood. Then he took up one of the blankets and wrapped that around himself while his robe was busy being occupied by the berries.

"Are you sure?" Robyn said, looking toward the entrance. "I don't like staying in one place too long."

"I know," he said. "But if we go down that ridge now, one of us or the horses could fall again. We have the vessel, but I'd prefer it if you wouldn't throw yourself into danger on purpose just because it's there."

She gave him a flat stare, and he couldn't help but smile. The corner of her mouth lifted, and she popped a few berries in. He looked aside and his eye caught on his damp riding robe on the floor beside him. A small emblem was sewn into the chest on the left. The royal crest: a silver shield with a crown above, and two crossed swords beneath. He ran a thumb over it.

"You're still worried about them," Robyn said.

She was watching. He nodded, setting down the robe.

"Then let's go," she said. "Now."

"No," he said. "You said it the other night, we can't do anything if we put ourselves in danger. Robyn, if I could save my parents this very moment, I would, but I can't. Right now, here, you are what matters. And I'm going to keep you safe."

A blush appeared on her cheeks, and she looked down at her hands again.

Lex sighed, turning away.

Robyn's voice was soft, smooth as a river. "Do you want to talk about it?"

He looked at her, and their eyes met for a long moment. He shrugged. "They love me, I know that."

She nodded, but didn't speak.

Lex went on, feeling as though a dam had broken inside him. "But since I turned sixteen, they've only ordered me around. Every interaction suddenly became kingdom business and marrying me off. It was like they didn't care what I thought anymore." Lex leaned against the cave wall and slid to the floor facing Robyn.

"I'm sure they only wanted what was best for you," she said.

"Of course they did," he said. "For me, and the rest of the kingdom. But they refused to listen. They'd never been that way before. Always they'd encouraged me to seek out new ideas, ask questions, speak my mind. I can't understand why they'd raise me that way but then follow so strictly to tradition when it came to something so ridiculous."

"You think marriage is ridiculous?"

He looked up at her. "No! No, not that. I mean, the tradition of nobility marrying within the nobility. I think I mentioned, it's not a law, only custom. But because that's how it worked for them, they were adamant that it work for me too. And it...didn't. Wasn't."

She cocked her head to one side. "Maybe they had someone in mind for you."

"Maybe," Lex shrugged.

"How do you feel toward them?"

"They're my parents," he said. "I love them. I wish I could tell them that."

Robyn smiled. "I'm sure they know.

"I hope you're right."

They sat in comfortable silence for some time, eating berries. A weight seemed lifted from Lex's chest now that he'd spoken of his parents. Rolling a berry between his fingers, he remembered his mother chiding him for eating too many, and his father smiling behind her, unbothered by the berry gluttony.

Lex's brows furrowed. He had to save them. Had to make it back in time.

"What's your favorite food?" he asked Robyn, trying to distract himself.

Robyn shrugged. "I haven't eaten as many different foods as I'm sure you have."

"Still, you must have something you prefer."

She closed her eyes and tilted her head back against the cave wall, exposing a strip of leather she wore around her neck. An old arrowhead hung tied to it.

"Venison. With seasoned vegetables," she said. "I had it once when I was younger. All I remember is how amazing it tasted compared to anything I'd had before."

Lex smiled. "That's funny."

"What's funny?"

"It's funny that you would choose such an expensive dish, that's all."

"And what would you choose?"

He picked up a handful of berries and held them out. "Sunsetberries."

"Berries?"

"Yes," he said. "I used to sneak into the palace gardens at night and pick them straight from the bushes. The cooks always got mad at me because it left less for them to make pies with, but they're so much better fresh." He paused. "Especially when you have someone to share them with."

She smiled, their gazes locked for a moment. Longer than a moment, Lex realized. And from across the room, his sight flickered from her eyes, to her lips, and he wondered what it would be like to kiss her.

He cleared his throat, breaking the spell. "Well, it'll be morning soon and this cave will get too warm," he said. "We should probably sleep while we can."

"Right."

He took the rest of the berries and tucked them away, then made a pillow out of one of their packs and lay down across from her. He closed his eye. If he kept it open he'd watch her, and that would be bad. So he held still, listening to her shift and get comfortable.

"Lex?"

A pleasant shiver ran down his spine. "Yes?"

"Would you blow out the candle?"

"Of course." He sat up and met her eyes. Her blue gaze stayed on him as he leaned forward and extinguished the light. He lay back, getting comfortable again. "If we leave at dawn, we should reach Belleci Palace by tomorrow morning."

"Goodnight, Lex."

"Sleep well, Robyn."

I stopped seeing Markus, stopped spending
time with my best friends.

25
CARINA

Carina clasped her hands before her as she kept pace with her father down the colonnade, a view of their city to her right where their forces were gathering to march. The sight sent a shiver down her spine.

Except for the occasional dinner or walk with her father, she'd been locked in her room for over a week. He didn't bother speaking to her, and she wasn't certain why he didn't just lock her up and keep her there. He knew she'd diluted the poison, so there had to be a reason she was still allowed some freedoms— if supervised excursions could be called freedoms. This was the first time she'd seen sunlight in days, and the heat was almost too much.

They took steps down to a lower level of the colonnade, and just when Carina expected them to turn and return her to her rooms, a messenger rode up to the front entrance, dressed in the blue and gold of the king's guard.

Beside her, her father quickened his pace. Carina followed.

ex444xxx

When they reached the entryway Carina stayed back, unnoticed, as the messenger hopped down from their mount and approached Valio, bowing and breathless.

"My lord," the man said.

"Antio," her father said. "What news?"

"Your concerns for the health of our king and queen have been heard, and actions taken, my lord. The royal Cures are checking their health on a regular schedule, and they have been instructed to take walks when they rise and before they sleep, as well as receiving small doses of Life magic at least once a day. Also," he paused, pulling a letter from his coat pocket. "This was intercepted just before it reached them."

Father opened the letter as Antio spoke, scanning the contents, then smiled. "Excellent. Thank you, Antio, the steward will see to your payment and then you are to return to the capital as quickly as possible."

Carina frowned as Antio hurried away. Then her father turned to look at her, as though only now realizing she was there, even though he'd summoned her for this walk. His brow furrowed. "Go back to your rooms," he snapped. "I have work to do."

Without another word, he hurried back the way they'd come.

From the side of the room, Adia approached and curtseyed. "My lady. I can escort you."

"Of course," Carina said, feeling dazed, the conversation between her father and this messenger swirling through her mind.

They began to make their way toward her rooms, but Carina paused when the messenger stepped out of a room ahead of them. A strange bravery bubbled up in her chest at the sight of him.

"Excuse me, sir?"

The man paused, then bowed when he saw who had called him.

"Your name is Antio?"

"Yes. And you are Lady Carina."

"I am. Can you tell me—" she cut herself off. "Why did you bring my father this report?"

Antio looked up, meeting her stare. His eyes were a deep brown, almost like her own, and there was a curve to his smile that she wasn't sure about. "I only know that I have been paid to do so, my lady. I have no idea what your father intends to do with the information I've brought him."

Something about his words felt ingenuine, but she couldn't discern why. "Very well. Thank you."

Antio bowed once more, then passed her by.

"My lady?" Adia said. "You seem concerned…"

"I am."

"For the monarchs?"

"Yes." Heart racing, she turned toward her rooms. "I need to speak to Damari. Send him to me, please."

Beside her, Adia had stopped, and Carina had to turn back to see her. The girl was only slightly younger. Pale, with dark hair and blue eyes, from the northern part of the Unbroken Lands. But now, in this moment, Adia's eyes were wide, and frightened.

"Adia, what is it?"

"My lady, I—I know you said you trust him, but…"

"Damari?"

Adia nodded.

Carina gritted her teeth. She finally found a person not under her father's control who she could trust, and now her servant—who she also trusted—was warning her against him without proof of anything.

"Adia. You will not speak of this again, is that clear?"

"Yes, my lady," Adia said, bowing.

"Find Damari, send him to my rooms."

"Of course, my lady."

Ten minutes later, Carina opened her door to find Damari standing before her, carrying a tray of food. She hurried him inside and he set the tray on her nightstand, then flopped unceremoniously onto the bed.

"The stupid head cook is making me actually work," he groaned. "I'm supposed to be undercover, not a real servant."

"Damari, we need to talk."

"Right," he said, sitting up. "What is it you needed?"

"My father just received a message. The man said the king and queen are healthy, taking walks, and receiving Life magic. Apparently he sent a letter of concern for their health? Why would he do that if he's trying to kill them and take the throne?"

Damari frowned, his brows coming together in confusion.

"And then the messenger wouldn't tell me why my father asked for this update. Shouldn't they be at least a little ill, if they've been taking the oil I made? He's changed his plan, somehow, but I don't know what he intends to do now."

"I don't understand," Damari said. "The messenger reported they're healthy, and your father seemed upset by it, right?"

"I...suppose."

"Then what's the problem?"

Carina pressed her lips together. What *was* the problem? Her father had been upset, yes, but hadn't he also been pleased at some part of the news?

"Carina?" Damari asked, placing a hand to her cheek. "What is it? You look ill."

"I'm fine, I just...I suppose it's fine. Maybe they'll be okay."

Damari smiled down at her, and the sight made her feel safe. Safer than she did while with her father, anyway. Adia was wrong.

Damari leaned down to kiss her softly. She tried to savor the kiss for a moment, his lips warm against hers. His hands slid across her back, pulling her close, until he squeezed a little too hard, putting pressure on her bruised ribs.

She cried, flinching away from the touch, leaning against him for support as the pain seared inside her chest.

"Carina," he murmured. "I hate seeing you like this."

She focused on her breathing, darkness sparking across her vision as she nearly fell to the floor. He lowered her, holding her awkwardly, as though he wasn't sure where to put his hands.

"You can't stay here," he said softly. "We have to get you away before he does something we can't heal."

Carina fought to bring air into her lungs, the pain seeming to slice her with every breath. She'd somehow been ignoring it earlier, but the grip of Damari's hands had brought on a new wave of agony.

Maybe...maybe he was right.

She'd never before, never entertained the thought of leaving. She'd attempted other things to escape, more permanent things...the memories flashed in her mind, of broken bones and aching body...her heart raced at the visions and tears burned behind her eyes...she shut them out. She couldn't think of it now.

But leaving...it never felt possible until now. With help, maybe....

"Your friends," she forced herself to say. "Can they...help?"

He stood, and she looked up to see him roll his eyes. "I have no idea. The last word I got was them saying they were splitting up to go for help." He turned to the tray of food and picked out a few berries and orange slices, bringing them to her. "No idea where they are now, not like they care much about me to let me know anyway."

Carina rubbed around the bruised spot on her ribs, trying to shove the pain away. "What do you mean?"

"They don't trust me," he said. "Robyn especially." He handed her a berry. "Here, eat."

"Thank you." She finally sat up straight, her pain subsiding a little.

"You know," he said. "A warm bath might help relax the bruised muscles."

"You may be right at that."

"I could prepare it for you if you'd like," he said, running a hand down her arm.

Carina shrank back. "Thank you, but...I think I'd prefer to call Adia for that."

Damari's eyes narrowed. "Did I do something wrong?"

"No, no," she said, quick to reassure him. "I'm grateful for your help, I just…I need some time alone to think."

"Oh," he said, his jaw tightening for a moment. "Fine, good. I'll…send for Adia, shall I?"

"Yes, thank you."

He turned away quickly and was gone without another word. By the time Adia returned to draw the bath, Carina was standing and had eaten, trying to parse out how she felt about many things…her father, Damari, the situation at the capital, Robyn and her friends…. Maybe a bath would help clear her head, because at the moment it felt as though her brain were clogged with fog, and she couldn't see a mucking thing.

My brother worried about me. I told him I was fine.
I thought I was.

26
LEX

Lex urged Pepper to gallop and his heart soared at the familiar sight before him. The sprawling granite complex of the Belleci palace stood a few hundred yards south of the Eiri River, surrounded by productive fields of grapevines, roaming cattle and sheep, and olive tree orchards. Already, three familiar figures with golden hair stood at the foot of the front steps. He pulled Pepper to a stop and hopped down in a hurry before he ran to greet them.

They were his second family. Though seeing them reminded him of the danger his parents were in, he set the thought aside to focus on how good it was to see them. Lady Belleci embraced him with surprised exclamations, while Kai bowed, and Millia curtsied, before he wrapped them in hugs as well.

"We knew you'd run away but Nick said you were going to the coast. What on earth are you doing here?" Lady Belleci asked.

"Where are Nick and Oliver?" Kai asked.

"And what is that hair doing on your face, highness?" Millia said, smiling slyly behind the rest of her family.

Lex held up his hands. "I'm fine, really, I…as for the beard, mostly I didn't want to be recognized."

"I've never seen you without your eye patch," Kai said, curiously examining the scars.

Lex's hand flew to his lost left eye. He hadn't put the patch back on? Memories flashed through his mind of rudeness and sly remarks people thought he couldn't hear. "I…I'm sorry, I didn't mean to—"

"Your highness," Lady Belleci said, stepping forward. "We don't care whether you wear your eye patch or not. If it makes you more comfortable, then by all means, put it on. But if you've become accustomed to not wearing it, that's fine too."

Lex let out a breath. He had grown used to not wearing it in the last few days, and he had Robyn to thank for it.

Robyn…

He looked back to the crest of the hill a few hundred feet behind. She was there, still atop her horse. Even from this distance he could tell she was uncomfortable. Lex waved for her to join them.

"Who is she?" Kai asked.

"A friend," Lex said. "She's helped me a great deal."

He kept his gaze on her as she rode toward them. She was tense, reminding him of her stance in that circle of bandits, right before Lex had attacked. When she stopped, a good twenty feet away, Lex approached, circling to the horse's left as Robyn dismounted so they were out of sight of the others. He offered a hand, and she tentatively took hold.

"Are you all right?" he asked, keeping his voice low so the others wouldn't hear.

"I don't know."

Lex looked over the horse's back to the Bellecis, then to her. "If you're uncomfortable here we can stay in the forest. I wouldn't mind."

She looked to him, her eyes slightly wide in surprise. "But you said they're your friends. Your family."

"As are you," he said, tightening his hold on her hands. "I would love for you to meet them, but if you'd rather keep your distance I underst—"

"No," she said, squaring her shoulders. "I believe you. Besides…if anyone tries anything, I have my daggers."

"Well, hopefully it won't come to that, but…look, once you get to know them, you'll love them. I promise."

She raised a brow. "That's quite a promise, Prince."

He smirked. "One that will be kept, Lady Outlaw."

Lex released her hands, wishing he didn't have to, and they approached the family, who waited patiently. From the corner of his eye, he saw Robyn look each of them over for weaknesses, strengths, motives, as she had when she first met him.

"Robyn, this is Kai and his sister Millia," he paused as they bowed. "And their mother, High Lady Angelina Belleci; the best strategist in the kingdom."

"Flatterer," Lady Belleci said. She came forward and opened her arms to Robyn, who stepped into the hug—albeit a little awkwardly. "A friend of Lex is a friend of ours," Angelina said. "It's a pleasure to have you in our home."

Robyn cleared her throat as they parted, looking uncomfortable and out of place. "Thank you," she said. "You are one of the few lordships who cares well for their people. On their behalf, I thank you."

Lady Belleci frowned, looking from Robyn to Lex.

"It's a long story," Lex said.

Lady Belleci smiled, brows raised expectantly. "Well, you can explain everything over lunch."

In the open corridors of the Belleci palace Lex found himself falling into step with Millia, the Belleci's oldest daughter. She was two years older than Lex and had been married for three years already.

"Where is Xanton?" Lex asked.

"Overseeing the planting of the western fields," she said. "He should be back by nightfall."

Lex nodded. "And, Kai? Anything exciting going on with him?"

Millia smiled. "He thinks we don't know, but he's been writing to Oliver since last year's Autumn Feast."

"Oliver?" Lex grinned as he turned to look back at Kai. The younger boy held Robyn's arm through his and seemed to be chatting her ear off. Robyn had the look of a small animal about to be pounced on, her eyes wide, striped face pale as she took in her surroundings.

"She's unfamiliar with this?" Millia asked.

"Yes," Lex said, turning forward. "She's survived the last few years on very little. I'm sure this is jarring."

"More than jarring, she looks terrified."

Frustration tightened his chest. "I should have talked with her about it before we arrived. How could I have neglected that?"

Millia laughed. "My lord prince, people rarely think selfless thoughts until one comes along who reminds us to do so. And even then, learning to do it as often as necessary can take time."

Lex frowned. "What do you mean by that?"

She raised a brow to him. "Does being around Lady Robyn make you want to be a better man? A better version of yourself?"

It felt as though all the breath in his lungs escaped him at that single question. He knew the answer right away, of course. But the surety with which he knew it was the thing that struck him like a blow.

Millia smirked as they continued walking.

They reached the main meeting hall where a table was set for them, and Lex made sure to rescue Robyn from Kai's clutches.

As they reached the table, Robyn finally spoke. "Was this meal prepared for only your family?"

Angelina turned. "No, lady. Our scouts reported you coming early this morning. We've been expecting you."

"Well, that's something," she muttered.

"I'm sorry?" Angelina asked.

"Nothing, my apologies."

Lex cleared his throat, placing a hand on Robyn's back and guiding her to one side of the table. She looked up at him with wide eyes, and he tried to tell her with a look that it wasn't nearly as bad as it could be. He'd seen far worse excess than this. Though, he told himself, that didn't make it right.

"Well, let's eat and you can explain what you're doing here," Lady Belleci said, letting a servant push her seat in for her. Lex did the same for Robyn, taking her hand to help her sit. It was a gesture he'd performed many times for other ladies, yet now it made his stomach twist into knots. And as he took his own seat to her left, he noticed a faint tinge of pink on her freckled cheeks, and the sight sent a thrill through him.

Trying to distract himself, Lex began to fill his plate. Beside him Robyn sat quite still. On the table lay seasoned chicken, baked fish, steamed vegetables of all colors, sweet citrus and berries, deep colored wine and clear water. There was even cake—had she ever had cake?

"Robyn," he whispered as he leaned toward her. "What would you like?"

She shook her head, frowning at the spread.

He took her cup and filled it with water, then placed a few cubes of cheese, some berries, and bread on her plate. "You've got to eat something. And we might as well save our own provisions if they're offering us fresh food, don't you think?"

She took a deep breath and nodded, taking a small bite of the cheese. She forced a smile at him.

"Well, Lex," Angelina finally said. "It's wonderful to have you here, of course, but to what do we owe the honor?"

Lex cleared his throat. "Well, as you may have heard, I left the palace a few weeks ago."

"Nick wrote to us," Kai chimed.

"Yes," Lex nodded. "Well, I left for a…a break, you could say, and I came across Robyn and her crew."

"Crew?" Millia asked.

For the next half hour, Lex related his escape, meeting Robyn and the others, their discovery of the meeting at Keep Valio, their infiltration, and escape—though he left out Carina's involvement, that wasn't his story to tell. Lex briefly explained

Robyn's organization, praising it highly, and finished with their plans to go against Valio.

"I sent messengers to the outer lords requesting loyal forces to meet at the southern curve of the River Tardus, to stand against him if he refuses to step down at my order."

Angelina held her hands clasped on the table, her face creased with worry. Millia twisted a napkin in her hands. Kai, however, spoke up.

"What about Nick and Oliver?" he asked.

"What about them?" Lex asked.

"Are they safe?" he said, his voice rising. "What if Valio takes over the palace? What if the knights refuse to help him? What if he finds out you're friends? What if he tortures them?"

"Kai, calm," Angelina chided.

Kai sat back in his chair, his breathing uneven and a scowl on his face. Millia laid a hand on his shoulder.

Angelina took a deep breath and said, "He's right to be worried, Lex. Maximus has acted oddly for years, but I never imagined he'd go this far. Besides that," she said, looking to Lex, "there are flaws in this plan of yours, my prince. You've got a force gathering, but what about a strategy? How will you attack if you need to? Or will you wait for him to attack you? Have you thought through any of this?"

"A bit," Lex said, holding back a smile. "But I was hoping you, being such a renowned strategist, could possibly assist us in those areas?"

The woman raised an eyebrow and began to chuckle. She nodded, squaring her shoulders and tucking her greying blond hair behind her ear. "All right. For now, I realize it's only late morning but you've traveled far and you two should get some rest. Tomorrow morning we'll meet in the library and talk this through. I'll send runners out right away to call my forces in, but it's going to take a day or so for them to travel here."

"A day or so?" Robyn asked. "How long, exactly?"

"From the farthest parts of my lordship? Nearly two full days," Lady Belleci said. "My knights are instructed to always be ready, regardless of peace or wartime. It'll take half a day to get the message out, and one for them to travel here. If I send runners now, I should have a sizeable force ready to march north two mornings from now. We will do all we can, Lady Robyn, but these things take time."

"We don't have time," she said softly. "The king and queen could be sick right now."

"We left Valios six days ago," Lex said. "If our estimations are correct, he could be administering the poison as we speak." Saying it out loud made a chill run through him, enough to raise bumps on his arms.

"I understand," Angelina said. "Still, moving armies is not an easy feat. We have to gather them from the outer reaches of our lands, then move as a group. Otherwise, they'll be unprotected, vulnerable, and not under my command."

Lex looked to Robyn, who straightened her shoulders. She gave a stiff nod. "I understand. I don't like it, but I understand."

"We should also send a message to your parents," Angelina said. "Telling them you're alive, and to arrest Valio. If they can do that much, our armies might not be needed."

Lex cringed. "I did send them one through some friends, but I'd love to send another. I'll write it as soon as I get to my rooms. Can you have a trusted messenger ready?"

"Of course," Angelina nodded. "And, since we'll be waiting for my forces to gather, why don't we have a ball? Music, wine, dancing, I think we could all use a night of fun before we risk our lives, don't you?"

"Mother," Kai said, shrinking in his seat.

Angelina continued. "Tomorrow night, as the lords and knights arrive, those here can attend, and we'll leave the following morning."

"Mother," Millia began. "Do you really think that's appropriate?"

Lady Belleci shrugged. "It's either that or we sit and twiddle our thumbs the whole time. I'd rather have fun." She stood and said, "For now, I think we're done here, and I have things to do. Follow me, I'll show you to your rooms where you can bathe and rest. Since we seem to have talked more than eaten, we'll send some food to your rooms instead."

Lex stood and offered a hand to Robyn. She took it almost naturally this time, and he relaxed a bit. He put her hand through his arm and they followed Angelina out of the hall, Millia and Kai behind them.

"A ball?" Robyn whispered. "Do these people have nothing better to do than waste resources?"

Lex frowned. "I wouldn't call it a waste. I'd call it boosting morale."

Her hand tightened on his arm.

"Especially here, Robyn. I've been to balls in all the lordships and if there's one I would call frugal it would be the Bellecis. And anything they don't eat or drink is given to those who need it, not wasted."

She rolled her eyes. "Still. How can she think of a celebration when your parents' lives are at stake?"

"It's a means of distraction, nothing more. She doesn't want to think about losing her king and queen—especially given that she knows them better than most. I'm certain she plans to come with us and help where she can."

"Help?" Robyn asked, looking at him. "How can she possibly help?"

"Did you miss that Angelina is the best strategist in the kingdom? Her late husband was often praised with that title but the real brains behind it was her. And women are trained in combat as well, if they choose to learn. Angelina is one of the best."

She looked away. "I find it hard to believe."

"Not everyone is as inept as I, you know."

"I never said you were—"

"Maybe not out loud," Lex said. "But you were thinking it."

Her cheeks flushed pink again, and Lex couldn't help thinking she looked beautiful that way…

"You're right," she said. "I did think it. But I was wrong."

Lex frowned.

"You might not be the best with a sword, Lex, but you've saved my life as many times as I've saved yours." She looked up at him. "I want you to know I'm grateful for that."

Lex smiled. "The pleasure is mine."

"Here we are," Angelina said ahead of them, opening a pair of doors.

The room was large, but smaller than his own quarters back home. It would still be too much for Robyn, he knew. The space was decorated in shades of deep green accented with gold. Lex turned to Robyn, whose eyes were wide, no longer with shock, but in awe.

"I thought you might like this room," Angelina said, a slim smile on her lips.

"I...I do," Robyn said. "Thank you."

"You're welcome," Angelina bowed her head. "Now, your bath is through here and already drawn, the wardrobe has clean clothes in many sizes which you're more than welcome to, Millia's rooms are right next door, and his highness," Angelina smirked, "will be down at the end of the hall."

Lex's face grew warm.

Angelina continued. "If you need anything, there are servants stationed in the halls, just send for us through them, or have them fetch whatever you need."

Robyn wrung her hands before her. "Again, thank you."

Millia and Kai bowed politely, leaving quickly. Angelina turned to go, pausing when Lex did not.

"Highness," she said, "shall we give the lady her privacy?"

"In a moment," Lex said, nodding to her.

She raised a brow, but bowed and stepped into the hall, leaving the doors wide open.

Lex turned to Robyn. "Are you all right?"

She straightened her back, defiantly. "Why wouldn't I be?"

Looking at her here, seeing her so determined to fit into his world, his hands itched to hold hers again. He clasped them behind his back and stepped closer to her. She watched him, one brow raised in what he thought was curiosity. "If you need anything...anything at all, even someone to speak to, please send for me. All right?"

Her bright eyes seemed to penetrate his soul, and he felt sure she could see every thought he had of her, that she would run away before he had the chance to prove himself.

She nodded. "I will."

He turned and went through the doors. Taking hold of the handles, he looked back.

"Robyn?"

"Yes?"

"These doors lock."

She nodded. He closed them, and waited. A moment later, the lock clicked into place and he heard her lean against the doors. He rested a hand on the wood, imagining her there on the other side. Capable though she was, he didn't want to just leave her. But, he forced himself to move away, his fingers seeming to reach for Robyn as they slid from the door.

I tried to be in predictable places so that I could see the high lord.
It wasn't long before I let him kiss me.

27
ROBYN

The library at Belleci Palace was unlike anything Robyn had ever seen. Well, the entire place was that. But this room, this single room held more knowledge than she'd encountered in all her life, peasant or outlaw. She was one of the few girls in her town who had learned to read. Her parents had hoped for a better life for her, and that hadn't worked out at all as they'd expected. Now she lived on the land and helped where she could. But this room....

The shelves rose to the ceiling, high as a tree grows. She'd seen the vaulted ceilings in other parts of the palace, but she'd never imagined *books* being kept so high. The ladders to reach them were thin and wobbly. She'd much rather jump from limb to limb on a tree than climb those spindly things.

Then there were the rows, and rows, and *rows* of shelves filling the floor space. These mostly contained scrolls and what looked like the Belleci's private records, but Robyn was able to run a finger along some few leather-bound tomes in their midst.

The place smelled of paper and ink and...old leather. Robyn was suddenly, painfully, reminded of her father. Shoe leather—used for sandals, here in Regania—always smelled deep, earthy, and somehow reminded her of sunshine. These books smelled ancient. Aged. Left alone for too long…much like her. She closed her eyes, taking a deep breath through her nose.

Focus.

She ran a hand over her hip, searching for the handle of her dagger, but it wasn't there. Instead she felt the soft deep green fabric of a formal chiton, wrapped by a sash of gold. She tensed, remembering now where she was, with whom, and what she had chosen to wear this morning. The wardrobe had been severely lacking in trousers, and so here she stood in a dress for the first time in years, in a library of all places, searching for a young man with a scarred face that somehow held more beauty because of its imperfections….

She shook her head to clear it and rounded the corner of one shelf to see that the center of the room was open, with a circular table atop a painting of the sun on the floor. It was surrounded by soft chairs and smaller tables, for what looked like casual reading. Robyn frowned slightly as she passed one of the chairs. She'd never had time for casual reading.

A thud at the central table made her jump, and she looked up to see Lex leaning over a gigantic book, turning page after page. He was wearing a glass lens over his eye, and that made Robyn pause. Did he need it for reading? She'd never seen him wear one before.

Without warning he slammed the book shut with a grunt, turned, and ran off down a branch of shelves, muttering something to himself.

What is he doing?

Across the space littered with tables and chairs, Lady Belleci stepped from the shelves. She smiled kindly and nodded. "Good morning, Lady Robyn."

Robyn narrowed her eyes. Lady Belleci had circled around, so as not to startle her from behind. Robyn knew it, and was grateful. She smiled. "Good morning. Your library is beautiful."

"Thank you. My husband made it a gift to me when we were married, and we filled it together. This collection is my most treasured possession. After our children, of course."

"Of course," Robyn said.

"Now," she looked around the room. "Where is that boy?"

"Here!" Lex said, rounding the shelves once more. This time he held three books, each smaller than the one he'd brought out before. He laid all three on the table and began flipping through pages, going back and forth between them.

Lady Belleci slowly approached Robyn. "I suppose we ought to let him have free reign until he finds what he's looking for?"

Robyn shrugged, purposely unladylike. "I've never seen him this focused on anything. Except perhaps his poetry; but I hardly know him."

"Really? Interesting."

Robyn frowned at this, but said nothing and didn't meet the woman's eyes. How Lex knew where to look to find what he wanted, she had not an inkling of an idea. As he ran off yet again she crossed her arms in annoyance. He was making a ridiculous mess.

"What are you looking for?" she finally asked.

He shouted back to her. "A story I read once."

"Why?"

"Because I think it has a good strategy!" His voice was now carrying through the shelves.

This time, she followed him. "I thought we were going to consult with Lady Belleci about strategy. And here you're trying to come up with one on your own?"

"Not on my own," he said from one row over. She'd guessed wrong, apparently. "I want to tell her my idea and see what she thinks. But I can't do that without—"

Robyn turned. Lex had come around the shelf to meet her and stopped, his eye wide and staring. Under his gaze she felt heat rush to her cheeks and wished she could turn off that specific reaction.

She squared her shoulders, falling into the proper etiquette she'd learned as a girl. The motions her father had learned when making shoes for nobility, and what he'd hoped might help earn Robyn a life of greater standing. Without a second thought she curtsied low, and was pleasantly rewarded by a look of astonishment on his face when she rose.

Lex blinked, then shook his head, a grin spreading on his face. "I must be dreaming."

Robyn tilted her head, hoping to give him a chance to avoid what she knew he was about to say. "Excuse me?"

"You, Robyn, you curtsied like a proper lady of court," he said, waving a hand like a lunatic.

"And?"

"And," he said, "I'm surprised, that's all. It's unexpected."

"Unexpected that someone of such low station could know anything about your high and mighty ways?"

Lex's mouth dropped open in surprise. "What? No, no I just meant—"

"You didn't expect the forest-dwelling outlaw to be able to *curtsey?* Do you hear how ridiculous that sounds?" she snapped. Gods, she hated dealing with nobility. "I told you once before, Prince, don't pretend you know me."

His face softened into a look of concern as he held her gaze. "I haven't forgotten."

The fight fled from her like a breaking dam. It was as though a hand had gripped her heart and closed it off from everything else in the world. Everything except Lex. How did he do that? She had been ready to run and leave him, now she stood staring at him, wishing she had some clever retort to make the growing feeling in her heart go away. Her face must be blushing furiously now, but Lex's expression didn't change. He stared into her eyes as she did his. Then his gaze slid to her mouth, and flicked back to her eyes.

She knew that look.

She left. Turned on her heel and got out of those shelves. There was no way she could stay; she knew what would come next if she did and she wasn't ready for that. Not now. Maybe not ever.

Lex was a good man, she knew it, and she'd gained a great deal of respect for him over their travels. But if he looked at her like that much longer, she wasn't sure she'd be able to keep her heart safely behind its walls.

Lady Belleci still stood in the center of the room, now sorting the books Lex had already brought out. Good, a distraction. Robyn stopped beside her and began to help, asking how she was categorizing them.

A few minutes later she heard a loud, "AH HA!" from where Lex had been, and he came running out.

"I found it!" he said, placing a book on the table between them. "Look at this," he said, pointing at a page.

Robyn leaned over and skimmed the text. "Lex this is a fable. A children's tale."

"Yes, it is," he lifted the book, waving a hand for emphasis of some kind. "But all fables are based in truth."

Angelina frowned. "I don't understand."

Lex frowned too, obviously annoyed. "Look, I just reread it to make sure I remembered. It's a story about a family of foxes who decided to work together instead of hunting on their own, right? Well, they send their fastest runners to the edge of the wood to act sick and weak, drawing the attention of a tiger. The tiger sees the foxes, goes after them, and the foxes run back into the forest where the rest of their family is waiting to attack. And when they all jump on the tiger at once, they manage to overpower it and win!" He tossed the book down on the table and held out his hands.

Despite herself, Robyn smiled. "Lex, I have no idea what you're talking about."

"Yes, please explain?" Angelina said.

Lex gave an eye-roll. "Bribery," he said, leaning forward. "Enticement. Using their greed against them. That's what we'll need to do. *If* Valio's at his palace, he won't have the man power to stand up to us. We'll arrest him and put him away no questions asked. *But*, if he's not at his palace, he'll be at *my* palace, in Galanis, right? A much more fortified city. So we need to draw him out of the city. I don't want to harm my people, and I don't want him blaming me for damage done to the city or anything else. We have to draw him out."

Surprised, Robyn found herself nodding.

"We station most of our troops here," he pointed to a map, at a particular curve in the River Tardus, about half a league south of Galanis proper—the place where their forces would meet. "We hide most of them, probably four thousand each, here and here," he said, pointing to two sections northeast and northwest of the river's curve. "Then, we take a small force, maybe seven hundred to a thousand or so, and go to Galanis to mount a weak attack. Large enough that Valio feels threatened and takes us seriously, but small enough for him to know he could wipe us out without trouble.

"He'll send out his troops, and we'll retreat to the river, where the other groups will surround on all sides. We'll get their attention there and I'll show myself, that way any who are loyal to me can defect to us, and Valio won't even know I'm there until the last moment."

Silence filled the room. Robyn frowned at the map, trying to wrap her mind around the plan he was explaining.

Beside Robyn, Angelina crossed her arms. "And you needed that book to explain this?"

Lex's face turned slightly pink. "I wanted to remember which story it was."

Robyn pressed her lips together, trying not to smile.

Lady Belleci frowned in thought. "I do think drawing them out is the best option, and this seems sound. Any stipulations?"

Lex nodded. "I don't want our force knowing who I am until I reveal it—IF I reveal it. If Valio gets word of where I am, he'll send someone after me. And to be honest, I like my head attached. That leaves you and the other high lords to lead the forces."

"There is another option…you are the rightful heir to the throne," Lady Belleci said, crossing her arms. "Surely, with the royal guard in place, Valio would step down if you simply go to the palace and announce yourself alive?"

Lex looked to Robyn and they exchanged a glance of understanding.

"He's determined not to, Lady Belleci," Robyn said. "And I think he's right. Valio is dangerous, and he's also smart. If Lex goes into Galanis, Valio will be surrounded by his supporters and Lex won't be able to arrest him."

Lex nodded. "If I recall correctly, he has the largest number of lower nobility and knights in the kingdom. If he takes them all to the palace with him, which I believe he will, they'll outnumber the royal guard. I've got to get the royal guard united with these groups from the outer lordships to have any chance. That means luring them out and showing myself outside the palace walls where they can easily switch sides."

Lady Belleci nodded slowly. "Lex, you did get that letter sent yesterday, right?"

"I did."

"Good. Maybe that will make the difference and we won't have to do this."

Robyn was smiling. She didn't know much about armies or war, but it *felt* right. It felt like a good plan.

"I like it," she finally said. "I think it'll work."

Lex met her eyes, and his face lit up with a smile. Robyn cursed that blushing mechanism again, but didn't look away this time. She smiled back.

"Thank you," Lex said.

Lady Belleci smiled as well. "And you said you needed my help."

Lex looked away nervously. "I will still, though. I can't do this on my own."

"Of course, your highness," she said. "You won't need to."

How sweet it felt, though it sickens me now.

28
LEX

Lex's palms were sweating. He'd never known that was a thing that actually happened to people. Nervousness was not familiar to him. He hadn't even felt nervous running away from home. He should've, he knew now, but he hadn't been at the time. Yet now here he was getting ready to go to a ball—the first ball he actually *wanted* to go to in his life—and maybe dance with a girl he was coming to care for more than he'd thought was possible—

Deep breath.

He looked himself over in the mirror. He had shaved his face for the occasion, and was glad he'd decided to. He felt lighter somehow, despite a couple of nicks around his scars. He only prayed he wouldn't be recognized by the people of this far southern lordship. The chiton he wore was deep blue, wrapped with a belt of tiny woven gold chains. His family's colors, though without any distinguishing marks.

What will Robyn think of me like this?

Finally feeling ready, he left his room and went to knock on Robyn's doors.

The doors did not open, but Millia's voice came from inside. "Go on down, highness. You'll see her when everybody else does."

"But—"

"I insist!"

He sighed. Hopefully they weren't putting her through anything she wasn't comfortable with. As she'd shown that morning, she knew more about his world than she'd let on before. He'd noticed her formal speaking when she became nervous, but never imagined she'd be so familiar with courtly interaction. He'd never seen anyone bow with as much elegance as she had in those bookshelves.

The ball was being held where they'd dined the previous day. A high-ceilinged room with one large chandelier hanging in the center; the granite floor was grey but polished to a shine. A group of musicians sat in a corner, setting their music out and warming up like a flock of birds chittering to each other. Tables lined one wall, covered with decanters of wine, platters of steaming vegetables, chopped chicken, fish, venison, soft breads, cakes, and pastries.

The rich smells made his head spin. A glass of wine would calm his nerves. As he took one, he promised himself it would be the *only* one. He had learned with the help of Nick and Oliver that he could not hold his liquor.

He circled the room as more people entered, and the musicians struck up a lively tune, the notes in perfect harmony and rhythm. The walls here were painted in murals of scarlet and gold depicting the Gods, and Lex was drawn to one image of all four standing in a circle, looking upward with their hands joined together. His vision went a little blurry, and he shook his head. The Belleci's wine was potent.

He looked to the door every few seconds as each person entered. Soon, a servant announced Lady Belleci's presence. She entered, regal as ever, waving and nodding as she greeted the knights, and their partners who had come to see them off. A moment later Millia was announced, and she entered looking beautiful in a chiton of soft green that brought out her eyes. She was accompanied by her husband, Xanton, a tall Callidian man with blue hair, dark skin, and a strong jaw. The couple were soon surrounded by friends and attention.

Lex's gaze returned to the door and, hidden by the commotion of the hosts' appearance, Kai and Robyn slipped in unannounced, and unnoticed by anyone but him.

A chill ran through him at the sight of her. The girl he'd first seen as a ruffian was there somewhere; the girl who had scared him, tested him, saved his life, and protected his mind. But in the same body stood a creature so unfamiliar to him that his heart raced in anticipation. He threw back the last of his wine.

She wore a chiton of deep blue that made her eyes sparkle like diamonds by comparison. The sleeves were left open at the shoulders, and her neckline framed the old arrowhead resting on her collarbone. A belt of silver chain wrapped around her waist, and from there the fabric fell loose to her ankles. Her pale hair was held back by a silver comb set with deep green emeralds, and with each step, he saw a tiny sheath wrapped in the straps of her sandal, a silver dagger handle coming from the top. He was surprised yet again when she approached with poise, and offered her hand to him in greeting.

He took it and bowed, placing a kiss on her knuckles. "Good evening, Lady Outlaw."

"Good evening, my lord."

"You look beautiful."

Her cheeks turned pink. "Thank you. I feel rather…exposed."

Lex opened his mouth to say something, but the image he'd locked away of her bathing in the canal near Valio's palace suddenly slammed back into his mind, and his face burned. He cleared his throat. Thankfully, Robyn seemed to feel as awkward as he did.

"So many people," she said. He saw her eyes dart toward the exits: front of the room, back of the room, kitchen doors.

"Robyn." He tentatively placed a hand on her back, and she turned to face him.

"Yes?"

"It's all right. You're safe here."

"*Ahem*," a voice sounded behind them.

Lex turned to see Lady Belleci. "Pardon me," she said, "But this young lady has to tell me more about her organization."

Lex smiled. "That's right. And, I'd like to know how you manage not to get caught." He clasped his hands behind his back.

She blushed again—*by Life, that looks good on her*—and began to speak. The more she did, the more casual she became. She went on about the details of her crew's work, and Lex could tell she was proud of this.

"Everyone needed something," she finished. "It was only a matter of piecing together who had what."

"And how do you transport?" Lady Belleci asked.

"By wagon," Robyn said. "Some of the towns donated what they could to our cause and we were able to obtain them for a low cost from the builders. As for how we're not caught," she smiled at Lex, who beamed, "We have a former royal scribe in our company. He used to work for the Master Vessels in Galanis, but was outlawed for passing a bit of contribution money to a poor family without permission. He forges papers for us, and we've never once had anyone question them."

Lex laughed. He was beginning to see why nobility was not trusted. "You've been running an illegal operation right under our noses. Incredible. And, for the record, pardoned."

"Thank you." She smiled. "I couldn't do it without my crew, though. I organize things, they're the ones who make it happen."

"It's brilliant," Angelina said. "I wonder, Lady Robyn, could I get your opinion on a few things?"

Robyn's face drained of color. "What things?"

"Not to worry, dear," Angelina said. "I'd like to discuss our exports and see what you think. We'd be happy to donate what we can to your cause."

Robyn blinked, looking from Angelina, to Lex, and back again. "Of course."

"I'll leave you two to talk," Lex said, and bowed himself away.

The center of the room was now filled with spinning couples, smiling and laughing as they circled the space. He was a terrible dancer, but watching them always made him jealous. He soon found Kai nearby, nibbling on a bit of bread as he leaned against a wall, back in a corner. He began to bow as Lex approached but he waved him off.

"Not here, Kai."

He elbowed him. "Looks like your lady is getting some attention."

He followed his gaze and saw Robyn still standing near Angelina, but with a couple of young knights having joined them as well. A strange heat flared in him at the sight.

Surely she wouldn't find the attention worth her time? Then she laughed at something someone said, and Lex's breath caught. She really was a vision.

"Jealous?" Kai asked, elbowing him again.

He tore his gaze away from Robyn to look at him. "Why don't we talk about you, little Kai?"

Kai's laughing smile turned to suspicion. "What do you mean 'talk about me'? And don't call me 'Little Kai', I'm not a child."

"Oh I know." Lex laughed, crossing his arms. "Sixteen! Marriage age. And you know what? I hear you have someone special of your own."

"I don't know what you mean." He looked away, his face flushing pink.

"Kai, Oliver told us he'd been writing to someone, hinted that he'd even *kissed* them, but he wouldn't say who. I got the feeling it was because Nick was around. And Millia says you've been writing." He raised his eyebrows at him, waiting.

When Kai finally spoke, he did so in a rush. "It was the Autumn Feast, at your palace. He'd always been nice to me, you know, like I was his little brother. Like you do. But at the feast it was like he finally…*saw* me, you know?"

Lex smiled, but didn't interrupt.

Kai hurried on. "It was while our families were busy celebrating. He asked me to go for a walk around the courtyard, and," he took a deep breath, a soft smile on his lips, "he kissed me. Under the peach tree by the fountain. But that was it! Nothing else happened. Mother called for me and I had to go." He slumped a little.

Lex grinned. "I'm happy for you both. I think he's taken with you."

"And...are you also *taken* with someone?"

Lex paused, knowing exactly what that question meant.

"Never mind," Kai said, waving it off. "Can I ask you a different question?"

Lex nodded, relieved he didn't have to answer the first. "Of course."

"Why don't you wear your patch anymore?"

Lex's hand shot up to his empty eye once more. Sure enough, it was bare. Had he really not put on his eye patch tonight? He'd meant to. He'd thought about it. He had told himself this was a formal occasion and required fewer...scars. But he hadn't worn it. What surprised him more was that until Kai had mentioned it, he hadn't even noticed.

"I...I suppose I forgot about it."

At that moment, Lady Belleci joined them with Robyn at her side. She turned to Lex and said, "Your lady has quite a sharp mind, highness."

"And sharper knives," Lex said.

Angelina smirked. "Lady Robyn, you are welcome back here any time."

Lex caught Robyn's eye and smiled. "Well done. You two must be thirsty. I'll get you some drinks." He turned and started across the room to the wine table. Taking two goblets he turned to see Robyn right behind him.

They faced each other for a moment, Lex searching his mind for something to say. Something witty, clever, not stupid.

Nothing came.

Robyn took one of the goblets and held it up in a silent toast. Lex mirrored her, and she drank. Lowering the cup, she licked her lips and said, "Lady Belleci said she doesn't care for wine tonight, so that's yours."

He smiled and took a sip, knowing he shouldn't. He felt far too familiar around her already, and the feeling in his chest was akin to a storm ready to break.

She walked along the wall to avoid the crowd. He followed, eyeing her neck when she tilted her head in thought. "I like your friends. They're nobility, but they're kind. You were right, the ball isn't as extravagant as I'd have expected. And Lady Belleci is willing to help me expand the organization I already have."

"I thought she might be," Lex said, putting off a casual air he didn't feel. "I used to think all of the members of court were like that, but my time with you has taught me otherwise." They stopped in a corner of the room, and leaned against the walls. "I hope Millia didn't make you uncomfortable, forcing you into a formal chiton and all…."

She smiled. "In all honesty, it feels nice to be properly bathed and dressed for once. Did you see these sandals? They're only leather, and yet so intricately designed." She lifted one foot and rotated it for him to see.

He inhaled as her skirts lifted and he wasn't sure why. He'd seen her in trousers; he'd seen her in far less. But for some reason, here in the ballroom with her in those robes, it felt like a very intimate thing. He ran a hand through his hair and took another gulp of wine.

Then Robyn pushed off the wall and took his goblet, setting it with hers on a table nearby. She turned to him and held out a hand. "Will you dance with me?" Her mouth tugged into a small smile.

Lex's mouth fell open. "Ah, well…er…I-I'm…you see, I'm not…I-I don't…dance."

Her eyebrows shot up. "The prince does not dance? And why not?"

He quoted what his mother always said: "Too much time in the library, and not enough on the dance floor?"

She smiled, looking rather mischievous. "Well, what are friends for if not to be silly with? Come on." She snatched his hand, and before he could object, they were in the center of the floor, dancers circling around them.

She took his left hand in her right, and placed his right on her back. "Now, you step forward, and I'll follow."

Lex's face burned. "How can you follow if I step into you?"

"Keep your arms firm and I'll feel you move. That way I'll know where we're going."

"How do you know this better than I?"

"I know many things better than you, your highness."

Lex's face burned. He swallowed the lump rising in his throat.

"The pattern," Robyn continued, "is two slow steps forward, and two quick steps to your left. Start with your left foot. When you finish the pattern, you repeat it."

Lex didn't move. He stared at her. "No, seriously, how do you know this?"

"Oh, honestly." She began to pull him through the pattern. He let her show him how to do it, but he still managed to step on her and trip himself. But she only laughed and made him do it again, and again, until he had mostly got the hang of it. He had to admit he felt far more comfortable dancing with Robyn than he ever had with anyone else. After a few minutes their movements became slow and repetitive.

"What will you do after all this?" she asked.

"All what?"

"This," she said, waving a hand in the air. "Marching with an army, stopping Valio, saving the kingdom," she laughed, and he couldn't look away. "Go back to the palace, I suppose?"

Her voice was tiny among the music and chatter surrounding them, yet it was the loudest thing to his ears. "I'll have to, eventually. I do have responsibilities there. But at first it'll depend on...things."

"What things?" Her hand tightened in his.

He looked over her shoulder. "Like I said before, I have to find a bride, or my parents will choose for me. I won't go back until I find her."

He finally looked to her and their eyes met. He hoped she understood. That he had feelings for her, wished she could feel the same. The air between them was thick and Lex cursed himself. Could he have made this any more uncomfortable? Then she blinked and looked away, scanning the crowd, the same way she scanned the forest for attackers. She looked like a princess. No, a queen.

He found himself staring at her lips. They were parted, as though she wanted to speak, and he had to stop himself from leaning toward them. He shook his head and cursed that second glass of wine.

Mid-step, he tripped, knocking her off balance. She fell into him. His entire being warmed as the scent of lavender flooded his senses. Waves of warmth spread where her body pressed to his, her hands resting on his chest. His arms were tight around her waist and he wasn't sure what to do. He stared into her eyes as she blinked twice, and he remained frozen in place until she pushed against him and stood straight.

She straightened her robe, looking around. He did the same, but no one seemed to have noticed. She let out a deep breath and said, "I think I should go."

His face fell. "Already? But you've only been here half an hour."

She stared at the floor. "I'm just not used to things like this. I think I...forgive me." She ducked around him and headed for the door. Even through the wine he knew he had to follow her.

Outside the ballroom he caught up as she ascended the stairs. "May I at least walk you to your room?" he asked.

She paused, looking him over. Then she nodded and began to walk at a slower pace.

Neither of them spoke, and Lex counted the steps in his mind. At the top of the staircase, he could see the doors to her room. He swallowed.

"Robyn...I'm sorry."

She laughed through her nose, her hands clasped tightly before her. "Why are you apologizing?"

"Because I know I made you feel uncomfortable. It was not my intention."

"I know." She stopped in front of her doors.

"I want you to know, if you…I mean…." He ran a hand through his hair. "Robyn, I set out to find a wife, and I found a friend. Whatever else there may or may not ever be between us, I want you to know that you *are* my friend. I trust you. I would never do anything to cause you pain, physical or otherwise."

She stood very still, her expression blank.

She's closing off, putting up walls.

He reached out and took her hands in his. She did not react except a slight squeeze of his hands in return. She didn't pull away.

"I truly enjoy your company," Lex said. "I don't want to steal you away from your forest, or your crew, or the good you do in the kingdom, but you are smart and kind. Hopeful and brave. Beautiful and so much more. I…when I go back to Galanis, please know that you are welcome there. I hope you'll at least come to visit?"

She took a slow breath and simply nodded.

He smiled.

She stepped away, her hands slowly sliding from his until their fingertips were all that touched, and he longed to take them back.

Only then did he fully realize, he didn't want to let her go. Not now, and not ever. Just before she closed her doors, she looked up at him. Her eyes were a crystal blue, like a pool of water at midday, sunlight reflecting on the ripples like stars.

"Goodnight Lex."

He heard the latch click shut, and waited for the lock. A full minute passed. He stepped forward and pressed his forehead and palms against the wood.

She hadn't locked the door.

When my sixteenth birthday came,
I was ready to be with him.

29
ZIVON

Shadows. Starlight. Assassination.

Cold tonight. Zivon pulled his cloak tighter, and hunched more as he passed guards who watched the palace perimeter. He walked with a fake limp, keeping his hood low over his face. The simple disguise had worked many times before, and did not fail him now. He carried a bundle on his back, four feet long and one foot thick wrapped with blankets and rope. The guards barely glanced at him.

It had taken hours for him to get to the city. And now he searched for the right building. The palace hill was not small. He would need to be on a roof for the arrows to reach the king and queen on their walk.

The building he entered was said by the locals to be haunted, which was beneficial for Zivon, as no one would enter while he was here no matter what they heard. Its true form, however, was a grimy deserted tavern, and smelled just as he would have imagined from that single description. Moldy air and rotted floorboards greeted him, dust and garbage parting before his steps. The stairs creaked under his weight, but he went on. Five stories, to the rooftop.

The clear air felt like cool water on a summer day after the tavern's rancid scents. He stayed low, and looked around. The palace had no surrounding wall, but was separated from the city by the River Tardus that ran as a moat around the hill upon which the palace stood, backed against a tall cliff. The palace itself was set up much like Valio's. A square with the front side missing, surrounding a garden, with open colonnade hallways between the rooms and buildings. Only this palace had multiple levels rising beyond, and three boxes within each other. A much grander edifice.

According to Master Valio's informant, the king and queen always took a walk around their courtyard just before bed, usually near midnight. Midnight would come in ten minutes, if Zivon's estimate was correct.

He laid his package at the edge of the building where a small wall stood four feet high, blocking him from view. The ropes loosed, he unwrapped the fabric to reveal a bow, and five poisoned arrows of Medelian make—sturdy desert wood, and arrowheads of sandstone. Arrows to start a war, Valio said.

Zivon strung the bow, testing the weight of it. He'd been an archer since youth, but never for humans. Not until Moriz's mistake forced him to work for Valio.

Part of him resented his son for that. If he had not been so foolish, Zivon might be at home with friends, celebrating a marriage, or a birth, or a coming of age. But Moriz had been young and brave. And when youth and bravery are not coupled with caution, foolish things happen.

Sounds came to him from beyond the rooftop. He rose up to check and indeed saw the king and queen exiting their private chambers at the northern end of the palace, guards standing back to allow them to speak privately. Zivon would have to wait until they were at the southern edge of the gardens before taking his shots. If he was lucky, he would take out both with one arrow. If he was not, it may take two or more. But no more than five.

Killing. He was about to kill. Not just any kill, but the leaders of a great kingdom. Certainly Regania had its flaws, and it did not have the special spices of Callidia or its firm foundation of faith in the Powers, but Zivon saw the good here. And killing the leaders would not bring that good out.

They were halfway.

Zivon nocked an arrow on the bowstring. The two monarchs were healthy, not poisoned as Valio had originally planned. As far as anyone knew, they were in no danger whatsoever. And here was Zivon, ending that.

Was he doing them a kindness, in some twisted way? What about the prince? That young man with the melted scars and eye patch so like Zivon's. He would be orphaned. Zivon closed his eye tightly. Leaving a child without family was a crime he did not wish to commit. Moriz had been taken from him. How could he take parents away from a boy?

Moriz's debt must be paid.

He opened his eye. The king and queen were in range. Zivon had been given an order.

He pulled the bowstring.

And shot.

It was easy, killing. It had become easy over the years.

He asked me to come live at his palace, I told him
I would send him my answer the next day.

30
LEX

Lex woke early the morning of departure, and not well-rested. On the bed beside him was his notebook and pencil, scribbles of words and nonsense bearing witness to how stupid he'd been the night before. He stood, going to the window, where early sunlight shone down on the many Belleci troops as they packed their belongings and prepared for a long march.

Robyn.

He put his face in his hands. He'd all but proclaimed his feelings for her the previous night. What must she think of him now? Would she speak to him? Would she trust him? He sat up in bed, trying to remember her reactions. The only thing he knew was she hadn't locked the door. At least she trusted him that much, but what would she expect now? An apology for behaving so ridiculously? For saying what he'd said?

No. He would not take it back. Drunk or not, he remembered what he said and he'd meant every word. He was incapable of lying while even slightly intoxicated, Nick had made sure he'd known that. He stood and looked out the window, resting his forehead on the glass.

Here he was worrying about Robyn when he should be worrying about his parents. Or neither. Worrying rarely did any good no matter the subject.

He dressed and gathered his things, then left his room to go find Pepper. But as he passed Robyn's doors they opened. She stopped in the doorway, and their eyes met.

Lex's stomach turned to knots. "Ah, good morning."

"Good morning." She came into the hallway and they fell into step beside each other. Robyn spoke without hesitation. "Are you worried at all? About what's waiting for us?"

"A little," he said.

"Do you miss your parents?"

His heart skipped, because he did. Despite his mind being occupied with strategy, and Robyn, and traveling, he missed them terribly. He wanted to get back, to know they were safe. He thought of his father's wrinkled hands, his mother's deep golden hair. Robyn was watching him. He swallowed.

"I just hope I get to see them again."

She looked away. "I know how you feel."

He stared for a moment, wondering what she meant by that. He cared for her a great deal, but he didn't know much about her past. "Well," he said, shrugging it off, "we have a whole week of traveling in which to worry, I'd rather not talk about it. I'm going out to the stables. Would you like to join me?"

"Lex?" She kept her eyes forward, still walking.

"Yes?"

"Thank you."

"What for?"

She breathed a small laugh. "Everything?"

278

He stole a glance at her. "That's quite a lot. I'm not sure I've done—"

"Thank you for being patient," she said abruptly, still walking, not looking to him. "For showing me people do care. I used to think being close to people only brought pain…"

He was grateful they weren't facing each other. If he'd been able to see her eyes, he might have done something stupid.

"But you've shown me it's not like that. Caring for someone means trust, even if it might bring pain, and…" she did stop now, at the edge of the colonnade, and turned to him, "I'm starting to trust you, Lex."

It took all his self-control not to reach for her. But he'd heard what she said. *Starting to trust*, not *I trust you*. He wasn't sure he trusted himself much, but he made an attempt to speak. "I would have your trust, my lady."

"Robyn, Lex!" Kai came, practically skipping up the corridor as though they were about to go pick flowers instead of march to battle.

Millia was close behind, looking far more composed. "Are you ready to leave? Your horses are in the stables."

"Thank you, both," Lex said. "Go on, we'll follow in a moment."

Kai looked from Lex to Robyn, a sly smile on his face, but Millia snatched his arm and said, "Take your time. We won't leave without you."

Lex nodded to them as they passed. As soon as they were out of earshot, he looked back to Robyn. It had taken a lot for her to say these things, and now she was shaken by the effort.

He smiled, hoping to calm her. "Perhaps you'll save my life again this trip."

Robyn's smile reappeared. "Or you, mine. We seem to make an interesting pair."

He nodded, and they began to descend the staircase. "How many times has it been now? Four? Five?"

"Only three for you, I think," she said, ticking her fingers as she listed them. "The assassin, the bandits, and those knights."

"And that would be…two for you, then? Escaping Valios, and that fall on the cliff?"

"Sounds right."

"Hmm, I appear to be winning."

Robyn laughed, and the sound sent a rush of joy through him. "Well, maybe I'll just fall out of a tree somewhere, and you can catch me."

"You," he said, "fall out of a tree? That'll never happen."

Why cent I think when she's
around? Was it the wine? I only
had one mucking glass!...didn't I?
Or was it two? I don't think I said anything
Tooooo stupid...did I?

God... her eyes are like stars.
That's mucking cliché is what it is...
But its true, anyone would say it, not just me.

I wonder if her hair is as soft as it looks...
Lands, I might never know after Tonight.

Stupid
Stupid
Stupid

I'm such an Idiot!

I went home and told my parents I wanted to accept.
They were terrified.

31
CARINA

Nine days since the meeting.

Carina's cheeks were stiff with dried tears. Her knees were pulled to her chest, arms wrapped around them. She sat on the floor at the foot of her bed. Pink sunlight filtered through the gaps in her curtains. Warm, bright light shining happily to mark the beginning of a new day.

It did nothing for her heart.

Her distilling equipment lay scattered, shattered, across her desk and floor, a memento of her father's outburst the evening before. It hadn't even been relative to the problem with the doctorbush oil, or anything to do with the monarchs...he'd simply been angry.

He'd been angry a lot lately.

She had stayed up all night, staring at the shards of her passion, eventually running out of tears to cry. Damari sneaked in with her food, though she ate little. He tended her injuries, tried to get her to sleep, but nothing helped. Not anymore. She'd eventually sent him away, not wanting the company.

King Stephan and Queen Larissa were dead.

The news had come only minutes before. Carina heard the guards speaking outside, and went to her door to listen. She wished she hadn't. She didn't want this. She didn't want to know.

The High Lords had been summoned to the capital palace, and Carina knew they would bring their armies with them. Her father would certainly be voted as steward until Lex was proved dead. She still held out hope that they could stop him. Or try to, if only to give her time to get away.

She had to get away.

There was a knock at the door.

"Come in."

"My lady," Adia said, "your things are loaded in the carriage. Your father said I could bring you down."

Carina stood on shaky legs. Without being asked, Adia helped support her. Outside, she kept her eyes on the ground as she walked, and climbed into the carriage. A fresh breeze from the mountains swept her hair back from her neck, but it brought no comfort. Her father stood on the back of the carriage, his knights gathered around the caravan. Carina could have moved to the window to see, but what would've been the point?

"My soldiers!" Valio cried, his strong voice carrying far. "I regret to tell you this news, but alas, it is my duty. Our beloved monarchs have fallen. Not to the illness that has beset them of late, but to an assassination."

Carina blinked. She moved to the window. What?

"In the dead of night," Valio said, "as the king and queen took their nightly walk, poisoned Medelian arrows were shot into their hearts. They died immediately, the Cures unable to heal them."

Carina's face went bloodless.

"I am off now to pay my respects to our late leaders. While there, the high lords of the council will vote a steward to rule until Prince Alexander's whereabouts can be confirmed. I do hope, that if I am to take that role you shall be as loyal to me there as you have been here. Spread the word, and join us at the palace within the week, to recognize the passing of great people, and ring in the rule of the new!"

Cries of support rang through the crowd of over two thousand lower lords, knights, and pages. Carina leaned back in her seat, a crease in her brow.

Through the opposite window Carina saw Damari loading a second carriage with trunks and bags. Their eyes met for a brief moment, sending her stomach into a knot of uncertainty. Then her father entered the carriage, blocking her view. The carriage began to move. She placed her hands in her lap and stared at the floor, days of silence ahead of her.

PART THREE

THE TARGET

They finally explained to me why they'd refused in the first place. He is dangerous, they said. He gets a thrill from hurting others.

32
LEX

Lex exchanged shouted bits of conversation with Angelina and Robyn as they continued north. They managed to climb the ridge, pass the cave they'd stayed in, and see that Glavan palace was empty save for servants who paid them no mind.

It was mid-afternoon of the sixth day, nearly halfway back to Galanis, when one of their scouts came back with an unsettling report.

"My lady!" the man shouted, running toward them.

Angelina reined in her horse and signaled the company to stop. "What is it?"

The scout leaned toward her and whispered, "Riders—from the capital." He gasped for breath. "They're wearing the royal crest—but, they're flying—Valio's banner."

Angelina's brow became stern, and she glanced at Lex and Robyn before she spoke. "Stay here with us," she told the scout.

"We don't want to cause an alarm. We'll meet them. How many?"

"Five, my lady," the man said.

Lex exchanged a look of worry with Angelina. Robyn leaned over and laid a hand on Lex's forearm, and he covered it with his own. That small reassurance of her presence made his heart warm. Neither spoke. Lex's muscles tightened beneath his scars.

They rode on, and after precisely seven and a half minutes the riders appeared. As the scout had said, they indeed wore the royal crest embossed on their black leather armor—the silver shield covered by a golden crown, with the Reganian crossed swords beneath it. And one of the riders bore a standard, raised on a long pole, depicting the Valio crest—a red banner with a black raven above crossed swords. Lex stopped his horse with the rest, pulling his hood low to avoid being seen. He realized his teeth were clenched, and tried to relax as the messengers approached.

The foremost among them addressed Angelina and said, "High Lady Angelina Belleci?"

"Yes," she answered.

The knight removed a scroll from his belt and opened it to read. "We regretfully inform you that King Stephan and Queen Larissa have passed on from this world. May their place in Vapris be assured and the Gods protect their souls. As our Prince is missing, it falls to the Lords of Regania to choose a Steward to rule in his stead until his whereabouts are confirmed. Please come to the palace with all haste to pay your final respects to our beloved late monarchs, and place your vote for our Steward. Sincerely, the High Priests of Regania."

What?

Lex was lost. Falling. It didn't make sense. His parents? Dead? It was a hoax, he was sure. Not real. Hadn't Carina and Damari been protecting them? Hadn't they promised the oil wouldn't harm them? He clenched the reins. His whole body tensed, and his shoulder cramped but he couldn't react.

A hand touched his arm. He didn't look to it. All he could do was stare at nothing, his brow furrowed, teeth grinding together, vision blurring with tears. If he moved, he would strangle these messengers. He had to stay calm. He heard Angelina's voice but couldn't hear the words. There were voices all around, but everything was muffled. Was he losing his hearing? It sounded like he was underwater. Like a part of him...didn't want to hear.

"—change course?"

"Yes. We'd wanted to check Valio's city first, but..."

"He'll be at the capital."

"Exactly. We'll stay here for the night. See if you can get him to eat and lie down."

The hand on his arm coaxed him from the horse. He swung his leg over and followed blindly. Robyn set him at the base of a tree, facing away from the main group. A blanket laid over him. Food was set on his lap. But he didn't eat. He sat, staring.

"Lex, you've got to eat something. At least drink some water."

Her voice was sweet. He obeyed. He drank and ate what she gave, but soon he threw it up. He knew these symptoms. Shock? He must be in shock. Something happened, and he didn't want to think about it. What had it been? It was too terrible. Before the sun was even down, he lay flat on the ground, staring up into the trees.

Dead?

Why?

His mother's face came into his mind's eye. He got his coloring from her; the golden hair, olive skin, dark blue eyes, all hers. He used to look into her eyes and tell her they looked like midnight. She would blush and tell him what a sweet little boy he was.

But he got his build from his father: slightly taller than average, no broad shoulders or thick arms to speak of—a scholar's body. Lex had never minded though. He certainly didn't now...not if his own image was all he had left of them, imperfect though it was.

Where were they? In Vapris, like the Vessels talked about? They wouldn't be sent to Muxai. They'd done too much good for that. Where was Vapris? Somewhere in the sky? Another land across the Western Sea? Or was it to the north? South? East? Could he follow, and find them? If only to apologize?

He was sorry.

His lip trembled. They hadn't even known he was trying to save them. Would they know now? Did it matter? They'd only wanted what they thought was best for him, and he'd deserted them. Didn't even say goodbye.

He couldn't sleep. It had been dark for five hours when a soft body cuddled up next to him beneath his blanket. He wrapped his arms around Robyn, cherishing her warmth.

"Lex," the sweet voice spoke again, "I'm so, so sorry."

His mistresses receive the worst...I can't write more.
It makes me ill to think of it.

33
CARINA

Carina walked the colonnades and porticos of the royal palace during the three days they waited for the high lords to arrive. It was an hour after dawn one day when Damari pulled her behind a tapestry where he'd found a hidden corridor. He drew her close in the darkness, hands tangling in her hair and clothes as he held her against the wall. His hips pressed into hers, his lips moving with too much force. Something was wrong.

She pushed him away to catch her breath, but his mouth did not pause. He moved to her neck, his hands trailing along her body in places she knew should be off-limits when they might easily be caught.

"Damari," she breathed, "what is it? Are you all right?"

"Carina," he said between kisses. "I am so much more than all right." He pulled away and put his hands to her face. "I have you." He kissed her mouth again hard.

With great effort, she pushed him away. "Damari, you've never been like this. What is it?"

He seemed only able to smile. "Nothing is wrong, why should anything be wrong?" He tried to kiss her again, but she kept him at a distance.

She stared at him.

His grin widened. "Yes, all right, everything is fine, but I do have something on my mind."

She raised her eyebrows, waiting.

He tried unsuccessfully to straighten his face. Then he cleared his throat and knelt in front of her.

Carina's eyes narrowed. "Damari…."

"Carina," he took both her hands in his, "I know I'm not nobility, and I don't have much, but—"

"Get up."

His face froze. "What?"

"I said, *get up*." She reached down to pull him up by his arms. When he stood, his face fell.

"But, I thought," he started.

"Damari," she said, taking his hands, trying to think how to word this so not to upset him. "I care about you, I do. But I'm not…not ready for marriage. Not yet. Maybe I would marry you someday. But the thought of it right now…it's too much.

She couldn't tell in the dim light but he seemed to be frowning.

"I am so grateful to have you here with me," she said, holding his hands. "And when this is all over, I'm going away, and maybe you can come with me. But for the sake of my sanity, I need to get through this first. Can you give me that? Time?"

He didn't react for a moment. It was like some part of him had been removed, his light snuffed out. Carina felt a chill run down her back, worry creeping in as Adia's words of warning echoed through her mind. But then, he nodded.

She squeezed his hands. "Thank you."

The palace courtyard was her favorite place. Fruit trees had bloomed and flowers were falling, casting petals across the ground where the wind whipped them around her with each step. She sat on a bench beneath a fig tree, considering taking a couple to eat, when she heard voices.

"Can you believe them?" It was a man, but he sounded young. A knight, perhaps?

"I honestly don't see a way around it," a second voice whispered, also a young man. "He's got more than three thousand knights loyal to him in the palace alone. Three thousand more in the city, and six thousand outside the walls, if the reports are right. We'd be trapped if we so much as tried. Not to mention he's got most of the lower clergy in his pocket, no matter what they might say to the contrary."

They were talking about her father. She stood and moved toward the voices, carried through a high wall of shrubbery.

"This is bad."

"But there's nothing we can do."

They fell silent, and she stood as still as possible, waiting for more.

"Do you think the prince will really come back?"

A sigh. "I hope he does, but I don't see how. Maybe it'd be better if he stays away for a while."

"Oliver says he'll come back. Nick too."

"Well, they know him best, maybe he will. But the royal guard is only a few thousand strong, and his other knights aren't gathered here. Valio and the other lords brought most of their forces, at least those who are loyal to them. That's what we're up against. At least fifteen thousand trained soldiers taking over the city. I don't see how the prince could get past that to make any difference."

Carina couldn't take it anymore. She walked away. So that was it, then. She'd be stuck here, trapped by her father's forces, to one day become queen of Regania.

A position she couldn't possibly want less.

As she entered the palace, her fists clenched in the folds of her skirts. There had to be a way to stop this.

Three days they'd been in the palace. Her father's allies were now present. Carina stood next to a window, the long drapes brushing against her best chiton of red satin trimmed in gold. She wasn't sure if she was meant to be here, in the King's council room, but no one had noticed her thus far, so she stayed.

Her father sat to the right of the head seat of the table, surrounded once again by his supporters. Before him, on a cushion of deep purple velvet, sat a small band of silver that served as the Steward's crown. She was only six feet behind him, and opposite her on the other side of the room, was her father's servant, Zivon. The Callidian stood relaxed but attentive. When their eyes met, he gave a slight smile.

The Master Vessels, gold stripes running down their sleeves to signify their positions as heads of their respective orders, stood around the empty chair at the head of the table. The Master Cure to the right in heavy robes of royal blue, a glass bowl of water held between his hands. Beside him stood the Master Shifter, a thin blonde woman in robes of deep green, who held a small olive branch freshly cut from the gardens. The Master Clarity stood left of the chair, wearing red and holding a rough chunk of granite in her thick hands. Lastly was the Master Virus, whose deep purple robes veiled and covered him entirely to allow him optimum access to shadows, the source of his power.

While the high lords chatted, waiting for the ceremony to begin, all four of the Master Vessels stood stiff and tense. And Carina knew: they didn't want to go through with this. These Masters surely knew what her father intended, but what could they do? They were outranked and outnumbered. Finally, the sun reached its peak and a beam of light shone through a hole in the ceiling. It fell directly onto the chair.

"King Stephan and Queen Larissa were beloved," the Master Cure said, his voice solemn. "For generations, the Galani family have ruled in peace and war, through famine and feasting, always thinking of the people before themselves. They would have wanted their son to take up their mantle, but…" he hesitated. "In his absence we are obliged to choose a steward.

This Steward will rule in the stead of Prince Alexander, until such time as he returns or is proved to have followed in his parents' wake." He paused, his eyes darting around. "It is...customary to have all ten High Lords present at this council—"

"However," Valio interrupted, "we have discussed that with the current unrest in Medelia, rumors of Fugeran spies infiltrating our kingdom, and the Somnurian's desires for an alliance, we cannot delay."

The Master Cure nodded, his face pale. "Yes, and now for the vote. If anyone would like to present a name for consideration, aside from your own, please do so now."

Lord Drako raised his hand and stood, his chair scraping the floor and making Carina flinch. "I would nominate High Lord Maximus Valio to the position of Steward. His leadership and drive to succeed will usher us into a grand new age." His eyes found Carina, and he raised an eyebrow to her. Bile rose in her throat.

Murmurs of approval came from around the table as Drako sat. The Cure waited a few moments, then said, "Would anyone else like to present a name?"

They collectively shook their heads.

"Anyone at all?"

Carina closed her eyes. He sounded desperate.

"Very well. Even though there is only one name, a majority is still required." He shuffled nervously. "All in favor of His Honor, High Lord Maximus Valio, taking the status of Steward in the absence of Prince Alexander, please show by the raise of your hand."

Seven hands raised. Unanimous.

The Master Cure swallowed hard, exchanging a worried look with his fellow Vessels. "So be it, then." He motioned for Valio to take the empty seat, where the sun shone bright on his black robes.

The Master Cure then set down his bowl, took up the small crown and, his hands shaking, lowered it onto Valio's head. One at a time, each of the Master Vessels knelt beside Carina's father and slipped a small amount of power into him from the sources they held. The water darkened, the olive branch wilted, the stone turned to dust, a small shadow...disappeared.

"By the power vested in us," the Master Cure said, "in the name of the Gods and their Creations, we proclaim you, Maximus Valio, Steward of the Reganian throne."

Carina curled in on herself slightly, trying to draw back, disappear into the curtains. How would Lex ever forgive her for letting this happen?

Then her father stood and surveyed the group. His gaze settled on the Vessels, who squared their shoulders and met his gaze, defiant.

"Master Cure, you say I am Steward and that we must confirm the prince's whereabouts before moving forward. But, has he not been missing long enough? Every spare soldier is searching for him. Surely, if he was alive and had a desire to return to the throne he'd have been found by now. Wouldn't you agree?"

Carina clenched her hands while the Vessels exchanged looks of worry. The Master Cure took a deep breath and put on a forced smile. "Not necessarily, my lord. Prince Alexander is very intelligent, he could easily hide from—"

"One moment, my friends," Valio said to the high lords. "Please, talk amongst yourselves."

Carina flinched as her father stepped toward the Vessels, right up to the Master Cure. They were equal in height and breadth, but her father seemed to tower over him in presence. She kept her eyes down, straining to hear.

"Do not make an enemy of me, Masters," Valio hissed to all of them. "You. Your sister's reputation is in danger should you deny me."

Carina looked up. The Master Shifter's face had gone pale. "H-how did you—"

"I make it my business to know secrets," Valio sneered. "And I know many for each of you. Now. You will crown me king, or I announce the shame of all your families to the world."

A moment of tense silence passed between the five of them. Then the Master Cure stepped forward to meet Valio's stance, a look of disdain twisting his features. "You will pay for this act, and these threats. The Gods will not stand for it."

"The Gods are no concern of mine." Valio turned from them and sat in his place at the head of the table. "As I said, Masters, wouldn't you agree that our dear prince has likely either run away for good, or been killed?"

"Yes, my lord," the four Vessels said. A chill ran down Carina's back at the monotone chanting sound of their voices together. It was obvious to anyone listening, that they did not approve.

Valio went on. "And therefore, shall we not crown a new king in his place?"

A moment of silence, then, "Of course, my lord."

Carina shuddered. Whatever her father knew about these families, it had to be horrific. Valio smiled. "How fortunate," he said, snapping his fingers, "that I already had my scribes write up the proper documents."

At the snap, Zivon turned to a side door and let in three scribes who carried ink, quill, and papers. When these were laid out, Valio gestured for the Master Vessels to come forward. They did, and one at a time each read the contract and signed it. Witnessing that they had allowed this to happen.

Carina shrank into the curtains.

As the last Vessel finished, her father stepped forward. "Friends," he said to the lords, "tomorrow morning I shall have my coronation. Please invite your families and armies to Galanis—oh wait, they're already here."

A chorus of deep chuckles met his words.

"Well, we shall have a celebration to remember. And that reminds me, we shall be changing the name of this city as well. Soon, Valios will be the name spoken of with the reverence and respect it deserves. My wax, please?"

The Master Shifter stepped forward. "My lord, this document requires a formal signature, not a seal."

Valio rolled his eyes, but did as told, leaning forward to sign his name at the bottom of the paper.

As he leaned away, Carina heard a sound from among the servants, as though someone had been punched in the gut...but none of their faces betrayed any emotion.

Her father stood. The scribes came forward and threw drying sand over the ink, cleaned up, and left the room. As the last stepped through the doorway, Zivon grabbed at his arm, gripping tightly. Carina stared at him. What had the poor man done to deserve such treatment? But suddenly as he had reached out, Zivon pulled back, his hand shaking.

The scribe hurried out, and Carina thought Zivon looked odd. His usual mask—for she could now tell it had been a mask—was cracked, revealing a stunned and confused man.

No one else in the room noticed anything amiss. As the lords stood and surrounded her father to offer congratulations, Carina stepped sideways and slipped through the door. Outside, she ran through passage after passage until she reached Damari's room in the servants' quarters. She pounded on his door until he answered.

"Carina? What is it?"

She shoved into the small room and paced in front of him, shaking as both fear and rage coursed through her. "My father, he," she shook her head, stopping to press it against his chest and cling to his shirt. "He's bullied the clergy into crowning him king! He's not going to be the steward, he's pushing Lex aside entirely!"

Damari pulled her close and tried to whisper, "It'll be all right, we'll figure it out."

She threw him off. "No! Aren't you listening? It's not all right, we can't let him do this! Think," she said, pacing again. "What can we do? How can we stop him? Alexander is the rightful heir, we need Alexander!"

"Lex?" Damari said, cringing. "Lex is no good to anyone. Just because he was born to the right parents doesn't mean he's what a prince should be."

She stopped and stared at him. "He is the prince! Our prince. Who better to stop my father than him?"

"Listen," Damari said, holding up his hands in surrender. "I have an idea I've been thinking about, but I can't tell you what it is yet. Give me a few days to see if it'll work. Then, if it doesn't, we'll try to get in touch with Lex. Agreed?"

Her eyes narrowed. "Damari you…why won't you tell me?"

"Because if I did, you'd want to help, and I can't let you do that. You might get hurt."

He ran a gentle hand down her arm.

"I'm only concerned for your safety, Carina."

She swallowed the argument she'd been about to make. Hesitant, she nodded. She cared about Damari; she trusted him. If he thought it was dangerous…. "Yes, all right. But we only have until tomorrow morning. My father's coronation is happening, and we have to do something before then."

He smiled. "I'll take care of it, I promise." Then he pulled her in for a hug again, and swooped down for a kiss.

When he pulled away, she left with a smile, but it didn't reach her eyes. The person she'd hoped to calm her had only heightened her anxiety.

I couldn't reconcile the man they spoke of
with the man who had lured me in.

34
ZIVON

No.

No...

No, no, no, NO.

"NO!"

Zivon finally reached the edge of the palace grounds, and crashed through the forest and underbrush of the mountain behind it. He couldn't have stayed in that room any longer. He'd gotten out as quickly as Mistress Carina, but for a very different reason.

He crumpled to his knees, leaning against a huge tree. Tears were already falling from his eye, the mountain air chilling them against his skin. His breaths came in gasps. Sobs racked his body, more pain flowing through him than he ever believed possible. He'd thought his threshold had been reached when Moriz died, when Zivon had discovered what he'd done. But this? This was infinitely worse.

Fingers shaking, he reached into his pocket for the note. The death order Moriz had carried out before trying to get away from the guild, before being killed himself.

Arianna Valio is near death. End her life. Enclosed, 500 gold crowns.

And the signature.

Maximus Valio.

Zivon could see it now. After Valio signed his name in the chamber and seeing it up close as the scribe left. The zig-zagged lines moving up and down, the single slash through the rest. Of course Valio would never have used his official seal on something like that, it would have been too easily traced. But his signature, the one thing rarely required of him, that, he could use. And that he did.

Maximus Valio had ordered his ailing wife to be killed? It made no sense. When Zivon had come offering service in recompense for Moriz's actions, Valio had seemed distraught.

Five years. Five years, Zivon had served this man in an effort to repay him. To somehow make up for what Valio had lost.

But he had lost nothing. He had disposed of it himself.

A waste. Zivon's service had been for nothing. All he had done was serve and help an evil man in evil deeds. Moriz's death was not avenged, and now Zivon carried a debt greater than any Callidia had ever known. He could never repay this.

That left only one option.

He would find Mistress Carina. Surely she knew nothing, was no accomplice to her own mother's death. Perhaps, if he spoke with her, they could find a way to stop her father. Carina, and the girl, the outlaw Robyn. And the prince, Alexander, with the missing eye. He had to find them, to apologize.

He'd thought, all these deaths, that he'd acted according to the will of the Powers. But it had been Valio's will, nothing more. Zivon could never gain forgiveness for his actions, but perhaps he could apologize to those he had hurt. Those, whose parents he had killed.

Valio could not be allowed to stay on the throne, could not be permitted to change or make laws, to lead this kingdom. Zivon would be the first to speak the fact that a man with that much blood on his hands should never be a king.

35
LEX

Lex didn't know how far they'd traveled since hearing the news, he had no idea how much farther they had to go. Only that it had been seventy-two hours of fog in his brain and an ache in his chest he couldn't relieve. He paid little attention to things like scenery, plants, life. His heart was painfully aware of the loss it had sustained. What if he let Valio kill him? Would he see his parents again? What would happen to the kingdom?

Nothing good.

The company was camped for the night. Someone said they should reach the river by tomorrow evening. Lex leaned against a tree on the edges of the firelight, ignoring the soreness in his scarred arm. Robyn perched above, watching, as she always did now. There was never a moment when he didn't feel her eyes on him. He knew she was worried about him. A few days ago he'd have given anything for her attention. Now, he only wished it hadn't come at such a terrible cost.

He hadn't spoken to anyone, not aside from crying himself to sleep on Robyn's shoulder each night. Something had changed about her. Before, she'd barely get close to him, and now she let him hold her as he fell asleep each night. It helped, finally having her in his arms. He wished he knew how long it would last; if it would last.

He looked up and caught her gaze. She tilted her head, so much like a bird, with a question in her eyes. He wanted to talk to her. To have her near, to be alone. Lex straightened, and motioned for her to follow him as he turned into the darkness, away from the rest of the company. He heard her hop down, and her soft footfalls as she caught up to him. When she did, her hand found his.

What changed?

She had a bag slung over one shoulder—one he'd seen her use many times while traveling. They stopped at a nearby stream and he lay down in the soft grass of the bank. She joined him wordlessly. He kept hold of her hand. If he let go, she might not let him take it again.

He ran his thumb across her knuckles and closed his eye, listening to the sounds of the river, the wind howling through the trees, cool against his scarred face. Small cracks and crinkles sounded in the trees nearby. The forest was a peaceful place. A place Lex had grown to love.

Robyn and her crew had a comfortable life here. They hadn't been forced to stop Valio. She'd done it because she knew he would put the kingdom in danger. She knew more about him than Lex thought was normal, and considering how nervous she'd been at Bellecia, he now guessed that Valio and his supporters were likely the only exposure to nobility she'd ever had. It was no wonder she hadn't trusted Lex at first. And in only a few short weeks, here she was lying beside him, holding his hand, giving him a lifeline.

He tightened his grip on her hand, gathering his courage. "Robyn?"

"Yes?"

"If I just stay here, in the forest...if I decide I don't want to do this...could I stay with you?"

She moved closer, laying her head on his good shoulder. "But you won't just stay here, Lex."

His eye closed at the pain in his heart. She was right. He couldn't *not* keep going. He wouldn't. His parents had given him everything they could, then he ran away from it all and left them to die. He knew it wasn't really his fault, but it felt that way. Now he had to make certain their deaths weren't in vain.

She sat up, leaning on her elbow, and laid a hand on his chest, sending a thrill through him. He turned to meet her gaze, grateful again that she was here.

"Listen to me," she said. "We gave our word that we would stop Valio. We didn't want him to succeed at anything, but now that he has he's more dangerous than ever. We have to get to him and fix this. We have to get you back on your throne and lock Valio away."

He sighed as she spoke. "You're right, of course. You're always right."

She put her hand on his cheek, and ran a finger across the skin beneath his scarred eye. With anyone else this might've bothered him, but this was Robyn. Her expression was one of sorrow and sympathy that had nothing to do with his appearance.

He lifted his hand to hers, leaning into her touch. She was so close, and the boundaries she had once had were seemingly gone. Lex's heart beat faster in his chest, and his gaze flicked to Robyn's lips, and back to her eyes.

"What about after?" he said.

"After what?"

"After all this. When we're done with Valio, everything's back to normal..." he trailed off, leaving his question unfinished.

Her hand slipped away. She turned to look out over the stream before them.

Lex forced a deep breath. That was answer enough. "I understand."

"Lex, let me explain."

"There's no need," he said, sitting up. "You've been through enough pain. You don't want to risk being hurt. I understand."

She sat up beside him. "Has anyone told you why I came to live in the forest three years ago?"

"I...no." He thought back over the conversations he'd had with her, Mitalo, Jianna. "No, Mitalo only said something happened, and you were forced to leave your home."

"Then you haven't heard the whole story."

His face fell.

"Here." She reached behind her, pulled a journal from her bag, and handed it to him.

He held it carefully. It was beaten and worn; the leather

scuffed in several places. He shook his head, handing it back. "I'm not going to read your journal, Robyn."

"Not even if I ask you to?" She didn't take it from his hands, but opened it and turned the pages. Her handwriting was messy, but legible. She stopped at a page near the middle, then looked him in the eye and said, "Please, read. But not out loud."

Lex gripped the book hard as he finished the entry, afraid he might tear it in two. He finally felt he understood her, what drove her to do as she had. Lex had never truly wanted to kill a man until this moment. Not only had Valio taken Lex's parents, but also Robyn's parents, her brother, and more. Her hopes, her innocence, her trust of the good things the world had to offer.... Lex closed his eye, focusing on the twinge of pain as his scars stretched. He set the journal down to keep from ripping it to shreds.

"He is a monster."

She said nothing.

"For what he took from you."

"From us." She slid her arm through his. "Lex, I hate Valio, I hated his man, I still do. For three years, all I've wanted was revenge. But now, seeing what he's done to you, I—" she paused, anger taking over her features. "I don't want it for myself anymore."

He laid his hand on hers. "I wish I could undo all of this."

"It doesn't get better," she said, "but I promise it gets easier to bear."

He nodded, squeezing her hands. "Thank you."

"To answer your earlier question," she said, "I can't say what will happen after all this is done. For three years I've been so worried about being fooled like that again...I've never been this close to anyone."

"You're scared."

She met his gaze. "Yes."

"I would be too."

They simply stared at each other for a moment. The silence was long, but comforting. Robyn ran her thumb across the back of his hand. The longing to lean forward and kiss her was more powerful than he'd ever felt.

"Robyn," he whispered. "I told you you'd be welcome at the palace, and I meant it. Now I've lost...well, I don't want to lose you too."

"I know," she said.

They returned to the camp hand in hand. And as he had the last few nights, he wrapped his arms around her, to wait for morning.

I was fifteen, eligible to marry in three months. I was being courted by a young man named Markus. He was handsome and kind, a friend of my brother's. I wouldn't say I had a grand connection to him, but I was content to marry him if it came about. One day, I came home to see a fine warhorse outside my home. I could hear shouting, and when my name was mentioned, I hid by a window to listen. My parents had received a proposal from the Lord of our land to take me as his mistress. His wife had recently passed away, and I had heard of him taking mistresses before. While it wasn't the marriage I'd always dreamed of, it was an opportunity few girls would get. I expected my parents to accept, but they did not. I didn't ask them about it, but sat conflicted as I watched the messenger ride away. A few days later, I was washing clothes in the stream nearby, when the High Lord himself approached me. He was respectful, very much a gentleman. He flattered me. I remember blushing, smiling; feeling, for the first time, a heat rise in my body. He made me feel like a grown woman. I see now how manipulative he was, tugging upon the emotions of an impressionable young girl. I was too inexperienced to understand what was happening. I stopped seeing Markus, stopped spending time with my best friends. My brother warned me about me. I told him I was fine. I thought I was. I tried to be in predictable places so that I could see the high lord. It wasn't long before I let him kiss me. How sweet it felt, though it sickens me now. When my sixteenth birthday came, I was ready to be with him. He asked me to come live at his palace, I told him I would send him my answer the next day. I went home and told my parents I wanted to accept. They were terrified. They finally explained to me why they'd refused in the first place. He is dangerous, they said. He gets a thrill from hurting others. His mistresses receive the worst... I can't write more, it makes me ill to think of it. I couldn't reconcile the man they spoke of with the man who had lured me in. Soon, however, they convinced me. We sent my refusal the next morning. I didn't see him at all that day, and went to sleep thinking he'd forgotten about me and moved on. How wrong I was. I woke in the night to my mother's screams. She shouted for me to run, to get away. Then her voice cut off. Ravin shoved my bow and quiver into my hands and told me to leave through the window. I tried, but a man entered before I could get out. "My Master summons you," he said. Ravin tried to fight him, but the man did not hesitate. I froze, watching my brother die in front of me. I tried to run, but the man grabbed me. My cheek was scratched in the chaos, but the most vivid memory I have is of something an arrow from the quiver I held and slamming the point into the man's eye.

I didn't see him at all that day, and went to sleep
thinking he'd forgotten about me and moved on.
How wrong I was.

36
CARINA

Her father was being crowned king. Carina stood to one side of the dais. He'd insisted she be there, going so far as to order brand new robes to be made the night before. The rosy-pink fabric itched at the shoulders and neck, and she fought to keep from scratching. Her neckline was loose, and fell far lower than she preferred. She felt like a caged animal, though no bars surrounded her.

To her left, her father knelt before the throne, while the four Master Vessels spoke in turn of his responsibility to the kingdom and the people. His face was bored. He sniffed; he wasn't listening. She twisted her hands in frustration. She'd meant to speak to Damari before now about his plan, but there hadn't been time. Whatever it was, it obviously hadn't worked.

The Master Clarity lowered the king's crown onto her father's head, then Valio stood and took his place on the dais.

"My people!" he said, smiling with distorted glee, "I humbly take upon myself this duty, and I look forward to many years of prosperity and joy! Let us begin them with a celebration and feast this day!"

The entire court shouted agreement, though many sounded forced. Then musicians, food, and drinks seemed to appear from nowhere. Carina backed away, hoping to sneak out one of the side exits.

"Lady Carina, would you care to dance?"

She turned to see a young man with his hand offered. He was tall—though not quite Damari's height—fair-haired, and had a bright smile that ended in a dimple.

"I, um...." She looked around for Damari but didn't find him. For now, she placed her hand in the young man's and forced a pleasant smile.

He led her out onto the floor and immediately began whisking her around. Then without warning, he drew her close and asked, "How do you feel about your father's new status, my lady?"

She blinked and stammered, even as he quickly backed away, giving her space. "I suppose..." She looked up at him. His eyes were shrewd, trying to tell her something. She leaned forward. "I think this is wrong."

The young knight smiled and pulled her closer. A mix of mint and saffron wafted off his clothing as he whispered in her ear. "My name is Nicholas. I am a friend to the prince, and I cannot believe he is dead. Forgive me, but your father has committed a crime today, and I hoped that you were innocent of the same."

She nodded, her cheek quite close to his chest. His hand on her waist held her steady as they spun. "Yes, I wish I could apologize for him, but he does not show an ounce of remorse."

Nicholas laughed, a deep quiet sound in his chest. "No, he doesn't seem the type. But not to worry, we'll think of something." As the music stopped between numbers, he stepped away from her and leaned down to kiss her hand. "I hope we speak again soon, my lady." Then he left, flashing a smile that said he was up to something clever.

She breathed a short laugh as he walked away, and found herself standing a little taller.

"Who was that?" Damari came up from behind her in a flurry.

She flushed, turning to face him. "One of the knights asking for a dance." She put her arms up for him to dance with her.

He danced well, to her surprise. "I didn't like seeing you with him, whoever he is."

A jolt of indignation shot through her. "Damari, you can't tell me who I am allowed to interact with."

"He's nobility," he hissed. "None of them can be trusted."

Carina stared at him. "*I* am nobility."

His eyes widened. "No, no, not you! You're different, Carina. You're not like the rest of them." He smiled nervously, looking her over. "You look lovely, by the way."

For not the first time since they'd met, she wanted to push him away. So she did. Shoving his shoulders, she strode toward a servant's door behind the thrones.

"Carina, wait!" Damari came to stop in front of her, blocking her path. "What did I do?"

She crossed her arms. She couldn't put it into words. It wasn't only his jealousy at Sir Nicholas. She stared at him. "Something is different about you, Damari. Ever since we got to the palace you've been acting…odd." Or had it been going on longer?

He frowned. "I…I'm not meaning to."

Behind, in the midst of the crowd, someone bellowed an awkward laugh.

"What about your promise? Did you find a way to stop my father? To reach Lex?"

He smiled. "I think so. Let's enjoy the celebration, and I'll tell you later."

She glared, shoving him aside and going straight to the rooms she'd been given here in the palace.

Whatever Damari had planned, she wasn't sure she wanted to know anymore. And she certainly couldn't sit in the throne room and watch her father a second longer.

That evening the throne room was empty save for Valio's men and a few of the royal guard. And, unlike during the coronation that morning, completely silent. Beams of setting sunlight filtered through the high windows as Carina walked down the center carpet, her shoulders back, head held high, and a tiny dagger in hand, hidden in the folds of her robes.

Her hands shook at her sides.

She wasn't even certain what she could do.

But she was done with not doing anything.

Reaching the throne, she knelt before her father. "You summoned me, your majesty?"

"I did," he said, standing. He wore robes of the finest red silk trimmed with black, the king's crown resting on his brow. He stepped down from the dais toward her. She stiffened.

"How may I be of service, my lord?" she asked without looking up.

She truly began to feel like prey as he circled her. "I've received word of a force," he began. "An enemy force within my own land meant to overthrow me. Do you know anything of this?"

Her initial shock was replaced by confusion. How could he know? She shook her head. "I don't, my lord."

He backhanded her face.

"DO NOT LIE TO ME!" His voice echoed throughout the hall, and every eye turned to see Carina's public humiliation.

She fell to the floor, her cheek stinging. She curled in on herself, gripping the dagger, trying to keep it hidden. A moment later, two sets of hands tucked under her arms and lifted her to her feet. Knights of the royal guard helped her up, one on either side. To her left was Nicholas. "Are you all right, my lady?"

She nodded. Fear kept her silent. Fear for herself, and for these men.

"And who are you?" her father's voice cut through to them.

The knights turned, and Nicholas spoke. "I am Nicholas Belleci, and this is Oliver Arena, sir. And I believe you have forgotten yourself, because that is no way to treat a lady of the Reganian court."

Valio laughed low as he spoke. "Oh, my dear sir Nicholas. This is no lady. She's nothing but a traitor."

Carina flinched at his voice, leaning more against the other knight, Oliver.

"My lord!" Nicholas's voice rang louder than before. "You will *not* insult this lady in such a manner!" Valio strode forward and landed a slap on the knight's face as well. But Nicholas stood his ground. He leaned forward to Valio and whispered, "I am sworn to the crown, not to you."

"My dear boy, I have the crown."

"Not rightfully. And mark my words, when Prince Alexander returns you will regret your actions."

Carina's mouth hung open. She'd never seen anyone stand up to her father like this. But it was short lived. Valio snapped his fingers, and his own men came forward. Nicholas and Oliver were surrounded.

They fought until they were restrained, and positioned behind Carina, forced to kneel on the ground. Guards came to Carina as well, taking her arms as though she might run.

She held the dagger against her chest, curled in on herself, as submissive as she'd ever appeared.

Her father came to stand next to her. "That's better," he whispered. "Now, Carina. I know you were lying to me, because my informant has been quite thorough in giving me every detail. Allow me to introduce you."

He waved a hand and from a side door was brought Damari. His hands were bound behind him, but otherwise he seemed unharmed. Then the truth hit Carina like a club.

"Damari?" she whispered.

He leaned forward, a blissful smile on his face. His eyes were wide and only for her. "Don't you see, Carina? We can leave. We can go away, like you wanted. Your father has what he wants now, and he'll never hurt you again. We can be married, he's promised me." His voice was so innocent, so sure, that Carina's heart broke for him.

Her father leaned forward to mutter in her ear, "Such a sweet boy, really."

Her head shook from side to side very slowly. "Damari...how could you? How could you do this?"

His face fell and he made to step toward her. A guard held him back. "But, I...I thought you'd be happy. We can be together now, Carina. You and me."

"Oh, no." She shook her head. "I can't go now, not while people are in danger."

His brows came together and his mouth opened like he might be sick. "You would...but...look what I've done for you. I'm the only one who's been there for you. Why would you choose them over me?"

She wanted to sink into the floor and hide away. He strained at the men holding him back, and a fear gripped her heart at the sight of him. She didn't know what to say. It was obvious to her now, Adia had been right all along.

Then, her father turned and leaned down to face her. "You really could do better than that, my dear."

She glared at him. Then struck out with her dagger.

She managed to slash once across his cheek, up and over his brow. She tried to bring the blade back down, but his hand gripped her wrist like a vice.

The entire room was still.

Her father's eyes were closed. Blood dripped from his brow, onto his cheek, and into his neat golden-grey beard. Slowly, he opened his eyes. They were hard and cold, filled with malice. His face and neck went red with rage.

As easily as she would've plucked a flower from its stem, he twisted her arm, sending the dagger to the floor. Carina screamed, and crumpled beside it.

Part of her registered him picking up her weapon, but she could only focus on the pain in her wrist.

"Bind her."

Her arms were yanked back roughly, and she struggled as men latched shackles onto her wrists, the pain from that twist still sharp. She wanted to shout to her father, ask for mercy, but she knew it was no good. She'd humiliated him, and now she would pay for it.

Out of the corner of her eye, she saw Damari trying to get free, held back by more guards. She thought she'd known him, but never would have predicted this. She didn't want him. Didn't want anyone. Couldn't trust anyone. More than ever, she wanted to run, but now she'd never get out. When the soldiers stepped away from her, she slumped under the weight of her bindings and stared up at her father.

He sat on the throne, leaning forward, one elbow perched on the armrest. "You will be tried for treason for that act. You are my daughter, and you are educated enough to understand my warning to act in your own best interest. This young man has already told me that the outlaw Robyn is in the force, and that there are likely troops from the other four lordships prepared to attack me. Now it takes nearly a week for a force this large to get here from those lordships, therefore they've been planning this for at least that long."

Carina let out a quiet breath of amazement. He didn't seem to know that Lex was with the approaching army. Damari had left that out.

"So I'll ask again," her father continued. "Will you tell me what you know of the army coming toward this city?"

She'd given the honest answer. She had guesses, but Robyn had never revealed the entire plan to her, there simply hadn't been an opportunity. Still…something in Carina's chest screamed to defy her father, even if it meant he killed her.

"No." Her reply rang through the grand hall. "But I will tell you this."

Her father sat back, a haughty brow raised. "Yes?"

She lifted her chin, and stared at him. "I helped them."

He watched her for a moment. Then shook his head. "It would be my luck that the moment you grow a backbone you turn against me."

Carina flinched. Somehow, that statement was more of a knife to her chest than anything he'd ever said to her.

"However," he went on. "I can appreciate defiance—even if it is from a traitor. I won't kill your friends yet, darling." He turned to the guards. "Take my foolish daughter and these three to the dungeons. Separate cells. I'll sentence them after this army is dealt with."

It took all of Carina's strength to keep her shoulders squared as her father watched her leave. They took her through a side door next to the thrones. The very spot where she'd stood that morning in her new uncomfortable chiton. She didn't fight anymore. Didn't want to hurt anyone else. Down a flight of narrow stone steps, and another staircase that zig-zagged deep into the mountains behind the capital.

Her shackles were removed. She was tossed into a cell, and locked inside. The place stank. The ground was covered in straw, and only a single cot stood in the space without any pillows and only a threadbare blanket, but at least it looked free of bugs. Now she scratched at her shoulders and neck, tearing at the offending fabric, trying not to scream.

She went to the door and, rising onto her toes, peered through the small barred opening. Across from her cell, she saw Nicholas's face in the window there. She opened her mouth to speak, but he shook his head and ducked. She followed his lead as more guards passed them from locking up Oliver and Damari.

Finally, a door slammed and silence fell. She peeked out again and made eye contact with Nicholas. "I'm so sorry, Sir Nicholas," she said, an ache forming in her chest. "I never—"

"Nick. Call me Nick," he said. "And it's not your fault. You did nothing wrong. It's your father who's mad. No offense meant."

She leaned her head against the door.

Nick whispered, "Don't worry. We'll get out of this, I promise."

She tried to smile, but couldn't. She nodded in parting to Nick, and turned away. Alone and cold, she lay on the small bed. She wrapped her arms around her chest for warmth, but could not sleep. They were all locked up in this dank dark place, unable to help their friends. And she couldn't help feeling it was her fault.

The cell was freezing cold. Carina wrapped the thin blanket around herself, trying not to smell it. She didn't know how much time had passed, but it couldn't have been long. She wished she had a window.

"No, my father already sent his men," Oliver said from his cell.

"And Liras?" Nick asked.

"I'm sure."

"If they made it to my place, I guarantee my family would come. I hope they're in that force."

"Me too," Oliver said.

"You like my family that much?" Nick said, a smile in his voice.

"Sure," Oliver said. "I mean, I practically grew up with you, right?"

"Uh huh. And there's not one particular person you're hoping to see?"

"Shut your mouth, Nick."

Nick laughed, and silence fell. It was some time before he said, "Lady? Lady Carina?"

She closed her eyes, not wanting to answer, but she did. "Yes?"

He cleared his throat. "You don't have to worry. We'll get out of—"

A loud clang sounded from down the corridor, cutting him off, and footsteps came near. When they stopped, Carina moved to peek out. A pale, dark-haired boy who looked fourteen or so stood at Nick's door and gave three quick knocks, followed by two slow ones.

"Enzi!" Nick shouted, his head popping up. The boy stumbled back, almost dropping the tray he held.

"Sleet, Nick, you scared me!"

"I keep telling you, En, weather terms are not swears."

"They are where I'm from, *sir*. Besides is 'sleet' really all that different from your 'muck' or 'life' or anything?"

"Not the same at all," Nick said. "So, I assume you have news?"

"Yes." Enzi handed Nick a piece of fruit. "Valio's called all forces in Galanis to prepare for battle. He has his own men and those of the other six lords who are here on his side. I'd wager he'll leave about two thousand in the city to outnumber the palace guard, but I'm sure he'll make the city guard fight, and that's two thousand more men. Altogether he'll have twelve thousand fighting soldiers."

"How many knights do the other lords have combined?" Carina asked.

Enzi spun toward her but Nick answered. "Less than that. Ten thousand if they're lucky. But it would take over a week to send messages to them and get them all here."

"But I just told you, that's exactly what Lex is doing," Oliver said. "A week ago, my father sent a carrier hawk to ask me about a message he got from Lex. Two outlaws had come to my parents and to Liras's asking for troops to march under Lex's command."

"It worked." Carina's hope began to rekindle. Then she sighed. "If we could only warn them that he knows they're coming."

"Where are they supposed to be?" Enzi asked.

Carina looked to Oliver.

He smiled. "The southern bend of the River Tardus."

Enzi nodded. "I can find them and warn them. I'll go tonight."

Carina felt anticipation rise, warming her heart. Then a thought occurred to her. "Enzi?"

"Yes, my lady?"

"Is there a standard for the king? Or armor? Anything that would help to show who Lex is?"

Enzi thought, but it was Oliver who answered. "Yes! In the armory. The king's banner for when he goes to battle. It's rolled up in the back corner of the shield room."

"Can you get to it?" she asked Enzi.

He nodded. "Of course."

"Take it with you to Lex. If he shows himself under that banner, with you at his side, maybe even in full armor, those knights will recognize him."

Enzi nodded. "I'll get the banner, my lady, and his leather armor that carries the royal crest."

Carina nodded. "Thank you. I think their survival might depend on your speed."

I woke in the night to my mother's screams.

37
LEX

They finally arrived at the river just after sunset on the twelfth day of their journey. Tired and sore though he was, Lex got a burst of adrenaline at seeing the forces of Liras and Arena already there, fires glowing in the dimming sunlight. Riding at the head of his own force as they approached the main camp, Lex, Robyn, and Angelina were met by Lord Arena and Lady Liras.

"Your highness," Lord Arena said as they both bowed low. "It's a relief to see you."

"And you as well," Lex said, trying to ignore the feeling of Robyn watching him. "How many soldiers do you have together?"

"Nine thousand, my lord," Lady Liras said.

Lex sighed. "That gives us twelve thousand total." He looked to Angelina. "Will that be enough?"

"Let's hope it is," she said.

"My lord," Lady Liras added, "your messengers have also infiltrated the city. Valio's taken over. He has all of his knights, plus many from his allies, all within the walls. They're threatening anyone who mentions your name or defies their orders."

Lex's teeth ground together. "How many?"

"Fifteen thousand at last count, sir," Lord Arena said.

Lex turned to Angelina again, and was surprised to see a smirk on her lips.

"You had the right idea, Lex," she said softly. "He won't send all of his forces out to fight us, but it should be enough to make a difference."

Robyn pushed her horse forward slightly. "Pardon me, lords and ladies, but could you tell me where to find my friends? They're the messengers who brought you the call to come here."

"Of course," Lord Arena said. "Mitalo and Jianna are camped on the edge of the force, to the west."

Robyn gave Lex a look, and he nodded. She turned her horse in the direction they'd said.

"If you'll excuse me," Lex said to his nobility. "I'll be back in a moment."

He caught a sly grin from Angelina before following behind Robyn.

When they found the siblings, Robyn practically leaped from her horse to hug them both, and Lex was shocked to feel a warmth grow in his chest at the sight of them. Jianna's smile was bright as she threw her arms around Robyn's waist, and Mitalo was as large as ever, though had a bandage around his shoulder.

Lex dismounted and approached, feeling oddly shy for some reason. "How long have you been here?"

"Only about four hours," Mitalo said. "How long until dawn?"

"Eight hours or so," Lex said, rolling his bad shoulder. His nerves were starting to get to him.

Mitalo nodded. "Good. The troops and the horses need rest. They marched with barely pause to sleep these last two weeks."

"Or bathe," Jianna said, running a hand through her matted hair.

"Now you know why I keep my hair short," Robyn said, smiling as she joined them.

"Look who's all bright and chipper," Jianna said. "Did you happen to find happiness on your travels, Lady Robyn?"

Robyn blushed slightly, her eyes flickering toward Lex which only made him blush as well.

"We have bad news, though," Mitalo said, frowning. "We sent scouts into Galanis to see what the situation was like."

"Arena told us," Lex said. "I'm hoping we'll have a strong enough force here to lure out at least some part of his army, maybe even him. If we can get him out of the city, we can capture him."

Nearby, above the bustle of the armies, someone began to shout.

"I need to talk to him, you don't understand. Let me go! Your highness! Prince Lex!"

Lex spun. Only one person ever addressed him with both his title and nickname. "Enzi!?"

"Lex!"

Lex couldn't believe it. Enzi was there, being held back by guards. As soon as Lex approached and lowered his hood, the guards finally recognized the prince they'd been traveling with. Lex waved a hand at them.

"So much for keeping my identity a secret."

Enzi grimaced. "Sorry, I didn't—"

"It's all right. Let him go," he said to the guards. They did, as Robyn appeared at Lex's side.

"I'm so glad you're safe," Enzi said, embracing Lex, who returned the gesture.

"And I'm glad for the same of you," Lex said.

"Who's this?" Robyn asked.

"Enzi, my manservant." Lex said. "And Enzi, this is Lady Robyn. She's...a friend."

Enzi smiled, then bowed to Robyn. "A pleasure, my lady."

Robyn looked to Lex. "I like him."

Lex smiled, glad of the playfulness. "So. How are things at the palace?"

"Not good, I'm afraid," Enzi said. "I came as fast as I could. I have a message for you from Lady Carina, and a warning."

"What is it?" Robyn asked.

Enzi let out a huff before saying, "It was Damari. He wanted to get Carina out, away from Valio. So he tried to strike a deal with him."

"What kind of deal?" Lex said, crossing his arms.

At the same time, Robyn asked, "What happened?"

"In exchange for Carina's freedom to marry and leave, Damari told Valio there was an army on the way to stop him. So...he knows you're coming."

330

Lex let out a breath and ran a hand through his hair. They'd been hoping for an element of surprise.

"Also…ah…" Enzi stammered.

"What?" Lex said. "There's more?"

Enzi nodded. "Valio tried to get more information out of Carina by threatening Damari's life. She gave him a little, told him she'd helped you, and he threw them both in the dungeons, along with Nick and Oliver."

They fell silent. Lex looked to Robyn first. Damari was one of her men. And along with sympathy, he saw frustration in her eyes.

"Does Valio know who's in the army?" Robyn asked. "Who's leading it?"

Enzi shrugged. "He knows it's the outer lords, but he doesn't know about Lex, I don't think."

"Let's keep it that way. We need all the advantage we can get." She turned to Lex. "And if we can prove to Valio's army that you're the prince, like you said, maybe they'll turn."

"Oh! I brought your banner," Enzi said.

"The royal standard?" Lex said in disbelief. "That's perfect."

"Also your armor. Both Carina's suggestions."

"I'm glad she thought of them," Lex said. "So Valio is expecting us, right? But he doesn't know when, or that I'm here?"

Enzi nodded. "That's my understanding."

"All right," Lex said. Perhaps there was still hope. "Is there any way you could get her out? Carina?"

"Maybe," Enzi said. He looked exhausted at the thought. "I'd have to hurry to do it before morning, but I think I could."

"Do it then, and you can rest as soon as you're done. I won't have you going into battle on no sleep." Lex said.

"Why not?" Enzi asked. "You will be, won't you?"

"Most likely; we'll get very little sleep tonight, yes," Robyn said. "Though I think we ought to encourage the soldiers to sleep for a few hours at least."

Lex nodded. "We should have time for that much. Thank you, Enzi. I'll inform the lords of the situation. Leave the armor and banner with me, and head back. If you can get Carina out tonight, do it."

She shouted for me to run, to get away.
Then her voice cut off.

38
CARINA

Carina lay on her cot in the darkness, a hesitant smile playing on her lips.

"Is it a person?" Nick shouted from his cell.

"No," Carina said.

"Animal?" Oliver asked.

"Of a sort, yes," she replied.

"Of a sort," Nick repeated. "You're making this harder than it should be."

"Insect?" Oliver asked.

"Yes!" Carina said.

Nick shouted. "What? Wait, does it have wings?"

"Yeeees," Carina said, dragging out the word.

"Yes," Nick said. "Aaahhhh…I don't know where to go from here."

"Colorful wings?" Oliver called.

"Yes!"

"Butterfly!" they both shouted.

"Correct!" she said, laughing.

"That was a good one," Oliver said. "All right, I think it's Nick's turn now."

"Finally," Nick said.

"It has to be something physical, though," Carina said. "Not an abstract concept, like justice or fear."

"You're ruining the game," Nick said.

The main door to the dungeons clanged as it unlocked from the outside, and Carina heard Nick and Oliver move back from their doors. Footsteps strode down the corridor, stopping in front of Carina's cell.

"Mistress?"

"Zivon?" Carina said, sitting up. Sure enough, the big Callidian man stared through her barred window, his face an expression of sadness. "What are you doing here?"

"A long story, that is," he said. "But I came to say…I am sorry. And I beg your forgiveness. I want to help you. I thought I was serving your father to repay a debt, but I discovered recently that he was the one…never mind. I want to help you. How can I help? Can I get you out?"

Carina went to the door. Behind Zivon, Nick and Oliver were watching.

"Zivon, I can't trust you." she said. "You have served my father faithfully for five years, never questioning his orders no matter what they were. Why now?"

He sighed. "The short version, then. Five years ago, my son was recruited into a guild of assassins, and his first job was an anonymous order to kill your ailing mother. When he completed the task, he asked to be released, but the guild said no, and killed him for questioning them. When I learned what happened, I collected the note, vowing to find out who gave the order to kill your mother. Vowing to meet them and ask why. Why my son.

"In the meantime, I went to your father to serve him, trying to make up for the loss of your mother. Then, yesterday morning, your father signed his name on those papers." He paused, looking shocked by the memory. "His signature was the one on the order, mistress. Your father ordered your mother killed. These five years I thought I was repaying a debt, instead I was only making the debt worse."

Carina's mouth hung open. Her father? Kill her mother? They had loved each other. And yet, hadn't he shown his mercilessness in killing the king and queen, and so many others with Zivon's hand? He may never have struck a killing blow— he always had others do his dirty work—but there was blood on his hands.

"How could he…" Anger swelled in her chest, stronger than she'd ever felt. Her hands gripped her skirts, and suddenly the last five years of her life seemed to click into place. She'd never been loved, only been used. She was a pawn to her father, nothing more. How had she not seen…

"Zivon?"

"Yes, mistress?"

"Do you know anything of my father's plans?"

"Not much," he said. "He plans to hold the city against attacks."

"You need to help Alexander," Carina said. "They will be coming to fight for the city soon, but if they have someone close to my father who can help—"

Zivon nodded. "I understand. I am that person, at least. How can I help if I am close to your father?"

"Poison?" Nick asked.

"He's too cautious to fall for anything like that," Carina said.

"Stab him," Oliver said.

"Maybe," Carina said. "But it would have to be at the right moment, or healers will get to him before he…" she trailed off. Was she truly talking so callously of murdering her own father? She shook her head. She had slashed his face with her own hand not hours before, had she not?

"Wait," Nick said. "What if you encourage him to fight? To leave the city?"

Carina blinked. Nodded. "Not necessarily him, he'd never risk his own life."

"I still think you should just stab him," Oliver muttered.

"Zivon," she said. "Could you encourage him to send his forces out?"

Zivon considered this. "A word or two is all it would take. And this will help?"

"I hope so," Carina said. "It will keep the citizens safe from the fighting, at least."

"Consider it done," Zivon said. "I will encourage him to be ready for any eventuality, even sending his men out of the city walls."

"And Zivon?"

"Yes, mistress?"

Carina squared her shoulders, a shiver running down her back. "You have my forgiveness. If you get a chance to kill him, I give you my blessing to do it."

Zivon gave a solemn bow in that special way of his, and without another word he left, shouting to the guards outside in an effort to seem angry. A distraction from his actual purpose. Carina forced a smile, trying not to think about her father, and how similarly ruthless she had just been.

Carina slept a little, but lay awake most of the night. It had been hours since Zivon's visit when the clang of the dungeon door sounded and someone came toward them. She moved to the back of her cell as a key played in the lock.

Enzi's head poked through.

"What're you—"

"Shhh, no time," he said. His eyes were red and he looked exhausted. "Lex and the others are fine. Come on, come with me."

She came into the corridor and waited as he opened the cells of Nick and Oliver before he whispered, "This way," and began to lead them away from the posted guards.

"Carina!"

She paused, turning back.

Damari peered through the opening of his cell. Carina cursed herself. She had forgotten he was even there. He hadn't spoken since they'd been brought down here.

"Lady Carina?" Enzi said. "Would you like me to bring him?"

She looked from him to Damari, to Oliver and Nick. Why was this *her* choice?

She knew the answer to that, however.

"Carina," Damari said again. "Please. You can't leave me here. I was only trying to help you."

Her hands curled into fists at his words. "Help me?" she asked. "By betraying the people I promised to help?"

"I told you," he said, his voice desperate. "I was only concerned with helping you."

"Then you don't know me like you thought you did," she said. "You can stay here. Lex can put you on trial for what you've done."

The expression on his face was pure shock. And as she walked away, Carina wondered whether he would shout, scream, alert the guards so that she wouldn't be able to escape....

He did nothing.

And for that, at least, she was grateful.

Enzi directed them farther down the tunnel of cells, opposite from the guarded entrance. Carina lost track of their movement as, turn after turn, he led them through the dim maze. Before long, her sandaled feet were cold and wet, sloshing through a thin layer of water, and the skirt of her chiton stuck to her legs. The stale, stagnant scent made her gag. She held a hand over her nose and mouth, but it did little to help.

TARGET

When she thought she would suffocate from the stench of decay, she saw a glow of light ahead of them. They'd ended up in some kind of drainage conduit. The opening, a grate in the ceiling above them, was secured by a padlock that looked much newer than the rest of the metal.

Enzi turned to Nick and said, "I'm too short, would you mind?" and handed over a key.

Nick reached up and unlocked the grate. He swung it upward and put his hands together, offering them to Enzi as a boost.

"What a gentleman," Enzi said.

Nick smiled. "It's what I do."

"I'll say." The smaller boy put a foot in Nick's hands and two hands on his shoulders. With a hop, Enzi was propelled upward and out of the tunnel.

"Don't let Andre hear you flirting with me," Nick said, grinning.

"Have you seen you? He'd do the same!" Enzi said, laughing.

"Next?" Nick said to Carina, offering his hands.

"What? You'll see up my robes!"

Oliver laughed. "Here, Nick, you go up first, I'll boost her."

Carina frowned as Nick took the boost and rose out of the opening.

"Why—"

"I have a boyfriend," Oliver murmured. "I promise I won't peek."

"You have a *what?*" Nick shouted down at them.

339

Carina flushed, noticing Oliver was as well, and she smiled as he gave her a boost, and Nick took her hand to pull her out, offering her a smirk before turning back to Oliver.

"Who's your boyfriend, Oliver?"

"Shut up, Nick."

Nick reached down to pull Oliver up, and Carina looked around. They'd come out in some part of the outlying forest. She could see the city walls a hundred yards in the distance. "How far does that tunnel go?"

Enzi shrugged. "I've never checked, but it hasn't been guarded for years. Anyone who tries to go in that way just meets guards. Come on, we've got to go."

He ran and they followed. Carina kept tripping on her skirts, twigs and leaves getting caught in it.

Nick noticed, and came to her. "Want a ride?" he said, holding out his arms. She paused, and without a struggle he picked her up, cradling her. A blush was surely coloring her cheeks, but she didn't complain. They did need to hurry, and it was much warmer in Nick's arms. They continued for another few minutes before Enzi stopped them by a group of horses. Nick set Carina on one of them, not bothering to set her on the ground.

"You all right?" he asked.

She met his gaze for a moment, and smiled. "Yes, thank you."

He gave a little nod before turning to mount a horse of his own.

Enzi pulled his mount in front of them. He rubbed his eyes and shook his head. "It's a short ride. We'll make it in an hour if we hurry. Stay close, keep me in sight."

The sky to the east was just beginning to lighten when Enzi pulled them to a stop near the wide and shallow River Tardus. The opposite bank had a rocky beach backed by huge boulders rising up thirty feet, like a cliff. They waded the horses across and were met by Robyn, Lex, and Robyn's two comrades whose names Carina couldn't remember.

The grin on Lex's face at seeing Nick and Oliver was almost childlike in its innocence. The three greeted each other with sobered embraces. Happy to meet, but knowing what was to come. There was something different about him, though. Carina stared for a moment and realized he wasn't wearing his eye patch. The skin that had covered over his left eye had the same texture as the rest of his scars.

A chill wind blew, and Carina wrapped her arms around her middle. She went to Robyn and said, "Hello."

"Hello, Carina," the taller girl said, looking around. "Did Damari come with you?"

Carina shook her head. "We left him in the dungeons. My intention was that...well, assuming Alexander wins, then Damari will be put on trial."

Robyn sighed. "I see. Well. Are you all right?"

Carina nodded, not trusting herself to speak more.

"Come," Robyn said. "Around behind these rocks. Lex!" she shouted. At her voice, he turned, a smile lighting up his face. Robyn said, "Bring them through."

"Yes, right. Come, this way," he rolled his shoulder and waved to his friends, then led everyone through a fissure in the rocks. Carina ran her hand along the stone as they passed beneath the cliffs. The solidity calmed her.

The tunnel opened on the other side to a meadow surrounded by trees. Fires dotted the ground, and Carina shivered. She wasn't very good at estimating numbers and sizes, but this was an awful lot of soldiers. Maybe Lex might have a chance.

A squeal rose up from the darkness and a blonde boy around Carina's age was running toward them. Nick came forward, arms extended, but the boy flew past him and into Oliver's arms, knocking him to the ground. Nick looked around to see them kissing, and turned away, rolling his eyes and muttering.

Robyn and Lex led the group to a large tent at the edge of the clearing. Ducking under the flap, Carina's eyes widened at the sight of a long table covered with a map, daggers holding down the corners. Lantern light shone from above, throwing shadows, making the space feel smaller than it was. A tall woman with greying golden hair leaned forward with both hands on the table, a crease in her brow.

"Mother," Nick said.

Lady Belleci looked up and smiled with relief, embracing her son.

Carina's heart ached at the sight, along with a small pang of jealousy that she quickly shoved aside.

As they surrounded the table, Lex called for their attention. "We've already divided the troops. Four thousand each to the east and west lining up north of the river." He pointed on the map. "The final third is divided again into one thousand of our best archers," he looked to Robyn, "and three thousand of our fastest runners. The archers will hide themselves among these rocks while Angelina leads the runners to the city walls to mount an attack. As soon as we have them following us, we'll lead them back here and stop. I'll show myself and call for them to change sides, followed by my personal challenge to duel Valio if he's there."

"Lex," Oliver said. "All due respect, but you'd lose that fight."

"That's what I told him," Robyn said, her arms crossed.

"It doesn't matter," Lex said, frustrated. "The goal is to get him out. He'll come, and I'll fight him. If Robyn gets a clear shot, she'll take it. And if I pretend to be weaker than I really am, maybe he'll get over-confident and I'll get a chance to take him."

Carina shook her head. "I'm sorry, your highness. My father is a great swordsman, yes, and he's also a coward. I doubt he'll come. He's more likely to send someone in his stead."

"Even better!" Lex said. "They'll see it's me and change sides, right?"

"Not all of them," Carina said. "He's promised land and gold to his followers, and those living under his allies are just as loyal, or afraid. The desperate ones will stay true to him."

Lex pressed his hands to his head. "Do you have any suggestions, Carina?"

She blinked, surprised he was asking her. "I didn't say it was a bad plan. I only wished to warn you that the entire army won't switch sides. You'll still have a battle ahead."

The air around them grew heavy. Carina shivered.

Lex sighed. "Well, whether the champions' duel happens or not, we will not go down without a fight."

"Cavalry?" Oliver asked.

"Not using horses," Lex said, shaking his head. "They'd only get in the way in those trees. We'll have swords and spears on foot, and whatever the archers can do from above. Once I've revealed myself and the fighting begins, the forces to the east and west will hit their flanks, taking some of the pressure off of our central force. Any questions?"

Carina looked up at Lex. "One thing," she said. "My father has a servant, Zivon. He has...done many terrible things in my father's name."

"The Callidian?" Robyn asked, eyes narrowing.

"Yes," Carina said. "Before we got out, he came to me to ask for forgiveness and offer his help. He is close to my father, and trusted explicitly. I believe he is being honest. He is there, in the palace, ready to help if you need him."

Robyn frowned, exchanging a look with Lex that Carina couldn't read.

"Thank you, Carina," Lex said. "Any ally is worth considering at this point."

A moment of silence passed, heavy with anticipation, and a hint of dread at what they were about to do. Then Lady Belleci spoke. "Well, that's that. Everyone into positions, runners march for Galanis in half an hour."

Carina stood still as everyone filed out of the tent. She was ready now. She had to tell them.

"Lady Carina?" She turned to see Nick next to her. He held out a sword. "I heard you are talented with the sword. Would you care to spar?"

His easy nature, his kindness, and that dimple of his made her smile. But she didn't take the weapon. "I'm afraid I can't."

"Why not?" he asked, his brow furrowed.

She didn't answer him. "Can you go get Robyn and Alexander?"

He backed out and called for them. When they came in, Carina straightened her shoulders, reminding herself she was among friends. Or, as close as she'd ever come to friends. She took a deep breath.

"I need to go."

"What?" the three of them said together.

"I can't stay here," she said. "I've wanted to leave for a long time—longer than I think I even knew—but I was too afraid of my father. I thought for a while I would leave with Damari, but..."

"He wasn't good enough for you," Nick said.

"That's not what I was going to say."

"Doesn't make it wrong," he said.

"Nick, come on," Lex said.

"Are you sure?" Robyn asked, stepping forward. "If we succeed here you won't have to worry about your father ever again. You could live in peace at your home."

"You don't even have to fight if you don't want to," Lex said. "Stay here. We'll send word if the battle goes badly and you can leave then if you wish."

Carina hesitated and stared at the ground. She could feel their eyes on her. She shook her head and looked up. "No," she said. "I've been hurt here, by more than just my father, and I…I need to start over." For some reason, she looked to Nick. His smile was back, and his eyes were bright. He gave a short nod, and she took it to mean, *you'll be all right.*

"Well, then," Lex said. "Despite leaving, you will retain your title, Lady Carina Valio. Your father might have committed treason, but you are innocent of his crimes. As prince, I—"

"As king," Robyn corrected.

Lex blinked. "Yes, as king I will make it official. You are Reganian nobility, no matter where you choose to live out the rest of your life."

"Thank you," Carina said. "Please give my lands to a worthy person. I don't want to stay there anymore."

"I will see it done."

Carina nodded.

"If you're sure, we'll give you the best chance we can," Robyn said. "You'll take one of the strongest horses, we'll give you everything you can carry for supplies, and a map…in case you decide to come back."

Carina nodded. "Again, thank you."

As they helped her get ready, however, Carina knew she wouldn't return. This place held nothing for her, and she wanted nothing more to do with it.

Ravin shoved my bow and quiver into my hands
and told me to leave through the window.

39
LEX

Lex watched Carina ride south, into the trees at the edge of their clearing, as the rising sun began to turn the sky pink and yellow with its coming. It was harder than he thought it would be, watching her go. When she was out of sight, he turned his back on the trees and found Robyn nearby staring at the same spot. Their eyes met.

"Robyn." He wrapped an arm around her shoulders and brought her to him slowly, giving her every chance to pull away. She did not. He held her for a moment before he felt her arms wind around his waist, and her head rest in the crook of his neck.

His face went warm, his whole body on edge. His textbooks had never mentioned anything about this.

After a moment, he pulled back to look at her face. Her trademark firm resolve was gone, and she looked like she'd seen a ghost.

"What is it?" he asked.

She shook her head, then turned and walked away.

He watched her go, not wanting her to. Wanting anything else to happen, anything but her walking away. He reached out and touched her arm.

"I could love you," he said.

She met his gaze, her expression stoic.

He felt a pinch in his chest that had nothing to do with his scars. "I could. I want to. And I'd be good at it. I mean…I think I could make you happy. And I want to, but…only if you want that."

Still, she did not move.

The pain in his chest deepened. Like a hole had appeared in his heart that could never be filled. He took a deep breath and swallowed hard. He nodded, understanding her silence, and walked past her toward the rocks. Maybe he would never marry. Never truly love. Maybe he would have been better off staying at the palace all those weeks ago.

No. He'd do it all again to have met her.

A cry rang out from atop the rocks, "Soldiers! Positions!"

Lex pushed his feelings to the back of his mind and crowded through the gap with the knights who remained, his muscles begging him to stop. Troops were running to get into position, and Lex ran north, crossing the river to the head of the central force.

Nick was there already, with Mitalo and Jianna, all in riding robes and trousers, around them the knights' leather armor was polished to shine in the sunlight. Angelina Belleci stood atop a huge boulder to their right, the rising sun behind her, creating a dramatic scene for the soldiers below as she addressed the company.

"Loyal Reganians! This day we march to Galanis under the orders of your prince, the rightful king! Our aim is not to damage our beloved capitol, but to threaten and bait those who have taken it. If we play the part well, Valio's army will follow us. We must make it back to the river before they attack. You must be prepared to run, and fight. Are you ready?"

"YES!"

The quick response gave Lex chills. All these soldiers were loyal to him. His chest puffed up in pride, before he deflated. Some of these soldiers would die today, but he hoped they understood why he asked this of them. He was sure that if left alone, Valio would run the kingdom into the ground. And in honor of his parents, Lex would do everything in his power to keep that from happening.

He followed as Angelina led the force north in an easy jog, feeling for the Amplia carving in his pocket. Robyn had made sure he had it earlier, and he was glad. He would've completely forgotten about it otherwise. They stopped a hundred paces south of the city wall, staying hidden in the forest. Lex's breaths came fast and short, and his muscles burned already.

The city of Galanis was glorious, its many levels rising up against the mountains behind, the clean bright buildings almost shimmering in the early sunlight. And with it in view Lex was surprised how much he missed it, a sudden longing caught in his chest.

I wish Robyn could see this.

349

"Split into groups of twenty and spread out," Angelina called out. "Attack as soon as you reach the city walls. Arrows, rocks, whatever you can to make them take us seriously. Go!"

As one, the soldiers of Regania did as she said. Lex kept himself hidden, not wanting to be spotted by Valio's force. Footsteps came up beside him, and he turned to see Mitalo and Jianna.

"You all right? Attacking your own sweet city and all?" Jianna asked.

Lex frowned. "I don't like it, but it's the best plan we've got."

"They'd better hurry and retaliate or I'll shoot down every muckin' lookout myself," Mitalo said. He and Jianna pulled longbows from the quivers on their backs and strung them.

"Try to avoid killing, please?" Lex said.

Mitalo and Jianna both stared at him, offended.

"We may not be as perfect a shot as Robyn," Jianna said.

"But we're a damn sight better than most," Mitalo finished.

They each took a shot, hitting soldiers on the walls in an arm or leg, adding to the chaos.

Most of Lex's forces were already attacking the walls at various points along it. Arrows from their bows and rocks from their slings as Angelina had commanded, and Lex saw someone chopping down a tree for a battering ram. Hopefully they wouldn't have to actually use it, but it would make a good show.

Then Lex noticed a thin young man weaving through the ranks, wearing the tattered blue robes of a High Cure. He looked familiar, and Lex stared as he came near.

"Highness," the man said with a nod and a wide smile. "Good to see you again."

"We've met," Lex said.

The Cure grinned. "You gave me a pregnant mare, and I gave you a not-pregnant one in exchange. Great deal for me."

Lex's jaw dropped. "What are you doing here?"

His clouded grey eyes seemed to shift as Lex watched. "I'm here to help. You still have that wood carving?"

"It *was* you! I—"

"Ah, just make sure you keep it with you, okay? Use it if you need it."

Lex shook his head. "What do you mean—"

"Look, it's a lot of power! Use it! Now get your people out of here. They're coming!" As quickly as he'd appeared, he ran off again.

"Who was that?" Mitalo asked.

Lex started to answer, but the alarm was raised inside the walls, and soon arrows rained down on those between the forest and the city. Lex grimaced in pain every time he saw a soldier fall, feeling the shots as though they'd hit his own body.

With that retaliation, Angelina ordered a retreat into the shelter of the trees, and the remaining fighters moved away. From there, they continued slinging stones and shooting arrows at the southern wall. Lex could hear shouting and bells from inside the city, and he was sure they were on the way out. When the mechanisms of the gate began to creak, Lex shouted to Angelina.

"Now! We have to run now!"

"Retreat!" Angelina cried.

All three thousand soldiers turned and sprinted southward. Lex pumped his arms and legs as hard as he could. His throat went dry, and his chest ached from the exertion. All around him his followers fled for their lives as hoof beats pounded the ground behind them.

Lex's heart fell. Horses. Hopefully the trees would slow them down.

Still, his small section of army ran on, tripping and stumbling on the uneven ground as they went. Shouts of pain or panic rang out around him. Lex flinched as his face was scratched by a tree branch. He clenched his jaw and pressed himself harder. He'd never run like this before, and wasn't sure how much longer he'd last. Then he saw the tower of rocks, on top of which stood Robyn and the archers. They took cover quickly as Lex and the army came into view.

He bolted through the trees until he reached the river, then ran across the shallowest point. Pulling his hood up to shade his face, he climbed—his left arm was useless now—to the rock he'd chosen earlier. It jutted out into the river, putting him in plain sight to anyone coming from the north. Here, he would meet this force as its leader.

As the last of his soldiers crossed the river and gathered against the rocks, the line of horses paused on the opposite bank. In the lead were six richly-dressed men sitting straight and proud on massive steeds. Lex recognized the high lords, but Valio himself was nowhere to be seen. He chanced a look back at the cliffs and saw Robyn scanning the line of men. She slumped and met his gaze, shaking her head.

Lex swore under his breath. Valio hadn't come, and he'd sent an army in his stead.

Coward. Like Carina had warned.

But Lex didn't have time to think. He had to turn the men against these lords. He waved to Enzi, who waited off to his right with the king's banner.

It was now or never.

Enzi came forward, and Lex removed his hood. A collective gasp rolled over the opposite bank as they realized who they were seeing. Lex's name and title were whispered through the ranks. He was content to wait for silence. When it came, he raised his voice into the dawn, and it carried across the river.

"Knights and soldiers of Regania. I am your prince, and rightful king. These men have lied to you under the direction of Maximus Valio, seeking to take power they have not earned. They worked in secret to kill my parents," his voice broke, but came back with more force, "and now they seek to kill me. The last thing I want is to lose honorable knights from the royal army. I offer you now the chance to surrender, or come fight under the king's banner."

"He lies!" One of the lords shouted, pointing a sword. Lex recognized Hector Drako's yellow and black crest on his tunic. "King Maximus has been nothing but generous and merciful to all of you! Our prince has been brainwashed by the outlaws and traitors we see surrounding him!"

"I've not been brainwashed!" Lex shouted back. He cursed himself for the childish retort. "I hereby challenge the traitor

Maximus Valio to a duel for the crown! If he's so confident in his position, let him come forward!"

Silence, but for the shuffling of a few men behind the six lords. Drako rode forward into the water. "*King* Maximus has business at the palace! Business that you should have been seeing to, until you ran away and deserted your position. You're a traitor to the crown for your actions!"

Lex flinched at the accusation.

The men on both sides of the river grew restless. Above him, he heard a bowstring pull back. *Robyn.*

"You speak falsehoods," Lex said, trying to keep his voice loud, but calm. "I have traveled the kingdom, and I now return to my city to find it against me? I say again to all of you: join me. Fight for me against Valio and his selfish whims. Those who do not will be punished for their actions."

"You have no power to make such statements!" Drako said, his face going red with anger. "It's obvious to me, and to anyone with sense: you've been bribed or threatened to be standing where you are, and you are unfit to wear the crown! We show no mercy! ATTACK!"

Like two waves, the soldiers on either side of the river surged forward and met in the shallow center, churned white water going everywhere. Lex looked to Robyn and nodded. She signaled her archers at the far east and west of the rocks, and two arrows with red ribbons trailing behind them were shot into the sky. At that signal, the other sections of the force would pull in to attack the flanks.

Lex slid down the rock to land in the river, sword out and swinging before he even registered lifting it. He saw arrows land in men all around him. Soon, the six lords who had led the charge were fallen, multiple shafts in their chests and necks. The sight made Lex sick.

Lex engaged a soldier who wore Valio's colors. The man growled as he came, swinging his sword through the air. Lex blocked, and spun the blade to throw him off balance. He ducked under another attack, took hold of the man's arm, and flipped him over his back. Once he was on the ground, Lex stabbed him in the chest.

He wanted to feel sorry for the kill, but there wasn't time.

Another attacker came toward him. He went for the arms and legs as much as possible. He managed to get one man subdued, but it wasn't long before the next was upon him. There was always another. He fought until his arms might fall off, his scarred muscles screaming for rest. Facing two men at once, he had a moment of fear. His thoughts froze. His throat tightened even as he swung his blade with abandon. How stupid was he to fight in a battle? Hadn't he learned he wasn't good enough for this?

Then arrows landed in each man, one after the other. He turned to the cliff, and saw Robyn meet his eye with a nod before she shot in another direction.

And that's four.

A roar from his left made him turn. Mitalo fought one man, and Jianna two. Lex spun toward his friends, taking down Mitalo's opponent from behind with a blow to his head. The two of them worked their way toward Jianna, pressing their backs together to keep their enemies in sight. Lex could see Nick and Oliver fighting nearby with the same strategy.

He was bumped from his right. He fought off his attackers and turned to see Jianna again taking on two new men. As Lex made to step forward, a spear came from above the soldiers' heads, straight for Jianna.

No.

Mitalo dove in front of his sister. The spear embedded in his torso.

"NO!" Lex shouted.

Mitalo—huge, imposing Mitalo, a man more alive than anyone Lex had ever met—fell to the ground. His hand clutched the staff, connected to a blade, that went through his chest. Lex ran to him. He could help him. He had the carving, all that power, he—

"MITALO!"

The cry came from above. Lex turned to see Robyn stare at her friend, raw pain clear in her features, before she moved to climb down the rock face. Lex swore.

"Robyn!" he shouted, but his cry was lost in the noise around him. He tried to get to Mitalo, but soldier after soldier stepped in front of him. Lex clenched his teeth, watching Jianna and another drag Mitalo's body out of the fighting.

Lex dug for the trinket in his pocket, feeling Life magic flow into him at the contact, strengthening him. Mitalo needed this, now.

"Robyn! NO!" Jianna shouted.

Lex looked up to see Robyn hopping from boulder to boulder. Her double swords were out and slashing as she spun past each attacker. A double swipe to a man's chest, and she looked up, meeting Lex's gaze.

An arrow whipped past her face, then someone behind fell into her, knocking her down the rest of the slope and into the mass of fighters, out of sight. Her voice cried out at the same time Lex flew forward. Time slowed as he ran, pushing men aside, not caring who he shoved. Where was she? She had to be okay. He had to get to her.

A hand clamped down on his shoulder, pulling him back. "ROBYN!"

But his shout was cut off. Another hand yanked his hair, pulling his head backward. He screamed in pain as a blade bit into his side, and his hand released the carving it held. A cloth was shoved into his mouth as the magic drained from him, and a dark sack was shoved over his head, sending him into darkness.

I tried, but a man entered before I could get out.
"My master summons you," he said.

40
ROBYN

Pain.

Robyn pressed a hand to her head to soothe the ache. When she tried to sit up, she collapsed back. Her ankle throbbed. She opened her eyes, blinking off the midday sunlight, and took in the damage. She found her left ankle sprained and a few bruises here and there, but otherwise, miraculously, she was unharmed.

She sat up and looked around. The fighting was over. Valio's forces must have either retreated or surrendered. Bodies littered the ground, the river dark with dirt, the sharp smell of blood hung in the air like a hanged man.

"Robyn!"

She turned to see someone coming toward her. It was Millia, the Belleci's oldest daughter, carrying a pack over her shoulder.

"Are you all right?"

"My ankle…" Robyn said.

Millia took a look at the lump, poking it and wincing when Robyn flinched away. "That's going to need a few weeks to heal. We ought to put ice on it, but I don't think we have any. Would a wet rag do? The river is fairly cold."

Robyn waved her off. "It's not that bad."

Millia gave her some water to drink, and that helped clear her head.

"They're getting ready to leave," Millia said. "I told them to wait until I found you, but we have to hurry."

"Who?"

"The others, everyone. They're going to get Lex. Take back the palace."

Robyn shook her head. "Lex? What happened to Lex?"

Millia's face paled. "They...Valio's men, they took him. I was watching from the cliff, they stabbed him and put a sack over his head, then dragged him off."

Rage built in Robyn's chest. If she ever found out who those men were.... She would go with Lex's friends, Oliver, Nick, and the others. She would take Jianna and Mitalo to—

Mitalo.

"Where is he?"

Millia frowned. "Lex? But I—"

"No, Mitalo." Robyn stood, unstable on her feet but determined. Millia ducked under one arm and helped her walk, but she didn't have to go far.

The spear she'd seen enter him was gone, a dark stain in its place. His eyes were closed. He sat still as stone, arranged as though he were resting against the cliff. Jianna knelt beside him,

staring, dead-eyed at her brother. She didn't look up when
Robyn approached.

Robyn swallowed, unable to speak. She pushed off of
Millia and went to the man who had been her closest friend and
protector for more than three years. A surrogate father for the
parents she'd lost. Kneeling beside him, she touched his face.
He was cold. She shook her head. "No," was the only thing she
could say, but it felt like someone else was saying it.

She covered her mouth, fearing she might be sick. Closing
her tear-filled eyes, she tried to remember him as he had lived:
large, animated, smart, protective. Then she remembered his
wife and daughter, and her heart broke again. She would have
to tell them. Would have to make sure his body went to them
for burial and funeral. She laid her head on his chest, letting her
tears mix with the blood that covered him.

How could this have happened?

"Robyn?" Millia said.

"Leave me," she said.

"But—"

"*Leave me alone!*"

Millia backed away. Robyn reached a hand toward Jianna.
In this, she knew, they would equally despair. Her fingers
brushed the other girl's hand, but Jianna pulled away and glared
at Robyn for a moment, before looking back to Mitalo.

Robyn's hands shook. She clenched her teeth, balled her
hands into fists and began to grind her knuckles into the dirt,
hoping to make them bleed. Hoping to hurt.

She stared at Mitalo's still form, and thought of Lex. The
man who mattered most in her life lay gone before her, and the

other who could matter was a prisoner in his own home. One dead, the other captured, injured. She closed her eyes tight and hunched over her knees.

What had Mitalo always told her? *Every storm passes*, he would say. He wanted her to be strong, to move forward with her life. To be happy, like her parents had been. When she'd asked him what she should do about Lex, he'd told her she was thinking too much. She had to follow her heart, be true to herself.

People had been telling her to be strong all her life. She gripped her hair with both hands, ready to yank it out. She didn't want to be strong anymore. Being strong only meant losing what you loved. Her family, her life, her friends…she wouldn't survive losing anything else. It was Valio's fault. He'd taken everything from her now. It always came back to him.

"You coming, ladies?"

The perkiness of the voice made her hands tighten into fists. She opened her eyes to scowl at the intruder. Nick, Oliver, and Enzi were mounted, pulling more horses behind them.

Millia laid a gentle hand on her shoulder.

Part of her didn't want to go. That part wanted to sit and cry and mourn for her lost friend until her tears ran out. But already, the prospect of going to rescue Lex had her mind working. She felt focused, her thoughts clear, now that she had a goal in mind.

Lex had asked her to stay with him. She knew what he'd meant, though he hadn't precisely said it. He hadn't needed to.

She closed her eyes, remembering. As a little girl, all she'd ever wanted was safety, stability. The knowledge that her next meal would be there, that she wouldn't have to worry whether she was cared for. Those dreams had made it easy to do what she'd done over the past three years, helping others to have that kind of security. Bringing food to those who needed it, blankets to others…it had filled the gap in a way she hadn't expected.

It was wonderful, yes, but now she had the chance at more. A partner who trusted her judgement, who was kind and earnest. A man who could love her, if she let him.

And Valio made her fear even that.

Valio's fault.

Valio.

She rolled her shoulders, testing her body, making sure that despite a sore ankle, she could still function. It hurt, but she could move. With luck, it would be enough to draw her bow one more time today.

She had a target to hit.

When they reached the city, guards on the wall attacked immediately. Arrows rained down on them, and the soldiers gathered beneath what few shields remained. Nick and Oliver had managed to gather and organize a section of their forces to help. According to reports, they now had about thirteen thousand soldiers—a thousand more than they'd started with, even after casualties. And Enzi, Lex's servant and friend, assured her that there were another thousand at the palace, waiting for Lex to appear.

Without a word to anyone, Robyn slipped away from the main force, winding her way between fighters and into the city. Her companions were focused on subduing Valio's defense, which needed to be done, but she had a higher priority. She'd only been to Galanis a few times, but it was enough to help her navigate toward the palace hill. Whenever she saw soldiers she ducked into an alley or behind a stack of crates. It took time, but not nearly so long as it would have with the army. And this way she felt like she was doing something, rather than waiting behind a line of swords.

After too long, she finally reached the hill. From behind a line of hedges, she saw it was surrounded by a river, with narrow bridges. She'd have to time her crossing right to avoid being seen by guards.

Unless....

She looked more carefully. Some of the guards wore red tunics with a black raven stitched on—Valio's men—and others wore blue, with a golden crown—Lex's guard. She didn't have to wonder which were her allies. But how would she make them believe her?

The truth would be best.

Taking a deep breath, she nocked an arrow and took aim. It shot through the bushes at one of Valio's men. Shouts from the guards came to her. A moment later, hands gripped her arms and shook her. The man was tall, and broad, and wore blue. Thank the Gods.

"Who the muck are you?!"

"A friend of your king!" she said, venom in her voice. "Let me go!"

"Why would you shoot the king's own men?"

"Because," she said, lowering her voice, "the one I shot is *not* the true king's man."

The soldier paused, eyes narrowing.

"Prince Alexander is alive, and has been kidnapped by the traitor Valio," she said. She had to be quick. "Tell your comrades, the rightful king is here, in the palace, and if you don't hurry Valio will kill him like he killed his parents."

The guard stared at her, obviously unsure whether to believe her.

"Please," she said.

"Andre!" a shout came. But it was from the city behind her, not the palace. The guard holding her turned to find the speaker, and Robyn saw Nick running toward them, Oliver right behind.

"Nick?" the guard, Andre, said.

"Let her go," Nick said, breathing deep to catch his breath. "She's telling the truth. At least, I hope she did. You did tell the truth, right?"

Robyn nodded.

Andre helped her stand, then turned to Nick. "The prince is alive?"

"Yes, and we have to hurry," Nick said. "Arrest anyone wearing Valio's colors who refuses to stand down. We're evenly numbered here, and the soldiers in the city are subdued. Mostly."

"Mostly?" Robyn said.

"We have to go," Nick said.

Together they made their way into the palace. Valio's men didn't look twice at them because of Nick and Oliver's uniforms, but the blue-garbed soldiers took notice. They all seemed to know these two personally, and trusted them when they quickly explained what was happening.

They'd gone down three hallways and two stairwells when Robyn's ankle buckled so badly she lost her balance, leaning against the wall for support.

"Lady Robyn?" Oliver said.

"I'm no lady," she muttered.

"We've got you," Oliver said, putting an arm around her and helping her stand.

"Come on, my lady," Nick said, taking her other side. "I haven't known you long, but I know he needs you."

These words buoyed her, making her blink tears of pain away. Lex needed her. She needed him.

Then they paused. Robyn raised her eyes to see why they'd stopped, and a wave of emotions swept over her. Fear, anger, rage, fury, a desire to leap forward and kill the man who had hurt her. Valio's mercenary. After three years he was here, right in front of her, and she had no strength to do anything.

"This way, come," he said, shuffling them through a doorway.

Robyn's fear boiled inside her, and she fought against the support of Lex's friends, but they followed the mercenary without a second thought. Another two doors, and they were in a silent chamber, one draped with heavy brocades and furnished with fine sofas gilded in gold. Nick tried to lower her into one of these but she went for the Callidian.

"You…you *murderer!*" Tears streamed down her face, but not from physical pain. This hurt was in her heart, and could never be healed. The memories of her parents, her brother, everything she'd lost that night…. Her throat tightened, her whole body shook, only Nick kept her standing. "You killed my family, you mucking son of a dog! You took *everything* from me!"

"Robyn," Nick said, holding her back even as she made pitiful attempts to dive for the man. She reached for her dagger.

Then the Callidian knelt on the carpet before them. His huge figure reminded her so much of Mitalo, and a stab of loss hit her chest once more. Then he raised his face to meet her gaze, and she saw tears in his eye.

"I am Zivon," he said. "I cannot tell my whole story, there is no time. But know this: killing your family was wrong. I knew that all along, but I believed following orders was more important. Valio is no longer my master. And I will do anything you ask of me, in order to prove my loyalty."

"Kill yourself," she said. He deserved it.

"Robyn," Oliver said. "He's trying to help. He's no good to us dead."

"Valio fooled him too," Nick added. "Like he has everyone else. And Carina told us he was on our side now, remember?"

Oh, she remembered. Remembered deciding Carina was a fool for believing him.

"I do not deserve to live," Zivon said. "I have done more in Valio's name than I ever have in the Powers', and I will never be able to repay that debt. But if I am to die, I will take him with me."

Robyn glared at the man until finally her legs gave out. She had to get to Lex before Valio…did something irreversible. She couldn't think in specifics now, it hurt too much. She wanted so badly to stab this man in his remaining eye, and leave him bleeding on this expensive carpet. Ruining it as he had her life. But Valio was the mind behind it. Valio had to come first.

"Help us kill Valio," she said. "Quickly. Give him no time to doubt your intent."

"This, I will do," Zivon said. "Follow me."

Ravin tried to fight him, but the man did not hesitate.
I froze, watching my brother die in front of me.

41
LEX

Ten.

Ten minutes since he'd been taken. Lex fought the ropes holding his hands behind his back. The wound in his side flared worse than fire, but he could hear his captors and knew where they were taking him.

Fifteen.

They were laughing, taking bets on how Valio would dispose of him. The ropes dug into his wrists. He was dragged, their hands gripping him under his arms, no sympathy at all for their fallen prince.

Twenty.

He recognized the sounds of the palace when they entered. How long would he last? He was injured, had dropped the Amplia figure when they'd taken him. He didn't have a sword, and no one to help him. He would be alone.

Twenty five.

What about Robyn? Mitalo…would they get a Cure to him in time? If she lost her best friend, would she be all right?

Thirty.

Lex was thrown to the ground, letting out a groan as his side exploded. The sack was removed from his head, and he pried open his eye, trying to ignore the pain in his side, but what he saw only made him want to close it again.

He lay on the floor of his own throne room, on the deep red carpet leading to the dais. With his head on the ground everything he saw was turned sideways.

Maximus Valio sat on the left seat of the royal throne, looking far more at home there than Lex had ever felt during his days of practice and training. Valio wore a sword, but no crown. Though he may as well have for the majesty pouring off him. He smiled at Lex, a malicious grin filled with the thrill of victory, his eyes bright with mirth.

Lex tried to move, to sit up. His body refused; the pain was too much.

Many hands grabbed him and lifted, making him cry out again before they set him on his knees facing the double throne, and tugged the cloth from his mouth, leaving his tongue feeling like paper. His breathing was ragged and painful, each gasp a new dagger in his side. The hands around him let go and he fought to hold himself upright.

Valio laughed. "Well, Alexander. Here we are. I'm told you accused me of murdering your parents, is that right?"

Lex did not speak. The truth about Valio was written in his features. Lex remembered Robyn's face the night she'd told him about the scar on her cheek. How hard it had been to read her whole story the day before yesterday. Had it really been only two days? It felt like another lifetime. Valio might not have done it himself, but he was certainly responsible for it. Lex clenched his fists. For the first time in his life, he felt no qualms about his desire to kill.

"Well, I can assure you they died quickly. The rock root poison works incredibly fast," Valio said. He stood and came forward, the hem of his robe trailing behind. "It was even painless. Or so I'm told; I wasn't there." He stopped right in front of Lex and bent down, looking him in the eye. "Now, I need you to tell me something. Where is my daughter?"

Lex glared at him, and was grateful for Carina's decision to run. "Gone."

Valio struck him.

Lex's head lolled back. He chuckled, facing the ceiling. "Was this what you did to her?" he said, his voice gaining strength. "No wonder she wanted to get away. You drove her out!"

Valio hit him again, and Lex fell to the floor. He grunted as his body curled into the pain, trying to lessen the blow, but it didn't make a difference. His blood already stained the carpet, his vision sideways and blurry again.

I can't do this alone...

"Alexander of Regania," Valio said, turning toward the throne, "you have committed treason against the crown."

"*What?*" Lex shouted.

"SILENCE!" Valio turned back, and his voice shook the room. "You have allied yourself with outlaws, assisted in the murder of six high lords on the battlefield today, assisted in the escape of three prisoners, and forfeited your right to the crown by running away. Do you deny these actions?"

Silence hung in the cavernous room while Valio waited for Lex's response.

He shook his head weakly. "You're a mucking bastard, you kno—"

"You are hereby sentenced to death."

Lex clenched his teeth. He wanted to shout, yell, scream at Valio that his claims were ridiculous, but he had no strength.

Hands gripped him, lifting him to his knees again.

A cry came from outside the palace, and Valio laughed.

"You see? My army is celebrating. They know as well as I that your little rag-tag band never stood a chance." He came near again, lowering his voice so only Lex could hear. "I will hunt down all your friends, one by one, and see that they never threaten me again. In fact, I'd be happy to let you watch as I torture them. It could be your personal entertainment."

"I won't let you," Lex said through gritted teeth.

"Kill him," Valio said, waving a hand and turning away.

One of the men drew his blade. Cold steel settled on Lex's throat. He opened his eye and saw Valio smirking, a glint in his gaze.

"I hope you know what you're doing," Lex whispered.

Valio's mouth twitched. "Oh, I do, little prince. I do." He nodded to the soldier, who shifted his blade.

Lex closed his eye.

A deep *clang* came as the throne room's double doors swung open. Bodies poured in from the corridor outside. The soldier about to kill Lex dropped his sword, and bolted. Lex gazed around, his vision going in and out of focus. He couldn't tell what was going on.

"How dare you desecrate my throne room!" Valio shouted. "Guards! Remove them!" Then he snatched the sword from the floor and put it to Lex's throat. His eyes were bloodshot with anger.

Thwip.

Lex frowned.

An arrow appeared in Valio's leg. The man screamed, staggering back, his hand going to the bolt.

"Robyn?" Lex whispered.

A hulking figure leapt over Lex and knocked Valio to the floor, rolling as they went.

Valio cried out again, pushing himself to his feet. The huge Callidian man who had kidnapped Lex all those weeks ago stood, and drew his sword. He advanced on Valio.

"What are you doing?" Valio said. "I am your master! You obey me! Or did you forget what your son took from me?"

The Callidian said nothing, but raised his blade, anger radiating from him. Their swords crossed, and Lex was shocked to see Valio—the arrow still in his leg—draw a dagger, and plunge it into the Callidian's chest. The hulking assassin gripped the hilt, glaring at his opponent. And, Lex could tell, barely hanging on to his life.

Valio backed away, looking exhausted but smug. Then in a flash, the larger man drew close, spinning Valio around, forcing him to his knees, and placing a blade to his neck.

"You will be executed for this," Valio said through gritted teeth. "I will make sure your family learns of your dishonor. You will never—"

A second arrow appeared in Valio's chest, cutting off his tirade.

The bulking man who held him leaned forward and whispered something in Valio's ear, before he staggered away.

Then a third and final bolt drove through Valio's eye.

His body fell backward, folding awkwardly to the floor.

Dead.

Thank the Gods.

The clinking sounds of swordfights around and outside the throne room were muted to Lex, and he imagined—hoped—most of Valio's forces would surrender soon. The Callidian with the eye patch stumbled over to where Lex lay.

"I want you—to know," he said, breathless, "that I am sorry. I took—too many lives. I will—" But he did not finish. Blood began to trickle from the man's mouth, and he fell to his side, as dead as Valio.

Lex closed his eye, ready to greet sleep. But someone knelt behind him, rolling him over.

"AAHH!" he cried, the wound in his side flaring up.

"I'm so sorry! Are you all right?"

Lex cracked his eye to see Robyn looking down at him looking weak and tired, but there.

"You're...you're all right. Thank Life, you're all right."

She gave a relieved smile as she pushed his hair off his face. Before he said anything more, she leaned down and kissed him. She tasted of salt and dirt, and her lips were cracked, but he didn't care. Her hair tickled his face. He had just enough energy left to wish he was more conscious for their first kiss, before his heart raced too fast, and his mind went dark.

I tried to run, but the man grabbed me. My cheek was scratched in the chaos, but the most vivid memory I have is of snatching an arrow from the quiver I held, and slamming the point into the man's eye.

42
LEX

Lex's first sense to return was smell. A musky, plant-like scent filled his nose, reminding him of his father. His sense of touch must have returned next, because he felt a tear slide from his eye to his ear, before realizing he was in a soft cocoon of blankets.

His mind told him he'd only been unconscious for a few minutes. Sound came then, as he made out whispers but couldn't identify the words. He opened his mouth and longed for water to rid the dry stickiness coating his tongue. He began to open his eye, then yawned.

"AAHH!"

Pain shot through him from his side, and a moment later hands were on him, holding him down. His teeth clenched together to keep from crying out again.

"He's waking up, hurry!"

375

Sounds of movement surrounded him but he could only focus on the pain. Then someone's hand gripped his right, and he felt the now familiar flow of Life magic entering his body, healing the wounds. The pain grew, all the healing being done quicker than usual, until someone took his left hand as well. Then, his mind cleared. The pain was still there—it was a lot of pain—but it was dampened. Enough that he could suck in a breath.

"Stay calm, highness, you're badly hurt," a man said. The one holding his right hand.

"You don't have to do that," another voice said.

"Get out of here; you're mad," said a woman to his left.

Lex opened his eye. The Master Cure himself, a tall middle-aged man in blue robes, held Lex's right hand in his, his other hand in a bowl of water to fuel the magic. To Lex's left, sat the Master Shifter, a short round woman in red with one hand on a large rock, the other holding his left hand. A third, much younger, man stood at the foot of his bed, black hair falling across grey eyes, and wearing the blue robes and white-striped sleeves of a High Cure. Lex squinted at him.

"I know you," Lex said, his voice like rocks scratching glass.

The man smirked. "We've met, yes."

Lex smiled back. "You're that Cure…the one who healed Robyn's horse."

The man nodded.

"You gave me—"

"Yes. We do need to discuss that, but it can wait for now."

Lex paused, understanding that they would speak in private. He looked to the Master Vessels. "Will I live?"

"Of course, highness," the Clarity answered, her voice high and practiced. "The wound did not pierce any vitals. It is painful, but should heal in an hour or two with diligent service."

"Sooner," the young man said in a sing-song voice.

"And...Robyn? She's alive?" The memory of her kiss was the clearest thing he could recall.

"She is fine, my lord," the Master Cure said. "She had a very swollen ankle by the time we saw her, but she should recover just fine."

"Can I see her?"

"Not yet," the younger Cure said.

The Clarity to his left huffed. "It is not your place to give orders, young Brother. Keep to yourself."

The young man arched a single dark eyebrow, but held his tongue.

"Casualties?" Lex asked.

"Few died, sir," the Master Cure said. "We were very lucky in that. From what Lady Belleci tells me, the men you brought from the outer lordships have mostly survived. Valio's men suffered more of a loss, but at least they've largely sought forgiveness for supporting him. As for the mortality rate, I'm told we only lost about four hundred lives between the two forces, though there are many more who have suffered great injuries, loss of limbs, even brain damage. We can gift small Clarity stones to most of those to help."

The young man cleared his throat.

"Have you nothing better to do than bother us?" the Master Clarity snapped at him.

"His highness needs support of close friends at this trying time," the man said. "I am his peer, I am here to provide that."

The Clarity rolled her eyes, and Lex couldn't help smiling, even as tired as he was.

"Highness," the Clarity said, "if you're feeling well enough, I think we'll let you rest. And you should eat something light. A nice warm soup, perhaps."

Lex nodded. "Whatever you think best, have the kitchens send it in."

"I'll see to it. We'll let you go in three, two, one." She and the Cure both released his hands, and the healing energy left. His mind clouded once more, making him even more tired.

"Drink this water, and I'll be back soon." She handed Lex a cup, nodded to the Master Cure, and left the room, scowling at the young man when she passed him.

"I'll come in to check on you every half hour, highness," the Master Cure said. "I'll leave this man to visit, as he seems intent on doing so, but please do not be long. You should rest. Let your body do its work."

"I shall, thank you."

The Cure bowed then, and followed the Clarity from the room.

Lex stared at the young priest.

The priest smiled, his cloudy grey eyes twinkling.

"Who are you?"

"No one of consequence." His smile widened.

"Liar," Lex said.

"No! You're supposed to say, 'I must know!'" he said, laughing. "I've tried using that line many times and no one ever gets it right. It's extremely frustrating. By the way, you need this."

With that, he came forward and handed Lex the Amplia carving he'd carried all those weeks. The moment it hit his hand, Lex felt Life flow into him once more. The process wasn't as painful, now that the deeper tissues had been healed by the Master Cure. He could feel his skin slowly coming together, tickling and prickling as it did so.

Lex took a breath, looking out the windows of the room to see daylight…. His internal clock told him it had only been moments since the events in the throne room.

"How long was I unconscious?"

"Only about half an hour, your majesty," the man said. "You started to wake almost immediately after you fainted, but the Master Clarity decided to keep you asleep until we got you into bed and situated."

Lex blinked and looked around again, only to realize he was in the royal suite.

His parents' rooms.

Something like an ache struck his heart.

For the moment, he did his best to set that pain aside. There were other things to address. He eyed the young Cure and raised an eyebrow. "Tell me who you are, sir. And be honest."

"You won't believe me."

"I've seen enough," he said. "I'll do my best."

The man nodded. "Very well. I am…a traveler. Of a sort. I've been making my way through these lands looking for something. I came across you by chance, and got myself involved here a bit more than I probably should have. But it worked out in the end."

"What's your name?"

"Not important."

"What are you looking for?"

"Also, not important."

"Yes, they are."

"No, they're not. These things don't concern you or your kingdom and I don't have to tell you anything." He stuck out his tongue.

Frustration welled up in Lex's chest. "I am the king, and you will do as I say."

"You're not king yet," he laughed. "And besides, I bow to no ruler, *my lord*. None but the Powers themselves."

Lex glared at him.

"And even that's debatable."

Lex sighed.

"Look," the man said. "I don't have time to explain everything, and it wouldn't make sense to you if I did."

Lex frowned, confusion clouding his mind. "You're already not making sense."

"See what I mean? Never mind." He waved a hand. "Someone's coming to see you."

A knock sounded at the door.

"What are you," Lex began.

But the young Cure was already walking to the doors. When he opened them, Jianna stepped through, and Lex gaped.

Jianna's usually laid-back demeanor was gone. She was clean, but looked unkempt, tear streaks lining her cheeks, her copper hair disheveled. But truly disturbing were the woman's eyes. Their usual light was gone, snuffed out.

"Jianna," Lex said, sitting straighter. "Are you all right?"

Jianna stared blankly at him, and Lex berated himself. *Stupid question.*

"What...how can I help?"

Jianna's gaze brought an unpleasant chill to Lex's skin. Then Jianna noticed the Cure.

"Get out," Jianna commanded.

The Cure bowed, but refused. "I am here to see to his majesty's needs."

"He doesn't need mucking religion," Jianna growled. "And I need to speak to him."

"Jianna," Lex said. "It's all right. This man can keep his silence. Say what you need to say."

Jianna looked between them, her breathing growing heavy. Then, without warning, she picked up a chair and threw it at the wall, letting out a scream of rage Lex never could have imagined.

The broken wood fell to the floor as Lex ducked into his blankets—which was stupid, blankets wouldn't protect him from a chair. But a moment later, he heard sobbing. He sat up to see Jianna kneeling on the carpet, shoulders slumped, fresh tears rolling down her face.

"Jianna," Lex said.

"He *believed*," Jianna said. "He had more faith than anyone. He helped people. He loved people. He had a little girl!"

Lex's throat tightened, tears burning behind his eye.

"WHY did he have to jump in front of that mucking spear?" Jianna shouted. "Why did *he* have to die? *I* should have died, not him! He at least had good reasons to live!"

It was one thing to see ladies of court weep at a tragic tale, or a child cry for a lost pet, even a young parent for a fallen child. But this woman he thought unbreakable, to see her so shattered, so broken...Lex didn't know what to say.

"Death is but a single part of the balance in the Gods' plan," the Cure said softly.

"I don't need your mucking plan," Jianna snapped. "He trusted in the Gods and they didn't save him. I sat by him for an *hour*, begging, praying for him to come back, but he didn't."

The Cure's head was bowed. "So sayeth Fina, all things come to an end."

Jianna stood so fast Lex barely saw her move. In a moment she had the blue-robed man pinned against the wall, choking him. "I'll bring your end if you don't shut your muck-drooling mouth."

"Jianna!" Lex called. "Jianna, let him go!"

It took a few moments, but Jianna lowered her hands, sneering and stepping away.

The Cure didn't seem bothered by the outburst, but the red marks on his skin said it hadn't been an act.

Jianna turned to Lex, her eyes blank. "Elena and Ceri will be here tomorrow. Your...officers, told me you need to hold court at sunrise, then we'll have the funeral in the afternoon, and your coronation will be at sunset."

"Busy day," Lex said.

"Given the current circumstances," the dark-haired Cure said, "the people are eager to have the situation dealt with, and a good king on the throne once more."

Lex nodded. "Very well. Jianna, please choose a spot in the palace cemetery. Anywhere you want, I'll authorize it. Brother Cure, can you please see that a proper coffin is commissioned, simple and sturdy?"

"Of course, your majesty," the Cure said.

After a few moments silence, Jianna let out a breath. "Thank you."

"Of course, my friend."

Jianna nodded, and left the room.

Lex looked to the Cure. "You're not very good at making friends, are you?"

He shook his head, rolling his eyes. "The only reason the Master Vessels hate me is because I was forced to shove my way into the palace to talk to you. No one would listen to me, so I got in on my own. Here," he gestured toward where Jianna left, "I was only trying to help."

Silence passed again. Lex had one other thing he wanted to ask, but was troubled by what the answer might be.

"Brother," he said. "Where are my parents?"

The man's eyes softened. "They are in Vapris, your majesty."

"Where is it?"

"All around us, my lord. Or so we're told. Their essence could be here in this very room, watching over you as we speak."

Lex tightened his grip on the carving he held, magic still strengthening him. "Can I use magic to see them?"

"I'm sorry, my lord," the priest said. "What Fina has taken, cannot be brought back by any power."

"I didn't ask if they could be brought back. I asked if I could see them."

The Cure's mouth opened, but he hesitated to speak. Lex waited while the man thought. "I'm told there is a way," he finally said, "but it requires great sacrifice. Fina is the Goddess of death. The power of death cannot be reversed. However, old records, scriptures, state that the entrance to Vapris will appear when one who holds all Four Powers performs a sacrifice to them, to the Gods. A sacrifice of one million souls."

Lex's face went pale. *One million souls?* He wasn't even certain that many people existed in all the Unbroken Lands. And even if they did, he would never be so selfish as to cause such death.

His parents, and Mitalo, were gone.

He blinked.

"Where is Robyn?"

The priest smiled. "I was wondering when you'd get around to—"

"Where is she?"

"In your old rooms, sire, probably sleeping."

Lex immediately slid out of the huge bed. Whatever power he held in that trinket, it was the only thing keeping him upright. He wore only linen pants, some bandages wrapped around his chest. He snatched a shirt before striding through private hallways to his former room.

There she lay. Her pale skin and hair a shock against his deep blue pillows. The Vessels who had been with him before stood here now, watching over her.

"Highness!" the Clarity said. "You should be resting."

"I'm fine. Give her this." He held out the carving.

The young Cure gripped his wrist before the Clarity could take it. "You may want to lie down first, my lord."

Right. Lie down. Lex went to a couch and used his free hand to shove all the books on it to one end. Then he lay, getting as comfortable as possible, before he handed the carving over.

The strength left him and he slumped against the soft sofa. He placed a hand over his side, and took up a book to read as the young Cure placed the figure in Robyn's hand. Lex watched as a healthy flush of color lit her cheeks, and he smiled.

"Bring up a tray of food," he told the others, his breathing labored. "And a pitcher of water. Then make sure no one disturbs this room except one of you three."

The two Vessels bowed and left. The young Cure came to him.

"I have to be going, my lord. I've got a very stupid sword that needs me."

"A sword?" Lex asked.

"I said what I said." He smiled. "But I wish you well, and I know that your lady here will recover. You've had them caring for you and held the charm long enough that you'll be fine. Let her keep it until she wakes, then place it somewhere safe."

Lex smiled, which was more like a grimace.

"Get some rest, majesty. There's enough power in that trinket to last a very long time, but do not waste it. Keep it for when it is most desperately needed. Do not use it otherwise."

"Thank you, friend."

The young man gave a wink. Then he left, and locked the doors behind him.

He released me, and I ran. I stole the stranger's horse and
rode through the night. A slip of a girl wearing a nightdress
covered in someone else's blood, tears streaking my face.
That was the morning I met Mitalo.

43
LEX

Lex stared at the sleeping girl in his bed until his vision blurred and he fell asleep. The rest of the day and night had passed when he woke to a small noise. He cracked his eye open to see the sky a softer blue than when he'd fallen asleep. Morning was on its way.

He blinked, and saw Robyn slipping out of bed on the far side from him. She wore a modest nightdress the same shade as her hair. She moved around his room, looking at his possessions. His books were scattered and disorganized, but other than that he felt rather pleased that the place was this clean. She found the water and food, eating until she was filled. Then she went to the open wall, lined with columns—the very one Lex had escaped from—and looked out over the city.

She was lovely. Brave, smart, honest, and loyal. Seeing her stand at his window made something in him leap with joy. He noticed she still held the carving in her left hand.

"Feeling better?" he asked.

She spun, eyes wide.

"Sorry," he held up a hand in apology. "I didn't mean to scare you."

She shook her head, a smile playing at her lips.

"You sure you're all right?"

She nodded.

"Good," he said. "Come sit with me?"

He pushed his legs off the couch and sat up, favoring his side. She sat next to him. He looked her over, checking on her ankle. Everything had healed completely, and he silently thanked the odd young priest for the magic in that trinket. Then Lex looked at Robyn's face and paused. Her eyes were a trap he could so easily get lost in.

If I marry this girl, I may not ever be coherent again.

He cleared his throat. "I'm glad you're all right. I woke yesterday and they told me you'd come to sleep in here."

"They offered it to me," she said. Then shrugged. "It would've been stupid to refuse an actual bed."

Lex smiled. "Well, I'm told you pushed yourself much harder than you should have." He paused. "Thank you for that."

She looked up. "For?"

"For coming after me. For stopping Valio when he was about to kill me."

"Right," she said. "I couldn't..." her voice trailed off.

Lex took her hand, not asking her to finish. "You saved my life again. That's…five, I believe."

"And you're still at only two," she said, smirking. "Better get on that."

She smiled. And his heart sank at the next topic he needed to broach.

"I'm sorry about Mitalo."

Robyn breathed in sharply. Her hand tightened in his and she stared at the other, still holding on to the carving, rolling it from palm to fingers.

"I'm so sorry," Lex said.

"For what?"

"I had that with me," he said, nodding to the figure, "I could've saved him. I tried, I was going for him, I had it out…"

"Lex," she said. "You were captured. It's not your fault."

"I could've—"

"Stop that."

He looked up at her. Her eyes bright and intense. "No amount of wishing can change what happened. You did your best, and so did he."

Lex nodded. "You're right, of course."

Robyn looked away, eyes on the floor. "He was like a father to me," she whispered. "His family—"

"Have been contacted," Lex said. "They should be here soon, and the funeral will be this afternoon."

She nodded, sniffed.

Lex reached for a handkerchief on the nearby table. She took it gratefully. He'd never seen her cry. He resolved then to never be the cause of her future tears if he could help it.

He still held her hand, and she held back. She dried her eyes, and forced a smile.

"Sorry, I haven't cried in a long time."

He squeezed her hand. "It's perfectly natural, and appropriate."

"Thank you."

"Of course."

Blush rose to her cheeks, and he felt his own go warm as well.

"My coronation is this evening," he said. "I'd very much like for you to be there."

She smiled. "Of course."

He couldn't look away. "Robyn, I—"

A knock came at the door.

"Come in," Lex called.

A servant entered and bowed. "Forgive me, your majesty, but court will begin in fifteen minutes and you will be needed for the trials."

Lex nodded. "I'll be there shortly."

The man bowed again, and left.

Lex let go of her hand, standing to put on his shirt.

"Are you truly needed right away?" Robyn asked.

He looked at her. She was staring at him. Her eyes asking a question he hoped he wasn't imagining. Something inside him sparked.

"I, ah…yes," he said, frowning. "We're putting on trial the families of the high lords who conspired with Valio. I don't imagine it will be much fun, but I am needed."

"Such is the life of a king," she said, standing. Smiling.

"I don't want to leave you," he said. "But I do need to go. I will see you this afternoon. Right?"

She nodded.

He smiled, a warmth rising in his chest. "Oh, I'll need you to lie down again."

Her brows came together, forming that line he now recognized. "Why? I feel fine."

"I know, but you won't when I take that charm away from you."

She looked down at it once more. "Right. I remember."

"I'm sorry. I'll need it for myself if I'm going to be of any worth to the trials this morning."

She moved to his bed—*the* bed—then held out the carving for him to take.

He did, and their hands brushed. Though they'd touched not seconds before, Lex felt a shiver run through his body.

She relaxed into the mattress as he took the carving, and he felt a wave of strength flow through him. Before she pulled away, he took her hand, and kissed it.

"Rest now, Lady Robyn."

The trials were tedious, but fortunately Lex didn't have to strip anyone of their titles, as those who had been the minds behind the rebellion were already dead. When that was done, he made it clear that Carina Valio was still nobility, and welcome to return at any time, but her lands would be presided over by another family whose rank he elevated.

Mitalo's wife and daughter arrived late that morning. Lex made sure to wear his very best: a flowing formal chiton of deep blue, with gold edging and clasps, with a white sash around the waist and over his shoulder. As the coffin was lowered into the ground, he stayed back from the rest of the group. He hadn't known Mitalo nearly as well as the others, and didn't want to be an intruder.

It wasn't a long service. The only attendees were Elena—Mitalo's wife—and Ceri—their daughter—holding hands, Jianna—who looked more composed than when he'd last seen her, but still haunted—Robyn, Lex, and to Lex's surprise, Lady Liras had come as well. They gathered around the coffin at Elena's request. She was a petite woman, dark of skin and eyes, with hair that seemed to shift from blue to black in the sunlight.

"If you don't mind, I would love to hear from each of you," she said. "It doesn't have to be a speech, but some small memory of him?"

Robyn spoke first. "He protected me. More than I ever knew. Looking back, I see it, but at the time…I'm glad I had him."

"His last words," Jianna said, her voice rough, "Were about each of us. He said, 'Tell Elena and Ceri I'm sorry, and I love them. He spoke of me," Jianna's voice broke, she paused. "He spoke of Robyn, how proud he was of her. He said Lex was a good man. Then he started talking about the forest, fights we'd had, things we delivered. He…faded out after a while and never came back." Jianna's eyes hardened at this, and Lex's heart broke inside him all over again.

Then it was his turn to speak. "Mitalo was brilliant," he said. "I respected him from the moment we met, though I don't think he returned it right away."

Lex saw Robyn smile a little at that.

"He was a great man," Lex said. "The world is a bit less bright without him."

They all stood in silence for a moment. Then Ceri spoke.

"I miss Papa."

Elena squeezed her daughter's hand, her voice breaking as she spoke. "I know, darling. So do I."

Tears pricked at Lex's eye.

"Excuse me," he said, nodding to them, blinking back the warm sensation. He walked up the hill of the cemetery to where the monarchs were buried. He found his grandparents' grave stones, and next to them were two sections of recently loosened dirt.

"Here I am," he said softly.

He knelt at the foot of his parents' graves and moved the dirt around with his fingertips. His lip trembled; his fist clenched around the dirt. He closed his eye. His shoulders began to shake.

Then Robyn was there. On their knees, she wound her arms around his neck, pulling him to face her. He wrapped his arms around her waist, holding on for his very life as his tears dripped onto her shoulder.

When he'd calmed, he pulled away, helping them both stand. "I'm sorry." He wiped his face then looked to her, forcing a smile. "I suppose I expected more than two mounds of dirt."

"It hasn't been long," Robyn said. "And I'm sure headstones weren't on Valio's list of priorities."

Lex nodded. "I'll see it done. Modest ones. They'd have wanted that."

Then she took his hand.

He looked at her, and saw their shared pain. She hadn't had anyone when her parents and brother died. She hadn't attended a funeral, probably didn't even know where they were buried. No one had been there to hold her, to offer support...and here she was giving that to him. "Thank you," he said.

She opened her mouth to speak, but said nothing.

He squeezed her hand tighter, wanting to pull her close. Wishing he could without scaring her away.

"Robyn?"

She turned toward him, hesitation in every movement. Then she leaned closer, rising onto her toes, and her lips met his. He flinched in surprise, but quickly relaxed at her touch. She tasted like sweet wine, and he wanted to drink forever. He held her close, his arms around her. His heart raced in his chest as she wrapped her arms around his neck.

How was a king supposed to function if he melted into a puddle? This girl, this woman, had such a hold on him.

As he pulled away, she gripped his hair, holding him close so their foreheads touched.

"Robyn," he said. "I want you to know—you have to know—I,"

"Your majesty?"

Lex blinked, looking up to see one of the palace stewards approaching.

"Pardon me, my lord," the man said, looking extremely apologetic. "I've been sent to bring you to prepare for the coronation."

Coronation. Right. Lex's breath came in deep gasps. He swallowed, and looked down at Robyn, whose breathing was also irregular.

"You'll be at the coronation?"

"Yes," she said.

"We'll talk after?"

She nodded.

A few months after I joined the crew, I noticed the needs of towns around us. It started small, and grew. I'm proud of what it's become.

44
LEX

His Royal Majesty, King Alexander Galani of Regania, stood from the dais where a larger, more uncomfortable crown than before had just been lowered onto his head. He honestly wasn't sure he'd ever get used to the weight of the thing.

As the four Master Vessels backed away, he turned to face the nobles and dignitaries who had gathered for the event. The crowd cheered. Lex nodded and smiled, but searched for one face only.

Robyn stood far to the right, against the back wall near a tapestry. Out of sight of everyone except him. She beamed, her approval and pride clear in her eyes, creating a warm glow in Lex's chest that had nothing to do with magic.

From behind Lex, the Master Cure stepped forward, raised his arms and said, "Let the celebration begin!"

People moved around to accommodate musicians, long tables were brought in, followed by food and drinks, and it wasn't long before people were dancing and laughing. Lex watched it unfold with amusement. As the music began, he hopped down the small steps and made his way toward Robyn.

No sooner had he stepped down than he was accosted by members of the court. Men shook his hand, patting his back and offering advice he didn't want to hear. Mothers pushed their daughters forward, and those daughters batted their lashes, smiling but not meeting his eye.

"Your majesty!"

Lex was forced to pause as a dark-haired young woman stopped directly in his path, curtseying low.

"Lady Naomi," Lex said, glancing past her. "Enjoy the celebra—"

"I hoped to speak to you, my lord," she said, standing. "Privately, perhaps?"

Lex finally focused on her, noticing the way her chin tilted down, her lips in a slight pout. She was beautiful, and he knew her to be a kind person and well-liked among her people. But her eyes were on his scars, and the gaze felt so different from the one he'd grown used to these past weeks.

He came forward and took her hand in both of his. "It's lovely to see you," he said. "But I'm afraid my time is otherwise committed tonight. Enjoy the celebration." He patted her hand, and moved away.

But when he reached the back wall, Robyn was gone. He spun around, searching the crowd, his heart beginning to race inside his chest. He found Jianna nearby. "Where's Robyn?"

"Last I saw she headed out there." Jianna pointed out the double doors of the throne room.

"Thank you." Lex ran through the crowd again.

It took five more minutes to reach the doors. He tumbled out into the colonnade and, looking to the guards at the door, he said, "Do not let anyone follow me, understand?" They nodded, and he spun again, looking for any sign of Robyn. He saw nothing.

"Robyn!"

"A young woman, sir?" one of the guards asked.

"Yes," Lex said. "Bit shorter than me, green robes, light hair?"

"In the courtyard, your majesty," he said.

"Thank you." Lex ran.

In the courtyard, he stopped. The place was manicured bushes, grass, flowers, and trees, lit only by moonlight and a few torches. A breeze wafted flowery scents to him. He walked now, looking back and forth, saying her name every so often.

Then he saw her, standing alone beneath the peach tree. Her chin held high, her arms wrapped tightly around her.

"Robyn?"

She didn't speak.

He took a step closer. "Are you all right?"

She nodded.

"Are you—"

"She was quite lovely," Robyn said.

"She?"

"The girl you just spoke to." She turned, and he could see her eyes were shining in the dim torchlight. "A proper lady of court."

Lex frowned. "Lady Naomi? She...she is a good person but, what about her?"

Lowering her arms to clasp her hands before her, she took a deep breath and let it out slowly. "I'm sorry, I...maybe I shouldn't stay here, Lex."

Agony struck like a bolt of lightning through his chest. He'd known it was a long shot, known his life was so different from what she was used to. What was making her think this? He shook his head. It didn't matter. If leaving was what she wanted, then....

He stepped closer, clasping his hands before him to mirror her. "If you want to go, I can have our best horses put to a new wagon for you. Fully supplied and ready to leave by morning. Consider it a parting gift."

She looked up at him, her eyes still bright. And in them he saw confusion, and a small amount of hurt. "You would just let me go?"

Lex swallowed a lump in his throat, and suddenly the thing he'd been so excited to say to her terrified him.

"Please don't misunderstand my generosity for indifference," he said. "I want you here, Robyn. I want you here with me, by my side, for as long as you wish. Forever, preferably. But I will never force you to stay. Your love and understanding of this kingdom is beyond anyone else, my parents included. You..." he hesitated, closing his eye for a moment before continuing. "You would make an exceptional queen."

A light seemed to spark in her eyes at that. "Can I ask you something?" she said.

"Anything."

"Why would you choose me, when you could have any of them?"

"Robyn," he said, taking her hands in his. "Didn't I tell you, that's what my options were before I ran away and met you? I know them, I tried with them. And, while they're decent people, I don't want to choose any of them. It took more time to gain your trust than I ever thought I would spend on anyone, but you are so very worth it. You," he paused, laughing softly. "You are the most wanted outlaw in the kingdom. Wanted by me. You're mad, frustrating, beautiful, and brilliant, and I want every part of you."

She was looking at their hands, squeezing tightly, and all he wanted was to draw her closer.

"What about my crew?" she asked. "All the work we're doing?"

"You can continue it," he said. "Of course you will. And think of the good you can do from here. If you have access to royal resources, perhaps?"

She finally looked up at him, eyes wide.

How could she not know exactly what he was about to say? "I love you, Robyn. I tried not to fall, I tried to wait for you, but I couldn't help—"

"Lex?"

"Yes?"

"I love you too."

Something like fire burned in Lex's chest, but this heat was one he didn't fear. He brought his hands to her face, running a thumb along the scar on her cheek, her hands fell to his chest, resting there.

"It scares me," she said softly. "But I do. I want you, Lex. I'm terrified of what that means, but...I want it more than I've wanted anything in so long."

"Lady Robyn," he said. "You have nothing to fear."

He leaned forward. Their lips brushed softly at first, and then she sighed and her hands grasped his robes, pulling him to her. The sensation of her lips on his was like clear spring water to parched ground. He buried one hand in her soft hair and wrapped the other around her waist and, without thinking, he pulled away from her mouth and kissed her cheek, her jaw, her neck. Her skin was smooth, soft.... Then he paused. His heart thundered in his chest, and while Robyn still held tight to him, the muscles of her body had tensed beneath his hands.

"I'm sorry," he said, shaking his head. "I shouldn't have—"

"Don't apologize," she said, breathless.

He met her gaze.

Fire burned in the bright blue of her eyes. Unmistakable passion and desire.

She shook her head. "Don't ever apologize for making me feel the way you just did. It's terrifying, but it's also wonderful." She pressed a hand to his face, her fingers tracing his scars. "With you, I know I am safe."

He drew her close, simply holding her. She sighed and her body melted into his.

"If I stay," she asked, "will you promise to write more bad poetry about me?"

"*Bad* poetry?" He pulled back. "You said it was good! You said you liked it!"

"I said I was flattered," she said, her smile sharp. "I never said it was good."

Lex put a hand to his heart, feigning offense. "Well," he said. "If you don't like my poetry, there is one thing you could do to make up for the terrible pain you've just caused me."

She tilted her head in that way she always did. "And what is that?"

He brushed stray hair away from her eyes. "Will you stay with me? Be here, to save my life?"

She smiled, her eyes lighting up. "Until the very end."

EPILOGUE

A few days after leaving everything behind, Carina stopped at the first town she saw. Word had already traveled ahead of her: her father was dead.

She probably should've felt something when she heard.

Instead, everything was numb.

At the first inn she came to, she paid for a room and locked herself inside. Sitting on a bed smaller than any she'd ever slept in, she tried to feel...anything. She'd finally attained freedom, but it didn't seem real. Part of her wondered whether she would ever escape her father's shadow...surely he wasn't truly dead. He would appear around the next corner. He would demand she return home. The thought that he could, and that he might never again, terrified her.

Darling...

She jumped, spinning to face the wall. That was her father's voice. She'd know it anywhere. Her hands clenched the blankets beneath her...the voice had seemed so close, so real.

Shaking her head, she took a few steadying breaths. Her father had done horrific things. He had hurt people, more than just her. There was so little Carina could've done to stop him, but now...now that he was gone...maybe she could make up for it somehow. Protect, instead of harm. Help, instead of hurt.

DARCI COLE

Lex had asked where she would go. She really didn't have any idea, except that something was pulling her southward. Her mother's homeland of Medelios lay beyond the Cliffs of Antos, Maybe…maybe if she returned there, to the place where her mother had grown up, she could find a place. Find where she belonged….

A cry sounded from outside her window, like that of a child. Maybe even an infant. Carina stood, looking down at the street below, where a woman with a sword held her blade up to a man in tattered clothing, a small bundle in his arms.

Townsfolk were beginning to appear, surrounding the two—but no one did anything. Carina opened the window a crack.

"—told you too many times," the woman was saying, a grin coloring her voice. "You owe a debt, and it must be repaid."

"I did," the man in the center said, his voice a strangled cry. "I did pay it. Please, ask your master! He knows!"

"My master is the one who sent me," the woman said. "And he says I'm to take in your child until you can pay."

"Please," the father said.

Carina watched, horror catching in her chest, as the woman began to draw closer, her sword skimming the baby's blankets.

A rage roared inside Carina. The instinct to run away was there, to hide. To leave these people to their business and mind her own. She felt it, and with great effort, shoved it aside. She was not the same girl who had cowered before her father. She had fought back, fought him, and she would continue to fight.

404

She would not stand still any longer when there were people she could help. With those thoughts swirling through her mind she took up her sword, jumped out the window, and slid down the small portion of roof there. She landed beside the father, facing the woman.

She had the decency to look surprised, before Carina launched herself forward. Their swords clashed, and in the back of her mind Carina knew she had no idea who this woman was, what the debt was, or why this father was in trouble—but she was not about to let a child be separated from a parent who so obviously loved them. Not when both her parents were gone.

Tears burned behind her eyes as that thought fed her strength.

"Stop this!" the woman cried. "You dare defy the wishes of High Lord Askar?"

Carina said nothing. Her arms burned as she dueled, pushing the woman back, away from the father and his child. The woman wasn't trained, Carina could tell by her messy parries and sloppy footwork. But then Carina had only rarely dueled anyone outside of her training sessions, and fear tightened a knot in her chest with every motion.

The fight lasted less than a minute, before Carina saw an opening. She spun the woman's sword around, forcing it from her hand, before bringing the tip of her own blade to the woman's chin.

Carina's shoulders rose and fell with each heavy breath. Only then did she remember she was surrounded by spectators. Strangers, watching, people who would surely judge her if they knew her past...the urge to hide hit her like a punch to the gut.

But the baby's cries still split the night. Carina did not back away.

"You will leave this man alone," Carina said, her voice shaking, but her hands steady. "Askar is no longer in power here, as I'm certain you've heard by now."

The woman glared. "You have no power here either, girl."

"This land will be given to a new leader," Carina continued, her voice steadying. "One who the new king will monitor closely to be certain they will take care of their people."

"Who are you?" the woman asked.

"Me?" Carina said, shaking her head. "I'm no one."

With nothing more than a dirty glare, the woman went to retrieve her sword, before going to a nearby horse and mounting up. In moments, she was riding away. Carina held her sword at the ready until the woman rode out of sight, into the forest.

Only then did Carina lower her blade.

The townsfolk applauded.

Embarrassment brought color to her cheeks, but she couldn't help a small smile. For the first time in a long time, she felt a lightness fill her heart. Despite this being entirely outside her comfort zone, she had done some *good* here, hadn't she? Perhaps this father and his child could stay safe now, stay together. She nodded to them, then turned to go back into the inn, feeling distracted. She'd locked her door...she would need another key...

"Lady?"

Carina paused. A woman in her middle years smiled, bowing in respect. "Pardon me, but...we would like to remember you, honor you for your help. What is your name?"

Carina froze. "I…I'd rather not…"

The woman gave an understanding smile. "Some wish not to be known, and I understand that." She paused. "We'll call you our Jewel, for your beauty and strength."

That seemed even worse, but Carina didn't argue.

It didn't take long to get back into her room and re-lock the door. Letting out a breath, she propped her sword in the corner and looked at it for a moment. It had been made for her, by her mother, when she was only ten years old. Father had it re-forged to fit her as she grew but it had still never felt quite right. Functional, but not ideal…. Something was missing.

It wasn't only the sword.

Carina rubbed at her temples, walking back to the window she'd jumped from, looking at the section of roof there. Had that really been her doing? She'd almost felt like something had possessed her to act. To protect. But no, it had been her own choice. She'd always felt a need to protect: her servants, her father's mistresses, even the flowering buds around her home in Valios.

And doing so had always given her joy, like a spark that couldn't be extinguished no matter how many times her father stomped on it. She stared at her hands, then looked out, and up, to the darkening sky and pinpricks of stars appearing.

This was something she could do. She could help. And maybe, in some way, her doing so could repay the harm her father had done.

Her shoulders squared, and a smile lifted the corner of her mouth. She would make this right, help as many people as she could, make up for the wrongs of her father, be better than he'd ever allowed her to be.

She would find her place in this world.

Carina Valio will return in

SUMMON

Book Two of

THE UNBROKEN TALES

ACKNOWLEDGEMENTS

Wow. I'm genuinely having a difficult time processing the fact that I'm writing this out for real. I've practiced so many times, but that didn't prepare me for the rush of emotions I'm feeling right now.

First and foremost, I have to thank my family. I've been blessed with an amazingly supportive husband who understands all my weirdness and nuance. His help has been fundamental to making this book a reality. I love you, Brandon. Thank you for everything. Thanks also to my kids, who have put up with a messy house and imperfect mom as I've put so much work into this project, and still let me snuggle them.

Now. There have been so many people who have read and offered feedback on this book over the years, and I'm sure I'll probably forget some of them. For that, I'm sorry.

I have to start by thanking Marieke Nijkamp. They've been a force for writing disability respectfully, and have taught me so much and given invaluable feedback. Along with that, as the first person I ever pitched this idea to, they saw the potential and encouraged me to write it. They were also the reality check I needed as a brand new baby writer with my first novel back in

2012, and I will always and forever be grateful for their patience and support and love.

A huge thanks also has to go to my incredible critique partners and many beta readers who have helped over the years to make this book what it is, many of whom have read it multiple times: Gina Denny, Megan Eccles, Brett Werst, Rachel O'Donnell, Ruth Olson, Shauntel Simper, Jaylee Kennedy, Chessie ZAPPIA (whose name my phone always types in caps lock because I've yelled at her so many times), Stacey Leybas, Katy White, Emery Jonas, Janci Patterson, Kathryn McGee, Brianna Shrum, Annalee Shumway (Hi Mom!), Ryan Dalton, Amanda Shayne, Jenny Kaczorowski, KK Hendin, Beau Barnett, Angi Byam, Brittney Robbins Riggin, and Larissa Reed. (Deep breath. I hope I didn't forget anyone, and if I did, I'm so sorry!)

A special thanks goes to Elizabeth Otto (EMT and writer who helped with fictional injuries), Cait Petersen (archery guru), and to Angi Black and Sarah Blair for lending me some awesome names.

Thank you also to Kirk DouPonce for the gorgeous cover art he created for this book. I've imagined this cover so many times, and he out-did every iteration I'd ever had in my head. It's perfect.

More special thanks to Shauntel Simper and Ruth Olson. Both of these amazing women not only offered extensive feedback and reread scenes to help make them better, but they were integral in giving me the confidence to self-publish. They taught me so much, sent me the best resources, and pretty much held my hand through this process. Thank you both for everything!

I've been extremely lucky to have so many Advanced Readers volunteer to read and review this book, and I couldn't be happier to have them: Alyssa, Amanda Barnett, Amy Standage, Annalee Shumway, Brigham Bunker, Catherine A.,Chris Fowler, E.V. Jacob, Erica Davis, Gaye, Hannah, Jayden, Jeanette, Jessica, Jodie Heiselt, Kathryn, Lacey, Lauren Skidmore, Lynn Ball, Margaret Dzierzon, Marta Hatch, Megan, My Amazing Sister Brigette, Rebecca Mee, Rob West, Rosana, Sarah Blair, Sarah Marie, Shanamarie, Sophia Bidny, Stephanie Allen, Stephanie B. Whitfield, Theresa, and Tim Baughman Jr. Thank you all!

Lastly, I have to give a huge thank you to my sensitivity readers. Eileen Doherty Souza, Ruth Olson, Candace Cameron-Mitchell, Quinnell Flanagan, and Erica Miles; thank you for your insight honesty, and willingness to reread revised scenes and offer additional feedback. This book wouldn't be what it is without you.

I will forever be grateful to my Father in Heaven for pushing me along this path I feared I'd never be brave enough to take. Between Him, many guardian angels, and everyone listed above, I'm finally here. It's been a long road, with many twists and turns and bumps, but the journey has made me who I am, and I couldn't be happier.

FOLLOW DARCI
FOR UPDATES

SOCIAL MEDIA: @darcicoleauthor on Facebook, Twitter, Instagram, Tumblr, and TikTok.

NEWSLETTER: Receive emails updating you on Darci's writing progress and process and be the first to know about awesome deals.
Visit www.DarciCole.com to sign up.

PATREON: For as little as $1/month you can receive early looks at new books and projects as well as deleted scenes and bonus content for
The Unbroken Tales.
Go to Patreon.com/DarciColeAuthor

ABOUT THE AUTHOR

Darci Cole is an author, narrator, and podcaster in the fantasy genre. She and her husband run Colevanders: a wand shop catering to lovers of magic and cosplay. She loves Harry Potter, oracle cards, pretty dice, and Supernatural. While she spends most of her time wrangling children, she also enjoys beta reading for her friends and acclaimed authors. Darci currently lives in Arizona with her husband and four children.

CPSIA information can be obtained
at www.ICGtesting.com
Printed in the USA
LVHW012359290122
709583LV00006B/731